# SECRET SORROWS

Steve followed the direction of the old woman's gaze down the gentle slope from the house to the end of the point. Karen Fraser was seated in her wheelchair, staring out at the empty sea; an older woman, much more smartly dressed than the drab figure in the chair, stood motionless behind her.

"That poor girl should have been married several years ago, but the man she loved died in an automobile accident. She herself hasn't walked since, and her incapacity has made her mother as much a prisoner as she is. And there's a sorrow about Greg Christopher, too. Have you met him, by the way?" When Steve nodded, she continued. "I don't know what it is, but there is something there. Even one of our young sailors. I saw him standing on the beach very early this morning, all alone . . . ." Ethel sighed and resumed her gentle rocking. "Oh, yes, there has been sorrow here . . ."

Steve saw her pale blue eyes shimmer with tears behind the glasses she wore. The thin, almost translucent hand holding the fan was still. "I feel you have sorrow, too."

Steve spoke now without hesitation. "My mother took her life because of something I had done, something she could not accept."

"That was most unfortunate," Ethel mused. "And perhaps very unfair. Sometimes love can be too demanding. We do what we must—we must all live our own lives. Sometimes this brings sorrow, to others as well as to ourselves, but we can't change because of it. Those who love us should realize that, and accept it. Love must never become so possessive that it attempts to alter what we are, or it isn't love . . ."

# DAVID DRAKE

**LEISURE BOOKS**   &   **NEW YORK CITY**

*To*
*Gertrude Hildebrand*
*and*
*Nancy Cerullo*
*in gratitude for*
*a sister's love*

*The characters and events within these pages are fictitious. Hawkins' Cove does not exist, and the writer feels no need to apologize for any similarity to Asbury Park.*

A LEISURE BOOK®

Published by

Dorchester Publishing Co., Inc.
276 Fifth Avenue
New York, NY 10001

If you purchased this book without a cover you should be aware that this book is stolen property. It was reported as "unsold and destroyed" to the publisher and neither the author nor the publisher has received any payment for this "stripped book."

Copyright © 1985 by David Drake

All rights reserved. No part of this book may be reproduced or transmitted in any form or by any electronic or mechanical means, including photocopying, recording or by any information storage and retrieval system, without the written permission of the Publisher, except where permitted by law.

The name "Leisure Books" and the stylized "L" with design are trademarks of Dorchester Publishing Co., Inc.

Printed in the United States of America.

# Part I

# The Cloud

# CHAPTER ONE

The train was scheduled to arrive at Hawkins' Cove that afternoon at precisely 2:27. He had just been informed that they would quite possibly be almost on time, a remarkable achievement for that particular railroad line, of which the bewhiskered and bespectacled conductor, strolling down the aisle with his thumbs thrust into the pockets of his blue uniform, seemed justifiably proud.

Steve settled himself back in his hard seat, attempting to avoid the lumps in the badly worn upholstery, resting his chin in his hand. His book lay completely forgotten in his lap as he stared morosely through the dirt-encrusted window at the uninteresting little towns blurring past, typical slumbering shore villages with such highly unimaginative though appropriate names as Seaside, Ocean View, and Sprayville. One could almost have been a carbon copy of the other. Small frame houses and bungalows whitened by long exposure to the salty sea air, the gleaming brass weather-vane perched atop the spire of the small non-denominational white wooden church (a cross would have smacked too much of Papism), the general store with its sidewalk display of tangled fishing gear, the soft layer of white beach sand and crushed seashells that seemed to lie over every-thing, the cars parked at the small railroad sta-tion, the town square with its statue of some long forgotten hero covered with pigeon droppings, and its green patinaed cannon. Each town was posed against the same brightly colored, monoton-ous postcard backdrop of a calm blue sea which the glaring sun touched with dancing flecks of light that hurt his eyes.

Steve licked at the salty taste of perspiration on his upper lip. It was easily the hottest day of the year; despite the air-conditioning of the coach, which seemed to operate none too well, his shirt was sticking unpleasantly to his back. There probably would be an unattractive sweat stain on the back of his jacket when he stepped from the train, yet his sharp sense of (perhaps outmoded) propriety would not permit him to sit in his shirt-sleeves.

He drew a cigarette from his breast pocket, flicked a small silver lighter bearing the monogram "S.C.," and blew the smoke against the dust-and-insect-smeared window, watching it spread like a blue-white miasma about the car, while attempting to close his ears to the cacophony that surrounded him. Two small children, a boy and a girl, their mouths smeared with chocolate, ran screaming up and down the swaying aisle in an endless game of tag, ignoring the half-hearted admonitions of their mother and the undisguised irritation of those passengers whom they knocked against when thrown off-balance by the movement of the car. Just across from him, a gangling teenaged youth with tangled yellow hair, faded, tight fitting blue jeans and an incredibly dirty torn T-shirt bearing the legend "Led Zeppelin" raised the volume of his massive chrome transistor and mindlessly beat on the arm of his seat a wild tattoo of raucous, meaningless rhythm. Glancing with undisguised annoyance at the vapid, empty face, Steve wondered if the youth had ever been capable of a serious thought. Perhaps he was better off. Hadn't Medea said people go mad if they think too much? She had reason to know.

Directly behind Steve, two middle-aged housewives clad in pathetically youthful fashions continued in shrill and irritating voices their neighborhood gossip, advising all unfortunate enough to be within hearing that Mary Hughes really hadn't the slightest idea of how to raise children, that Ruth Springer was carrying on something scandalous with her handsome new neighbor (who, after all, had a wife of his own, the poor mousey little thing), and the marriage of the Spinellis was on the rocks.

The rhythmic click-clack of the train's movement was a dull, constantly recurring pain like a tooth-extraction when the novocaine has worn off. Steve scrunched himself lower in his seat, aware that his irritation was caused more by his own dissatisfaction with himself than by those about him. Here he was embarked once again on his annual escape (perhaps it would be proper to term it a flight), certain that what he most needed was a few days of peace and quiet and relaxation, away

11

from the many distractions of the city that made it impossible to think rationally. Would it really do any good at all? He had tried the same thing last year at just about this time, and when it was all over, nothing at all had been resolved. This year. . . .

Oh, hell, this year would be just the same and he damned well knew it. Why did he go on trying to fool himself this way?

The train clacked noisily over a causeway, and he found himself looking directly down into a small rowboat, bobbing gently in the calm, clear water like an apple in a rain barrel. Two men lounged in the boat with their fishing rods motionlessly extended, probably as a matter of form to justify their lethargic state. The younger of the two wore a very tight T-shirt with salt-whitened blue jeans and a blue captain's cap perched jauntily on his thickly curled blue-black hair; the older, bald man in the stern was stripped to the waist, revealing a barrel chest with sagging, fleshy breasts matted with graying red hair, and a broad back apparently long accustomed to the leathering influence of the sun; perspiration gleamed on the melon-pink top of his uncovered head.

Steve felt a sudden twinge of envy. The two fishermen seemed almost offensively content with their lot, undisturbed by any problems, worries, or frustrations. Was it really still possible to feel that way?

He again picked up the thick volume he had set aside more than once, and tried to interest himself in the emotional entanglements of the rather bland and insipid characters, but within moments the book had again slipped from his fingers and he found himself staring moodily, almost angrily, through the closed window. Had this trip always taken so long? Where was that relaxation and that sense of well-being that were supposed to be an integral part of every vacation, that eager anticipation of fun, excitement, adventure? The tight knot of tension and worry at the pit of his stomach had not yet unraveled.

He rose abruptly, tossing the book into the seat, and, swaying with the expertise of the frequent train traveler, made his way towards the club car. A young couple guiltily moved apart as he passed them on the platform between two cars; he smiled slightly, wondering that they should believe him the least interested. A fat woman squeezed past him in the second car, and he was momentarily assailed with the unpleasantly pungent odor of perspiration. He quickly looked away from the inviting eyes as her massive breasts pressed briefly against his chest.

The small tables in the club car were occupied by card players or postcard writers, and laughing, joking groups were gathered about the small bar; they glanced up when he entered, then ignored his presence. The noise and the smoke were unpleasant and depressing. Ignoring the openly interested stare of a fading beauty leaning against the bar, he moved on to the rear of the car and sank into one of the lounge chairs. Nearby, a smartly dressed businesswoman in an immaculate pink pants suit sat with a martini, her heavily ringed fingers casually turning over the pages of a fervent women's lib magazine. On the other side of the car an elderly man, the abandoned New York Times spread over his ample paunch, his rimless eyeglasses resting on his forehead, was sleeping with his head hanging over the back of his chair and swinging slightly with each movement of the train. His mouth was open, revealing yellowing dentures and producing a slight snoring sound, something like the angry droning of a trapped hornet.

The porter delivered Steve's iced drink, and he again automatically turned his attention to the passing landscape, blurred by the speed of the train like the hazy memory of some half forgotten dream. A tow-headed and remarkably dirty little boy with a frisky dog of indeterminable breed stood beside the track and waved vigorously as the train whizzed by. He had thought little boys had long since fallen out of that peculiarly American pastime, weren't their eyes now raised to those flaming rockets in the skies? They passed out of the area of fleeting sleepy towns and wind-rolled sand dunes and sped between tall, motionless trees to emerge in swampy marshlands dotted with pools of stagnant water. The bite of the liquor was warming as it slid easily down his throat, and he felt that with the help of a couple of these concoctions, his depression might lift before their hoped for 2:27 arrival.

Sudden laughter drew his attention to the opposite side of the car. A pretty blond girl in a bright print dress that did nothing to conceal her charms was engaged in the enthusiastic attention of two young sailors in spotless white uniforms. The darker of the two was seated on the arm of the girl's chair with a hand placed on her shoulder while his eyes eagerly explored the cleavage revealed by the gap in her low-cut blouse. The fairer of the sailors, seated in the chair beside her, seemed to receive little of the girl's attention.

With a wry smile, Steve thought back for a

14

moment, remembering himself as he had been (how many years before? . . . ten? . . . twelve? . . . fifteen?) in that same white uniform with the blue insignia. He understood the Navy was finally getting around to changing the traditional uniform; a lot of the sailor's sex appeal would surely be lost! He had never been much of a sailor, bored by the dull routine of his work, demeaned by the sharp class differences, degraded by the crudeness and vulgarity of the men with whom he was forced to live. Above all, he resented the total lack of privacy in such a life, sitting beside lip-smacking drooling strangers while eating his meals, taking communal showers with roughhousing nudes, emptying his bowels into a metal trench with men farting and shitting beside him. He had never made friends easily, and his aloof attitude was resented by those with whom he was forced to associate. That had been an intensely lonely time.

No, it was not only that time that had been lonely; he was merely making excuses for his own isolationism. Actually very little had changed, and he often wondered why. That sense of loneliness had never left him, despite the changes of time and age. He was no longer the rather scrawny, shy and awkward youth of a decade and more ago. He was now past his thirtieth year, reasonably successful in a routine and uninteresting office position, and considered by many to be pleasant, friendly and attractive. And yet, his loneliness remained undiminished; that apparent friendliness was merely a facade. He still spent far too much time by himself. Oh, he had tried all the usual supposed remedies—travel, friends, love affairs—but all had failed him disastrously. The first such failure had made him a divorced man. The second had taken the life of his mother.

The remembrance was disturbing; he generally avoided thoughts of the past. He shook his head as though to clear it of such unpleasantness, drank quickly and ordered another glass from the passing porter, whose obsequious attitude failed to conceal a certain contempt for this heavily drinking white man. The woman reading the magazine happened to glance up and catch his eye; his automatic faint smile was answered with a frigidly raised eyebrow and an abrupt return to her magazine as clear indication that she was not an easy mark. The sleeping man choked suddenly, awakening himself. He looked about somewhat sheepishly, reached to his head to feel for his glasses, and promptly returned to his contented nap. Another small town whizzed by like a smeared canvas, too swiftly to permit Steve to read the name on the station platform. It didn't really matter, of course. All these towns had the same emptiness, the same vapid dreams, the same joys and sorrows, the same lonely people searching for reasons where there simply were none to find.

A portly man somewhat past his middle years, wearing a dark business suit sprinkled with ashes and a badly knotted necktie, settled his ample frame into the chair beside Steve and opened a copy of the Wall Street Journal, placing a glass of Scotch on the small stand beside him. He breathed heavily, with an irritating rasping sound, and pursed his moist lips as he examined the newspaper.

At a rippling laugh from the pretty blonde he lowered the Journal, staring myopically over the gold rims of his glasses with sudden interest. He

16

watched the young people for a moment, then sighed and slowly shook his head as though remembering past experiences or lamenting lost opportunities.

"Great to be young," he muttered through thick lips; even his voice bore the sandpapered tone of too much tobacco. "Yes, siree." He turned to Steve and leaned closer, as though speaking in the strictest confidence; his breath was stale with a tobacco odor only partially relieved by strong breath mints, and the collar of his white shirt was discolored with perspiration. "Does you good to see something like that, don't it?"

Steve smiled slightly, uninvitingly, but said nothing. He was not particularly interested in conversing with strangers. (Perhaps that had been one of his problems, he suddenly thought.)

"Sure does. Yes, sir. Sure does." The man's laughter rumbled from the depths of his fleshy stomach as he extended a huge hand blotched with large brown liver flecks; he wore a massive digital watch and a heavy school ring with a ruby stone. "Name's Clayton. Bernie S-for-Sam Clayton. Wall Street."

Reluctantly, Steve took the hand in his own; it was firm, but unpleasantly moist. "Steve Conroy."

Clayton pulled from his pocket a long black cigar that immediately made Steve think of excrement; he bit the end, spat noisily, and spoke as he wetly rolled the cigar in his mouth.

"Twenty, thirty years ago, would've been doing the same goddamned thing myself." He struck a match and frowned with concentration as he touched the flame to the cigar. "Some real nice, ripe stuff, too, let me tell you. Yes, sir." The cigar

17

securely burning, Clayton leaned back in his chair staring enviously at the young threesome, his watery blue eyes appreciatively eyeing the girl's partially exposed breasts. "Hell, tell the truth, still do it now, whenever I get a chance. Surprising what you can pick up on the train, you know, 'specially if you've got a compartment. That's why I always travel this way. Costs a little more but, shit, why pass up a chance? Those two young studs will be in there before this day's over. Girls really go for uniforms, don't they? Specially sailors. Sailor suit shows a lot more than the other services, gives a girl an idea of what she's getting. Yes, siree, sure is great to be young." He laughed too loudly and looked at Steve again; the cigar was beginning to stink. "What the hell, why should I be saying this to you? You'll probably be into something yourself before this night's over. Going to the shore for a while? Hawkins' Cove?"

"That's right," Steve admitted, switching his position slightly so as to avoid the puffs of foul smelling smoke. Then, still not wanting to appear too unfriendly, he added, "Sometimes it's good to get away for a while. Relax. Have some fun."

The man leaned closer, his left eye closing in a lewd wink, and grasped Steve's leg just above the knee, giving it an almost painfully tight squeeze. "That's right. Have some fun. That's the ticket." He chuckled. "Got a nice piece of stuff hidden away somewhere down here? Something the little woman don't know about?"

Dirty old man, Steve thought; next he'll be wanting details. "No problem. I'm not married."

The man's guffaw, exploding out of his vast flesh, blew thick cigar smoke about him as again he gave Steve's leg a hard squeeze. Steve winced and moved his leg away. "Hell, that's the ticket for sure, boy! On a trip like this, nobody's married, right? Say, where you stayin' at the Cove?"

Steve hesitated, then decided it was unlikely that this overbearing extrovert would be putting up at the same place. "The Cloud."

Clayton made a moue of distaste and shook his head, withdrawing the wet cigar from his mouth and staring accusingly at the ragged, gleaming end, as though it had somehow failed in its purpose.

"The Cloud? That old peoples' home? Hell, no action there. They don't even have a bar. Me, I always stay at The Buccaneer. Air conditioned, nice rooms, good food, and a real swinging bar; you can pick up a piece there just about any night. Don't cost too much, either. Say, maybe we can get together for a drink some evening." He winked again, and Steve suddenly had a bad taste in his mouth. "Don't worry, I won't cramp your style!"

Steve half-heartedly returned Clayton's laughter but pointedly made no response to the unwelcome suggestion. He quickly finished his drink, made some comment about getting his things together, and returned to his own car, where he sat gloomily staring through the crusted window until the train finally arrived at Hawkins' Cove just ten minutes late.

Released at last from the tedium of travel, Steve lowered his large suitcase from the overhead rack and moved to the rear door of the car, where the two sailors and the girl were already stationed, waiting for the train to come to a stop. He followed the girl to the platform as, her young breasts bouncing, she laughingly sprinted down the steps, adroitly avoiding the helping hands of the sailors.

Steve gasped when the hammer of heat struck him, and felt bands of perspiration instantly burst out on his forehead. The station was the end of the line, and the whitened boards of the empty platform were suddenly filled with people. Catching sight of Clayton ponderously descending from the bar car with two large pieces of luggage, Steve quickly made his way to the taxi stand at the further end of the platform.

"Taxi, mister?"

The driver stood leaning against the open door of his yellow cab, clad in a sweat-stained Hawaiian sportshirt and ragged cut-off jeans. His thick legs were hairy and muscular, and curls of black hair at his throat gleamed with perspiration; a toothpick emerged from a corner of his mouth.

"Right. The Cloud, please."

"Mind if I wait for some other fares?"

Steve hesitated. "I'd rather you didn't. I'll make it up to you."

The driver shrugged, shifting his toothpick to the other side of his mouth. "Okay."

Steve tried to ignore the insistent pain in the back of his head and the stickiness of his shirt as the cab moved from the station and swung towards the blueness of the horizon. The sun had baked the interior of the car, and the warm air blowing through the open windows and ruffling his hair carried with it little of cooling comfort. When the ocean suddenly came into view, Steve squinted in the glare and quickly reached into his pocket for a forgotten pair of dark glasses. His monosyllabic responses to the cabbie's inevitable

20

remarks about sports and the weather brought an end to any unwanted conversation.

The long stretch of beach was as thick with people as a stain on the pavement becomes covered with ants, a huge jumbled mass of not particularly attractive flesh in various stages of burning. Sitting, standing, walking on the soft sand, the sun-worshipers displayed too-skimpy swim suits emphasizing swollen paunches, bouncing or sagging breasts, buttocks that seemed to roll with a tide of their own. Sun umbrellas flashed vivid red, green and yellow. Deeply bronzed lifeguards sat self importantly on their raised wooden perches, surrounded by the usual coterie of admiring young girls in bikinis, carrying on inane conversations, while running their eyes over rippling muscles and tapering forms. Occasionally the lifeguards would glance out to the water where bathers clung to guide ropes and permitted themselves to be raised and lowered by the waves that seemed to roll rather sluggishly towards the beach, as though even they had been effected by the enervating heat; one of the lifeguards proudly expressed his authority by blowing his whistle at a man who had ventured too far beyond the ropes.

A wooden jetty, pointing its long finger out towards the hazy horizon, was lined with fishermen dangling their lines in the calmer waters beyond the surf. A large ferris-wheel, its cages swaying slightly as it moved in continuous circles, rose through an opening in the roof of the Casino. On the horizon was a faint dark smudge, a lone ship headed for some unknown port.

The Boardwalk swarmed with strollers while the benches were occupied by those content to sit quietly and stare out to sea with that fascination that is part of mankind's most ancient heritage. There were several minature golf courses with small windmills and carefully trimmed obstacle courses, and the screams of children rang out from the swooping and spinning rides of Kiddieland.

The sharp, tangy freshness of the sea air, filled with the mysterious odors of a world in which man would forever be a stranger, was tainted by the smells of roasting frankfurters, sweet cotton candy and salt water taffy, popcorn and French fries. A bright red balloon floated out to sea, a patch of crimson against the blue-white sky. Somewhere in the distance Steve could faintly hear the mechanical rhythms of a carousel.

Steve's attention was drawn to a small family group strolling slowly along the Boardwalk, and for a moment he seemed to be viewing a part of his own past. There were his parents walking slowly down the stretch of boards, hand-in-hand, perhaps reminiscing about the past or dreaming about the future while he, a boy of ten years, played tag with his eight-year-old sister, dashing about between the legs of the grownups, screaming with the sheer ecstasy of freedom.

A mist passed before his eyes and he sank back again into the seat, passing a weary hand over his perspiring forehead. No. No, of course not. These were people he did not know. This was a different family, a different time. That was all too long ago, surely part of someone else's life. The eight-year-old sister was grown into a wife and mother, her life carefully patterned along traditional prosaic lines. The father had been dead these fifteen years, taken from them at too young an age. And

the mother . . . the mother . . . so still and so white
. . . so very still. . . .

The cab moved on past the large domed Casino
that marked the end of the most commercial area
of the Boardwalk. Beyond this were fewer shops
and concessions, and the Boardwalk was less
crowded, the benches now occupied primarly by
elderly couples sitting silently, staring out to sea,
perhaps remembering dreams and hopes that
time would now not permit to come true. The
beach was largely deserted, save for an occasional
young couple strolling slowly along, shuffling
their bare feet through the warm sand while discussing dreams that they could still believe might
become reality. Small birds with curved beaks
played tag with the surf, and white seagulls
arched themselves against the sky.

The ground rose slightly just where the Boardwalk finally came to an end, and a small peninsula
of land jutted towards the horizon, rising to a bul-
bous end like the body of a whale. Upon this point
loomed the dark Victorian house, a reddish-brown
mass against the cloudless sky, and Steve felt a
sudden pleasurable warmth; it was like coming
home again to see those pointed gables outlined
against the bright horizon. The cab turned into
the peninsula and pulled to a stop before the
house.

"Be a buck and a quarter, mister," the sweating
driver announced, turning around and extending
his unclean hand; his initial friendliness had faded
when Steve ignored his expert opinions on the
prospects of various ball teams.

Steve handed him the fare plus a more-than-
generous tip; the cab farted some black smoke,

made a screeching U-turn, and headed back to the more lucrative area of the Boardwalk.

Steve stood for a moment on the walk before the house, listening to the cawing of the gulls, the sibilant hissing of the sea dashing against the black, wet rocks. The tall house was sharply delineated against a sky that had suddenly become somewhat hazy; there was the shadowed hint of a dark cloud rising slowly upon the horizon, like the sudden appearance of black pirate sails. The sea was becoming choppy; Steve wondered if a storm were approaching. It might break the suffocating heat. With its ornate carvings, pointed gables and tall windows, the house was like the memory of another, gentler age. A black telescope glittered in the sun on the otherwise vacant Widow's Walk. The words THE CLOUD were blazoned in fading golden letters above the broad verandah. For the first time that day, Steve felt his depression ease. It was good to be back.

Taking his suitcase in one hand, he started up the gently sloping, curved walk lined with seashells, leading to the verandah. A youngish woman with a light blanket about her legs despite the heat was seated to the right of the entrance; as he mounted the four wooden steps, she looked at him and smiled slightly, somewhat vacuously.

"Good afternoon."

"Afternoon."

"Looks like a storm coming up, doesn't it?"

He nodded. "Yes, it does. Guess I made it here just in time."

She smiled again, although the pale blue eyes remained empty, as though totally untouched by the friendly politeness of her lips, almost as if they belonged to quite another face. Forgetting him, she turned and gazed indifferently out to the swiftly graying sea. Steve hesitated for a moment, decided there was no need to say more, and entered the house.

The sombre darkness of the exterior of The Cloud was belied by the cheerful brightness of the lobby, cool and lofty, extending up the entire three stories of the structure. There were potted palms, over-stuffed chairs and sofas; on a table near the door was a lamp with a stained-glass shade. Steve thought again that a true Victorian would feel very much at home here.

Margaret Hawkins—Miss Meg to her constantly returning clientele—was standing behind the desk placed beside the curving stairway, engrossed in one of her ledgers. Miss Meg was an ample woman, plainly but well dressed, her gray hair carefully arranged, rimless spectacles firmly placed on the bridge of her generous nose. A small brown mole near the left corner of her mouth might, in a different age, have been considered a beauty mark; she thought of it as a blemish, but it did not disturb her. Perhaps never a beauty, Margaret was a warm and comfortable woman, and that was all she ever aimed to be. She looked up as Steve approached, and the stern aspect of her rather fleshy face suddenly melted in the charm of her broad smile; women more than half her age would have envied her those even, pearly teeth.

"Why, Mr. Conroy, how very nice to see you!"

"And how nice to be seen!" he responded in one of their traditional bits of badinage. "How are you, Miss Meg?" he asked, setting down his luggage and extending his hand, which became lost in the large, soft hand that absorbed it.

"Oh, I'm just fine, thank you," she responded, turning the ledger for him and handing him a nib-pointed straight-pen; her voice was surprisingly soft and gentle for a woman of her size. "It certainly is nice to have you back with us again, Mr. Conroy."

"Thank you," Steve replied, entering his name in the ledger. "You know it's always a little like coming home. And how is Mother Hawkins?"

"Oh, Mother is just fine, too, thank the Lord. Getting older, of course, but then, don't we all, if we're lucky enough?"

"And Johnny?"

With an expression of unashamed pride at this mention of her young son, Margaret closed her green eyes and nodded her head with the easy complacency of a sleepy Buddha. "Oh, that boy! Never changes. As always, running around down there on the beach somewhere and everlastingly dreaming about that someday-boat of his. But here, let me show you to your room. Ed hasn't come back from his lunch yet, so I suppose I'd better play the bellhop."

"Oh, really, that's hardly necessary," Steve objected. "I should certainly know my way about by this time."

Margaret vigorously shook her head, setting her pearl drop earrings into swinging motion. "No, no, no. You are like one of our own family here, but you are still a guest, and a guest must be shown to his room." She grunted slightly, raising her ample bosom and pulling in her stomach as she moved between the desk and the wall. "You will have the second floor front; I remember you always liked that room."

She started up the broad, curved, stairway;

picking up his bag, Steve followed her, smiling contentedly, pleased at this inevitably warm and friendly greeting. Their progress was extremely slow, the large woman leaning heavily on the graceful metal railings, gasping with the physical effort of the climb, carefully raising one leg after the other.

"People always say . . . I should put in an elevator . . . like in those big fancy hotels . . . down on the Boardwalk." She stopped and looking back at him, shook her head again; the pearls bounced almost with indignant anger against her pale cheeks and her eyes became suddenly stern with disapproval. "No, no, not here. We like this place to be like your own home, and what home has an elevator?"

The stairway curved in a broad arch against the white wall to the wide second floor balcony, onto which the various rooms opened. The stairs continued to a third floor, from which the narrow additional stairway led up to the Widow's Walk. It was a spacious and attractive area, brightened by circular windows that looked out upon the sea. Here and there along the wall, carefully placed on small wooden shelves, were models of sailing vessels, remarkably well carved and proportioned, Johnny's work. A large crystal chandelier swayed slightly in the stairwell, casting daggers of light upon the walls; it had come to them from Bavaria, and the Hawkins family had always been particularly proud of it.

They finally reached the second floor, where Margaret paused once again to catch her breath, pressing her ringed hands to her considerable bosom and inhaling deeply, like a surfacing diver. "Oh—I swear—those stairs do get steeper every

27

year!" She laughed at her own discomfort and fanned her face with a handkerchief from her pocket; Steve caught the slight, familiar scent of lilac. "And this heat! No elevators, but air-conditioning might be something else again. They say you shouldn't need it in a house that faces the sea in three directions, but the winds don't always blow the way we would like!"

She guided Steve to a door on their right, opened it and with a firm step marched across the room to draw back the golden draperies from a pair of French doors, flooding the room with bright sunshine.

"Well, now, here we are. Now I can really say welcome back. There are fresh towels in the bath, and the sheets were placed on the bed just this morning. I hope you'll enjoy your stay with us."

"Thank you, Miss Meg; I always have, you know."

With another smile, Margaret bowed herself from the room, closing the door softly behind her. Steve surveyed the now familiar room with complete satisfaction. It was large and airy, with solid, comfortable furniture and a large bed which he knew from past experience to be wonderfully soft and comfortable. There were paintings of sailing vessels on the walls and models of the same —Johnny's work again—on the dresser and the bookshelves. There was a small door leading to the bath and the large French doors opened to an iron-railed balcony overlooking the sea, with a fine view of the Boardwalk just to the right. A small radio was set on the table beside the bed, but he was rather pleased to note that Miss Meg still had not installed television sets.

Steve stood for a moment in the center of the

silent room, smelling the freshness and purity of the sea air (the heavier food odors from the Boardwalk never came this far) suddenly feeling very happy to be back here and alone again in these silent, comfortably familiar surroundings. He stepped out onto the small balcony and felt the gentle touch of blown spray on his warm, flushed face. The sounds of the Boardwalk reached him faintly; the figures in the distance looked like walking puppets that had lost their strings. Returning to the room, he quickly unpacked his bag, placing his shirts and underclothing in the large dresser against the wall, his toilet articles in the bathroom; he removed his shirt and sat before the open balcony doors, feeling just the breath of a welcome breeze brush across his bare perspiring chest.

So, here he was again. And now, the eternal question: what next? How long before this brief flight, like all the others before it, became only a frenzied attempt to fight off loneliness and somehow pass the long, empty hours? How many days and nights did he intend to sit here just like this, alone, telling himself that he must take hold of his life again and give it some direction, not tomorrow, but right now, before it was too late?

He sighed and, leaning his head back against the chair, closed his eyes for a moment. Perhaps it was already too late. He was now past his thirtieth year. He didn't even really know what he wanted out of life. Had he ever known? Had there ever been dreams? The hazy fancies of childhood were long forgotten, lost in the limbo of someone else's life.

Dreams. He didn't know what the hell there was to dream about.

He rose somewhat wearily from the chair and removed the rest of his clothing, preparing for a cooling shower and change. Perhaps it had been a mistake to come here after all. That was his inevitable thought at about this time. But he had so badly needed to get away from it all, from the office where he did his dull and meaningless work, from the cloying solicitude of a sister who tried too hard to understand what she could never hope to comprehend . . . and from all those painful reminders.

The sun glittered on a sea that had turned to silver, and he looked across again to the distant, crowded Boardwalk with its multicolored river of slow moving humanity. Hadn't they all, basically, whether they admitted it or not, come here for the same reason that had brought him? They all wanted to get away, to forget. Perhaps he need not really be so alone.

# CHAPTER TWO

Having seen her welcome guest to his room, Margaret started slowly down the stairway, leaning heavily on the metal bannister, feeling again the weight of her body and the increase of her years. There had been a time when these stairs had presented no difficulties whatever, when she could manage them easily and with a spry, light step. Lord, she had actually used to run up them half a dozen times a day without even so much as a pause for breath! Well, she had been younger then, and much lighter. Why did time become so unkind to those he marked with his cold touch?

She wanted to go and sit with Mother for a while, and hoped Ed had by now returned to his post behind the desk; age had slowed him in recent years, too, but it just didn't seem right to leave the desk empty, even though no other visitors were expected just now. Mother would be waiting for her; it was that time of day. It was so comforting to both of them to sit alone together and remember. She smiled. Oh, and there was so very much to remember, here in this great old house. The very boards spoke of remembrance; the walls breathed of the past. She paused and looked down at the highly polished lobby floor, the graceful potted plants with their broad leaves, the dark burnished wood of the doorways. She listened to the silence marked only by the everpresent rhythmic sound of the sea. The house was warm with love and memory.

Captain Nathaniel Hawkins had built the great house on the point about a hundred years ago, long before this section of the coast had suddenly blossomed into a popular summer resort. Captain Nathaniel was one of the most successful of that wonderfully hardy breed of seamen who piloted their great sailing ships to all the farthest corners of the globe, and his house was the most tangible symbol of his success. Exquisitely furnished with products from all over the world brought back in the hold of the Captain's own ship, it quickly became something of a showplace. He called it The Cloud after his ship, although its dark color bore no resemblance to the white purity of his vessel and the house looked more like a rain cloud against the clear sky. It was said no one could spread a better table than Helen Hawkins, and not even the Ancient Mariner could spin a salty yarn like Captain Nathaniel.

The Captain was typical of his breed: a big, booming, hearty and good-natured man standing almost six and a half feet in his stocking feet. He had been raised by the sea, and the sea was the only life he knew or cared to know. From an early age, his flaming red beard was sprinkled with gray, but his bright sea-green eyes, like a reflection of the broad surface of his own world, remained ever youthful. Aboard his vessel, he was considered a hard taskmaster, but a fair one, and he was justifiably proud of possessing both the trust and affection of his weatherbeaten crew.

The Captain's wife was a small, slender auburn-haired Puritan from New England, member of a collateral branch of the Captain's own large family. She, too, had lived her life by the sea, and it had never occurred to her to marry any but a seafaring man. She was physically dominated by her giant of a husband, whom she quite unashamedly adored with that dignified and rather formal devotion of the time, addressing him always by the title of "Captain" and never by his given name. Despite her appearance, there was in Helen neither meekness nor timidity. While Captain Nathaniel was the undisputed master of the bucking bridge of The Cloud, his tiny wife was complete mistress of the land-based Cloud, and even the burly seafaring man bowed to her will in the raising of their two children. Daniel was dark and stormy like his father, and Ethel, six years younger, a sparkling, laughing little girl who resembled her mother and was, next to the ship itself, the greatest love of her father's life.

The Hawkins family for some years lived in an idyllic manner in their splendid new mansion by the sea, somewhat isolated from the rest of the world, surrounded by the natural elements they had come to love, hearing only the music of the surf and the harsh calling of the gulls. The Captain continued his profitable voyages to distant lands. Whenever he was due to return, Helen, with an excited little Ethel in tow,

33

mounted the short flight of steps to the Widow's Walk and peered eagerly through the single searching eye of the black telescope for the first sight of those familiar sails. There was no fear in this vigil; Ethel knew Captain Nathaniel would always bring his ship safely to harbor.

Sorrow first touched them when young Daniel, then but fifteen years of age and on his very first sea voyage, was lost in a typhoon in the China Sea. It was the harbinger of difficult times for the Hawkins family, for the great clipper-ships floating like enormous graceful swans over the cold green seas of the north and the sparkling blue waters of the south, were all too soon replaced by clumsy but efficient steamers. Standing on the windy expanse of the Widow's Walk and peering through the salt-encrusted old telescope, Helen would see squat, ugly iron monsters pouring great columns of black smoke from obscene funnels, where she had been so long accustomed to smooth white sails and gracefully dipping prows.

Captain Nathaniel refused to accept this revolutionary change in his world. It surely could not last for long; people would return to their senses and realize steam was only a passing fad. Everyone was so easily fooled by what was new. Wind had moved ships since man had first ventured on the sea. He, for one, had no intention of altering his way of life for this meaningless and temporary change.

But the Captain was wrong. The black smoke that now stained the clear horizon was the inerradicable writing of a new era upon the sea. Man no longer had to depend on the whims of weather for his progress across the great oceans.

Those who refused to move with the time could only be left behind.

As the sailing expeditions became fewer and steamships took on more and more of the available cargo, the Captain's wealth inevitably began to dwindle, and there came that terrible day when even his great ship was lost. The Captain returned from his last voyage a sadly broken man, facing the terrible reality that there was no longer a place for him in the world and the life he had loved.

Whether it was the loss of his beloved ship and his hard won fortune, or the disappearance of a way of life that seemed to him so much cleaner and finer than that the sea now offered, it proved an unbearable burden for the Captain. One balmy summer evening, when a slight zephyr breeze was blowing to fill the canvas of ships that would sail no more, he climbed to the Widow's Walk and there put a bullet through his head. It was his adored Ethel who found him there, one arm about the blind-eyed telescope as though linked with an old and faithful friend, the salty air gently ruffling his red-gray beard, his open eyes staring sightlessly out towards the sea that had been his life and had finally conquered him only with the connivance of his own kind.

(Margaret paused halfway down the stairs to catch her breath and correct the position of one of Johnny's little ships on its shelf against the wall. She was intensely proud of her son's work, and insisted that his carvings always be displayed to their best advantage.)

With the sudden death of Captain Nathaniel, life became increasingly difficult for his widow and her young daughter. For a time they were even faced with the prospect of losing the house itself. But it was just at this most opportune time that the resort . . . named Hawkins' Cove in honor of the dead Captain . . . sprang into existence because of its suddenly discovered superior bathing and fishing facilities, and with this the Hawkins family and their beloved home were saved.

Helen determined to save her home by converting the great old house into a comfortable, family-style hotel, retaining the name The Cloud. To see her father's pride and joy, the very place where he had died by his own hand, turned into a home for strangers was to Ethel almost an act of sacrilege. On the very day the golden name was placed above the verandah to identify the house for those who had known nothing of it in the past—a branding that turned her home into a commercial enterprise—Ethel, then an attractive and determined young woman, left Hawkins' Cove vowing never to return. She went to Boston, where she married a distant relative who also bore the name of Hawkins and gave birth to three children—two sons, both of whom died at an early age, and a daughter, Margaret, born when Ethel was already well into her forties.

Ethel kept her vow for nearly twenty years, and it was only her mother's death that finally brought her back to her old home. Standing once again on the rounded point of land before the house, feeling the salt spray on her face, remembering the time-gilded days of the past, she realized she could never leave again, and announced her intention of remaining at Hawkins' Cove and continuing with her mother's plans.

Now nearing her ninetieth year, Ethel Hawkins

still lived at the old house, the management of which had long since been assumed by her daughter. Ethel's husband, whom she now only vaguely remembered, had been gone for three decades, but she herself was still reasonably alert and active. Perhaps there were times, when the white moon was brilliant on the calm sea and the night air carried with it the fragrance of distant lands, when she tended to slip into the past and remember her home as it had been when the clipper ships ruled the seas. Nonetheless, she became accustomed to the strangers and found herself entering their lives and looking forward each season to the return of regular patrons who were now almost like members of the family.

There was one part of the house to which Ethel never returned, not even on her first visit there after twenty years. No one could induce her to ascend to the Widow's Walk where, so many long years before, she had discovered the bleeding body of her father. In spite of its obvious attractions to guests at the hotel, she insisted that the Widow's Walk be closed and, with few exceptions, no one was ever permitted upon that sacred platform.

Margaret had followed the family traditions by marrying a cousin of the same name in the constantly spreading Hawkins family. Upon his death, she had returned to Hawkins' Cove and The Cloud for good. Her son, Johnny, was now just past his sixteenth year.

As a hotel, The Cloud had been considerably less than a financial bonanza, particularly after the ultra-modern hotels with their greater convenience arose in competition. It was situated too far from the main Boardwalk; lazy vacationers did not like walking ten minutes to reach the bathing areas when the larger hotels were situated directly on the Boardwalk itself. Simple but excellent meals were provided, boarding-house style, at the communal table in the large dining room for those guests who did not care for the noise and the greater expense of the Boardwalk restaurants. The Hawkins family had never been teetotalers, and choice wines were always served at dinner; although there was no actual bar or cocktail lounge, liqueurs were always available to guests in the sitting room. Nor were the comfortable rooms air-conditioned as in the larger hotels, but the house's exposed position with the sea on three of its sides, attracted pleasant breezes the other hotels did not enjoy.

Despite the lack of modernity, Margaret managed a comfortable enough living for herself and her young son, and over the years she developed a strong sense of pride in what she offered at The Cloud. There was always those seekers of peace and quiet to whom the seaside did not necessarily have to provide a carnival atmosphere, and for these the old house was ideal. It was efficiently run by a small staff, most of whom had been with the Hawkins family for a good many years, and its guests were assured of comfort, pleasant surroundings and more personal attention than could be provided at the larger hotels.

Margaret reached the bottom of the stairs and stood for a moment of quiet contemplation before the glass case in which stood a large model of the ship that had been the beginning of all this, that great vessel with the smooth lines, the proud sails, the tangled rigging and the full-breasted figure-head at the prow. She sincerely believed that even her grandfather the Captain would not have been ashamed of what had been done with this house. It was a happy place for all who came to it; surely he would have wanted that. His spirit was still very much in the high-ceilinged rooms.

There were several patrons who returned year after year to spend a part or even all of the summer at The Cloud. The largest room on the top floor was occupied by Greg Christopher, the young man who directed the popular Seaquarium down on the Boardwalk; he was the only year-round resident aside from the Hawkins family themselves. Steve Conroy generally arrived for a week or two some time during the summer; he had often come here as a child with his sister and their parents. Then they received the overflow from the other hotels, those who, lacking advance reservations, could not be accommodated and were directed to The Cloud as the only place that might have room for them. At first disappointed, many soon found themselves so content that they, too, became frequent visitors.

The Hawkins family had their own apartment in the first floor rear; Johnny, who spent the summers working as a lockerboy down at the beach, filled his room with memorabilia of the sea and his family, of which he was intensely proud. The Hawkins apartment had originally been the only one on the ground floor, but now a second apartment just off the lobby was occupied yearly throughout the summer by Linda Fraser and her daughter, Karen, a rather dowdy young girl in her late twenties. The Frasers had been spending their summers at The Cloud for some years, and this unusual arrangement had been made when Karen had been permanently crippled in an auto accident a few years earlier. They arrived in late June and remained until Labor Day. Linda's husband would arrive for a brief stay toward the end of the season, for the Hawkins Festival.

Ed had returned to his position behind the desk when Margaret reached the bottom of the stairs. He apologized for his tardiness, having fallen asleep after lunch. Margaret smiled at the small white-haired man who had been with her since she had assumed management of the house; these brief naps were becoming more frequent.

"That's all right, Ed," she assured him. "This heat is enough to make anyone sleepy."

She seemed about to say more to the thin-faced old man, his light blue eyes watery with age, then changed her mind and arched her back with weariness.

"Oh, those stairs! How I used to run up and down them a dozen times a day! Well, I'll be with Mother if you should need me for anything. I don't suppose she's gone out yet, has she?"

Ed shook his head. "I haven't seen her." He smiled, revealing his yellowing teeth. "But then, I've been asleep!"

Margaret paused at the entrance to the sitting-room, looking back at her old employee, whose head was already beginning to nod again as he seated himself behind the desk. How had he suddenly become so old? Did he wonder the same about her? What would become of him? She wondered how much he had managed to set aside over the years; certainly not a great deal, considering his earnings. He had more than once, in years passed, received offers from the Boardwalk hotels where his earnings would have been considerably higher, but he had remained loyal to the Hawkins establishment.

The large, sun-filled sitting room was vacant; her patrons were all either at the beach and Boardwalk or resting in their rooms during this hottest time of the day. She always found comfort in this room; it was pleasant, cheerful. Not quite as bright and polished as the other hotels, certainly, but comfortable.

The sadness suddenly returned, that heavy sorrow that had become so terrible a burden since the visit of Martin Levine to the house just a couple of weeks ago. She sighed and put a hand to her forehead. What would happen to them all?

And above all, what would happen to Mother? As Margaret walked through the sitting room toward her own apartment, she wondered how she could possibly tell her aged mother, whose pride in the house was even greater than her own, that this would be the final season for The Cloud, and that before long her beloved home might no longer stand on the out-jutting of rock from which it had so defiantly faced the sea for over a century.

# CHAPTER THREE

Johnny was at work at the bath-houses that afternoon. Wearing only a pair of white bathing-trunks
that set off the deep golden tan of his strong,
young body, and an open white cap with a trans-
parent green visor, he sat on the bath-house
balcony, the chair tilted back and his feet resting
on the iron railing before him. This was his
invariable pose, something he had figured out for
himself through very careful calculation and
manipulation. By sitting just exactly at this point
on the balcony and tipping his chair at exactly the
right angle, he could manage to look out to sea
without having his view marred by the strollers on
the Boardwalk and the baking masses on the
beach. The railing on which his feet rested was
level with the guide-ropes that marked the farthest
permitted extent of bathing, and thus he could see
only the sea and the sky.

Although Johnny made his summer earnings on

those who visited the beach and patronized the bath-house, he had no liking for those who came here. These people had no true understanding of the sea, merely using it for their own little pleasures, staining the smooth white beach with masses of smelling, sweating flesh, the women stretching out on the sand to bake themselves like mindless lobsters, fat middle-aged men ogling scantily-clad young girls, mothers screaming at their misbehaving children, lifeguards blowing their whistles at those venturing beyond the safety of the ropes. Only in solitude could one really appreciate the magnificence of that vast world of water.

The seafaring blood of the Hawkins family had fully reasserted itself in Johnny. He was tall for his age as were all males of his family, and darkly handsome, with a thick shock of generally unruly black hair and intense green eyes. His lips were perhaps a bit too full and sensuous for his liking but his jaw was strong and firm, his teeth even and white. He was, at this age, inclined to lankiness, but his body was strong. In her periods of mind-wandering, Ethel sometimes confused him with her long lost brother Daniel.

There was only one truly passionate love in Johnny's young life, and that was for the sea. His great-grandfather Captain Nathaniel had always been his only hero, and a large oil painting of the Captain's clipper-ship, its white sails pregnant with wind, hung on the wall just opposite his bed. The walls of his room were lined with books about the sea, and in one corner was the large table where he worked on his ship models.

The boy spent much of his time sitting quietly and alone at the very end of the spit of land on which the house stood, his arms curled about his raised legs, his eyes fixed on the glittering waters of the sea. Although generally liked by those of his own age group, he was considered slightly strange. He had no interest in, or time for, anything but the sea. His blood seemed to move with its surging tide as the blood of his friends moved with the savage rhythms of modern music. The sea was his all.

Johnny was quite certain he had been born in the wrong time. He would never be able to experience the wonders of his great-grandfather's world, the rise and fall of a clipper ship's deck beneath his feet, the surge of power as the graceful figurehead thrust her shining face thirstily beneath the green waters, the sharp flapping of the wind in the great canvas sails. That beautiful romantic era was long vanished, to be relived only through old prints and paintings, romanticized writings and films that could only hint at the excitement of the time.

It was Johnny's most persistent dream to have a boat of his own some day. Oh, nothing very large, of course, just a sloop or a schooner that he could manage by himself, something powered that could take him into the sea for greater distances than the small, battered rowboat tied to the decaying wharf at the far side of the house, something to give him that indefineable, affinity between man and the sea that was the hunger of his life. Sternberg's in town had just exactly what he wanted, a trim, white and gold 24-foot sloop that could take him anywhere he might want to go, but the price was still beyond him, and he had constantly refused his mother's offer to lend him the money.

No, this was much too important, too personal,

and he knew he would have to make it somehow completely on his own. He worked conscientiously at the lockers, where the bulk of his earnings came in tips, but the boat still seemed a rather distant dream. All those at the house were aware of his ambition, and sometimes the guests would fabricate special little errands for him to run that would give them an excuse to hand him an extra dollar or so. Some purchased his ship models, although Johnny often felt the miniatures were too much a part of himself to sell to others. It all helped, but still it was not enough. Once the summer was over and he returned to school, his earning powers would drop sharply.

No one seemed more understanding and helpful than his great friend Greg Christopher, who gave him five dollars for every interesting sea specimen he brought to the Seaquarium. But those were sometimes rather difficult to come across, particularly during the summer months when the influx of bathers and fisherman drove so much of the sea life further from shore.

The Seaquarium was Johnny's favorite place on the Boardwalk. Here he would stand for hours at a time on the edge of the huge tank with the rippling water reflected on the green walls, watching the seals at play, the ominously languid movements of the great gray shark, the lazy crawling of the tortoise, the ugliness of the horseshoe crabs with their hard backs, spiney tails and many spider-like legs.

Sometimes he would follow his friend Greg and the group of interested customers to the plate glass window-cases set in the walls of the second floor gallery. Here were the small, deceptively innocent piranha with their little razor-sharp teeth, the electric eel with what looked like fluttering frills along the sides of its body, the angel fish, puffers, seahorses.

Or he would examine the seashells and wonder at the fabulously delicate shapes of these peculiar marine creatures, the fragile white shell of the tiny creature that could bore its way through the thick sides of man-eating clams, the bright green and pink ferns that looked like delicate fans, the chambered nautilus about which someone had once written a rather silly poem they had learned in school. Johnny had no fear of sea creatures, no matter what their size; to him, they were all friends.

Greg Christopher very quickly became the new hero in the boy's life. Johnny had not yet passed beyond the age of hero-worship. Although twice his age, Greg treated Johnny like an equal and a friend, and often they would spend the first or the last hours of the day seated together on the deserted beach, feeling the salt of the cool sea air on their faces, watching the sand crabs scurrying home, wondering at the glorious touch of gold on the sea as the sun sank behind the horizon. The waves carried bits of driftwood that might have traveled clear around the world, washing them up onto the beach and then carrying them out again on the next tide, as though the flotsam were under some Flying Dutchman curse and fated to be rejected by all the beaches of the world. Here and there were green-black splashes of seaweed stretched like bloated corpses on the sand. There would be a wonderful stillness in the world. Sometimes they would talk together about the sea, or perhaps they would not say so much as a single word, content in their own company and in the beauty that surrounded them.

This was Johnny's world, all the world he ever needed or wanted, and those were the golden hours of his days. He often wondered what the world had been like in those distant ages before the arrival of Man, when the great thundering sea covered even more of the land than it does now, when the world was silent save for the crashing of the great breakers, in a world of scudding gray clouds and tumbling green-white water.

"Locker boy!"

The sharp, angry call brought Johnny abruptly out of his reverie. He lowered the chair and picked up the keys from the floor beside him. A balding middle-aged man with excessively hairy legs stood impatiently at the far end of one of the aisles, irritatedly brushing at the sand on his swim suit.

"Come on, boy, move your ass, will you? I haven't got all day!" He brushed vigorously at the loose grains of sand clinging to the graying hair on his sloping shoulders. "God damn sand! Come down here for one day and itch with sand for a whole week! Come on, boy, God damn it, open up, will you?"

"Yes, sir!"

Johnny turned the key and the little wooden door opened revealing the bare white-panelled walls and bench, the hooks on which hung a pair of wrinkled brown slacks, a tan sportshirt, and shit-stained underwear; the portly man forced himself into the little room and, without bothering to close the door, began to twist and squirm as he pulled the wet bathing trunks over his ungainly body.

48

"God damn ocean! Ain't even fit to piss in! Every God damn summer we have to come down to this God damn place. What the hell does anybody want with so damned much water, anyway? You can't swim in it, it's too damn rough. You can't sit in it, it's too damned cold. All you can do is stand in it and let it knock you down. Damn salt gets in your eyes and you can't see a damned thing. Crabs bite your toes. Damn waste of time, that's what it is, a God damned waste of time. Not next year, by God! Next year, we go to the mountains, and this whole God damned ocean can go to hell!"

Johnny kicked the door shut with his foot and returned to his perch overlooking the sea. He noticed the weather was changing sharply and rapidly. The sky had begun to darken, as though a piece of black gauze had been placed in front of the sun, and already stretches of empty sand were appearing on the crowded beach. The heat had become even more intense. To the west, the blue-white sky was blended with a darker and more ominous shade of blue, and there was a hint of blackness just below the horizon. Irritated parents, anxious to commence the homeward journey before the storm broke, began to call their sullen, stubborn children from the water.

Johnny leaned back in his chair, placed his bare feet up on the railing, and his eyes once again moved across his own private world.

By the time Steve left The Cloud, now more comfortably dressed in white slacks and a light sportshirt, the sun had already disappeared behind a haze of yellow-gray clouds rolling in from the West. As he headed for the Boardwalk, he saw the merest flicker of lightning on the horizon, followed after an appreciable time by low, scarcely audible thunder.

The shop keepers on the Boardwalk, their practiced eyes ever alert for sudden changes in the weather, were busily moving their exterior displays indoors, and the beach had already become an almost vacant expanse of littered sand. The bathing was obviously over for the day, although a few young diehards were still stretched out under the sunless sky, as though defying the weather to interfere with their pleasures. The beach cleaners walked along with their pointed sticks, stabbing the litter of candy and ice-cream wrappers as though they were personal enemies, while the lifeguards shuffled across the sand with folded umbrellas under their arms. As the storm came closer, the heat increased.

Steve strolled slowly along the gradually emptying Boardwalk, his hands plunged into his pockets, no objective in mind, oblivious to the suddenly threatening weather. He enjoyed these first hours at the sea, before the onset of ennui. He paused for a moment at the railing and looked across to the graying horizon, inhaling the sharp, fishy smell of the ocean. The blue-green water had turned a dull gray, and the waves seemed to have regained some of their vigor as they crashed heavily against the sand. Gulls walked along the water's edge, pecking at the minute creatures washed up by the waves.

Steve left the railing and walked on down the Boardwalk, pausing for a moment to watch a party of miniature golfers driving small white balls across a Lilliputian landscape. Passing the bath-house, he saw Johnny sitting on the balcony, staring out to sea. He raised his hand and waved, but the boy apparently could not see him. Inspecting the colored postcards with their standard views of the too-blue sea and the crowded Boardwalk, he decided it was too soon to send one to his sister, and there was no one else he cared to remember.

It was really too soon for anything just yet. It was not yet time to start thinking. For the first day or so, he would at least attempt to enjoy himself. Serious thinking could come later, once he had managed to unwind that knot in his stomach and clear his mind of the tortured confusions that befuddled his thinking. He would swim, sun himself on the beach, amble along the Boardwalk, play miniature golf. He would have a drink whenever he felt like it, drop in to see a movie, maybe even take a ride on the Ferris wheel. Christ, how long since he'd spread his legs around the painted form of a carousel horse?

Other things would have to wait. For now, he would try to forget his aching loneliness, try to erase from his mind the terrible picture of his mother lying so strangely still, her face whiter than he had ever seen it before, her eyes closed. . .

He was startled when his thoughts were interrupted by the first drop of rain on his warm cheek, and he quickened his pace to the Casino. A brilliant flash of lightning, followed almost instantly by an ear-shattering clap of thunder, indicated the storm had come up quickly, and brought screams of surprise from women and children as the skies suddenly opened and a torrent of rain cascaded down upon them.

The great glass and steel Casino was a bedlam of noise and confusion. Disheartened vacationers gathered in small unhappy groups, the women with their hair hanging in wet strings, the men tired and impatient. The Casino was not completely waterproof; here and there sprays of rain fell upon them, and small puddles began to form on the floor. The echoing sounds raised by the ringing games of chance, the monotonous music of the carousel and the yelling children were deafening and the atmosphere was depressing.

Leaning against a hot-dog counter and apparently not at all dispirited by the change in the weather were the two sailors Steve had seen on the train, together with their blond girl friend and another attractive brunette. Their faces were flushed with youth and pleasure.

It was growing darker now, with frequent flashes of lightning that momentarily dimmed even the brightness of the flashing colored lights within the Casino. Steve made his way through the grumbling crowds and stood at the closed window, staring out at what had suddenly become a pettishly angry gray sea. Here it was somewhat quieter. Great yellow-streaked clouds covered the sky, and the line of the horizon was lost behind him.

Steve seated himself in a bamboo rocking-chair, lighted anther cigarette, and stared thoughtlessly at the tossing white-caps. He angrily banished every vagrant thought that entered his mind. He was not yet ready for thinking.

Was he ever ready for thinking? Would he ever really be ready to grapple with the problem of his life?

He knew suddenly that this would be the same as his last visit here. Every tomorrow would be the time to start thinking, to tangle with the problems that had sent him here. And every tomorrow would be the wrong tomorrow to begin. He would again postpone the unpleasantness of serious thought until the very last moment.

And then it would be too late.

# CHAPTER FOUR

Unable to secure a room at any of the larger hotels on the Boardwalk, the two sailors were also staying at The Cloud, although neither of them was particularly pleased about it. But whereas Paul could always manage to adjust to even the most unexpected developments, Michael was much more vocal in his displeasure; as a matter of fact, he had all along been not particularly enchanted about this entire outing to the shore, and had already expressed his dissatisfaction several times during that day.

"I just don't see what we can get here that we wouldn't be able to get in the city," he complained again as he unpacked his few necessities and placed them with his customary tidiness in the dresser drawers.

Paul stepped from the shower, vigorously rubbing himself with a large fluffy white towel; his thick black hair, glistened with wetness, a single curl dangling over his forehead. "Maybe nothing at all," he admitted, "but here we have a better chance of getting something, that's all. Hell, the city's got sailors up the ass. How many have we seen here? Just a few. You gotta take the competition into consideration."

Michael looked wryly at his friend's naked form, the powerfully muscled and perfectly proportioned body, the startlingly handsome face with its light blue eyes and ready smile, and enviously compared Paul's tremendous virility with his own slender blond boyishness.

"I do, maybe," he complained. "You don't know the meaning of the word."

Paul tossed the towel into a chair and threw himself on the bed, luxuriously stretching himself. "Hell, we're gonna have a ball, Mike. Don't we already have dates?"

"We've got something, I guess, but I don't know what. I don't like these 'bring a friend for my friend' dates. You know what you're getting. The friend might weigh two hundred pounds and have bad breath."

"Who gives a shit about her breath, as long as she's got everything else you want?" Paul chuckled. "Look on the bright side; she might be even better than Chrissy."

"Then you'll probably take 'em both."

Paul laughed. "I always share with you, buddy. Tell you what: you can take your pick." With one energetic bound, he leaped from the bed and reached for his clothing. "If you wanta take a shower, better make it snappy."

Paul began stepping into his clothes, while Michael removed his own and headed for the shower. He paused at the doorway and turned to his friend. "And don't call me Mike," he cautioned. "You know I don't like it."

Paul grinned. "Okay, Michael, Michael it is. Some guys just gotta sound fancy."

Michael disappeared into the bathroom and the sudden thunder of water drowned out other sounds. Paul whistled as he slipped into the crisply clean underwear, then drew on the tight-fitting white trousers, pleased at their promising and inviting cut; never hurts to show a little, he thought again. Careful to avoid wrinkling, he drew the jumper over his head and fastened the black kerchief, drawing the knot up close to his throat, wondering what he would look like if they really came across with the new uniforms they were always talking about. A few careful touches with the brush and he was prepared for what he hoped would develop into a satisfying evening.

"Hey, Michael," he called into the bathroom, "I'm going on downstairs. Meet you outside."

"What you say?" Michael called over the roar of the shower.

"Meet you outside!"

"Right!"

Still whistling, Paul stepped from their pleasant third floor room and started down the stairs. Pausing at the railing, he glanced at the chandelier casting dagger-prisms of colored light, and at the broad marble floor of the lobby, and felt himself suitably impressed. He looked with interest at the ship models as he started on down the stairway, reading the identifying plates beneath each one—Emerald, Coquette, Flying Cloud, Ann McKim—and admired the delicacy and apparent accuracy of the carvings. At the bottom of the stairs, in a special glass case, stood a much larger and more intricate model of The Cloud, with Nathaniel Hawkins indicated as its captain. He wondered vaguely at the change in fortune that had converted a home like this into a hotel.

When Paul stepped through the lobby and out to the verandah, the girl who had been seated there on their arrival was still in her chair near the door, a light brown blanket covering her legs. Paul threw her the same carefully appraising glance he automatically had for all women. A bit too old to be of much interest to him, he decided. Late twenties, maybe even early thirties, hard to tell with such a lifeless face. Plain, too thin, nose a little too long, not much of a figure that he could see. He wondered what just a bit of color would do for her, just a slight sparkle of life in eyes that looked too worn and sad for her years. There was something about the set of the mouth and her thin lips that indicated smiles did not come to her easily. She looked up at him, briefly, then turned her eyes away as though she had not even seen him. He stood for a moment leaning against one of the pillars and lit a cigarette, wondering if she appreciated the fine, strong figure he presented. He noticed it was growing much darker over the sea.

"Storm coming," he commented.

After a moment she replied, "Yes, I imagine so." Her voice was not unpleasant, soft, somehow sad.

"Hope my buddy and I can get to the Boardwalk fast." He looked down at himself and wondered if her eyes followed him. "These uniforms can get to be a real mess when they're wet. Don't suppose there's any kind of bus that goes by here?"

She paused again, as though uncertain of the propriety of speaking with him. Was she one of those old-fashioned broads who needs an introduction, or had she heard too many stories about sailors?

"I really couldn't say," she responded. "I've never really noticed. I seldom go down to the Boardwalk. You could always call a cab, I suppose."

He shrugged his shoulders. "Don't really seem worth it, for that distance. Guess we'll be able to make it all right. Good to do a bit of running now and then, anyway."

"It's your decision, of course."

Her voice had become suddenly, unexpectedly hardened and he threw her a sharp glance, irritated by the sudden attitude of indifference. Women generally paid Paul more attention. This one scarcely seemed to know he was there, and couldn't care less. He shrugged again. Didn't really mean that much to him. A little younger, she might have presented a challenge. Not much of one, of course; he generally got what he wanted without much trouble.

Since the girl was obviously not inclined to friendliness, Paul stepped from the verandah and walked down the slope and along the empty beach to the end of the peninsula. The sea had grown rougher, and the breakers crashed noisily onto the shore. Not a bathing beach, the peninsula was lined with sharp, spume covered rocks. The whitecaps had increased in size and number. A dead fish of some kind lay just out of reach of the waves. A short distance to the north, a rock jetty pointed out to sea, and the waves battered the wet boulders with curtains of lacey white foam. The air was fresh and bracing. Paul squatted a few feet from the rising tide, careful not to soil his uniform, and scratched absently in the sand. His face became suddenly more serious as he battled again with the light but uncomfortable pricks of his conscience.

He knew he should have gone home on this brief leave, rather than come here, strictly interested in his own enjoyment. It had been more than a year since his last visit to the city where he had been born and spent most of his life. But what was there for him now in that sewer where he had been raised? His father had been in prison for the past two years after conviction for armed robbery, and would be kept there for another few years at least, since this was by no means his first offense. Nor was there any reason to hope that this new period of incarceration had changed him in any way, except perhaps to make him more brutal and angrier with the disastrous course of his life. Paul's older sister, still unmarried, had just undergone her third abortion, as always not even really knowing who had placed her in such a condition. His mother was still doggedly trying to drink herself into an early grave.

Paul tossed a pebble into an incoming wave; it disappeared as though cast into a hungry maw.

It was only his mother he really cared about, that worn, weary, battered woman who was finding it ever more difficult to cope with the unfairness of her life. How often she had promised to stop her drinking, if only he would agree to come home more often to see her, but the last visit, during his Christmas leave, had been a total disaster that he did not ever want repeated. He still remembered with a cringing sense of shame her pathetic attempts to make him feel at home. Never before had the cramped, dark fifth-floor walkup with the peeling walls and dripping sinks been so clean. In a corner, its tired branches already sagging and its needles falling in a green-black shower on the white cloth beneath, stood a pitifully small Christmas tree, its colored balls and shreds of dangling tinsel only adding to its attitude of loneliness and despair. At the top of the tree a pink-gowned angel spread wings in blessing, and beneath the tree was a cheaply made manger scene. His mother had spent the entire afternoon at having her graying hair done, trying to smooth the drink-created wrinkles in her face. But the dark pouches were still there, the trembling of the hands, and her eyes constantly moved toward the cabinet where he knew a bottle was carefully concealed under the linen sheets.

On the very day after Christmas, Paul had returned to the apartment to find her once again in a drunken daze. She had pleaded with him, on her knees, the tears coursing down her worn face, to forgive her this one lapse. She would never do it again, it was just that she was so nervous, so anxious to please him. He had left her there, weeping on her knees, and returned to his ship. He hadn't been home since, simply ignoring the pleas in her frequent letters, which he always diligently answered, as though nothing had gone wrong between them.

It wasn't that Paul had no feeling for his family. He and his sister had once been quite good friends, until the increasing despair of their home life led her to the streets and into one sordid entanglement after another. He had never really had much use for his brutal father, that burly, broad-shouldered

61

Greek with his constant need for money to satisfy his gambling debts. More than once, his mother had physically borne the evidence of his violent rage. It was gambling that had finally driven him to crime, at which he was no more successful than at anything else in his life. In his own way, Paul still felt a strong need to love his mother, that saddened woman trying to find in drink a forget-fulness of the squalid life she lived. But even love could not survive the stultifying pity he felt for her, and the embarrassment of being in her company.

Paul realized that the basis of his problem with his family was simple fear, fear of the kind of life they led, fear of the sordidness that surrounded them. He wanted to get away from that ugly world before the cancer of it infected him as well, the sordidness of the Greek-Italian slum, the dirt engendered by a sense of hopelessness that seemed bred with his mother's milk. Throughout his life there, he had seen too much that had frightened him, even aside from the terrible erosion of his parents' relationship. He had seen friends beaten and knifed by rival gangs. Other friends had been sentenced to long prison terms when their desper-ation turned them to crime, not as much for the necessities of life as for the urgency to express their burning anger. He had watched others writhing under the horrifying impact of drugs that numbed the mind and helped them, briefly and at a terrible cost, to forget the bleakness of their lives.

And all of this frightened him, filled his days with fear and his nights with terrible dreams. He needed to break out of the imprisoning mold before it was too late, to save himself from the depressing fate that was endemic in the stinking slum where he had been raised.

He had enlisted in the navy on a sudden impulse, following a particularly ugly battle between his parents that had ended with his father carted off to jail and his mother briefly committed to the alcoholic ward of the local hospital. This was the end; he could bear no more of it. Strolling the streets of the city, lost in fear and confusion, he had seen the recruitment poster and, almost without thought, entered and offered his services.

He had never regretted it. Life in the navy suited him. He liked the order, the dependable routine, the cleanliness and the cameraderie. It seemed to lend a purpose to his life, and for the first time he awakened each morning without the crushing burden of not knowing what problems would have to be faced. It had been two years now, and he was still enjoying every moment of it.

Paul smiled as he tossed another pebble into the breaking crest of an incoming wave. It had been fun, too, more fun than he could have imagined. He gave a slightly lascivious chuckle. The girls really went for sailors.

Paul had never been particularly vain about his looks; some people were born handsome while others were born ugly, and it had simply been his luck to be one of the former. He was young, virile, and good looking, both face and figure cast in the classic Greek mold. While he took no credit for this bounty of nature, Paul could see no reason why he should not take full advantage of it. He had first learned the pleasures of sexual release when he was only thirteen and he and several of his companions of the street had taken the young girls from the local orphanage up onto the dark roof of the tenement building and had their way with them. Time and surroundings had changed this for him now. No more sweaty couplings on baked rooftops or in dark, dirty hallways smelling of cooked cabbage. A new world of opportunities had opened to him, and he took full advantage of it. It was part of being a sailor.

This made him think of Mike—Michael, he corrected himself—and he mused again on the attraction of opposites. Michael, his closest friend, was in almost every way his opposite. A farm boy from Ohio, blond where Paul was dark, small where he was muscular, Michael had come from a decent family dominated by the strict, narrowminded religious attitudes of midwestern Protestantism. Movies were considered sinful, his reading was closely supervised, television was not even permitted. Michael's mother was a staunch prohibitionist and his father would never think of approaching the dinner table without necktie and jacket. Their home was a large three-storied frame building, white with green shutters, impeccably clean and tidy, where the word 'shit' had never been uttered. Michael had his own spacious room, with college pennants tacked to the walls and photographs of his sports heroes on the desk and dresser. A large willow wept silently just outside his window, casting its shadows on the white ceiling of the room. Paul had once spent a few days with Michael there; it had been like the realization of a childhood dream.

Paul rose from his haunches and walked farther down the beach, to the very point. A wave broke too close to him and left a smear of wet sand on his well-polished shoes; with a muttered oath, he pulled a white handkerchief from the tight waist-band on his trousers and wiped the shoe clean, then carefully refolded the handkerchief to cover the stain and restored it to its place.

It was a strange thing about these nice, wholesome all-American kids. Maybe too much religion did it to them; it seemed to turn them mad for sex. With all his different background, Michael was as avid for sex as Paul himself, although there was always a slight difference in his attitude, for Michael was possessed of a strong sense of middle-class morality that never disturbed his friend. Paul was never bothered by anything he did; pleasure and satisfaction were his only criteria, and he had no patience for moralizing.

It was different with Michael. Enough of his proper background remained to cause him occasional uneasiness about the promiscuity of naval life. He sensed it as a base betrayal of his sheltered, religious upbringing. He had at first been disturbed by Paul's candid approach to sex, and by the constant stream of obscenities that filled his conversation. But he could not be long in the service and retain such attitudes. It was perhaps more difficult to overcome his inbred sense of sexual guilt, and he would often feel shame at the thought of that clean, neat room at home with the shadows of the willow and the bed he had never yet shared with anyone.

But Michael was learning. The drive was strong and could not be denied. The sense of guilt never lasted long and never interfered with the next exciting opportunity. He was a good Joe.

Paul looked up sharply, wondering if that sudden cold touch on his cheek could be the first drop of rain. He turned to the house and saw

Michael starting down the verandah steps. He waved to him, pointed toward the Boardwalk, and started off in that direction.

# CHAPTER FIVE

From her position on the verandah, Karen Fraser
watched the sailors walking quickly toward the
Boardwalk, and she was instantly reminded of
Jeffrey. This was not unusual. Everything
reminded her of him. He was part of every scene,
every thought, every remembrance. They had
once been here together, had walked along that
stretch of sand, felt the same sea air cool their
flushed faces. They had strolled arm in arm,
gazing at the sea while dreaming of a future that
was not to be. Everything in Karen's life was connected with Jeffrey.

How long ago had it been? The passage of time
tended to confuse her, for it was all one, and there
was now little difference between the days.
Present and future had no existence for Karen.
There was only the past. The world was dead, and
she was part of its corpse.

Karen spent all her summers at the old Hawkins

home, and she seldom left the house throughout the duration of her stay, venturing only as far as the end of the point on which the building stood. She preferred to spend her afternoons seated on the verandah, reading and remembering.

People often wondered about the white-faced, crippled girl who spent all her time staring sadly out to sea. When they learned her story, they felt sorry for her, and this pity from strangers was now the only remaining joy of Karen's life. She was always eager to accept a sorrowful word, a sad smile, a tender touch of the hand. One day before the two sailors left here, she would have their pity as well; they had probably not yet noticed that the chair in which she sat was wheeled. She would accept their unspoken pity quietly and with just the slightest touch of humility, not really with gratitude but as something to which she was richly entitled through the great shining tragedy of her life. She accepted this pity from everyone, friend and stranger alike, carefully storing it away like a child's treasure, to bring her warmth and comfort in the dark lonely hours of which her life was now composed, a perpetual reminder to herself and to others of the dreadful loss she had suffered. Pity was all that mattered now. Pity and remembrance. That was all she wanted or lived for.

The door opened and her mother stepped onto the verandah. Linda Fraser was still an attractive woman though now well into her fifties, chic and fashionably dressed; it was only by looking very closely that you might discern the dark shadows of weariness beneath her eyes, the exhaustion in the lines about her mouth. She stood at the top of the steps for a moment, peering with some concern into the darkening sky, then turned to her daughter.

"I thought I might just run into town for a bit, dear, and pick up a few little things, before the storm. I'm sure I'll have enough time. Why don't you come with me, Karen?"

Karen smiled her carefully sad smile and shook her head. "Oh, no, I don't believe I will, mother."

Linda hesitated, realizing insistence was quite useless, but always anxious to try, in the hope that one day the result might be different; she looked at her daughter and frowned.

"We could call a cab, and then we wouldn't even have to worry about the rain at all. It really would do you a world of good, Karen; you know you haven't left this house since we arrived."

The girl shook her head again, with a slight trace of irritation at the repetition of the offer. "No. I don't think so, mother. I'd really much rather just sit here."

"Well . . ." Linda had known from the start of the conversation that there really had been no point even in asking; Karen never went anywhere. "Is there anything I can get for you?"

"You might pick up another book, if you should see something really interesting. I've just about finished the one you brought the other day."

"Of course, dear."

"A love story."

"Yes, of course." Karen never read anything else. "Well, I won't be long, I'm sure; perhaps I can get back before the storm breaks."

"Oh, don't worry on my account, mother." Linda recognized in her tone that slight touch of pathos that Karen had so carefully cultivated as a part of her constant ploy for sympathy. "I'm sure I'll be quite all right. You just enjoy yourself."

After a moment's hesitation, Linda started down the steps, casting an uncertain eye to the sky. Karen watched her mother until she moved out of sight. She smiled with a trace of satisfaction. No one had more pity for her than her mother, and that was a great comfort to her.

"Would you like a nice glass of cold lemonade, Karen?"

Karen turned to see the large matronly figure of Margaret Hawkins looming over her, holding a small wooden tray with two glasses of lemonade in which floated slices of green lime. Smiling, Karen took one glass.

"Thank you very much, Miss Meg; I was getting a bit dry."

Margaret placed the tray on a small table and, taking the other glass for herself, sank into a chair at Karen's side. The big woman always suffered severely from the summer heat, and a large stain of perspiration soiled the back of her print dress and created unsightly wet patches under her arms. She wiped a large kitchen towel over her face; she carried it everywhere during the summer to dab at the curtains of perspiration that constantly trickled down her forehead and beaded her upper lip.

"It's really fearfully close, isn't it?" she asked. "Perhaps the storm will cool it off a bit. I feel so sorry for everyone when it rains on weekends, and it does seem a pity that the weather so often has to be bad for them. You can't blame them for complaining."

Karen smiled slightly. "People like to complain about the weather. Weekend rain ruins their good time, but if it rains when they have to go to the office, they complain just as loudly about the inconvenience. I suppose it's unfortunate that the rain can't restrict itself to the very late hours of night or the very early hours of morning. It did that in Camelot, didn't it? But I imagine there are people who would be inconvenienced even then."

They sat silently for several moments, sipping their drinks. There were two toy ships on the horizon, steaming northwards, their black smoke rising in motionless columns against the graying sky.

"I see there are a couple of sailors staying with us," Karen mentioned.

"Yes. They weren't able to get a room at The Buccaneer, so they came here. I'm afraid they really aren't very happy about it. They seem like nice boys. I like having men of the sea in this house, but you can't blame them for preferring the larger, more modern hotels, particularly the young people." She smiled as she raised the glass to her lips. "Men of the sea! That sounds rather antiquated, doesn't it? I suppose they call them sailors, but it just doesn't have the same ring to it."

Karen drained the last of her lemonade and set the glass down on the table. "Well, if you don't mind, I believe I'll just go inside for a bit. I've something of a headache; the heat, I suppose. A nap might make me feel better."

"Of course, my dear. Can I help you?"

"No, no," Karen quickly responded. "I can manage quite well, thank you. I'm used to it by now."

Slowly, Karen wheeled herself into the quiet, empty lobby and turned to the left, to the small apartment she shared with her mother. The windows had been closed and the room was uncomfortably stuffy. There were no cigarettes in the case on the coffee table, but she found some on the writing desk against the wall. Blowing the smoke from her lips, she lowered the lighter to the desk and, in doing so, caught sight of her reflection in the large mirror on the opposite wall. She turned her chair and sat for a moment, drawing slowly on the cigarette, looking at herself quite objectively, as though examining a stranger, turning her head for different views.

Karen had never been a really pretty girl, although her features were regular and pleasant enough, stamped with what is often termed "character," a phrase kindly supplied where there is an absence of beauty. The girl in the mirror looked older than her years. Unmarked by makeup the face seemed almost ashen. Her hair was a mousey brown; she wore it loose and untended, and she noticed now there were already a few strands of gray. That pleased her. She was still far too young for gray hair, and people would attribute it to her great sorrow. She had often wished she might have managed to have her hair turn completely white after the events of that harrowing night. She wanted to look plain and sorrowful, and had managed to defeat all efforts of mother to improve her appearance. There was no longer any need for an attempt at charm and beauty, and it would not suit the image she meant to present to the world.

She snuffed out the cigarette and wheeled herself into her own room, closing the door behind her. The room was small and tastefully furnished, but deep in gloom. Karen seemed not to notice the extreme closeness of the air as she moved her chair to the stereo machine and switched it on. The music was soft and melancholy.

Karen wheeled herself across the room and turned on a small light standing before a vase of white flowers on a table against the wall farthest from the windows. The light shone upon a life-sized painting of a young man wearing a white tennis sweater with a red and blue stripe across the chest. The pose was awkward and artificial, the smile insincere, the flesh tones too robustly pink and the eyes blue and overly large. The basically attractive features seemed idealized, like the portrait of a mythological Teutonic god, with its curled light brown hair, straight nose, and sensual lips. An attempt had been made to give the eyes depth and expression, but they resembled only the rude stare of a child. The portrait had obviously been done from a poor photograph or from a particularly idealistic description.

Karen moved her chair back from the wall and, with her hands folded in her lap and an expression of almost religious adoration on her face, she stared intently at the painting, her eyes softly carressing the well remembered features. Her head moved slightly in motion with the languid music. Her lips parted and her eyes misted.

The first drops of rain struck the windows of the room, but Karen failed to hear them. In her small circle of light, she resembled an enraptured devotee before the ikon of a saint. Only the veil was missing.

The sudden rain-squall brought an effective end to the afternoon's activities on the beach. The Boardwalk was deserted, the boards washed clean. The sea had become rough, but it seemed not an angry roughness; thunderous, yet somehow jovial, the sea welcomed the touch of rain to add to its vast watery empire.

Johnny sat in his chair overlooking the sea, sheltered from the rain by the overhanging eaves. There were calls of 'so-long,' and 'see you' behind him; the lockers were closing for the day. Now and then a gust of wind blew a mist of rain into his flushed face. He had already changed from his swimming trunks into his jeans and T-shirt; he would be leaving shortly, the last as always.

"Christ, you'd think there wasn't enough water out there already," a voice said behind him. "Gotta have more from the sky."

"The clouds picked it up from the sea to begin with," Johnny commented, defensively. "Rain's good sometimes. Cools things off. Cleans 'em." He breathed deeply, the tang of the sea and the freshness of the rain sharp in his nostrils. "Just smell that ocean! Cleanest smell in the world." He straightened in his chair and supported his chin on his arms as he leaned on the railing, staring across the rain-spattered Boardwalk and the empty beach to the sea; his friend Jimmy leaned against the wall. "Look at those whitecaps, how the waves stand still for a moment before they sort of turn in on themselves and tumble down on the beach. Think of all that water. . ."

They both moved quickly back under the eaves as a sudden gust of wind blew the rain in on them; the thunder of its fall was loud on the wooden roof. The rain struck the Boardwalk and ran in small rivulets between the boards. Jimmy drew a cigarette from his pocket, offered Johnny one, and lit up for both of them, making no comment on his friend's remarks; everyone at the lockers knew

74

how hung-up Johnny was about the sea. The best thing to do was just let him talk himself out. He never really expected any answers, anyway. Jimmy was a year older than his friend, tall and husky, proud of the hair sprouting on his chest.

"How'd you do today?" he asked.

Johnny reached into his pocket and loudly jingled a considerable amount of loose change. "Pretty good; too bad the storm stopped it. How about you?"

Jimmy turned his head and glanced carefully down the empty, rain-drenched wooden aisles with their rows of half-open doors, then dug his own earnings from the pocket of his jeans. In the mass of silver there were a number of dollar bills. Johnny glanced at him in surprise, then an expression of suspicion crossed his face; he turned again to the sea without saying a word.

Jimmy stuffed the bills back into his pocket and leaned against the railing, looking at his friend with a half-amused expression of superiority. "Don't be a dope, Johnny. Why the hell do you want to work for quarters when you can get some bills? Why don't you get smart?"

"Maybe I just don't think it's so smart," Johnny said, his voice betraying the beginnings of anger.

"What the hell's the harm?" Jimmy demanded. "So some of the guys get a little excited if you look at 'em when they're naked. You just open the door a crack and take a look at them. How does that hurt you? It's good at least for a buck, every time."

"You didn't get all that just for looking, Jimmy."

Jimmy flushed a bit, shifted his position uneasily, and laughed with a slight trace of embarrassment. "Oh, all right, so look, is my hand rotten just because maybe I give 'em a little feel once in a while? It's real easy money."

"Maybe I'm satisfied with the money I get just doing the work I was hired to do. This is a bathhouse, Jimmy, not a place for queers to come to when they want a kid to play around with."

"Oh, shit, who's talking about playing around? I never really do anything to them, even if they ask me to." He moved closer and lowered his voice. "And sometimes you don't even have to do anything at all."

"What do you mean?"

"Look at this, will you?"

Jimmy drew his hand from his other pocket and revealed the corner of a five-dollar bill. Johnny looked at him with undisguised amazement.

"Five dollars. Where'd you get that?"

"Shh! Not so loud!" Jimmy hushed, again glancing uneasily about them and shoving the money back into his pocket. "The easiest five bucks I ever made in my life. Couple of guys came to me just about noontime and asked if they could have just the one bath-house together. I told them there were plenty of empty bath-houses, and they're too small to hold more than one person; cost is the same, anyway. Then one of them took me aside and said he and this other guy had just met and they were hot for each other but they had no place to go, and if I'd let them use a bath-house and saw that nobody came near the place for just ten minutes, they'd give me five bucks."

Johnny rose so quickly that his chair fell over. "You're crazy!"

Jimmy shrugged. "Aw, shit, who's ever gonna know about it? It was a slow time of day, lots of empty houses, nobody around. I took them down to the last one, they went in, I closed the door behind them and just kept my eyes open for about ten minutes. Nobody ever came near the place. Then they both came out again, in their trunks, slipped me the bill and went to the beach, and nobody knew the difference."

"You know what they'd do if they ever found out?"

"Who the hell's gonna find out? All those guys want is a few minutes to have a little fun. They've got it done before anybody else even comes near the place."

Jimmy thrust his hands in his pockets and walked nervously up and down as he talked, his face flushed with anger; the rain was heavy again and the sky had darkened further. "Don't be a goddamned idiot! Didn't they kick Harry out on his ass when they found out some of the women were paying him to go into the lockers with them?"

"Shit, Harry couldn't keep his fool mouth shut, always bragging about how good he was and how hot all the broads were for him and how they all paid him for a quick screw. That was his own fault." He grasped Johnny by the shoulder and turned his friend to face him. "Look, Johnny, as long as these two guys stick around here and need a place to play around with each other, I can make five bucks a day just for letting them use a two-by-four bath-house for a few minutes. I get the five bucks, and they have a good time." He leaned against the railing, crossing his arms over his broad chest and looking at Johnny with an assumed air of worldly wisdom. "For Christ's sake, Johnny, when the hell are you gonna wise up, anyway? You gonna be a wide-eyed innocent kid all your life? These things happen all the time whether you like it or not, so why not get in on it? You're always mooning over that Goddamn ocean like it was a girl or something, always talking about buying yourself that boat in Sternberg's window. Well, you got the dough yet? You gonna buy that boat before the end of season?"

Johnny shook his head, saying nothing.

"Like hell you will. You sure won't get it by picking up a quarter tip here and there. Hell, this is the way to do it, Johnny! Let some of these horny queers have their fun, and you'll have that boat before you know it. Let 'em have a single bath-house if they want it, look them over when they're bare-ass, and let them show off how big they are. Play around with 'em a little if they want it, and you'll have more money than you know what to do with. Hell, Johnny, ain't it worth it?"

Johnny leaned heavily against the railing; a gull swooped close to the heaving surface of the sea and then soared again into the gray sky. "No, I don't think it is."

Jimmy laughed and slapped him on the shoulder. "Never change, do ya, kid?" he asked in a tone of smug superiority. "Well, think it over, Johnny. You're my buddy, and I'll let you in on a good thing any time. Good looking kid like you, hell, you could make plenty. I'm going for some Fries. Come along?"

Johnny shook his head. "No. Guess I'll go on home. See you in the morning."

There was still no sign that the rain was letting up, and Johnny vaguely wondered if it might not be an all-nighter. The bath-houses were deserted now, barren wood aisles with here and there a door hanging ajar, the whitened boards drenched with rain. Johnny was alone. He seated himself again, leaning his chin on his folded arms, gazing out to the gray swell of the sea, his eyes serious, his expression more intent as he thought again of Jimmy's suggestions.

At sixteen and some months, Johnny was neither innocent nor particularly prudish. He had all the drives and interests of the healthy, young male, and never denied himself the opportunity of expression. He had passed beyond the youthful thrills of mutual masturbation, and had experienced several sessions with the resort's well-known willing girls under the pilings of the jetty. He enjoyed perusing dirty pictures and listening to sexual stories; standing here on the balcony and looking down at the beach, he would freely join the other locker boys in their lewd remarks about the bathing beauties.

But what Jimmy was talking about was something entirely different.

Johnny had known for some time about Harry and his sexual actitivies with women in the bath-houses, before they became the scandal of last season. Harry was twenty-two years old, chief lockerman, handsome, with an impressive body-builder form that he took care always to show to its very best advantage. He gave free reign to his powerful sexual drive and saw nothing particularly wrong about accepting money from "lonely old dames who either never had it, or who've forgotten what it was like," who asked him into their lockers with them, but the management was not amused when Harry's activities resulted in a threatened cry of rape. Harry was immediately fired, with a stern warning to stay away from the bath-houses and the Boardwalk.

"This ain't no whore-house! Anybody does crap like that, and he's out on his ass!"

Johnny couldn't quite see that there was much difference between what Harry had done and what Jimmy was doing. Neither action was really anything new, but Johnny himself had always steadfastly refused to become embroiled in the practice. It had nothing to do with a sense of outraged decency or code of morality. He had the natural youthful contempt for "queers," and that contempt could easily have excused him for accepting money to look at them in the nude. He would under no circumstances agree to go any further, of course, in spite of what Jimmy had said and done. You did things like that with your playmates when you were still innocent and curious kids, but once you became a man, as Johnny felt he had become, that sort of thing was over, unless you wanted the tag of "queer" on yourself. It just wasn't right.

In addition, Johnny simply could not see placing his job in jeopardy for the sake of a few extra dollars, no matter how welcome the money would be and how easily made. Should he be caught in that sort of thing, he would be instantly dismissed. He didn't want to risk it.

He frowned. Jimmy said he was just being a dumb kid. Maybe he was right, after all. Maybe he was afraid for no reason at all. Others were getting away with it; Jimmy wasn't the only one. Johnny had more than once walked away from conversations of the locker-boys, chortling with contempt over the queers who proudly exposed themselves, comparing what they had seen, mocking the urge for self-display and bragging about how much more well endowed they were than the fairies.

And what Jimmy had said about the boat was true, of course. The season would soon be over, and there was little chance that he would have raised the necessary bucks for the down payment. He would have to go back to school and wait at least another year. He thought of Jimmy's newest friends. Five dollars! It didn't really hurt anybody, did it? If they want to be that sick, maybe it was up to them. He wondered what they looked like. Probably fat, bald and hairy.

A gust of wind blew the rain in on him, and Johnny shivered at its suddenly cold touch. The summer was nearly over when the rain held such a chill. It had been a short season.

# CHAPTER SIX

At the Seaquarium the great chamber was dark save for the minimal light filtering through the thick glass windows and the underwater lights in the vast tank. The rippling water cast a yellow-green reflection on the walls.

Gregory Christopher stood at the edge of the pool, grasped the iron railing in his hands and leaned over, staring down through the shimmering green water. The giant tortoise lay like a massive encrusted rock in the far corner; the ever-restless shark was a darkly ominous patch of gray, mysterious in its gracefully silent movements. The horse-shoe crabs crawled along the bottom like creatures from some alien world. Partitioned by a strong steel netting into their own safe compartment, three baby seals, only recently acquired, bobbed on end, only their bewhiskered faces rising above the calm water.

Greg walked completely around the pool, his

steps echoing loudly in the empty chamber, his practised eye glancing into the shadowy corners to make certain that all was in order. The seals barked noisily as he passed them, but the harsh sound faded as he started up the dark stairway, sure footed and unhesitant despite the lack of light, to the small second floor acquarium. With a quick, familiar glance at the lighted cases set into the walls, he moved into the shell room.

The large windows here faced the sea, and he paused for a moment, glancing down at the Boardwalk. The storm had passed, but the rain would linger for a good part of the evening. Both sea and sky were still slate-gray, the clouds pregnant with rain. A young couple walked by beneath him, hand in hand, clad from head to foot in matching yellow plastic rain-gear, and Greg smiled at the portrait of young love so completely indifferent to the discomforts of the elements. He turned out the light, returned to the first floor, and closed the stairway with the heavy steel chain.

When he stepped onto the Boardwalk, the rain had fallen off at least temporarily into a light but chilling drizzle; the horizon was lost behind a gray haze. The Boardwalk was silent and deserted save for a few strollers hardy enough to ignore the rain. There was a teenagers' dance at the large auditorium, featuring another of the primitive rock groups with a ludicrous name. As he passed he could hear the loud cacophony of their music and the shouts of their excited audience. He made a slight, involuntary grimace, and stepped off the Boardwalk, headed for The Cloud.

Although born and raised in a small town completely surrounded by green Pennsylvania hills, Greg had always felt a deep fascination for the sea and the creatures who made their home in its supposedly silent depths, and his work absorbed him completely. At thirty-two, he combined intelligence and a natural charm with a pleasantly attractive appearance that often drew the attention of women in his groups, attention which amused rather than flattered him. He had been director of the Seaquarium now for the past five years and was proud of the reputation he had created. Admissions had increased permitting purchase of some particularly interesting exhibits. He put on a good show for his visitors, his talks were lively and informative, and he was always willing to answer all the questions put to him regarding the sea and those creatures on exhibit. Unfailingly polite, he yet remained aloof and apart, disinterested in personal involvements of any kind, concerned only with the continuation and improvement of the Seaquarium.

Johnny Hawkins was the single exception to this carefully reserved business-like attitude. Greg had watched the boy grow up in the past few years, and had always been aware of his keen interest in the sea, but it was only during the early part of this summer that this interest had become an obsession with the boy. Johnny had started visiting the Seaquarium every day without fail, to watch the feedings and listen again and again to Greg's carefully prepared lectures. His lively, darkly handsome face seemed to be lighted by the green sea when he bent over the tank, and the shading seemed natural to him. With his sharp interest, his questing mind, his inherited love of the sea, the boy might prove to be a born icthyologist, and Greg constantly encouraged him in every way, talking with him when they sat together on the beach, detailing the responsibilities and the problems of the Seaquarium management. He might one day come in very handy at the Seaquarium; he had already on occasion assisted Greg in the feedings. Should the exhibits continue to expand as they had in the past couple of years, Greg might require another assistant in addition to the three boys already on his payroll. He had been meaning to talk to Miss Meg about sending the boy to the School of Oceanography up the coast. She would listen to him, he was certain. Margaret was pleased and flattered by the interest Greg showed in her son.

The dark mass of the point loomed against the dreary grayness of the sky. Although it was not yet dark, the storm had created an unusually early twilight, and several lights shone through the fine curtain of the rain. He felt a sense of warmth and comfort. Greg had often considered buying a place of his own somewhere along the beach, but was now so comfortable at The Cloud that he had continued to delay the project and finally had abandoned it altogether and become a permanent fixture at the Hawkins house.

Margaret was standing in the doorway, her hands on her ample hips, staring out to the dark sea as though looking for the ghost of a ship on the horizon, when Greg mounted the steps to the verandah. She smiled with pleasure at sight of her favorite guest. "All night rain?" she asked.

"Afraid so," Greg replied, wiping the drizzle from his forehead. "Good night to sit in a warm room with a drink and a good book."

"Wish Johnny would think of that," she remarked, glancing down to the almost deserted

Boardwalk as though looking for her son. "At least, the part about the room and the good book. I swear I don't see that boy all day long. He's probably sitting out there somewhere on the beach, getting soaked through and through and ignoring it all. Did you ever see such a boy?"

Greg smiled as they turned together and entered the lobby. "He's a good boy. He comes by his love of the sea naturally, you know."

"Oh, yes, yes," Margaret hastily affirmed. "He's a good boy, and I must admit I'm proud of him, even if I do say so who shouldn't. I just wish once in a while he would remember he has a home." She sighed heavily, her bosom rising. "Well, I suppose I would rather have him sitting out there on the beach by himself than at that dance with all that rocky-rolly nonsense. Remember, last dance they had ended in a riot and they had to call the police?"

Greg laughed as he headed for the stairs. "Well, now, I've seen that little foot of yours tapping away with the best of them at times!"

"That was music," Margaret complained. "This is nothing but a lot of noise." She laughed suddenly. "And you have better things to do than to watch the movement of an old woman's foot!"

"I expect you to save me at least a dozen dances at the Festival," he reminded her as he started up the stairs. "I won't take no for an answer, now."

Margaret put one hand on the bannister and looked at him, laughing her rich, full-bodied chuckle. "The floor's too small; with me on it, there wouldn't be room for anyone else!"

Greg laughed again and continued on up to his room as the door opened again to admit a windblown Linda Fraser, burdened with numerous boxes and shopping bags that threatened to spill to the floor.

"Oh, dear, I was so hoping the rain would hold off until I got back from town," she complained, blowing a wisp of gray hair that the rain had caused to fall from its careful position. "I was completely out in the open when the downpour began, and then I had to wait just the longest time for a cab. Never can get one when you want one, isn't that what they say? Or is that policemen?"

Margaret closed the door behind her; the marble flooring gleamed with drops of rain. "Can I help you with those packages?"

"Oh, no, thank you, Miss Meg. I can manage, once I get myself just a bit more organized. If you'll just be good enough to open the door for me . . ."

"How would a nice cup of hot coffee go?" Margaret asked as she opened the door to the Fraser suite and turned on the light.

"It would go just marvelously," Linda assured her. "Thank you so much. Surprising how chilly it's become all of a sudden; you wouldn't think it was still summer. Well, I'd best get out of these wet clothes or I'll catch cold."

Margaret rushed off to the kitchen for the coffee, while Linda dropped her parcels into the chair near the door. "Karen! Karen, dear, it's mother. I'm back!"

She removed her hat and, pausing before the mirror, patted her hair back into place and dabbed at her wet face with a handkerchief. The door to Karen's room was closed, and when Linda knocked there was no response. When she quietly entered the room, she found it in darkness, save for the small light under the portrait. Karen slept in her chair, head resting against its back and her mouth slightly open. The record had ended and the needle made an irritating swishing sound as it moved back and forth across the empty grooves.

Linda turned off the machine and looked at her sleeping daughter, her eyes disturbed. Karen had been smoking heavily, and the room was hazy. Linda raised her eyes to the lighted portrait, and her face became stern and unpleasant. Her hand was firm and her mouth set when she reached out to turn off the small lamp beneath the portrait. She flicked on the ceiling light.

"Karen, dear," she whispered, gently taking her daughter by the hand. "It's mother, Karen. I'm back."

Karen stirred slightly and opened her eyes. "Oh, hello, mother; I must have fallen asleep. Why, you're all wet." She glanced to the closed windows. "Is it raining?"

"It has been for some time, dear, although it has let up quite a bit. It's really become quite nasty. Miss Meg is bringing some good hot coffee. Won't you come out into the sitting room and have some with me, dear?"

"All right, mother. But you'd better change your things, first."

"I'll do that, dear," Linda responded, in the patient tone one uses toward a child. "I'll be right with you."

Linda left for her own room, leaving Karen seated where she was. The girl looked after her mother for a moment, smiling her sad smile, and then reached out to relight the lamp under the portrait, before wheeling herself into the sitting room.

* * *

A large, heavy-limbed tree grew directly beside the old house on the side away from the Boardwalk, its sturdy old trunk standing firmly between two of the house windows, its arched branches rising as high as the Widow's Walk, in some instances almost touching the balconies on the rooms of the upper floors.

The light drizzle of rain had brought an early darkness, shrouding the tree in gray mist; the light streaming from the windows on either side of the tree merely made the darkness more intense. It would have taken a sharp eye to notice the peculiar movement of the branches, which swayed slightly even though there was not even the suggestion of a breeze. Something seemed to be moving upwards under the cover of the concealing branches, climbing laboriously toward the strong limbs that brushed against the house itself. A closer inspection would have revealed that there were four of these forms, two apparently male clad in white and two young females clad in form-fitting colored slacks. The males, who manipulated the climb with considerable ease, paused now and again to reach down their hands and give aid to the struggling young girls, perhaps not quite so accustomed to this exercise. There were constant hushed cries for silence during the climb.

It was not really a difficult climb at all. The tree, which had perhaps in its long history been used in this way before, seemed to extend its broad branches to aid the climbers, and it was not long before the two males dropped down onto the balcony opposite their room and helped the girls out of the tree. The four quickly disappeared into the room.

This was the only manner in which Paul and Michael could resolve the dilemma of escorting the girls into their room for the evening's entertainment.

When Steve left the bar of The Buccaneer later that evening, somewhat unsteady on his feet, the rain had finally stopped, but a chilling mist filled the air and the sky was still heavily overcast. His head was swimming, there was a peculiar dry heaving in his stomach, and a choking taste of cotton in his mouth. He crossed over to the Boardwalk and seated himself on a bench, indifferent to the clammy wetness that seeped through his trousers. It was already too dark to distinguish the horizon; he could see only a world of deep blackness. The sound of the surf came to him from beyond an ebony wall; strange to think there was a great ocean just out there, and another kind of life far beyond.

He felt drowsy, and his head began to nod. The rhythmic sounds of the surf were soothing. Looking out towards the sea, he could catch a sight of an occasional splash of white as a larger wave crashed down upon the empty beach. What would it be like, he wondered, to walk into the sea, to let the enfolding waters sweep you into peaceful oblivion? The movies made it look so dramatic. Fredric March dropping his bathrobe, as if it really mattered, and Joan Crawford nobly entering the surf, head high, to the weeping tones of the *Liebestod*. Surely there must be an easier way to die. Despite the desire, there must be a last moment of battle, a final hopeless struggle against the choking waters.

He started slightly and quickly shook his head. These were dangerous thoughts. Still swaying a bit, with that nagging pressure throbbing at the back of his head, he rose from the bench and headed back towards The Cloud.

He had had too much to drink, but what the hell! He had actually enjoyed himself for a time this evening, and that was something of a rarity. The Buccaneer bar was, as Bernie S-for-Sam Clayton had advised him, a real swinging place, and he had enjoyed the noise, the lights, the raucous music, even the singer with the loud, brassy numbers from the Gay Nineties. What was her name? Beatrice. No, worse than that. She was billed simply as "Bea." Gay Nineties. He had a sharp mental picture of his mother, when he was still a child, sitting before the radio and listening to Beatrice Kay in a Gay Nineties program on the local radio station. His mother.

Well, anyway, the evening had been fun, and good for him. He would suffer for it in the morning, but that would pass. No harm was done. He told himself that again. No harm was done. As long as this sort of thing didn't happen too often . . . He shied away from the thoughts that came to him.

The Cloud now loomed before him, in darkness save for the lights that always burned on the verandah and in the lobby. Walter, the night clerk, was seated behind the desk with a paperback. He looked up briefly when Steve entered, somewhat surprised at his condition. Steve stood for a moment at the foot of the stairway and the red carpeting seemed to writhe like a sinuous crimson serpent, then started up the stairs; he stumbled halfway up the flight and sprawled full length, falling with a loud crash. A door opened on the third floor and Greg Christopher stepped from his room to peer down the well of the stairway. Seeing the form stretched out on the stairs, he was about to go down to provide whatever assistance might be needed, when he saw Walter rushing to the rescue.

"You all right, Mr. Conroy?"

Steve nodded, embarrassed, as with Walter's help he raised himself with some difficulty to his feet. "Yes, yes, Walter. Okay. Must have tripped. Sorry. Thanks, Wal'er."

Walter returned to his reading, looking carefully behind him, as Steve resumed his ascent, somewhat more slowly now, leaning heavily against the bannister. Greg stepped back from the railing and watched in silence, out of Steve's range of vision.

At the head of the stairs, Steve nearly tumbled back down the entire flight, saving himself by a quick tightening of his grasp on the railing. He paused for a moment, perhaps not quite certain of his bearings, then entered his room, closing the door softly behind him. Greg stood at the railing for a moment longer, then silently returned to his room.

Steve didn't bother to turn on the light. He removed his shirt and let it fall to the floor, then stood for a moment at the open French doors, looking out to the dark sea; the moon broke out at last through a thinning veil of cloud and shone upon a surface that was again calm and peaceful. He put a trembling hand to his forehead and narrowed his eyes, trying to keep the wavering beach and sea in their proper perspectives. He took a step towards the bed, reeled, and fell heavily against the corner of the dresser, wincing slightly at the sudden pain that shot through his back. He suddenly realized he was indeed extremely drunk, and knew he was about to be sick. He staggered out onto the balcony, leaned over the railing, and vomited into the sand below. Exhausted, wiping at his wet mouth with a handkerchief, he leaned back against the wall and felt the evening breeze on his face.

Now that the storm had passed, the night was extremely quiet. The dark clouds were beginning to break and there was an occasional sight of the pale moon. By morning the weather would probably have cleared. Another day would begin. Another endless day in the seemingly endless cycle of days. Another long period of loneliness and self-recrimination, of bitter memories and lost hopes. Another empty day.

The moon cast its silver upon the sea, as though some philanthropic giant had cast down diamonds. Steve gazed listlessly at the calm water and wondered again about death, a sleep without dreams, free of the nightmares that constantly plagued him. A forgetfulness.

Was that, then, why he had come here?

No! He would not, could not. There had to be something else ahead for him, some reason to hope, to dream, to look for happiness.

He turned from the balcony and staggered back into the room, standing for a moment in the semi-darkness, feeling helpless and vulnerable, his eyes searching for something he feared they would never find. His hands were raised to the blackness in a voiceless appeal, but there was no one to answer.

With a sharp cry, he fell sobbing onto the bed.

The single lamp between the two beds cast only a dim light, and much of the room was left in shadow. On the table beside the lamp stood a whiskey bottle, three-quarters empty, and two empty glasses. The sailors were stripped to their trousers, their bare chests gleaming in the yellow light, strong and bronzed. Michael and Frances were engaged in an embrace on the bed near the door. Michael's hands fumbled eagerly inside her opened blouse, and Frances moaned when she felt his hard body rubbing up against her.

Paul and Chrissy were seated side by side on the other bed, facing the open balcony doors which showed a patch of brightening sky. Both held a drink in one hand; Chrissy, giggling, sipped from the glass as Paul ran his lips across her cheek and hair, darting his tongue into the curved shell of her ear.

"Don't do that!" she cried in startled pleasure. "It tickles!"

"Shhh!" Paul cautioned. "Gotta be quiet. Throw us out of here if they knew we'd brought you up here."

He had one arm draped about her narrow shoulders, the hand toying with the buttons on her pink blouse; he had already determined that she was not wearing a bra. Her free hand was lightly rubbing the inside of his thigh, moving ever closer to his swelling crotch.

"Oh, baby," Paul sighed as he ran his hand down her breast, feeling the hardness of a nipple through the light material of the blouse. "Oh, baby, let me have 'em!"

She smiled archly and, taking another sip of her drink, giggled again. "Well, you know where they are, honey!"

His fingers trembling with excitement, Paul undid the buttons of the blouse and slid it from her shoulders. The full young breasts with the dark nipples stood up in shared excitement. Quickly, Paul set his glass on the table and both his hands closed over her breasts; he bent his head and ran his warm wet tongue over the nipples. She gasped with pleasure and, moving her hand further up his thigh, grasped him tightly. He set her glass down on the table and tried to press her down onto her back.

"No . . ." She suddenly resisted. "No, I don't want to."

"Come on," he muttered through teeth clenched with desire, trying to keep his voice low. "You can't stop me now; I'm going crazy!"

She placed her hands on his perspiring naked chest and made a weak attempt to push him away. "No. I don't want to. Besides, it's late. We've got to go. And somebody might hear us."

"We're not gonna make any noise. There's plenty of time. Your friend isn't ready to go any place."

Michael, already brightly naked, was helping Frances out of her clothes. The sight of his aroused nudity and Frances's obvious willingness excited Chrissy and she suddenly ceased her resistance, falling with an inviting sigh back onto the bed.

"Wait," Paul said hoarsely. "Wait right there, baby!"

He rose quickly and, staggering slightly, went

into the bathroom and noisily relieved himself, not bothering to close the door. Quickly, eagerly, he stepped out of his trousers and shorts, leaving them on the floor where they fell, and returned, naked as his friend, to the bedroom.

Johnny ambled slowly along the beach, his hands plunged deep into the pockets of his jeans, the new evening breeze ruffling his long dark hair. It had grown very late by now. The Boardwalk was quite deserted. Tonight he could imagine that all this silent, sibilant world belonged to him, the soft, cool sand under his feet, the gentle, peaceful ocean before him, the breeze that might have traveled halfway across the world to touch his warm cheek. As he walked, an occasional wave washed up to him, gently kissed his feet, and returned to the sea. It was like a silent compact of friendship between them.

He walked with practised step along the wet rocks on the jetty, not for a moment losing his sense of balance on the slippery surfaces, and sat there, hugging his knees to his chest, tasting the salt spray on his lips, his young eyes thoughtful as he stared into the friendly darkness.

Johnny was uneasy, thinking of his conversation with Jimmy. He wanted to forget all the coarseness and vulgarity of life on the beach and just be alone with the sea, here where it was dark and quiet and he could be lulled by the gentle sound of the breaking surf.

He knew he was not really mature enough to cope with Jimmy's proposition for making extra money at the bath-houses. He could not be really certain what was right and what was wrong in such matters. His experience had not prepared him for anything quite like this. Black was black and white was white. But always? What about the shadings of life he had always heard so much about? He sensed this matter now before him might be something important, and something that required a good deal of serious thought if it were to be satisfactorily resolved in his mind. Jimmy stressed there really could be no harm in such matters, but Johnny wasn't so sure. Was he afraid of something? Was he perhaps merely uncertain about himself? Yes, there could be harm. He knew that.

He looked out again to sea and thought of his boat. With Jimmy's help, perhaps that dream could become a reality. If he accepted Jimmy's suggestion, he might still have that boat by the time this very season ended. Would it really be so wrong? Would the end justify the means?

There was no use in brushing the matter aside. The offer had been made, an offer that would give him what he wanted more than anything else in the world. Should he do it? Should he accept money for looking at naked men, perhaps even for 'doing things' to them? That phrase was still vague and indecisive. He wasn't really certain what it meant, although he had his suspicions. He began to realize how completely naive he really was. Too much of a dreamer. By his age, he should know all there was to know about such things.

He pictured some of the fat, hairy, disgusting men who came to the bath-house. How could he. . . . Well, of course, they weren't really all that bad. No, that was surely the wrong way to think about it. If it was the wrong thing to do, it was the wrong thing to do all the time, not just some of the time.

He stared out to the dark horizon and could almost see himself out there, rising with the swell of the tide, smelling the sharp freshness of the air, looking over the side and seeing life swimming past him. . . .

He turned to glance at the darkness of his home rising on the jutting spit of land. He came from a virile and masculine family. The Hawkins men were men in the fullest sense of the word. He was certain none of them would ever have done such a thing as he was now contemplating. What would they think of him? It would be like being a traitor to his own race.

But, of course, nobody need know about it. None of the family, none of the guests at the house, above all not Gregg. He frowned, thinking of Greg. Could it be kept from him? Oh, he could trust Jimmy well enough, he was certain, but what of himself? Wouldn't it show on his face?

Only then did he realize the moving trend of his thoughts. It was as though he had already decided. No . . . He hadn't . . . Of course not . . . Had he?

A cloud passed before the moon and a sudden chill made him shiver slightly. The sea had again become black and slightly ominous, as though it sensed the confused darkness of his thinking. The bad weather was not yet completely gone; it would return before the dawn. Johnny shuddered and drew his legs more closely to his chest.

The sky clouded over again, and the rain returned. Throughout the remainder of that silent night, the gentle drops fell, a more soothing and apologetic rain than the torrent that had fallen earlier that evening. The smooth surface of the sea was roughly pitted by the large drops; a light breeze provided the rhythm for a dance of scraps of paper. It was very quiet. The Boardwalk was dark; wet canvas covered the rides in the Kiddieland, and the painted horses of the carousel were frozen with fear of the dark.

Like a brown monolith rising from the ancient sands of the beach, the old house of Captain Nathaniel Hawkins slumbered. The rain fell gently on its roof, polished the leaves of the tree on which the sailors and their whores had climbed for their exercise in fornication, blew in on the verandah where a crippled girl wove her hopeless dreams, and washed the spot where the Captain had shed his own blood.

# Part II

# Dreams on a Summer Night

# CHAPTER SEVEN

On the topmost floor of the old Hawkins house, directly beneath the empty Widow's Walk which for so many years now had echoed to nothing but soft ghostly treads from the past, Gregory Christopher lay in a dream that had its beginnings in a small Pennsylvania town called Corryville, population at the last census some two thousand, six hundred and sixty-nine. . . .

Greg hadn't really intended to go back there at all; there was certain to be unpleasantness and perhaps even serious trouble connected with his return. Logic told him to stay away, simply to forget the town and let the town forget him, but who can so easily forget the home where he has spent the happiest, most carefree days of his life? Can one forget the memories that play so large a part in making us the kind of person we are? In spite of his uneasiness, he was driven back there.

Perhaps it was because he was very tired, with a

soul-searing weariness that filled every moment of his day and made his nights interminable. He needed rest, a place to forget what he had experienced in those terrible years of war, somewhere to remind him that the basic values of life still existed somewhere, the decency, the love, the caring about others. What better place than the home where he had first learned all these values as a child?

Perhaps he was wrong. It might not be too bad. They were decent people, most of them. They would understand. Perhaps his fears were groundless. He was a native son.

He stepped off the train on a pleasantly cool morning when the sun still shone brightly on the green fields and the small steepled town nestled sleepily in the valley ringed by low mountains. He instantly sensed the peace of the place. The town seemed asleep; there was scarcely a sound. He used to think of it as a world of its own, and perhaps he had not been far wrong. Perhaps it remained completely unaware of the world beyond that rim of mountains. He breathed deeply of the pure air; a bird perched on the station-house steeple sang a welcome. An omen?

He walked slowly and not without difficulty down the platform . . . he was not yet very expert in the handling of his crutches . . . and hesitated before the station lunchroom. In the window there was a photograph, flanked by two small American flags, of a clear-eyed young soldier who bore a marked resemblance to Greg. He knew the picture well; a print of it was in his bag. There was a black hand printed sign beneath the framed picture, the letters not quite even:

Raising his eyes and peering through the dusty, streaked window which also held posters advertising a Church bazaar and announcing an upcoming meeting of the Citizens Committee for a Better Corryville, Greg could see Bill, his fiancee's teenaged brother, behind the counter, leaning his chin in his hands as he browsed through a magazine which would almost certainly deal with the sporting world.

Gathering up his courage, Greg slowly entered the lunchroom; the juke box in the corner was blaring one of the tunes of the day, and neither Bill, deeply engrossed in his magazine, nor the single middle-aged male patron sipping his coffee at the counter, heard the door open. Greg paused briefly in the doorway, looking with a sense of comfort at the long familiar scene—the white counter with its covered displays of pastries, the small round tables with the wire-backed chairs, the gleaming jukebox against the wall, the pinball machine in the corner. He moved slowly and quietly to the counter, placed his bag on the floor, and carefully lowered himself to one of the red-covered stools, leaning his crutches up against the side of the counter. He was reminded of the times he and Dolores had come here for a snack after a movie . . . Too long ago.

"Coffee, please," he said softly.

"Right with you," Bill replied, not raising his head.

With his eyes still riveted to the magazine, the youth absently reached for a cup and placed it under the coffee-spout behind him; he flipped the magazine over to his other patron, pointing to a particular photograph.

"Now, that's what I call real fishing gear!" he announced enthusiastically. "I gotta get me a reel like that one of these days!" The coffee overflowed the cup, he spilled out a small portion and carefully approached Greg, trying not to spill any more of the liquid. "Here you are, soldier," he said, "one cup of good, hot coffee."

As he placed the cup on the counter, he raised his eyes for the first time and looked at his new customer. He stopped speaking, his hand still holding the saucer.

"Hello, Bill." Extending his hand, Greg added, "Good to see you."

Bill's light blue eyes narrowed and firm lines of disapproval suddenly marred the pleasant friendliness of his rather homely face. He abruptly and clumsily lowered the coffee to the counter, spilling some of it into the saucer. He ignored the outstretched hand.

"Fifteen cents."

Greg looked at the boy for a moment, hoping to find in his face the merest glint of the old friendliness he had always seen there, but failed. The eyes were hard, the mouth firm, as though Bill were looking at a stranger he could not trust. Greg lowered his hand, reached into his pocket and took out a dime and a nickel. Bill looked at the extended coins but made no move to take them. When Greg placed them on the white counter, he picked them up with an exaggerated expression of distaste.

"How are you, Bill?" Greg asked.

"Fine. Just fine." Bill's eyes ran impudently over Greg's uniform. "You look pretty fit." Glancing at the crutches he smiled slightly, unpleasantly, and harshly added, "Watcha do, Greg? Trip yourself up?"

Greg looked self-consciously down at his legs, flushed slightly, and said nothing. After sparing him one further look of open contempt, Bill returned to his other customers.

"How about another coffee, Ben?"

"Sure thing, Bill." Ben set the magazine aside and noticed the other occupant of the counter, running his eyes over the smart, clean uniform. "Just in, soldier?"

"That's right," Greg replied after a moment. He did not recognize the man; he was of middle-age, dressed in worker's clothes and had a friendly, somewhat weathered face.

"Live here in Corryville?"

"Yes."

"New here myself," Ben informed him. "Came to work for the railroad. Nice little town. Real friendly people. Always find that in these small towns." His eyes wandered to the row of ribbons on Greg's breast. "Vietnam?"

Greg sipped his coffee and mumbled, "That's right."

Ben sucked his teeth with an unpleasant juicey sound and shook his head. "Must 'a been rough."

Greg nodded and said nothing. Bill turned and placed another cup of coffee before Ben. "Depends on the way you look at it, Ben."

Greg quickly raised his head and looked directly at the boy. But Bill only returned the look with a challenge. Greg quickly finished his coffee and prepared to leave. As he eased from the stool, one of his crutches clattered to the floor; Ben immediately stooped to retrieve it for him.

"Here you are, soldier."

"Thanks."

Greg placed the crutches under his arm, picked up his luggage in one hand, and glanced again at Bill, who was staring at him with undisguised amusement. Greg seemed about to speak, then changed his mind and started for the door.

"Can you manage the door, soldier?" Ben asked.

Bill suddenly slammed his magazine down on the counter with the sharp retort of a pistol-shot. "For Christ's sake, Ben, save your sympathy for somebody who deserves it. You're looking at Corryville's own yellow-belly."

Greg, his back already turned, froze where he was; he felt perspiration spring to his forehead.

"Yellow-belly?" Ben asked.

"Sure," Bill replied, leaning against the back counter and crossing his arms while he looked at the broad back of the man in uniform. "That's Greg Christopher. Brother of Bob Christopher, biggest hero this town ever had. Nothin' like his brother, though. This yellow bastard went over to the Commies to save his own skin."

His interest deeply sharpened, Ben turned on his stool to look at Greg, a different expression now in his eyes. "You don't say! So that's what they look like! Never would have believed it."

"Sure, looks like a real red-blooded American, don't he, Ben? Trouble is, ain't just the blood that's red."

Greg swung through the door, letting it slam shut behind him and, with Bill's sardonic laughter still sounding in his ears, stepped again out to the station platform. Breathing heavily, the perspiration gleaming on his flushed face, he paused for a moment, his eyes closed, his fists tightly clenched and beating futilely against the wood of the crutches.

Was this the way it would be? Would they all look at him the same way? No, he shouldn't have come back! He had known that all along. He should have expected something like this, and worse. This was just the beginning. He looked at the steel tracks of the railroad, gleaming brightly in the sun. He should wait right here for the next train to take him away, anywhere, either direction; it didn't matter, just away from the hatred he knew he would find in this town.

He shook his head. No. That wasn't the answer. It couldn't be. His home was here. His family was here. He had every right to be here, as much right as anyone. He would have to come back sooner or later. Get it over with.

On the platform a dozing white dog of indeterminate breed occasionally raised its tail, and a thin young man in a black leather jacket sat on a bench against the far well, carving the form of a horse out of a piece of wood, the knife shooting small shavings into the air to join the circle of white wood at his feet. Greg recognized him at once, although he hadn't seen him for some time. Dick Fittelli. They'd been to school together, had played together as children. He owned the cab parked at the end of the platform. Greg approached him, trying to muffle the sound of his crutches.

"Your cab free?"

Frittelli quickly stuffed his whittling materials into the pocket of his jacket, rising as he did so and brushing off his trousers. "Sure thing, mister. Where to?" He raised his face and recognized his prospective fare; his expression instantly lost its business-like friendliness. "Oh. Greg."

Greg smiled, as though nothing had happened during the intervening years and they were merely old friends meeting again. "How are you, Dick?" His tone was deceptively, hopefully light.

"Sorry, Greg." Frittelli replied without responding to the question, or posing a like question of his own. "Thought you was somebody else." He sank lazily back to the bench, drew the whittling materials from his pocket and resumed his carving. "No, I ain't free, matter of fact. Waitin' for a fare. Thought you was him. Sorry."

Greg hesitated. "What about your other cabs? Hear you've got a real fleet of them."

The driver pointed with his knife to the vacant parking spaces. "See for yourself. All of 'em out on calls. Won't be back for some time, I guess." He looked up with a sudden hardness in his eyes. "Wouldn't be at all surprised if they don't get back all day long."

Greg indicated his crutches. "It's pretty rough to walk all the way home on these."

Fittelli shrugged his shoulders. "Well, that's the breaks, I guess. Too bad, Greg."

Exhausted by the long walk from the station, Greg hesitated before the house where he had been born and raised. Leaning heavily on the crutches, wiping the perspiration from his face, he looked at the broad verandah where he had played as a child—the swing where he and Dolores had often sat in the evenings was still there, the apple tree from which he had twice fallen and broken the same right arm, the little flower bed he had so carefully tended, now somewhat overgrown. The window there on the second floor at the side of the house was his bedroom, where he had sat during balmy summer nights and dreamed his childhood fantasies of traveling to distant jungles and becoming a great white hunter, or of making amazing discoveries in the burning sands of Egypt, of sailing his own vessel through the pearl-like islands of the southern seas. It all looked the same. Had nothing changed at all?

Yes. Something had changed. Bob had shared in all those dreams. He would not be here.

Greg made his way slowly to the front door. His hand went to the doorbell, then he lowered it and grasped the metal knob. The door was unlocked; the Christopher house was always open to their many friends. Slowly, he turned the knob and pushed the door open.

The foyer and living room were empty and he stood there for just a moment, breathing in the air of familiarity, happy to be home again, to have shut the outside world away with the closing of the door behind him. There was a new runner on the stairs leading to the upstairs rooms; the blue looked more cheerful than the brown he remembered. The Statue of Liberty on the newel post had been replaced with a graceful Venus light, such as he had recommended years ago. Aside from that nothing had been changed.

Let it be all right, he sighed. Oh, let it be all right.

He could hear the clatter of dishes in the kitchen. After a further moment's pause, he walked passed the stairway and to the kitchen doorway. His mother was at the sink, busy with the luncheon dishes. She hadn't changed much. A bit more gray in the hair, perhaps, a few more pounds about the waist. She wore a bright print

111

dress and no apron. She had always enjoyed doing the dishes, never considering it the chore so many other women did. Somehow, he had expected to see her stooped under the weight of one son a hero and the other a coward. It had been nearly three years.

"Hello, Mom."

In the act of placing a washed dish on the drying rack at the side of the sink, Irene Christopher paused. She raised her head just slightly, as though looking out into the backyard where her two sons used to swoop through the air on the tire swing hanging from the bough of the great oak under which they'd often had their summer picnics. The only sound was a slight ripple of water as the washed dishes slipped back into the suds. She turned slowly, reaching for a dish towel.

"Gregory." She looked at him, absently drying her hands, then put one hand to her forehead and brushed back a straying lock of hair. "Oh, Gregory!" Those warm, familiar arms opened and in one quick swoop she had her son in her arms. "You're home! You're home!"

They held the embrace for a long and wonderful moment, then Irene stepped back. "Let me look at you, son! Oh, but you're thin, Greg! You're so very thin!" She put a gentle hand to his face; the fingers trembled slightly. "And you're pale!"

He smiled. "Just a little tired, that's all. I couldn't get a cab at the station, so I walked all the way." He answered her unspoken question. "My leg's much better, but it still gives a little trouble."

"Sit down, son; sit down."

Greg eased himself into one of the wooden chairs at the table, placing his crutches against the sink; his mother sat opposite, taking his hands in hers. It was difficult, again, to believe that anything had changed, that so much time had passed; they had often sat here just like this.

"But are you all right, Greg?"

He nodded. "Oh, sure, I'm fine. Really." He looked towards the living room; this would be the most difficult moment. "Where's Dad? I didn't see him . . ."

A sorrow-cloud briefly concealed the happiness in his mother's eyes. "He's been away on a business trip since yesterday; won't be back before Tuesday, at the earliest. Maybe later."

"Mom . . . How does he feel . . . about me?"

There was the sparkle of tears, and her lower lip quivered. "He hasn't once spoken your name, son, since we heard."

Greg took the worn hands tightly in his and looked at his mother, his eyes earnest and pleading; this would be important to him. "Mom, I'm not . . . not what they say I am."

"I know that, Gregory," Irene responded. "I know my son. I knew both my sons. I knew you would never . . . Well, I'm certain that whatever was done, there was a reason for it, and it couldn't possibly be the way some people said."

"What about the others? The neighbors? Our friends?"

She bit her lip again. "You must know it isn't going to be easy for you, Gregory."

He nodded. "Yes. I know. I never expected it to be. Dolores?"

Irene shook her head. "I honestly don't know. She loves you, Greg, you know that, even now, although she's too confused to realize it. They all

113

make it very difficult for her. She doesn't know what to believe, or what to do. Her brother especially never lets her forget."

"I don't suppose Bill will let anybody forget," Greg said, somewhat grimly. "I've already had the pleasure of seeing his reaction, at the lunchroom. He always used to like me, you know. We got along real well together, and he was excited at the thought of having me for a brother-in-law."

"He just doesn't understand these things, Greg. He's still only a boy. To him, every man in uniform must be a hero, like Bob." Once again, at mention of her dead son, a darkness crossed her face. "This town worships Bob, Greg."

" . . . So did I."

"Were you with him, when he . . . died?"

Greg put a hand to his head; the pain was returning. "Yes." There could be no real harm in such a lie.

Irene leaned her face on her hand and turned away from Greg, staring again into the backyard as though her sons were still playing there. If only you could call back the happier days . . .

"They've raised a plaque to him. Right in the City Hall. There's talk of a memorial fund, and changing the name of the park or the high school, even a statue in the square . . . Did they hurt him very much? Was he really very brave?"

Greg looked into that most gentle of faces. "I wish you could be as proud of me as you are of Bob."

"But I am, I am," Irene insisted fiercely, again pressing her hand to her face. "I'm proud of both my sons. And I thank God that at least one of them has come back to me." For a moment, she seemed

114

in imminent danger of tears, then she lifted her head sharply and a no-nonsense tone entered her voice. "But you must be hungry; let me get you something." She rose quickly and opened the door of the refrigerator. "There's some cold chicken." She smiled slightly and there was a catch in her voice. "There's always cold chicken in everyone's refrigerator, isn't there?"

"I'm really not very hungry, Mother. What I want is a shower. The train was . . ."

"Mrs. Christopher?"

Greg stopped speaking when he heard the front door open and the so-familiar voice calling to his mother. He had imagined that voice in a thousand nightmares over the past months, soothing him, reassuring him of her unwavering love. He caught his breath in surprise and anticipation. Startled, Irene closed the refrigerator door and looked at her son, her face revealing concern.

"It's Dolores."

"Are you here, Mrs. Christopher?"

"I'm out here in the kitchen, Dolores," Irene responded, her eyes on Greg.

"Mother's ready to . . ." She was talking when she entered the kitchen, bright as a spring morning, beautiful as he remembered her, the years of his absence merely sharpening that beauty in his eyes.

When Dolores saw Greg, she stopped. Instinctively, her bright green eyes filled with pleasure and she took a step towards him; her lips seemed to tremble slightly. Then she stopped, hesitated, and the light faded; doubt, confusion and uncertainty replaced the pleased surprise. She stood halfway across the kitchen, looking at the uniformed figure, searching his face, her hands at her sides, wanting to go to him, but held back by her own fears and uncertainties.

"Hello, Dolores," Greg greeted, raising his head and looking at her, feeling the pain of finding her even lovelier than his dreams.

"Hello, Greg." Her eyes were still on him when she spoke again to his mother. "Mother's ready to go downtown if you are, Mrs. Christopher."

"Yes . . . Oh, yes, I did promise I'd go with her. I'd quite forgotten all about it."

Irene moved quickly, before either of them could object to their being left alone together; she paused for a moment at the rear door after she had tossed her apron onto a chair, looking at their frozen figures, her eyes pleading. Please let them both understand, let them both be kind, don't let all of this be lost. She closed the door softly behind her.

"Won't you sit down, Dolores?" Greg asked after a moment of awkward silence. "Forgive me for not getting up."

Uncertainly, Dolores took the chair Irene had vacated. "You're looking well, Greg."

"So are you." He moved a hand out to hers where it rested on the table; she quickly moved hers away. "Dolores . . ."

She rose quickly from the chair and stood at the sink, her back to him, nervously wringing her hands. "I don't know, Greg."

"I'm the same person I was when I went away."

"Are you?" She turned and looked at him for a moment, her eyes earnestly searching, looking for the man she had loved through most of her young life. "Are you the same, Greg? They say you're a traitor."

116

"Do you believe them?"

For a moment, her eyes softened and her lips moved soundlessly; confusion returned as she shook her head. "I don't know what to believe. You look the same, you sound the same. But are you? Hasn't something changed? Traitor is an ugly word, Greg, in any land and in any time. They say you spoke out against your own country in order to save your life. Did you do that, Greg?" She waited for a reply, but he remained silent. "I'm asking you, Greg. Did you do that?"

"Dolores . . . Sometimes there are reasons . . ."

"I'm not asking for excuses! Did you or didn't you?"

He was silent a moment longer. "Yes. I did."

Her eyes widened; the faith that had supported her was gone. He had not even tried to deny.

"Then you're not the same, Greg. Not at all."

"Dolores . . ."

She shook her head, refusing to listen. "No. I tried very hard to believe in you. I told everyone it just couldn't be true. It must have been a similarity of names, or a wild story someone had just dreamed up. I wouldn't listen to them. My Greg could never be a coward or a traitor. He could never do anything so despicable. He was a strong, intelligent man with ideals and dreams. He was a man to be proud of!"

"You've got to trust me, Dolores."

"Trust you? When you've admitted it's true?"

"Things happen, Dolores," he attempted to explain. "Sometimes there are reasons . . ."

"Reasons!" He flinched at the sudden contempt in her voice. "Are there reasons that can make you turn against your own people, your family, your friends? What happened to Bob, then? Did he forget those reasons? Or was it that nobody bothered to tell him about them? Is that why you've come home and he hasn't?"

Greg reached for his crutches and rose clumsily, unsteadily to his feet; he caught the fleet expression of sympathy on her face as she watched him. "You've got to listen to me!"

"Do you know what has happened in this town, Greg? Do you know how things have changed? There are no more sports heroes, no matinee idols, there's only Bob Christopher. Benson's store sells photos of Bobby for a quarter apiece; Bill has one on his dresser, and I can't tell you how proud he is of it! The fourteenth of May is as big a holiday as the Fourth of July, because that was Bob's birthday. Teen-aged girls who never even knew him wear his picture in their lockets. They've even suggested we change the name of this town to Robertville. Did you know that? Absurd, isn't it? Bob is our own personal hero, the small-town boy who went to war and died in a Red prison camp rather than give in to the Communists. You should have seen their faces when they heard of it, Greg —the pride, the love, God, the adoration! Our own private hero!" She walked to the screen door and stood with her back to him. "And you should have seen those same faces when they heard how you . . . his own brother . . . had saved yourself!"

Greg stood before her when she turned again, leaning on his crutches, his arms hanging limply over them, staring at the floor, his face down, his eyes pained.

"It's a pity you couldn't have seen my face," he remarked.

"Greg! Don't ask for pity! Only Bobby deserves that!"

"I don't want pity!" He looked up at her, angry at the tears that had started to his eyes, at this sign of weakness when he most wanted to be strong. "I want love!"

"And do you think you really deserve love?"

"You thought so, once."

The words brought back memories that Dolores had tried too long to subdue—the drives in the car, the parking on the mountainside to look at the moonlight, their first date, the first dance, that first wonderful kiss. She could not remember a time when she hadn't loved Gregory Christopher . . .

"I wanted to love you, Greg. Oh, God, how I wanted to be proud of you! Every girl wants that of her knight in shining armor. I wanted to talk about you the way people talked about Bobby. I wanted to see your picture on Bill's dresser, wanted to hear him boast about his future brother-in-law." She was crying now, the tears streaming freely down her cheeks, her throat working convulsively to get the words through the sobs. "Do you know what you've done to us, Greg? Your father has resigned from all his civic committees, because the shame of having a son who was a traitor is greater than the glory of having one who was a hero. Your mother has left all the church organizations and stays in the house day after day so she won't see her friends with their cluckings of sympathy. And I . . . I . . ."

She threw her hands to her face, and the tears flowed through her fingers. Greg looked at her, helpless and silent, waiting to reassure her, wanting to take her in his arms as he used to do, and comfort her, feeling the closeness of her, letting his love warm her. He couldn't. That time was gone,

119

and he knew it was gone forever. He said nothing.

She lowered her hands again and looked at him through her tears, all the bitterness, fear and loneliness stinging in her voice.

"Why didn't you die with your brother?"

She ran from the room and he heard only the sound of her sobbing and then the slamming of the front door. He stood for a moment where he was, his face white, his hands trembling. He swayed slightly and put one hand out to the table to steady himself; the other covered his eyes.

It was all coming true, and it was growing worse. No, there was no place for him here. But where could he go?

Turning, he limped into the living room. Its sameness was almost a mockery: the all-American-television-room, the comfortable winged chair where his father always sat with the evening paper, the couch where his mother settled herself with her sewing, the window-seat where he and Bob had so often sat together and played their little games. The room was painfully filled with memories; ghosts seemed to surround him. It was too quiet, too familiar, and yet too strange. It could never be the same again.

His eye fell on the mantel and the silver-framed photographs of his younger brother, the original of that in the window of the railroad station lunch-room. They had been closer, perhaps, than many brothers, sharing their joys, their dreams, their triumphs and their sorrows. The familiar face, the smiling eyes, the white scar on the right forehead just at the hair-line (a football injury, of course; that was part of Bob's Americanism, too), all so familiar, and now gone forever. He rested his head against the mantel, his fingers lightly touching the picture.

"It's too much, Bobby," he sighed. "It's too much to ask of me, or of anyone."

Sleep did not come easily to Greg that night. He lay through the long hours tracing the shadows of the tree outside his window cast on the ceiling by the bright silver of the moon. It seemed to him that the branches were long, lean fingers pointing at him accusingly, calling him despicable, coward, traitor. The very silence of the house seemed unnatural, a condemnation of his presence. There was the sound of an occasional car moving down the street, the sharp yapping of a dog. Everything else was silent, comfortable. The town slept, the smug and self-confident town so sure of its own righteousness, a world away from the terrible things that had happened to him and for which they all so bitterly accused him. The American dream. What was it but merely a desire to be serene, comfortable, unchanging? Those who changed were condemned; no matter what the reason, all things must remain as they were.

Just after the clock struck two, Greg threw back the covers, reached for his crutches, and moved slowly and quietly down the stairs. He entered the living room, switched on the small light by the couch, and poured himself a stiff drink at the liquor cabinet. He was sitting on the window-seat, staring into the silver-blue night, when Irene, tying a robe about her, her eyes heavy with sleep and her forehead knitted with concern, entered the room.

"Gregory? Is that you?"

"Yes, Mom."

"Are you ill?" she asked as she entered the room. "It's very late."

He turned from the window and tried to smile convincingly. "No. I'm all right."

"Can I get you something?" Turning again to gaze into the darkness, he shook his head; she moved closer, her voice gentle. "What is it, son? Is something wrong?"

"I still have a little trouble sleeping sometimes, that's all." He sipped his drink and turned his head away. "I have dreams . . ."

Irene sat beside him, disturbed, and looked at her troubled son. "What kind of dreams, Greg?"

What kind of dreams? Dreams of mud, dreams of bursting shells, dreams of limbs torn from healthy bodies, dreams of blood spurting from the remains of what had once been a human being, dreams steeped in the flowing crimson of life's sacred fluid. Could he tell her of those dreams? He did not reply at once, when he did, his voice was low, still touched with the horror that had come with him half way around the world.

"Oh, dreams. Dreams I could never even tell you, Mother."

"But it's over now," she reminded him. "You're home again."

"I wonder," he mused. "Is it really over? Will they ever let it be over . . . for me?" He sighed and rested his head against the window-frame. "Home. I used to laugh about all the sentimentality connected with that simple little word, the way people always spoke of it, the songs, the pastiche of sweetness and light, the cloying wholesomeness. I don't laugh any more." He paused for another moment, then spoke so softly that she hardly heard him. "They hate me here."

"No. Don't say that, Greg."

"It's written on every face. It burns in every pair of eyes. I walked home from the station, down a row of neat middle-class homes with green lawns and cars in the driveways, a street where I had played as a child, down which I had gone to school, and everywhere along the street, people I had known all my life turned their backs. I could feel them staring at me, and there was friendliness in none of them. I could feel the resentment. Paul Dietrich was mowing his lawn; when I started towards him, he turned and went back into the house. Paul and I went camping together every summer from the time I was twelve years old. Mrs. Ferrante looked right through me. My first job was delivering newspapers on that street. Everyone was so friendly then, waving to me, stopping me on hot summer days for a soft drink . . ."

"They'll get over it, Greg," Irene insisted, trying to sound more convincing than she really felt. "People do forget."

"I wonder. They forget what they want to forget. Which one of us will they forget first . . . Bob or me. My good has been interred with Bobby's bones."

They were both silent for a moment. A late car turned the corner of the street, its headlights flashing briefly through the window, lighting Greg's strong profile. It seemed to him he could feel his brother's presence in the room.

"Gregory . . . why did you do it?"

It was the question he had been waiting for; he would hear it often in the days to come. He finished his drink, hobbled on one crutch over to the cabinet for another, and spoke with his back turned. "I'm sorry, Mother. I just can't tell you."

123

"Were you afraid?"

The remembered fear shot through him suddenly, like the touch of a hot poker, and he winced. "We were all afraid, always."

"Did you believe those things?"

He shook his head. "No. Of course not."

Irene was trying desperately to understand. This was her son, her own little boy, grown to confused manhood. She owed him not only love, but understanding as well. Her entire nature called for it. But his words were of no help.

"Then, why?"

He placed his glass on the mantel, beside Bob's photo, and faced her. "You say you believe in me. Keep on believing, Mother! Trust in me, no matter what anyone says. I can only swear to you that things just aren't the way they seem. I've got to have someone who will believe!"

She looked at him for a moment, this only son remaining to her, then rose from her seat, walked to him and lightly kissed his cheek. "I'll always believe in you, Greg. I know my boy better than anyone else. But now it's very late, and you must get some sleep. Come upstairs, dear."

"You go on up, Mom. I'm really not very tired. All the excitement of coming home, I suppose. I just want to be alone for a while."

She smiled again, touched his cheek and moved slowly out of the room to the stairs. "Good night, son."

"Have a good sleep, Mother."

He looked after her tired figure for a moment as she went slowly up the stairs and out of sight. Then he limped back to the window-seat with his drink and again stared into the loneliness of that dark and silent night. . . .

124

. . . . Phil Jenkins was really in no respect a hard or an unfeeling man, and he enjoyed a position of the highest respect and trust in the small community of Corryville, not only as president of the only local bank but for his many philanthropic activities as well. He was good for the town. He wanted to be liked, and he worked hard for the welfare of his town and for the consolidation of his own position. He had succeeded. One of the most constantly repeated jokes in town was that Phil stood for Philanthropic.

Above all, he liked things to be orderly and uncomplicated. Life should progress smoothly with a minumum of problems. Problems only gave him headaches and threatened to tarnish that image he had so painstakingly erected for himself.

And right now he was faced with a really major problem, and the name of that problem was Gregory Christopher. Phil had come to know Greg very well over the years, both as his one-time employer and as his prospective father-in-law, and he had always liked the boy. The news of his shocking defection in Vietnam had hit Phil hard. Like so many of the townspeople who remembered Greg, Phil had at first refused to believe the story. No boy from Corryville—good, clean, American Corryville—could possibly do what Greg had reportedly done. It was obviously some kind of mistake. But then there had come the incontrovertible proofs, the account of Bob Christopher's heroic death and Greg's blatant cowardice. Here was a problem that could not be evaded. Corryville, his own little town, had produced a man who was both a coward and a traitor.

And now, that problem was here and smack in

Phil's lap. On this mild morning, there could be only one reason why Greg should be out there waiting to see him. He wanted his job back.

He had every right, of course, at least in the normal sense of things. Greg had done very well at the bank before his induction, and there had been moments when Phil had quite contentedly imagined Greg, as his son-in-law, following him both as the bank president and as a new pillar of the community. That, of course, had all been before the—problem. As a former serviceman, Greg was fully entitled to have his job back. Corryville took care of its boys in uniform.

And that was the crux of the problem, for under no circumstances could Phil take Greg back. No, not even if he wanted to, and he really wasn't too sure of that. The stockholders would never stand for it, and Phil was certainly not about to risk his own position by going to the defense of a traitor, whoever it might be. Phil would have to turn him down. He might have to be unpleasant about it, and he didn't like that. It hurt the image. Well, rather that before one man than before the entire town. It might even do him some good, defending the good old American way and all that. He would play it as it came.

When Greg entered the bank president's office, leaning heavily on his crutches, Phil moved around the desk with a forced geniality and extended his hand; it was the first hand offered Greg since his return.

"Hello, there, Greg. How's the boy?"

"Fine, Mr. Jenkins. How are you?"

Phil glanced with some surprise at the crutches, and felt just a slight stirring of hope; could this perhaps change the situation? "What's with the crutches, boy? Didn't know you'd been wounded."

"I wasn't," Greg replied, slightly embarrassed. "There was an auto accident in 'Frisco. Nothing serious; it's getting better."

"Oh, I see." After a brief awkward moment, Phil added, "Well, son, sit down, sit down." When Greg had seated himself, Phil offered a box of cigars, which Greg refused. He spoke abruptly.

"I've come to see about my job."

Phil moved around the desk and returned to his large leather seat of authority; he always felt more secure there. "In a bit of a hurry, aren't you?"

"I'm restless," Gregg confessed. "I want to get back to work. It was my understanding when I left that the job would be here for me when I came back."

There it was. No beating around the bush. The problem was squarely before him. Phil picked up a letter opener and began to trace lines on the green blotter on his desk.

"Well, we certainly try to take care of our boys all we can, of course. But I should think you'd want a bit of a rest, first. Isn't there something about getting back into civilian routine again, a sort of period of adjustment?"

"I don't need it." Greg was not going to let him brush the problem aside quite so easily. "I at least want to know what to expect."

"Well, we've got to give it a little time, Greg. We have to be fair to your replacement, perhaps find another spot for him here at the bank . . ."

"You're stalling, Mr. Jenkins."

Phil raised his head as though his face had been slapped, and the point of the letter opener dug into the green fabric. His eyes narrowed; he disliked such open opposition. "I don't care for your tone."

"Do I get my job back?"

"You're hardly in a position to make demands, Greg."

"My work here has always been satisfactory," Greg reminded him. "I had several promotions before I left. Why can't I come back?"

Phil turned away, swiveling his chair to glance out at the comforting scene on Main Street. His eyes moved back to Greg and strayed absently over the campaign ribbons on his uniform. Catching the glance, Greg flushed and began to ease himself out of the chair.

"I expected better from you," he commented quietly.

"Wait. Sit down, Greg."

Greg hesitated, then sank again into the seat and looked at his former employer, his eyes somewhat harder than when he had entered the office. "Yes?"

"I'm going to level with you, Greg, for your own good," the bank president said. "You were always a good boy, a real nice kid. The whole town liked you and your brother, and I don't deny I was pleased when you and Dolores got on together. But times change, and people change with it. The past can't always be with us. Things just aren't the same. People see you in a different light now, and it's not a flattering one. They don't like what you've done, and in spite of my fondness for you, Greg, I don't mind telling you that I don't like it either."

"You say the past is the past," Greg remarked. "What you're talking about—or, rather, talking around—is part of the past."

Phil shook his head. "That's something entirely different. Maybe it isn't exactly fair to remember the bad and forget the good, but that's the way people are made. A crime isn't forgotten once it's over. I can tell you what you've done will never be forgotten in this town. You might be able to escape from it in a larger city, but not in a town the size of Corryville, where you're known to everybody and where everybody knows what you did."

"The board of review took no action against me," Greg reminded him.

"Maybe not, but they didn't exonerate you, either. We don't particularly care what others say."

"How can people judge when they may not even know the entire story?"

"We're talking about a highly emotional matter, Greg, and perhaps that does make people a bit unfair. They don't have to know the entire story. All they need is the plain basic fact of what you've done, and they have that. It's not a rumor, it's the truth, and you haven't made any attempt to deny it. You see, Greg, you forgot something very important. When you got into that uniform, you lost your identity. You became a soldier. Millions of young men fullfilled their duties, and you were expected to do the same. But you didn't. Your own brother died doing so; you should have been ready and willing to do the same."

"Not everyone can be a hero," Greg commented, rather bitterly. "Have you forgotten there were many opposed to the war . . ."

Phil reached into the humidor and lit a cigar, his face for a moment disappearing behind a haze of light blue smoke.

"That's completely irrelevant here. I had no

sympathy for them, either, but they weren't in uniform. There are always those opposed to any war. Weakness is unpleasant in any man; in a soldier, it's unforgiveable. Believe me, you would be no more welcome here if you were one of those peacenicks who ran off to Canada. But there's a difference. Their cowardice hurt no one but themselves; yours hurt us all. It's true not everyone can be a hero, but that doesn't give you the right to be a coward. The fact remains you accepted the responsibility and failed in it." He pointed his cigar at Greg. "I have only one suggestion for you, Greg. Leave this town."

"But I've lived here all my life!" Greg protested. "I was born in this town; it's my home!"

"Not any more. You repudiated this town, and it won't take you back now. The people just don't want you here any more. You've become an embarrassment, and people just don't like being embarrassed. Greg, you're a smart boy. You can make good someplace else—any place else. You've always wanted to live by the sea, study sea life, that sort of thing, haven't you? Do it. Go to school, learn about those things, take up a new way of life. But leave Corryville now, before it's too late."

"And just what do you mean by that?"

"People are talking about you, Greg, and the talk is growing louder. It's ugly talk. They don't like to see you walking down their streets. They want something done about it."

"The days of lynch mobs are over, I should hope."

"There are other ways of forcing unwanteds out of town. Think of your folks, Greg."

130

Greg lowered his head and said nothing. The room seemed uncomfortably stuffy.

"You really have no choice, Greg. You'll find no work here."

"You won't take me back?"

Phil shook his head. "No, I can't help it, Greg. I couldn't take you back even if I wanted to, and I don't mind telling you I don't want to. I don't make the policies of this bank, I merely carry them out. The Board of Directors won't risk the good will of their depositors."

Greg rose to his feet and slipped the crutches under his arms. "Well, I suppose I should thank you for seeing me."

"I don't want you to get hurt, Greg," Phil said. "I remember other, better times. Don't try to fight the whole town; you can't win." Greg continued on his way to the door. "Have you seen Dolores?"

"Not since the day I came home," Greg replied flatly. "She's broken our engagement."

"Oh? I didn't know. I'm sorry."

Greg opened the door and turned again, smiling slightly. "Are you really sorry, Mr. Jenkins?"

Phil realized he had stabbed his blotter to shreds.

Greg entered the house, went directly to the liquor cabinet and poured himself a drink as his mother, dressed to go out, entered from the kitchen.

"Greg?"

"Yes?" He recapped the bottle.

"Did you see Phil?"

After a moment's hesitation, he turned and looked at her. "Oh . . . no, no I didn't. He was too busy to see me today. I'll go back in a day or so.

There's really no great hurry about it."

"No, of course not," Irene agreed, drawing on her gloves. "Dinner will be a little late tonight, dear. Your father should be home at any time. I'm going shopping." She looked at him as he raised the glass to his lips. "You never used to drink so much, Greg."

"I never had so much reason to." He was immediately repentant of his harsh tone. "I'm sorry. I'm a little tired."

Irene returned to the hall. "I'll be back soon, dear. Try to get some rest."

When the door closed behind her, Greg placed his drink on the mantel and loosened his collar. His eyes traveled about the room, and he wondered if it would ever feel like home again. Reaching for his glass, his hand touched the photograph of his dead brother. He picked it up and looked at it as though he had never really seen it before. There was a very strong resemblance between the two of them; anyone would have taken them for brothers.

"Look at it well."

Greg turned quickly to find his father, suitcase in hand, standing in the doorway.

"It's the face of a hero."

Greg carefully replaced the picture on the mantel. "It's the face of a dead man," he said softly.

"It's the face of a man who knew the meaning of honor."

"I think," Greg said, glancing again at his brother's face, "in the moment of death honor really didn't seem so terribly important to Bob."

"And yet, he didn't try to keep death away." Edward Christopher walked into the room and looked closely at his sole surviving son; he placed the suitcase against the wall. "I'm surprised you came back here."

"This is my home," Greg reminded him, startled by the blunt statement and the tone in which it was spoken.

"When did you remember that?"

"I'm your son."

"I had two sons. One was a hero; the other was a coward. They're both dead."

"You don't mean that."

"Bob is more alive in my heart now than you can ever be," Edward stated. "I will not have a son who is a coward and a traitor."

"Are you so certain I'm either?" Greg asked.

Edward hesitated, looking at him. The rather fleshy face bore the mark of weariness and overwork and Greg suddenly knew how deeply his father felt about what had happened. At the same time, he realized there was a wall between them that nothing, not even time, would ever be able to remove. They had once been friends.

"Do you think I wanted to believe it, any of it?" Edward asked. "Is it easy for a father to believe such things about his son? I called them liars. Yes, I even fought them, when the talk became too much for me to bear." He walked past Greg and looked at Bob's photograph. "You were the little boy who used to come home dirty and ragged from your rough games in the vacant lot down the street, who dressed up all bright and shiny for Sunday School, who made us so proud when he came home with the first few dollars he'd ever earned. Your mother and I nursed you through measles, scarlet fever, one cold after another. You always took such care of your brother . . ." He raised his face to the mirror and met Greg's eyes. "Do you think it was easy to believe that boy could go against the teachings of a lifetime, could turn traitor to his country and spout Communist heresies to save his own life? Do you think that was easy, Greg?"

Greg took a halting step towards his father and then stopped, leaning heavily on his crutches, looking at Edward in the mirror.

"And how do you think it was for me?" he asked. "How easy it is for people to condemn! You sit here in your comfortable, warm homes and you spout about death before dishonor! Do you know what it is to be surrounded by brutal forces in a hostile land? Do you think we didn't want to die? We would have welcomed it! But they wouldn't let us die!" He paused for a moment, held by his father's eyes; he trembled slightly under the stress of his emotions. "Do you know what pain is, Dad? Horrible, terrible, searing pain? Not the kind of pain that you feel from a toothache or a stomach-ache or a hangover, but the kind of pain that rips into your soul so you don't know who you are or what you are or what you're doing or saying, and you don't give a damn? Do you know the thousand and one ways of hurting a man? I mean really hurting a man, Dad. Do you know what it's like to have your testicles put into a vise and squeezed until it feels like they're going to burst? To have bamboo splinters inserted under your fingernails and hot pokers forced into your rectum? You shudder to hear about it, but can you ever begin to imagine the pain it causes? Do you know, any of you, how a man can be destroyed and yet still live when all he wants is to die?"

"Don't ask for pity, Greg."

"God damn it, it isn't pity I want, it's understanding!"

They faced each other, one face stern and bitter, the other agonized and pleading, perspiration glistening on their foreheads. They seemed strangely alone in the world. Edward suddenly turned away, to the liquor cabinet; his hands trembling, he poured himself a drink. He spoke with his back to his son.

"Love dies very hard, Greg. I'm not an unnatural father. I loved both my sons. But there are some things even love can't survive. Had it been anything else, I would have stood at your side and defended you with my very last breath. But this! At the very moment of your brother's death, you stood up and denounced him, your home, your family, your friends, everything decent that has been taught you all your life. . ."

"You mean I dared to speak against middle-class white America, flag waving, apple pie and Grandma's house over-the-river-and-through-the-trees. . ."

"Yes!" The word was an explosion. "Yes! They may seem a bit dull to you, but they were your life, and there's still nothing wrong with middle-class American morality and patriotism. You spoke against them all, and now you expect us to forget all that and take you back, you expect to go right on enjoying everything that you condemned. Do you really think it's going to be that easy?"

"Do you think it was easy for me, any of it? I spoke to save my life. Should I let a matter of semantics destroy me?"

"Damn it, you were a soldier, an officer!" Edward turned to face him again, his own face crimson with anger. "You weren't just a puny,

135

weakling kid! Bob was three years younger than you, but he was more of a man than you can ever hope to be!"

Greg turned to the mantel, almost losing his balance in the swiftness of his movement. "Bob! Bob! I'm sick of hearing about Bob!" He swept his crutch across the mantel, knocking Bob's picture to the hearth, where the glass shattered. Without his crutch, Greg tottered and fell to the floor, sobbing. "I'm sick of all of it!"

Edward looked down at his weeping son, staring for a moment of silence as though at a stranger.

"I want you out of this house, and I don't ever want you to come back."

With these words, he started for the hall. Greg crawled to the couch and tried to pull himself up on it to his feet.

"Do you know?" he cried, his face twisted with the agony of remembered pain. "Do you have any idea what those bastards can do to a man?"

The sharp cry stopped Edward; in the doorway, he turned.

"Perhaps I should ask Bobby that."

For a moment longer, he coldly looked down at his son, and then turned and started up the stairs. Raising himself to one knee, watching him move slowly and steadily out of sight, Greg called after him. "You don't know! You don't know!"

Greg sat up abruptly in the bed, breathing heavily; his naked chest was bathed in perspiration and his hands trembled. Relieved to find it had been only another dream and not an actual reliving of that terrible time, he sighed and put a hand to his face to wipe the sweat from his forehead and upper lip. Throwing back the covers, he stepped out of the bed and over to the window. Fumbling in the darkness, he took a cigarette from the pack on the dresser, lighted it, and stepped out onto the small balcony.

Rain was falling again, but the roof overhung his perch and he managed to keep dry. The night was still very quiet. Leaning against the wall, he gazed out to the dark sea, invisible save in the tumbling of waves onto the beach, mingled with the velvet blackness of the sky. The ran fell softly, almost musically; there was no breeze.

After that terrible confrontation with his father, there had been nothing for Greg to do. Over the tearful protests of his mother, he had left Corryville and, after a period of schooling and study, found his way to Hawkins' Cove. He was now quite content, immersing himself in the work he had come to love.

He had not seen his father nor had any contact with him since that painful day, but he kept in touch with his mother, and twice during the past year she had come to Hawkins' Cove to visit him, without Edward's knowledge. She had become a painfully lonely woman, for she had indeed lost both her sons, and that loneliness at last was beginning to age her; her hair was almost white, her smile was strange and sad. It was true that Edward would not permit Greg's name to be mentioned in the house, but some day, Irene constantly insisted, his father would understand and relent. Some day all of Corryville would understand and then he could return home again.

Greg knew that wasn't true, and so did she. He could never go back there now. They would always look upon him as the coward who had stood before a microphone and uttered Communist heresies while his own younger brother had preferred death to dishonor. Only Greg himself knew the complete truth, and he would never reveal it to anyone. Let them forget him, as he had now quite forgotten them.

He really didn't even care any more, and that made it easier. He would not have gone back if he could. He had found a new home and was reasonably happy. He remembered the past from time to time, and there was still moments of loneliness, but it was getting easier all the time. None of them were really important to him any longer.

Somewhere in the silent house, a clock struck three. Greg flicked his cigarette down into the sand and returned to a mercifully dreamless sleep.

# CHAPTER EIGHT

Steve tossed uneasily on his bed, his mind still befuddled by all he had drunk during the course of the evening. The breeze had freshened a bit and the curtains at the open French doors floated out into the room. The rain splattered softly on the balcony. Still partially dressed, he lay face down, one arm dangling over the side of the bed, his breathing heavy, his face lined with the unpleasantness of his own painful ever-recurring dream. . . .

. . . He was led into the cold, cluttered, cheerless room, white and trembling, more than a little frightened by what had happened to him. A uniformed police officer sat at a battered desk littered with papers, determinedly filing his nails, and another sat beside the water cooler, deeply absorbed in a girlie magazine. When Steve entered, the policeman at the desk glanced up with very little interest.

"Take a seat," he suggested.

Steve took the hard wooden chair beside the desk, sitting on its very edge as though afraid of making himself comfortable, his hands nervously clasped between his knees. Tiny beads of perspiration stood out on his upper lip, and he felt somehow reluctant to lick them away. The only sounds were the monotonous ticking of the clock on the wall, its daggars stabbing the time at shortly before two o'clock in the morning, and the irritating rasp of the file drawn back and forth over the cop's nails; the water cooler belched a bubble. Darkness showed outside the room's only window.

Steve looked at the red-haired officer at the desk and tried to speak calmly, but he had to clear his throat before the words would come.

"What's going to happen to me?"

Not raising his head, the officer shrugged. "Depends. Probably too late for night court. Probably have to hold you 'til morning."

"I'll have to spend the night in jail?"

"Won't kill you. Give you time to do a little thinking. Might help." The officer looked at him for the first time, his watery blue eyes still showing little real interest. "First arrest?"

Steve nodded wordlessly.

The officer raised his feet to the carved and scratched top of the desk, crossing them at the ankles; Steve noticed the sole of his right shoe had worn thin and his blue socks dropped over the tops of his shoes.

"You don't really look the type," the officer said. "We get lots of 'em in here, you know. Not all like you, though. Some of 'em real fairies, swishes, limp-wrists. Even had a couple last month all in drag. Yeah. Drag. Dresses, lipstick,

140

beads, all the fairy trimmings. Tried to make up to us. Said they'd do anything we wanted if we'd let 'em go. Disgustin'." He hesitated a moment, looking at Steve with the first signs of interest. "Guy like you, though, I dunno. Dressed good, decent-looking, pretty smart. Looks like you'd know better." He shrugged again. "Can't always tell, I guess."

Steve lowered his eyes and stared at the floor.

"Gotta watch yourself," the officer cautioned. "If you gotta do that kinda thing, pick on your own crowd, but Jesus, don't go makin' a pass at a cop!"

"I didn't know he was a—cop."

"Sure. That's why you gotta be careful. Never can tell who's a cop and who isn't. What you wanna play around with in your own place is maybe your own business, but a guy's gotta be nuts to try a pass in a public place."

The officer at the cooler, not raising his head from his magazine, chuckled as he turned another page. "Must have wanted it real bad."

The door opened and Joseph Hirsch, dignified, white-haired, his eyes still red from this early rising, entered the room, carrying a leather briefcase. He paused a moment when he saw Steve.

"Hello, Steve."

Steve raised his eyes briefly, then looked away. "I'm sorry to get you out this time of morning."

"That's all right, Steve." Hirsch sighed, then turned to the officer at the desk. "Where's the arresting officer?"

"Went for a cup of coffee. Be back in a minute."

Placing his briefcase on the corner of the desk, the lawyer next asked, "How did it happen?" and, somehow, Steve found a certain measure of comfort in the businesslike tone of his voice.

The officer shrugged. "Same old story. Pass in a men's room, notes, obscene suggestions. That sort of thing."

Hirsch seemed startled by the account and looked questioningly at Steve, who flushed under his gaze. "It's his first arrest."

"Yeah. So he says."

"Ain't it always?" This from the officer at the cooler.

Hirsch ignored his comment and turned again to the officer at the desk. "Can't you give him a break?"

"You know it ain't up to me. Chief says no. Too much of this kind of thing nowadays; too many fairies around. Gotta crack down. He's got to go up before the judge in the morning. I got nothin' to do with it."

"Where's the chief?"

"Gone home."

The attorney hesitated, trying to think of some other angle. "What about night court?"

The officer aimed his nail file at the clock. "Too late. They'll take him over to the Fifty-Third Street station; the wagon's waiting until you're through with him."

"Can I see him alone for a minute?"

The officer dropped the file to the desk and rose to his feet. "Yeah, sure. You know his rights." He moved to the door, nudging his companion and motioning with his head. They both left, closing the door behind them.

The room was silent for a moment; the ticking of the clock seemed unusually loud. Steve was staring absently at the floor; his mouth was dry, his lips parched, but he lacked the strength to walk over to the cooler. The collar of his shirt was darkened by perspiration. Hirsch looked at him for a moment, frowning, uncomfortably avoiding his direct gaze. He took a cigarette case from his pocket and offered it to Steve, who took a cigarette, accepted a light, and resumed his former pose.

"It's a bad business, Steve," the attorney announced.

Steve spoke softly, in a monotone of despair. "You never think things like this could really happen to you; it's always someone else, isn't it? He had a partner with him, and when we walked past him, the officer told him to hit me over the head if I tried to get away. They say that to gangsters, bank robbers, murderers." He raised his head and looked at the lawyer through eyes red with strain and worry. "I'm not a criminal, Mr. Hirsch."

"You've broken the law, Steve."

"Seems to me it takes two to break a law like that. I . . . I had encouragement, or it could never have happened."

"Nobody says the law's perfect. We're still basically a Puritanical society, Steve. So-called sexual divergence scares the hell out of us, and our laws are archaic. But they're still the laws, and if you break them, you have to accept the consequences."

"What will they do to me?"

"That depends on the judge. Some are harsher than others in something of this nature. I don't suppose it should go very hard on you, though; it is a first offense. But that isn't really what's important, Steve. You'll have an arrest record, maybe even a conviction."

143

"The officer said I should just plead guilty. Throw myself on the supposed mercy of the court, I guess he means."

"Sure, he would say that. It makes the entire procedure so much quicker for him, but not for you. Conviction on a charge of sexual perversion isn't pleasant. You'd better just leave it all to me."

For the first time, Steve rose from his seat and crossed to the dark, unshaded window. The glass was streaked with dirt, and a serpentine crack ran down the left side. He could look down into the dark street below, brightened only by the circle of a single streetlamp. No lights showed in any of the buildings and the sidewalks were empty. A lone cab cruised by.

"It's all been very humiliating."

"I could suggest mental treatment."

"I'm not sick," Steve quickly rejected with a decided shake of his head. "Look, believe me, Mr. Hirsch, I'm ashamed about all this, and I don't suppose I'll ever understand quite how this mess happened. It certainly has never happened before. But that's as far as my shame goes."

"I'll have to tell your mother, of course."

Steve turned from the window. "Can't you . . ."

The lawyer interrupted him with a decided shake of his head. "No, Steve, I can't. She has to know the truth. I don't relish telling her; it's going to be very hard on her. She idolizes you." He rose from the desk and picked up his briefcase. "Well, there isn't very much I can do here before morning. I'm sorry, Steve, but it just can't be helped. You'll have to be locked up for the night."

"Locked up." He sank again into the chair, despair on his white face. "Am I really that dangerous?" Was this really happening to him?

The door opened again and a tall, beefy plain-clothesman entered the room, looking at them for a moment with an air of smug superiority before announcing, "I'm Grote. Arresting officer."

"I'm his attorney. Family's attorney."

An unpleasant grin crossed the officer's long face. "Didn't take you long to get here, did it? Experience?"

"It's his first arrest."

"Oh, sure it is." The officer dropped into the chair behind the desk. "Where the hell do all the two and three time losers come from, I wonder?"

"Can't you give him a break?" Hirsch asked, although realizing the utter futility of his appeal. "He comes from a good family. Has a good job. Widowed mother. It's going to be rough."

The officer tilted his hat on the back of his head; the band was heavily stained. A toothpick wavered between his thin lips. "And I'll just bet she don't even know Sonny here's a queer."

"Why give him a black mark?"

"Save the hearts and flowers, will ya? I didn't give him a black mark; he gave it to himself."

"What if something like this happened to a boy of your own?"

The officer's face became uglier in its hardness; his small eyes glowed with contempt. "If I had a son who was a fuckin' queer, I'd beat it out of him if it killed 'im."

Obviously nothing was to be gained by appealing to the officer's better nature. "He says you encouraged him."

"I don't give a shit what he says. Let 'im prove it. He slipped me some nice dirty notes."

Grinning, he looked at Steve. "You really do those things, kid?" Steve looked away and the officer laughed.

Hirsch looked at him for a moment longer, dislike unconcealed in his expression, then turned again to Steve. "Well, there's nothing I can do until morning. We'll straighten this out."

After Hirsch had left, the two other cops returned. Settling in a chair, the first officer took a sandwich and a bottle of diet soda from a paper bag. He looked with distaste at the bottle.

"Christ, I hate this rotgut, but Flo says I'm gettin' a tire."

The arresting officer yawned, stretched, and rose to his feet. "Guess I'll go on home. Sally's waitin' up for me. See you tomorrow." He left without another glance at Steve.

His departure was followed by silence. Steve felt suddenly deathly tired.

"Sally his wife?" he asked, feeling a sudden need for sound.

"Yeah."

"Lucky girl. What does he do now?" Bitterness entered his voice. "Go home and tell her how brave he was tonight, exposing himself to the queers?"

The officer chuckled. "Yeah, Grote's a bit hard-boiled sometimes, I guess."

From the cooler, the other officer glanced up briefly from his magazine and commented, "Nobody asked you to make a pass at him. Jesus Christ, Grote sure isn't a beauty!"

His brief flare of nervous spirit effectively squelched, Steve again lowered his head and resumed his study of the floorboards. The room smelled stale, with an unpleasant odor of ink. A

146

few minutes later, he was taken out to the street where a large black patrol wagon waited for him. He stepped inside and seated himself on one of the benches lining the sides of the vehicle, grateful to be the sole occupant. The wagon moved at a brisk speed through the dark, silent streets of the sleeping city. It had rained earlier, and under the street lamps wet pavements glistened; sprays of water rose on either side as they moved quickly through a large puddle. A car moved up behind them, and Steve quickly slid down towards the far end of the wagon, hoping he had not been seen. He sat with his shoulders hunched, his hands in his pockets, wishing he could run, wishing he could cry, wishing he could somehow relive those terrible few moments. He watched the empty streets slip by, unaware of light or movement, feeling only his own deep misery.

When the wagon came to a stop, he was conducted into another sombre police building. A burly sergeant at the high desk indifferently relieved him of his possessions, belt and shoe laces, and he was taken through a door to a row of cells. A gaunt, incredibly dirty jailer, his teeth stained with the juice of the tobacco he was vigorously chewing, entered his name and the charge against him in a large book that made Steve think of the ledger used by the Recording Angel.

"Another one, huh?" the jailer asked, spitting a dirty brown stream onto the floor. "Must be a full moon; always brings 'em out."

Steve and the officer followed him to a cell, which he opened with one of the keys clanking on a large metal ring fastened to his belt. "Inside, baby."

"Gonna get pretty cold tonight," the officer

commented. "How about a blanket?"

"Locked away for the night. Too much trouble to get one." He smirked at Steve, shifting the tobacco wad to the other side of his mouth. "If you get cold, beat your meat; I'll sure as hell bet you know how." Laughing at his own witicism, he slammed the barred door and turned the key.

Steve stood at the door, his hands grasping the cold bars, listening to the fading footsteps. Silence followed, utter, complete; the other cells were all apparently unoccupied. He looked at the barren, narrow cell, which contained only a hard metal plank, intended as a bed but without a mattress or a blanket, and a dirty, chipped toilet bowl lacking a seat. He shuddered slightly, for it was already quite cold.

A window, small and barred, gave onto the cloudless night sky, dominated by a large, bright star. Ludicrously, he found himself thinking of Pinocchio. When you wish upon a star.

His embarrassment had been replaced by a strange new fear. How had this terrible thing happened to him? A few drinks . . . No, that was begging the question. He was not anywhere near drunk; he'd had no more to drink this evening than usual. He had dropped into the men's room at the station, and when the well-shod foot in the booth next to his moved invitingly closer, he had thought it amusing to respond. He'd heard about such happenings. Was that all there was to it? A joke? Something to laugh about? No one was laughing.

His fear now ran deeper than this. It was a fear that this incident revealed something about himself that he had not known or even suspected. Had his actions expressed an unspoken desire and interest? Arrested on a charge of public homosexual activity, an attempt to make contact with another man for homosexual reasons. He had, in what he wanted to believe was a prank, made obscene suggestions to a man who had turned out to be a cop!

Or was it more than that? At the age of twenty-five, was he to understand he was a homosexual? Was this where he had been heading since the ugly ending of his brief, tumultuous marriage two years earlier? Why had the marriage been unsatisfactory? Secretly, he had blamed his wife; perhaps she as secretly blamed him. Incompatability. Was there more behind it than that? Had his life gone wrong because he had not accepted his true nature? But there had been nothing before, nothing of any importance. . . .

His hands tightly grasped the iron bars and he placed his feverish face against them. A cold breeze struck him through the open window and he shivered. He felt numb. . . .

At 10:20 the following morning the foul-smelling jailor opened the cell door and motioned Steve out. His clothes rumpled, his eyes red from lack of sleep, he followed another officer to the front desk, where his property was wordlessly returned to him, and out to the patrol wagon. There were several others seated on the benches this time; three teen-aged hoodlums grinning and joking as though the entire business were a lark, and a sullen brooding black man bleeding profusely from an untended gash in his hand. Steve silently took his place at a safe distance from the others, and the wagon started on its way to the courthouse. When it came to a stop, a patrolman motioned them out. At the curb stood a tiny wisp of a woman, her gray hair flying uncombed about her head. She stared with fascination at the prisoners as they stepped from the wagon, her eyes alight with senile amusement.

"What these boys do, eh?" she demanded loudly, drawing the attention of several passersby. "Rob a bank? Mug some poor old lady? Kill somebody? That black rape a nice white girl, eh?"

Steve followed the others in the courthouse and into another row of cells, filled with those awaiting entry into the courthouse. He sat on the cot, his hands clasped between his legs, staring unseeingly at the dirty cement floor. A welcome numbness had come over him, and he was now scarcely aware of his sordid surroundings. He was tired, rumpled, unshaven, and ravenously hungry. He tried not to think, determined to take whatever came to him. This, too, will pass away. The cells were filled, mostly with young delinquents who had obviously been here before, heaping abuse and obscenities on the officers, the courts, each other, everyone in general. Steve scarcely heard them.

It was more than an hour before Grote, his arresting officer, appeared and removed him from the cell. He was taken to a large room on the third floor and photographed with a numbered tag about his neck, finger-printed for a second time, and conducted to yet another large cell with others about to be summoned into the courtroom, derelicts and hopeless drunks primarily, some asleep curled against the wall or the bars. Two blacks lay in a corner bleeding from open wounds into a small drain in the center of the sloping floor. One old man seated against the wall was mumbling incoherently to himself, spittle dribbling from his mouth and running down his unshaven chin; a filthy boy on the far side of the cell had urinated in his trousers, leaving a dark stain down the inner part of one leg.

When Steve's name was called, he was conducted into the large, almost empty courtroom, and was relieved to see Joseph Hirsch, the only familiar landmark in this sordid sea into which he had fallen.

The brief hearing was a confused jumble that he could never afterward recall with any clarity. He had a vague recollection of standing, nervous and dry-mouthed, before the judge, of muttering "not guilty" like some character in a B movie, which even then struck him as ridiculous under the circumstances that had brought him here. The courtroom was hot and uncomfortable; the flag behind the judge was a blur. Hirsch spoke for a few moments, too softly for the rest of the court to hear, and Steve caught references to good family and upbringing, an excellent business position and a widowed mother. The judge mentioned something about psychiatric treatment, and then he heard the words "suspended sentence" and he was permitted to walk out of the courthouse.

Steve hesitated a moment before the house, with his hand on the cold brass knob of the white door. He had been wandering aimlessly about the city for several hours, dreading the moment when he would have to go home. Now he was simply too exhausted to stay away any longer. He had neither washed nor eaten all that day, and hunger was beginning to make him feel light-headed; he desperately needed sleep. When he passed a mirror, he found it difficult to recognize himself in the glass. He opened the door and stepped into the house.

Dorothy Conroy was lying on the couch in the living room, a wet cloth on her forehead. Within closed windows the shades were drawn as though she had wanted to seal herself off from the prying world. The sunlight through the shades cast a yellow light into the tastefully furnished room. Steve stood quietly in the doorway until his mother rose slowly to a sitting position on the couch. She looked worn and haggard, older than he had ever seen her before; her eyes, unusually large, were raw from weeping and lack of sleep.

"Where have you been?" Her voice was harsh, a sibilanty accusing whisper. "It's been hours."

"I don't know." He vaguely waved his hand. "Walking . . ."

She looked at him, her face marked with fear of the unasked but necessary question, which she finally managed to put into words. "What . . . happened?"

"Suspended sentence."

She threw her small, narrow hands to her pale face. "Thank God! Oh, thank God!"

Steve took another step into the room and extended his hands to her in a form of supplication. "I'm . . . sorry."

Dorothy looked at him, and there was something almost frightening in the wildness of her eyes; she rose slowly to her feet and faced him, slowly wringing her hands. Her pace was unsteady as she approached him. Steve was somehow surprised to notice that she was really a very small woman.

"What did you do, Steve?" she asked, her voice

taut and almost unrecognizable. "What did you do with that man, that policeman?"

He walked to a chair and sank into it, reminding himself of his weariness. "Please, mother . . ."

She moved closer to him; her face was pale with fear and anger. "I want to know! I've got to know! What did you do, Steve?"

He shook his head, feeling an almost overpowering desire to fall asleep where he sat; the room seemed to be swimming before his eyes.

"Nothing, mother. Nothing."

"Nothing? They don't put you in jail for doing nothing!" Her voice was rising to a pitch of hysteria. "You've been in jail Steve! In jail! What did you do?"

He closed his eyes and leaned back in the chair. "I won't want to talk about it, mother!"

"But I want to talk about it!" Her face was livid as she bent over him, one hand convulsively squeezing a tear-dampened handkerchief. "You're my son! What are you? I raised you decently. I gave you everything a person could need, a good home, love, anything you wanted! How did this . . . this thing get into you? Where did it come from?"

"Please, please . . ." Steve thrust his hands through his hair, closing his eyes to the fury before him.

"I've always lived a clean, decent life, and so did your father! Oh, yes, he told me there were people like that, dirty, filthy, obscene people who found pleasure in . . . in filth! But I would never believe him. People are people, not animals. But now . . . my own son! Oh, God, how glad I am that your father isn't alive to see this day! Why couldn't I be dead as well?" She moved away from him, pacing the floor, constantly wringing her hands, her eyes darting about the room, as though looking in the familiar furnishings and surroundings for answers. "I've been lying here all night, all day . . . how long has it been? Since Joseph called, I've been sitting . . . waiting . . . I've been nearly out of my mind, thinking, wondering what to do. First I thought maybe I should kill you and myself, too, and put an end to it all, and then I thought of my poor, decent girl . . ."

Steve quickly raised his head. "Mother, for God's sake, stop this!"

"Oh, Steve, what have you done to me? Do you want to kill all the love I feel for you?"

He looked at her for a moment before replying, his voice dull, in sharp contrast to her own strident tones; she seemed someone he had never known before. "Can love really be killed, mother?" He rose and walked to the windows, staring around the edge of the drawn shade into the familiar street; then he turned and faced her again. "Look at me. Am I really any different? Am I less a son, less a brother, than I was last year, last month, yesterday morning? Do I look any different?"

"A murderer seldom looks different after he has murdered!"

"Oh, for Christ's sake, mother!"

"Don't blaspheme, Steve!" she shouted at him. "Haven't you committed sin enough without adding blasphemy?" She turned and began to pace the room again. "Oh, my God, my God, what am I going to do? How can I ever rest or have peace of mind again? My son . . . my son . . . is a . . . pervert!" She spoke the dreaded word in a horrified whisper. "I've loved you so, I've idolized you!"

"You've idolized your own image of me!" he

insisted. "In your mind you've created the perfect being you wanted your son to be. Nobody could possibly live up to that image, myself least of all."

"But how could you do this to me?"

"I haven't done anything to you! This has nothing to do with you. I don't live my entire existence within these four walls!"

She stopped and turned with a sudden, quick movement, and he was startled to see the light of hope gleaming in her reddened eyes. She seemed to think for a moment, and her mouth worked with a sudden excitement.

"Yes. Yes, of course." She spoke slowly, as though still forming her new thoughts. "That's what it is, isn't it? You could never have picked up . . . such things . . . in this house. It's in the city that you have found this kind of filth. Those people you know, people you've never brought to this house. Bad friends. Bad companions. And you drink too much, Steve, you know you do." Her voice had acquired a new strength; she had found a needed belief. "That's what it was! You had too much to drink, and you didn't know what you were doing. Those friends of yours led you to this!"

Tired again, he shook his head. "No, mother . . ."

But she refused to listen to him now; she had found a glimmer of hope in the darkness of this dreadful day.

"Now we know what to do, how to stop this thing, this evil, from growing . . . You must never drink again, Steve, no, not ever again. That's what broke up your marriage, you know, oh, yes, it is, I know it is, Christine told me about it more than once. Promise me you'll never touch another drop as long as you live. You know I've never really liked it; drink is a terrible thing, and it makes people do terrible things . . . Never again, Steve, never. And forget those wild friends of yours. They're no good, and can only bring you trouble. They all drink too much, and they lead you to do the same. They don't come from good homes, I'm sure. They live too freely, doing too much as they please. Forget them. When you're through with work at the end of the day, come right home to me. Oh, Steve, you've got to promise me these things!"

A clock chimed, and he automatically tried to count the number of strokes, but they all became a mere blur of sound. He had lost all conception of time.

"Oh, let me sleep at night, Steve!" The pleading voice continued, drumming into his tired consciousness. "Can you imagine the terrible dreams—the nightmares—the fears I'll have whenever you're away from this house? If you love me, Steve, you must promise!"

His mouth was dry and his head was pounding. There suddenly came to him the picture of a filthy boy urinating onto a stone floor. His mother's face came closer, her eyes wide and staring, her mouth open like a red maw lined with even dentures; her breath touched his face, warm and unpleasant. What had happened to his world? He had to get away, up to his room, he had to sleep, rest, he had to be alone. He could no longer do battle against all the world.

"All right, mother!" he cried in a tone calling for release. "All right! I promise!"

Her face came closer and he felt her moist, quivering lips on his cheek. "Oh, I didn't really mean all those terrible things I said, you know that, dear. I was so terribly upset! You're a good, decent boy; I know that. I guess sometimes things can happen . . . bad friends, too much drink. We'll forget all about this now. We'll put it out of our minds, and your sister will never even know about it. Oh, Steve, if anything were to happen to you . . ."

He moved away from her, suddenly repelled, knowing he had to be alone, now, now, now, and started slowly up the stairs. "I'm terribly tired, Mother. I'm going to have a shower, and go to bed."

"Of course, dear, of course." The happiness, the joy in her voice was somehow frightening. "Oh, we're going to be very happy together, dear, you'll see. I promise you that. I'll do anything . . ."

"Yes, mother, yes . . ."

"Go to bed now, dear. Have a good sleep." With a touch of the ridiculous, she added, "Pleasant dreams."

She watched him, her face aglow with triumph and satisfaction, as he made his way up to his room.

Things went well enough for a short time after that. Frightened by the nightmarish incident, Steve was willing to alter the pattern of his life in order to prevent even the slightest possibility of a recurrence. He went to the office each morning at nine, returning home promptly at the end of the day's work. He drank nothing, he saw no one, he abandoned all of his former friends, although they were totally innocent of any involvement in his problem. He no longer went to the theatre, or to the movies, or even out to dinner. The fear controlled and dominated his life. He found himself agreeing with his mother's hopeful theory as to the causes of that dreadful evening. There was surely nothing really wrong with him; he was as normal as the next man. Hadn't he even been married once? The failure of that marriage had resulted from temperamental difficulties—and, yes, perhaps from drink, although he would have strongly refuted the suggestion at any other time— and not from sexual incompatability. This thing— it had been the result of drink. He would play it safe. He would drink no more. And sex would play no further part in his life. It could be done. He would merely suppress all such thoughts. That was the safe way.

For Dorothy, the entire matter therefore proved a blessing in disguise. She had probably never been happier than during those weeks that followed that terrible time. Always a fiercely protective and possessive mother—driving her daughter Ruth into an early marriage in order to make a life of her own—she had resented any of Steve's contacts and activities away from home. Now all that was changed. Now Steve belonged entirely to her. They needed no one else.

It could not last, of course. The strain of his new life soon began to tell on Steve. He lost weight, became nervous and irritable; even his work at the office began to suffer. Dorothy made frantic, almost pitiful attempts to brighten matters for him at home. She plied him with his favorite foods, she deluged him with little gifts of things she knew would please him, but nothing could conceal from Steve the fact that he was now living an overly-sheltered life dominated by a frightened, possessive mother. He was living like a gigolo, a young boy pampered by an older woman, who also happened to be his mother. His manhood strained at the unnaturalness of this position. Inevitably, the time came when he could tolerate it no longer.

He stopped for a drink at a cocktail lounge near his home early on a Friday evening. Just one little drink, that was all. Surely there could be no harm in that. It had been a particularly trying day, hot and uncomfortable, and his nerves were on edge. Just one little drink.

But he had been away too long. The first drink re-awakened something in him, some pleasant memory of more comfortable days. He found the surroundings pleasant and restful, the dim lights, the soft music, the subdued conversation. It was all so pleasantly familiar. After all, he was a grown man, and his life was his own. A drink now and then couldn't really hurt anything. Not that it was going to become a habit, of course. He ordered a second drink, and then a third. Just imagine a man of his age hesitating to buy a drink because of his mother's attitude! Ah, now he was feeling so much better, so much more relaxed.

When he finally returned home, his gait was slightly unsteady and his breath was strong. Already concerned by his unusual tardiness, Dorothy immediately realized he had broken his promise to her. The scene that followed was ugly and painful for them both, with tears and recriminations, shouting, wringing of hands, and direful predictions of what would become of him now that he had returned to those old evil ways. When it was over, Dorothy lay sobbing on the couch and Steve had closed the door to his room behind him. It was obvious that his pride now left him no choice; he would have to leave.

When he came down the stairs with his suitcase

the following morning, his mother was waiting for him in the living room. She had again spent a tormented, sleepless night; she was nervous and her eyes were red from crying. Steve felt a moment of weakness at sight of her pitiful vulnerability. It could not be helped. At least she seemed now resigned; either the tears had stopped or there simply were no more to shed.

"You're really going, then?" she asked.

He nodded. "Yes. It's much better that I do. For both of us."

She looked at him, her light eyes swimming, and sank slowly into one of the wing chairs. She raised a thin hand to brush from her face a strand of gray hair; Steve afterwards remembered the theatrical touch.

Her voice was tired and somehow different when she said, "I've become an old woman, Steve." The sunlight streamed through the window and etched deeper shadows in her face. "Every time you leave this house, I sit in fear, wondering what might happen. You don't know how often I awake in the night from some horrible dream in which I see you do the most terrible things . . ."

Steve walked quietly to the window and looked out onto the flagged terrace where they had sat together on so many comfortable summer evenings. The grass needed trimming, and one of the prize rose bushes sagged. Perhaps he should have seen to these things before leaving. He could come back and do them.

"That's why it's best this way," he said. "I'm a young man, mother, and I simply can't live like an old one. I've got to do as I please, even if I should make mistakes. The life I've been living these past

160

weeks is unnatural for me. I have to be on my own."

"I'll worry about you."

"I know you will. For a while, anyway. And it won't do any good for me to tell you not to. You'll get used to it, in time. I . . . I do promise there won't be . . ." he was finding the words very difficult to say " . . . any trouble."

She rose and walked to a vase of flowers on the piano, absently fluffing and re-arranging them; Steve wished he could stop thinking this was like a scene from an old movie. "It seems wrong to have you leaving this house." Her back was to him; her shoulders trembled slightly and he could hear the tears in her voice. "We were always such a close, happy family. There are so many memories in this house." Her voice softened with heavy remembrance. "Christmas Eve, trips to the shore, the springtime picnics, all those wonderful, wonderful times." She turned, tears coursing down her cheeks. "What happened to all that?"

He reached out and took her hand in his; it was damp with her tears. "We can't stay children forever. Time creates changes for all of us."

She tried to smile, unsuccessfully. "Yes, of course. But if only it all could have lasted a little longer . . ."

"There's still Ruth. She's never far away."

She nodded. "Oh, I know. I know. Ruth thinks you should have done this a long time ago. Of course, she doesn't know . . ." She tried again to smile. "But you're right, Steve, of course. You've got to do this. I mustn't be selfish. It's just that I have always loved my children so deeply. I mustn't try to live your life for you, Steve. I just hope it isn't my own fault, any of this . . ."

"I've got to catch a train, mother."

He quickly kissed her cheek and, taking his suitcase, walked out into the foyer.

"Steve!"

He turned. "Yes, mother?"

"You'll call me, won't you? You'll come and see me, as often as you . . . like? This is still your home."

"Of course I will, mother. Of course."

He took his bag, opened the door, and was gone.

It was that same night, at the East side hotel where he planned to stay until he found an apartment of his own, that he received a phone call from a nearly hysterical Ruth. It was difficult to understand her . . . something about their mother . . . the kitchen floor . . . open gas jets . . .

He rushed back to the silent house he had left only that morning, but it was already too late. Sobbing, distraught, his sister took him into the bedroom and there his mother lay, her eyes closed, all the care and worry gone from her gentle face. He wanted to speak to her, to make her understand, to tell her that his leaving hadn't meant he no longer loved her, but the words would not come, and now it was too late.

A sudden sharp squall of wind blew the rain in upon Steve. He moaned lightly, tossed in his sleep, raised a hand to his face to brush at the sudden wetness. His eyes opened and he stared up at the dark ceiling, momentarily bewildered by his surroundings, until he heard the sound of the surf outside his window and then he remembered. He reached out for the cigarettes that were always at the side of his bed for just such nights as this. The flame of the lighter showed the fatigue and the sorrow in his face. Drawing deeply he lay back and let the rhythm of the surf and the patter of the rain lull him into a temporary calm. He was aware of a pounding in his head.

The ground would be cold on such a night as this. He hoped the rain would fall gently on that low mound of earth that marked the place where his mother slept.

# CHAPTER NINE

Linda Fraser stirred uneasily in her sleep. The windows of her room were wide open, for Linda firmly believed in the benefits of fresh air, and a stain darkened the carpet where the rain had blown in; the lace curtains, ruffled by the slight wind, writhed like spectres in the darkness. Linda generally slept quite restfully—she always referred to it as the sleep of a clear conscious— but on this night her rest was strangely disturbed by troubled memories of the past.

Marriage and family were really all that mattered to Linda Fraser, and they were important to her not only for herself, but also for those dear to her. She firmly believed family was the entire basis of a sane, well ordered society and an acceptable civilization; if all the world were more concerned with such mundane matters, there would be less time for wars. She was often gently ridiculed for this simplistic point of view, but such

chiding never bothered her. Some people had
religion and the church; Linda had family and
home.

Her own marriage with Charles Fraser—although it had been arranged by her family when
she was still in her teens and Charles a good ten
years older than she—had been, aside from the
usual minor incidents and problems, almost bliss-
fully happy all through their thirty years together.
The marriage of her own parents had been equally
satisfying, at least as far as their daughter had
seen, and this was all the evidence Linda required
to come to her unshakeable conviction that
marriage and family were the one necessary
element in a truly happy and successful life. (She
always considered marriage and family as one, for
she could not conceive of one without the other. A
sterile marriage seemed to her one of the Biblical
abominations, and her only regret was her
inability to bear more than one child.)

The birth of her only daughter, Karen, had
given her a new goal in life: to insure that her
child would one day experience that same contentment in life that she herself had always known. It
was a constant source of concern to her, the only
shadow in her happy world, that Karen
apparently was doomed to a life of spinsterhood.

It was not that Karen Fraser was a particularly
unattractive girl. The problem was that Karen
simply did not seem to care very much about
herself. The basic ingredients were undoubtedly
there—the fine Fraser bone structure, the friendly
eyes—but they were left untouched, like a block of
promising marble somehow ignored by a sculptor.
Karen could have done a great deal with herself
had she applied just a touch of makeup to her

rather pale, thin face, done something with her mousy hair, and dressed with a bit more imagination. Oh, those dowdy tweeds and formless blouses, like an old maid school teacher in a small English town! Karen seemed determined to avoid attention. She had always been that way, even during her high school days, when most young girls first awaken to the romantic possibilities of life: her studies seemed always to be her only true interest. This irritating attitude persevered into her adult life, through college and into the advertising agency where, thanks more to her own capabilities than to her father's considerable influence, she held a fine position.

Karen thus remained the despair of her mother, who constantly urged her to assume the position in society to which she was entitled by her family's more than comfortable means. Karen turned to Linda's constant pleas a deaf ear.

"I haven't time for such nonsense. There's far too much emphasis placed on appearance and social position. I happen to think there are other matters of much greater importance. It's all such a waste of time. There's too much to learn, too much to understand to waste your life on such triviality."

By the time Karen reached her twenty-fifth birthday, after most of her friends were already married and properly raising families of their own, Charles Fraser had resigned himself to the fact that his only daughter was a born spinster and would continue to spend her evenings seated opposite him with her crossword puzzles. Even traveling abroad, Karen spent most of her time prowling through the time-dusted museums and abandoned palaces of Germany, Austria and

France instead of tasting the social opportunities offered.

Although depressed by Karen's total lack of cooperation, Linda was not as willing as her husband to surrender her hopes. "After all," she insisted, "Karen has a very fine mind, and for the right kind of man, that counts for a great deal." Then she looked at her daughter in the plain dark dress, with her dull hair worn tight against her skull, and sadly doubted her own words.

It is possible that Linda occasionally felt a slight twinge of guilt about her daughter's behavior. Perhaps she herself, with her somewhat prim and proper attitudes, had not set the perfect example. If that were the case, Karen was certainly carrying matters too far. Linda had certainly never for a moment condoned a cloistered existence. The nagging sense of her own responsibility was sometimes quite disturbing.

Neither Linda nor Charles was capable of grasping the truth of the matter; possibly Karen herself was not totally aware of it.

The simple fact was that Karen happened to be painfully, psychopathically shy, terrified by the thought of entering the battle of the sexes and competing for male attention with those she knew to be physically far better equipped than she. She totally lacked those sexual ploys which many women are able to exercise through sheer feminine instinct. Above everything in life, Karen most dreaded rejection, and she feared nothing more than personal humiliation. Rather than risk those dangers, she was content to stand aside in a world of her own. She could tell herself that life was, after all, just exactly what she wanted it to be.

Sometimes she almost believed it, yet even Karen was not without her own romantic fantasies. When she heard the infectious laughter of young lovers, she could sense a complete happiness that she would never find for herself.

Her dreams became an important part of Karen's existence. She would often sit at her open window on warm nights, when the brilliance of a seductive white moon in a cloudless sky stirs thoughts of romance. Staring down into the whispering shadows of the gardens, she would imagine herself strolling arm in arm with a handsome young man, feeling his touch and seeing the adoration in his eyes. And she would wonder then what life might have been like, had she possessed the courage to find out. She could never give herself the strength to try.

No one knew of these fantasies, and Karen often attempted to dismiss them from her mind as something impure and indecent, and not merely the natural, healthy thoughts of all women, for these reveries disturbed her carefully preserved indifference to the outer world. No, it was too late for that sort of thing now. She could not change, and she refused even to run the risk of trying.

She encountered Jeffrey again one afternoon in the bookstore near her office; they both reached for the same volume on Western civilization. He muttered an apology, handing her the volume, and was about to move away but then turned back, peering closely into the face she tried to avert from this sudden close examination.

"It's Karen Fraser, isn't it?" he asked.

She looked into his deep brown eyes and felt something she had never before experienced, an excitement, a strange inner stirring. It seemed to her she saw him standing under the rose arbor in her garden.

"Why, if it isn't Jeff Williams!"

They had known each other most of their lives and had played together as children, gone to the same schools, graduated at the same time. Jeff had always been a serious scholar and they had got along well together, but unlike Karen he was also an all-round student, interested not only in study but also in sports, in theatre, in all that was part of young student life. Participating in all such activities, he was one of the most popular youths in school, and in their later school years his path crossed Karen's less frequently. Although Karen secretly conceded to herself the possibility of a school-girl crush, there had never been anything but casual friendship between them, and Karen had never even dared dream of anything more; Jeff was too busy dating the more attractive girls of their class. Immediately after graduation from high school, he had gone to college in another state. Karen had not seen him since that time, although his scholastic and sporting achievements were frequently mentioned in the local newspapers.

He was tall, with the compact figure of a sportsman, thick waved brown hair, and a smile that lighted his face and created deep creases on either side of his mouth. He was charming and personable. And through most of her lonely life, he had figured as the Prince Charming in those dangerous fantasies that so disturbed her.

Standing among the book stalls with their brightly jacketed volumes on history and biography, they quickly covered the missing years.

Jeff had returned to his home town to settle down and open his own real estate firm. No, he had not yet found the right girl, although not from lack of looking. Karen thought nothing of the remark; no one had ever yet indicated she might be the right girl for anyone. There was little enough to tell about herself, and that was quickly done. Before they parted, Jeff asked if he might call upon her some evening. Karen said of course he might. She knew full well he would never call. He was merely being kind and courteous. She had already reached the stage of spinsterhood where people were always being kind and courteous. It didn't mean a thing.

But Jeff did call, and that was the beginning of it all. They went out together not once or twice, but several times, and then frequently. Jeff became a constant visitor at the Fraser home. They went dining and dancing, to the movies and the theatre, to sporting events in which she attempted to feign an interest and show as much enthusiasm as he did. They went to Hawkins' Cove for one wonderful weekend, and since it was only Karen, there was very little whispered talk about it. They found they had much in common, shared many interests and enjoyed the same activities. Their hands touched and the contact lingered. Their talk grew more personal, then intimate. Their eyes met with special meaning. They kissed.

And suddenly there was a new Karen Fraser, such a Karen Fraser as no one had ever expected to see. She began to take a greater interest in herself and her appearance. She permitted her mother to take her on one of those marathon shopping-tours so dear to Linda, and her face sparkled with a new

171

excitement as she bought herself a fashionable new wardrobe containing more youthful, colorful and form-fitting clothing. She paid her first visit to a beauty salon, and her face glowed with color; it was difficult to decide what was due to cosmetics and what to a reawakened joy in living. Her eyes sparkled with warmth, her hair acquired a sheen and luster, she walked with more confidence and style, suddenly revealing an attractive figure no one had ever suspected she possessed. Markedly friendlier to others, she was even heard to laugh.

The inner changes were even more spectacular. For the first time in her life, Karen was experiencing a sense of happiness. Life had suddenly changed for her as the bud of a flower opens to the warming kiss of sunlight, and for the first time the phrase "the future" held some sense of promise. Suddenly all those hopeless fantasies were actually coming true. She need not always stand on the lonely sidelines of romance. Why, life really could be exciting, after all!

Linda watched these developments very closely, and felt a deep satisfaction as her plain daughter blossomed into an attractive, assured young woman. Hadn't she always predicted it would happen one day? After all, Karen had a really fine mind, and Jeff's attentions had brought out in her other, unsuspected qualities of womanhood. She said nothing to her daughter, knowing full well that Karen would speak to her when the time should come, but she freely and frequently expressed her hopes to her husband.

"Something will come of this, Charles," she predicted. "I just know it; I feel it. Karen's found herself, at last. She's become a woman."

Pleased as Linda by their daughter's sudden

transformation, Charles was inclined to a bit more caution. "Well, I certainly hope you're right," he assured her. "You know I hope so, Linda. She's not getting any younger." He sighed. "But I wouldn't be too certain about anything where Karen is concerned."

His words brought a sombre expression to Linda's face. "Of course, I wouldn't want her to be hurt . . ."

"Oh, Karen can take care of herself," her husband assured her, sounding more confident than he felt.

Charles frowned, glancing over at the table on which Karen had been accustomed to work on massive, intricate jigsaw puzzles; it stood now forgotten in a corner of the room, still covered with the jumbled pieces of an incompleted, totally confusing French impressionistic painting.

"I certainly do hope so, Linda," he whispered again.

As the weeks passed and Jeffrey became more and more a fixture at the Fraser house, Linda's confidence increased and her hopes became a certainty.

The climax came on an early autumn evening. Jeffrey had been out of town for some days, but had returned to escort Karen to the Harvest Ball, one of the major social events of the season. As Karen sat before the dressing table in her room, she at last confided in her mother who stood behind her, ready with expert advice on her make-up, advice which Karen now scarcely needed. Karen looked charming in a light green gown cut how to emphasize the fine smoothness of her shoulders and bosom. Linda wondered how they could ever have thought of Karen as a homely girl.

"Perhaps I shouldn't say anything, mother," Karen confessed. "I really can't be absolutely certain, but I know there has been something on Jeff's mind the past couple of weeks, something he's having trouble discussing with me." She raised her eyes to the mirror and they sparkled with a light Linda had never before seen there. "He wants to have a talk with me tonight, something very important that can't wait any longer."

Linda instinctively clasped her hands together and seated herself on the bench beside her daughter. "Oh, my dear, do you really think . . ."

"I'm not sure," Karen quickly cautioned her again, but Linda noticed that her daughter's hands trembled slightly. "I may be wrong, and I don't want to raise your hopes, but . . ." She turned to her mother, smiling. "I think he's going to ask me to marry him."

With an excess of maternal emotion, Linda caught her daughter in her arms and they embraced for a moment in a silence punctuated only by sighs of hope and pleasure. Then Linda drew back and looked at her.

"Do you love him, Karen?"

Karen hesitated for a moment before responding, and her eyes held a strange mixture of hope, happiness and wonder.

"I never thought love would have any place in my life," she responded softly. She turned again to the mirror and stared at the transformed reflection, as though seeing herself for the first time, examining the features of this stranger who now suddenly dared to speak of love. "Jeff has brought me something I've never known before. An excitement, a zest for life. I suppose I never realized love could be like this. Everything seems suddenly so much brighter—the color of the sky and the grass. The world smells fresher and purer. I seem to notice things I've never really seen before—oh, the clouds in the sky, a bird on the branch of a tree, a flower raising its head out of the tall grass—so many, many things that suddenly have a new meaning for me, all because of Jeff. I just love being near him. I feel warm and comfortable, secure, and I want him to like being with me. I know I want to be with him always." She turned again to her mother, and in the voice of a child asking of someone older and wiser, added, "Is that what love is like, mother?"

Linda placed a hand to Karen's cheek. "It's the way I've always felt about your father, my dear."

Karen put her hand over her mother's. "I only know that I'm really happy for the first time in my life."

It was after one o'clock in the morning when the telephone rang beside her bed. Linda had slept fitfully. Her mind was too full, she was too excited by hopes and dreams for her only daughter's future happiness. She lay for what seemed hours, staring up at the ceiling, her eyes tracing the twisted network of shadows cast by the branches outside the window; the shadows moved slightly, almost sinuously, under the touch of a soft breeze. The night was silent save for the gentle sound of her husband's breathing from the bed beside her own.

Linda felt content, fullfilled, as though she had at last completed a long and hazardous mission. Karen would be happy now. She had at last found love and would never again be lonely or unwanted. A new life was about to begin for her

175

daughter, and Linda let her mind wander over the happiness the future years would now bring to them all.

It would be a beautiful wedding, of course—they could well afford to give Karen the very best —and then they would have a house of their own, and in time there would be children. She was going to be a grandmother! The chronology amused her. She had been a daughter, she was a wife and mother, and soon she would be a grandmother. The progression of years neither frightened nor displeased her. She would be a doting grandmother, carrying pictures of her grandchildren to be shown about on every possible occasion, until people would begin avoiding her out of sheer boredom.

It was just at this moment that the bedside telephone rang, its strident tone tearing through the comfortable silence as a knife tears through a bolt of cloth. The noise startled her, jolting her out of the joyous future.

The phone rang again and Charles, muttering sleepily, fumbled for the receiver in the midst of the third ring. Linda put out her hand and lighted the lamp between their beds. She was aware of a sudden tightness in the muscles of her stomach.

"Hello? Hello?" Charles mumbled with undisguised irritation, preparing his scatching remarks for a wrong number. "Hello? . . . Yes, this is Charles Fraser. . . ."

Linda moaned and stirred in her restless sleep at The Cloud in Hawkins' Cove, her forehead creased with a sudden frown; her hands clenched and unclenched on the light blanket that covered her. Even as she slept, her husband's words seemed to echo in her ears, those terrible words

176

that could never be forgotten and that had forever destroyed all those hopes and dreams. . . .

"Linda, there has been an accident . . . Karen and Jeff . . . The car went off the road at McGarry's Point. No, no, Linda, no, Karen is all right. She's in the hospital, but thank God it's nothing serious, just bruises. But Jeff is dead. . . ."

There followed those long, anxious days when Karen, numbed by what had happened to her, lay silently in her hospital bed, staring vacantly at the expanse of green lawn outside her window, saying nothing, her face empty and that wonderful light forever extinguished. It was only after she had again returned home that Linda and Charles learned the sequence of events of that terrible evening.

Karen's dream had come true, all those lonely fantasies dreamed in the shadows of a garden touched with moonlight. Jeff Williams had proposed marriage, and in the intensity of his love had urged an immediate elopement. Dazed by the happiness of the moment, Karen had instantly agreed. Perhaps they had simply been too filled with their own happiness to notice the condition of the roadway at McGarry's Point, a dangerous curve even in the best of weather, made more treacherous by a day of rain. The car had broken through the guardrail and tumbled over and over down the incline, brought to a stop by a large oak tree. Karen had been thrown clear, but Jeff had been trapped in the car. He was dead when they pulled him from the wreckage, his spine shattered.

The weeks that followed the accident were a terrible time for all of them. Linda often feared for her daughter's sanity. Karen refused to leave her room or her bed. She lay in total silence, unmoving, her face an expressionless mask, staring vacantly at the walls and ceiling. Books lay unopened beside the bed and Karen refused to listen to music or turn on the television. She would not see any of her friends, and, as the weeks passed they stopped calling. It was as though the accident had forced Karen into a state of shock from which she found it impossible to remove herself. Her own physical injuries had been relatively minor, but her mind could not grasp the enormity of what had happened.

Almost two months had passed before the doctors realized that Karen had lost the ability to walk. When they finally managed to force her out of bed, Karen collapsed to the floor, screaming with pain and unable to raise herself to her feet. The closest examinations failed to uncover a medical explanation; although badly bruised, the legs had not been broken, and the swellings and contusions had faded. Yet Karen cried out in pain when forced to stand, insisting her legs simply would not support her without creating unbearable agony throughout her body. She agreed to leave her bed only on the acquisition of a wheel chair.

This discovery brought about another peculiar change in Karen. Wrapping about herself a dark mantle of sorrow, she reverted to her old sheltered life. Once again, she was referred to as "poor Karen," but she was now surrounded with quite a different kind of pity. There was sympathy for her now not because she was so plain and dull that she had never experienced love, but because she had loved and lost. Her crippled condition had become a permanent reminder of her sorrow.

What disturbed Linda was that Karen slipped

so readily into this mournful role. She resumed the habits of her past life as though Jeff had never been more than a part of her romantic dreams, but now her sorrows about life were deeper and more intense. She resigned her position at the office and spent all of her time at home. The gay clothing was packed away, the cosmetics were removed from her dressing table; the dark dresses and tweed suits reappeared and the mousey brown hair framed a face wan with an unforgettable sorrow. The old puzzles were brought out again, and Karen the Spinster became Karen the Widow.

But with a rather ominous difference. For Karen did not forget Jeff and would not permit others to do so. She talked a good deal more now than she used to, and all her talk was of her lost love. She even laughed over the good times they'd had together, and that laughter was laced with a touch of hysteria; she chatted as though only the past had meaning for her, and sometimes as though she did not even realize Jeff was dead, as though a happy future still faced them both, as though he had merely gone away for a time and would one day return.

Her bedroom became a shrine to his memory. She set up on the wall a rather poor painting made from her favorite photograph of him. On a small table beneath it a lamp burned continuously and a vase always contained a fresh supply of flowers. Here she now spent much of her time, thinking and reminiscing, on her face a curious smile blending happiness, nostalgia and heartbreak. She refused to go anywhere without this reminder of the dead past.

It was while watching Karen at her peculiar devotions one day that Linda felt the first stab of fear. There was something grotesque about all this, something that went beyond ordinary grief, beyond the tragic loss of her intended husband, something that was both unhealthy and unnatural. She could not, at first, understand just what made her believe this, until one afternoon at Hawkins' Cove when she found her daughter asleep before the mournful shrine. . . .

Linda stirred in her sleep and awoke. The house was very silent, but she could hear the gentle patter of the light rain. She turned over and tried to sleep again, but slumber had gone for the night. The room was uncomfortably warm, the air close; she could taste perspiration on her upper lip.

She slipped from the bed and went to the open windows, staring out at the darkness of the indistinguishable sea. She brushed the hair back from her forehead and felt the touch of a welcome breeze. It was beginning to rain harder again. She wondered if Karen had been able to sleep. Probably. Sleep came to her easily now; she was happier in her dreams.

Linda frowned again, remembering. Happy. Sad. The two emotions were still part of Karen, but wasn't she experiencing them in reverse? Her very sorrow seemed to make her happy, and only when she talked of her tragedy was there an expression of pleasure on her face. When a girl has lost the man she was about to marry, shouldn't there be a certain pain in discussing him, a sorrow in remembering him, even after years had passed? Karen was never so happy as when speaking of the man she had briefly loved. The sympathy of others seemed to have given her a new purpose in life. Surely this was wrong, very wrong. . . .

Karen moved almost convulsively in her sleep and a muffled cry escaped her lips. Her eyes opened suddenly and instantly sought the portrait. The dream had ended, that dream that came to her so often in the silent loneliness of the night.

She lay still for a moment, clasping and unclasping her hands in a gesture like that of her mother in the adjoining room, staring into the soft brown eyes of the portrait, remembering, remembering, and then, with another sharp cry, she buried her face in the pillow and found relief in tears.

# CHAPTER TEN

When Greg flicked his lighted cigarette over the balcony, Michael, in the room beside his, saw the glow descend in an arc and disappear into the darkness. He heard Greg's light step as the older man returned to his bed. Naked, the young sailor stood on the dark balcony outside his room and felt relief in the cool sea air after the hot, sex-laden atmosphere of the room behind him.

Michael had never even seen the vast expanse of ocean before his naval enlistment. All his life he had been on the Ohio farm his family had owned and cultivated for several generations, never going farther away than Chicago and the sea-like Great Lakes. He loved the great old house with the green shutters against the white-painted boards and the wide encircling verandah, the peaceful expanse of broad farmland that surrounded it, as he loved his kind and understanding parents and the good people who had always been part of his life. It was a safe and a gentle world, and its problems were minor; life was warm and secure.

But of course he had always known there were other worlds to experience, not necessarily better, perhaps uglier and perhaps not, and he wanted to see something of these worlds before finally settling down to the kind of life his family had always known. He had figured a time in the navy was the best way to "see the world." A strange choice for someone as land-bound as himself, everyone said, but it provided an entirely different kind of life and he had never regretted the choice. He had seen much, and now felt he was satisfied. When his enlistment was over, he would be perfectly content to return to the farm in Ohio and settle down again, probably for the rest of his life.

His introduction to the navy had, however, come as something of a shock to him. It was not that the work was hard or difficult—he had never minded that—and to a farmboy, rising in the early morning darkness was a way of life. What disturbed him was the unexpected revelation concerning the nature of people. After his conservative mid-Western upbringing, it took some adjustment to live in a barracks with a number of lusty young males from every part of the country and every stratum of society. He was embarrassed by the casual nudity, and startled by the constant repetition of obscene language. Still a virgin when he entered the service, Michael was discomfited by the air of crude, vulgar sexuality that now surrounded him.

After a few uncomfortable weeks, his sense of guilt passed and he was able to swear and curse with the best of them. Once the rigors of boot-training had been completed, he began to enjoy himself, even finding pleasure in that sea duty which most sailors attempt so vigorously to avoid.

He was assigned to a destroyer (tin-can, he corrected himself; he was not yet really at home with naval lingo), a small ship given to frequent unpleasant motion in the great troughs of the Atlantic, but more relaxed and informal than the regulation bound larger vessels. (Less chickenshit; he reminded himself of proper terminology again.) He suffered one brief period of exhausting seasickness, and never encountered that agonizing malady again.

The midnight to four watches in the radio shack were wearing but generally interesting. He spent most of this time at a typewriter, the earphones clapped to his head, transcribing the jumble of dots and dashes into intelligible conversation. When work was slow on the midwatch, he would sit and shoot the bull over coffee. Sometimes they would go down to the galley, through compartments of sleeping men, dark chambers lighted by red hurricane lamps, to requisition a pre-dawn snack. There was a warm cameraderie about the life that he found pleasant and comfortable.

There were other duties to pass the time when not on watch—keeping the living quarters spotless for frequent inspections by the skipper, repairing the radio equipment (his mechanical training on the farm's tractors had made him adept in handling all kinds of machinery), studying for an advance rating and another stripe on his sleeve. In the evenings he would go back to the fantail to watch the night's movie or sit in the ship's library with a book, or after a refreshing shower sit in his crisply laundered shorts and T-shirt and write letters home. It was an undemanding life, a clean one, and not unpleasant.

His first cruise took him to the far northern waters, and he enthusiastically explored and photographed the bleak hills of Newfoundland and the narrow, old-world streets of Halifax with the silent ruins of the old fort perched above the city; it was like a touch of Europe, a different and older civilization. Then he had seen the cold shores of Greenland rising defiantly from the white-spumed green sea. When relieved of his watch, he would bundle into his pea jacket and, seeking the comparative shelter of a gun-turret, stand alone on deck, his hands plunged deep in his pockets, his hat pulled over his ears, watching the tumbled gray-green waters of the misnamed continent. On Thanksgiving Day they had crossed the Arctic Circle and received the small blue cards noting the time, the place and the ship, and certifying membership in the exclusive Order of Blue Noses.

The tropical waters of the Caribbean, his next cruise, were like a lush world gone mad with color. Where the northern Atlantic had been a uniform, leaden gray-green, the Caribbean was a warm, clear blue, lighted by touches of dancing phosphoresence that lifted like gossamer veils of light at either side of the moving ship's prow. You could lean over the railing and look down right into the sea, almost to the very bottom, watching the brilliantly colored fish swimming by, ignoring the metal monster that had invaded their world. During the day the water would be suddenly marked by the gleaming wet humps of porpoise; the sunlight sparkled on their black backs for a moment before they disappeared again into the warm water. The sky was clear and cloudless and you wondered if this blue were its real color or if it was merely reflection from the blue sea, or perhaps the other way around. It was warm, with breezes bearing the gentle scents of this exotic world. It was surely something like Paradise.

During a liberty in Puerto Rico, when they happened to be walking together down the ship's gangway and fell into conversation, he and Paul had first become friends.

The square in Ponce was a dazzling flash of color under a hot yellow sun. Young girls, in frills and bows, walked slowly in one direction around the square while the young men, also clad in their best, walked as slowly in the other. Men and women, girls and boys, eyed each other as they passed, and with each revolution, their paces slowed until, mutual interest aroused, the girls and the boys joined, linked arms like old friends, and then disappeared from the square for more private pleasures. Michael and Paul, amused by this old-fashioned courting charade, seated themselves on a bench under the shelter of a large bush covered with shining green leaves and enormous crimson flowers, and watched the sexual game.

A small boy, not more than ten years old, his black hair long and uncombed, his bright-eyed face streaked with sweat and grime, his ragged clothing torn and encrusted with dirt, stepped up to them.

"You like good time, sailors? You like good hot screw?"

Amused, Paul raised a foot onto the bench and, leaning his chin on his knee, grinned at the boy. "You gonna give it to us?"

"Got good hot sister," the boy responded, sitting on the bench beside them and grinning with a mouthful of strong, perfect white teeth while he swung one foot back and forth. "She give you real good screw. Do anything you like. Nice and dirty. Let both of you screw. Sailors like her. Ask 'em. Only cost two dollars. Each," he quickly added to avoid any confusion.

Paul smiled again and shook his head. "No thanks, kid. We can get our own stuff."

The boy leaped from the bench and stood before them, nodding vigorously. "You screw me? Give me American cigarettes, you screw me. I pretty much good, too."

Paul drew a cigarette from his pocket and handed it to the boy. "Here, you fucking delinquent. Now get lost."

"You no screw me?" the boy asked, surprised; Michael, who had been listening with shocked fascination, wondered if there was a touch of disappointment in the young voice.

Paul shook his head again, still smiling with good humor. "We no screw you. Not our type. Go find a Marine."

The boy clenched the cigarette in his grubby fist and dashed from the square; they saw him approach another group of sailors across the street and begin his sales pitch. Michael watched the child with an expression of confusion, while Paul seemed merely amused.

"Jesus Christ, imagine a kid that age offering his sister to a sailor!" Michael remarked. "When I was his age, I didn't even know there was such a thing

188

as sex. I thought you used it just to have something to hang onto when you took a piss."

"Oh, don't blame the kid," Paul urged, stretching and yawning; the unrelieved heat of the sun made them both sleepy. "Money's not easy to come by in these parts. Shit, we had the same thing going on that garbage pile where I grew up."

"But you don't approve of it, do you?" Michael asked, genuinely surprised.

Paul shrugged. "Why not? What the hell? What's wrong with it? To a lot of dames, that's a money box they've got between their legs. You can't blame 'em for using it. And without them, where would we horny little sailor boys be?"

"Would you offer your own sister like that?"

Paul laughed, his strong teeth flashing in his tanned face. "The classic question. What if it was your own sister? Shit, my sister hasn't got time enough for her own clients, without having me find more for her."

Two young girls passed them, walking arm in arm, bright flowers stuck in their hair, casually flicking their brightly colored skirts with one hand. They slowed, turned their heads and unashamedly smiled at the two sailors lounging on the bench. One of them quickly, as though accidentally, fluffed up her skirt high enough to reveal that she wore nothing beneath it. The girls smiled again, and continued on their way. Paul nudged his companion.

"Come on," he said in a voice suddenly tense with the excitement of sexual promise. "That's our stuff right there."

They rose and set off after the two girls, who noticeably slowed their pace, then stopped completely when they realized the instant success of their overture. They giggled to each other as the two sailors approached. Paul conducted the bargaining, in a mixture of pidgeon-English and sign language, for the girls spoke little English. Two dollars each, no less. Anything the boys wanted. But it would have to be quick. The ship would be gone tomorrow, and they could not devote too much time to one customer; they would have to please as many sailors as possible in the course of this one day and evening.

Paul hailed a cab, and the four piled into the rear seat for the brief trip to the girls' home. It seemed they were sisters. Their English vocabulary was composed of four letter words picked up from their sailor clients, but none of the foursome was interested in the niceties of conversation. Concetta was sixteen and her sister Maria a year younger. Both had been prostitutes since the age of twelve, and they indicated their desire and ability to please. Both girls were extremely thin and small-breasted, clad in the lightest of clothing. Michael complained of the unpleasant odor emanating from their heavily perspiring bodies but Paul, who already had his active hand under Concetta's dress and was making her squeal delightedly with the work of his fingers, shrugged his shoulders.

"So what the hell? They're no movie queens, so what? They've got just what we want. We'll give 'em a quick ramming, get our rocks off, and dump 'em."

Michael was perspiring as much as the girls. This was going to be his first time. He was afraid Paul might realize this.

The houe was a small unpainted clapboard structure in a narrow street just outside of town

190

that stank of exposed garbage. A motley group of people, of all ages, lounged on the sagging porch in various stages of undress, from a small girl just able to walk to an ancient crone smoking a stinking pipe in a chair. No one seemed at all surprised at their arrival. They all smiled with pleasure when the two girls walked up the broken stairs, followed by the sailors; Michael's embarrassment obviously did not infect Paul, who seemed rather to be enjoying himself as he bounded up the stairs. Michael cringed slightly as an enormous armour-plated beetle scurried out of his path and dropped into the rank growth of weeds beside the stairs. A half-naked boy covered with a solid layer of dirt, rushed up to Paul and placed his hand on the white sleeve of his uniform.

"You got American cigarette, sailors?" he begged. "You give me American cigarette?"

Paul obligingly handed the boy a cigarette, and he and Michael followed the girls into the dark, airless house. The old crone in the rocking chair called after them, "You fook 'em good, poys; you fook 'em real good!"

The room was incredibly dirty and littered, with paper peeling from the walls, chairs tottering on three legs, an upholstered sofa from which the stuffing had exploded and dragged like entrails on the floor. On a large round table in the center of the room lay dirty glasses and several half-empty whiskey bottles. An unwholesome odor prevailed. The girls, smiling eagerly, opened another door to a bedroom which Michael didn't care to examine too closely. Without a word, the girls began to undress. Michael hesitated, looking at the soiled and rumpled double bed; he suddenly felt very little desire.

Untroubled by the squalid surroundings, Paul was already stepping out of his trousers; he smiled when he saw Michael's hesitation.

"Come on, buddy, don't be so damned finicky. A whole division of shipmates have probably been in this bed already, but what the hell's the difference? Every guy should get laid in a rotten place like this once in a while; it's good for the pride."

"They look like syph-bags to me," Michael complained, unenthusiastically undoing his trousers, and hoping that the nervousness of his voice wouldn't betray him.

"We'll get our shots as soon as we get back aboard ship," Paul promised. "Just take your pants off; leave your blouse on."

"I hope the bed doesn't have bugs," Michael muttered.

Maria latched herself to Michael; he tried to look away when he saw her stepping out of underwear that might once have been white, but was now a mixture of gray and certain other unpleasant shades. Concetta (who had previously given evidence that she wore no such encumbrances) reached for the half-naked Paul.

"Oh, sailor-boy, that for me! You geeve Concetta all of this, yes?"

"Till it comes out the other end, you goddamned whore," Paul promised, smiling, not understanding the words; the girl giggled with excitement.

The two whores stretched out on the bed, their small breasts firm with desire, their eyes hungrily exploring the half-nude sailors. Breathing hard, they spread their legs invitingly. Michael noticed with distaste that Maria's pubic hair seemed to have been rubbed away.

When they left the house shortly after, Paul noticed there was something of a strut to Michael's walk. He smiled, careful to conceal his amusement. What do you know? The kid had lost his cherry! Where the hell had he been all this time?

The evening marked the beginning of the close friendship between Paul and Michael. That cruise took them to various Caribbean ports, and in each of them Paul and Michael automatically went ashore together in search of women. Michael suddenly found himself moving in a daze of hot, exciting sexuality, and for the first time he understood why such activity was the primary topic of conversation among his ship-board buddies. He now joined the ribaldry, freely describing his activities, boasting of his conquests.

But there were other, more lasting aspects of his relationship with Paul, more than this giddy descent into excessive sexuality. While Paul introduced Michael into his own promiscuous world, Michael also raised Paul to other interests he had not known before. Prior to their assocation, Paul had cared for nothing but drink and women. While these still remained the paramount interest of any shore leave, there were now other matters as well. In Guantanomo Bay they went horseback riding through dense green forests such as city-bred Paul had never seen. In Port-au-Spain, they examined the narrow streets of the city with its gayly painted houses that seemed to reach out to kiss each other in the uppermost stories. Under a swaying palm tree they lay on a beach of pure white sand. The ship moved on to South America, and in Rio de Janeiro they climbed Sugar Loaf and gazed at the Christ atop Corcovado; they even visited the opera house and the palace of the former Emperor. While their evenings were dedicated to sexual conquests, their days included natural wonders and monuments that had never before engaged Paul's attention. Thus the new friendship brought unexpected benefits to both of them.

Michael soon managed to subdue the nagging feelings of guilt over his current life, so far removed from the routine experiences of the farm-boy. It was a dilemma common to many in service who suddenly found themselves in a totally new world that provided unlimited sexual opportunity. It was fun, it was exciting, he was a long way from home, and Michael soon found himself as avid as Paul. . . .

The rain had stopped again now, and the only sound was the dull, monotonous dripping from the eaves. The heat hadn't been broken by the storm, and as he stood on the balcony, Michael could feel the trickle of perspiration. He threw the cigarette down to the sand and, grasping the railing of the balcony with both hands, leaned over and looked down to the beach. He breathed the clean, fresh air. There was a dark form sitting on a bit of drift-wood right at the water's edge. Who would that be out there all alone at this time of night?

There was a stirring in the room behind him; Michael turned. Chrissy moved in her sleep, pressing her body closer to Paul, absently and perhaps automatically running her hands over his naked flesh as her dreams recalled the recent ex-perience. Michael turned away again; the sight

194

suddenly displeased him. There was a moving light in the sky; probably a low-flying plane.

"Can I have a cigarette?"

"I thought you were asleep," he commented as Frances stepped onto the balcony.

"Too damned hot. For sleep, anyway," she added with a giggle. "How about that cigarette?"

He stepped back into the room, moving silently on his bare feet, secured a cigarette from the dresser, handed it to her and lighted it.

"We shouldn't be standing out here like this," he cautioned. "Somebody might see us, and we're not exactly dressed for company; besides, we aren't supposed to have anyone in our room."

Frances shrugged. "So who's gonna see us, anyway? Anybody out at this time of night has no right talking about anybody else."

"There's somebody out there." Michael indicated the dark shadow on the beach.

She shrugged her bare shoulders again. "That's only Johnny. He lives here. I don't think he ever sleeps. All he ever does is look at that damned ocean. Day and night, looks at that damned ocean as though it ever looks any different. I think he's a little scrambled in the head."

Michael leaned against the railing, feeling it pleasingly cold against his bare buttocks. The clouds were beginning to break, and he had a fleeting view of the bashful moon. The house was completely silent; apparently all were sleeping. The eaves had ceased the chatter of their dripping. He found himself suddenly feeling very much alone, wanting someone to talk with. He looked over the blurred whiteness of the girl; an occasional drag on her cigarette outlined her face

195

and part of her firm breasts.

"Do you live here, Frances," he asked, "or do you just come down for the summer?"

"I've always lived here. Born in the house I live in now."

"Must be nice, living near the ocean."

She shrugged again; it was the inevitable response to all questions. "Oh, sure, it's nice enough, I guess. Especially in the summer, when the sailors come down. Then it's real nice. Don't get as many as we should, though."

He wished he might, for just a few moments, escape the ever-present aura of sex. "Must be quiet in the winter, though."

"Quiet? Shit!" Michael cringed; he could never accustom himself to such language from girls. "You should see it! Nothin' doin' at all. We have to fall back on the local yokels for our fun, same damned tired old stuff night after night. Bores the hell out of you."

The moon broke suddenly through the clouds and brightly illuminated her naked body, touching with silver the swell of her breasts. The inviting darkness between her legs renewed her appeal. Michael wondered about the girl's truthfulness in claiming to be twenty years old. Looked no more than eighteen, at the most; he had become something of an expert in judging the age of naked women.

"Do you have a regular boy friend?" he asked, still anxious for conversation. "I mean, one you might want to marry some day?"

"Oh, sure," she replied, flicking the cigarette over the balcony.

"What's his name?"

"His name? Ray."

196

"Is he nice?"

Again there was a shrug; her breasts bounced with the movement. "Oh, he's all right, I guess." She moved closer to him. "He gets real jealous when I go to bed with other guys. He thinks he's the only guy who should screw me, and if I spread it around, I'm a whore. Shit, I never take money, so that means I ain't a whore, don't it? It gets dull, doin' it with the same guy all the time. He's not so much, anyway. Not as good as you are. You're a lot bigger, too." Her hands caressed his smooth chest, brushing at the perspiration. "You got a nice chest, you know? Ray's chest is all hairy. Some girls like that, but not me; I like a chest like you got." She quickly bent and pressed her lips to his left nipple; he felt the gentle bite of her small teeth. "All you got is nice," she whispered, her mouth still pressed to his chest. She forced his legs apart and moved in to him. "Let's do it again, honey. Once more. We can talk any time."

The girl was right. Silent, suddenly eager, he moved her up against the wall. They could talk any time. . . .

Sitting alone on the beach, Johnny glanced up and saw the two white forms, more sharply outlined against the darkness than they realized, merge into one against the wall on the top floor balcony, and he quickly turned his eyes away. He wondered how the occupant of that room had managed to get a girl up there; if his mother knew about it, there would be hell to pay. He didn't like it much himself. After all, this was still his home, not just a place for men to take their chippie whores. They should do that at the big hotels where nobody cared. He had no idea who was

197

occupying that particular room—he generally showed little interest in the guests—and somehow it did not occur to him that it might be a married couple.

The sea was quiet again, following its brief outburst of temper during the storm. The moon broke through a hole in the ragged clouds, and the broad expanse of water before him became suddenly alive with dancing specks of light. The sand was still damp from the rain, and the driftwood on which he sat was soggy, but he scarcely noticed the discomfort. The log had been imbedded in just this spot for as long as he could remember. He often wondered where it had come from, and in his younger, more childishly imaginative days, he had woven colorful fantasies about it. They said all the seas of the world were in reality just one vast ocean, and that every drop of water in the sea traveled all about the world and finally returned to the place from which it had started, only to begin the long voyage all over again. The Gulf Stream swept close to the land here; this bit of driftwood, whitened by salt and riddled with the holes of hungry parasites, might have come from one of the pirate islands of the Indies.

Digging his bare toes into the wet sand, he again thought of his boat, all his own, and of the many hours he could spend on the sea, rising and falling with the tides, smelling the fresh air, listening to the cawing of the gulls and the soothing shush of the waves.

The summer was nearly over now, and Johnny suddenly felt—knew beyond question—that he had to have that boat before the end of the season. It cost more than he had managed to put aside, but he had to have it. Now he knew there was a way. . . .

He rose and began to walk slowly across the damp sand, with his hands plunged deep into his pockets. The moon had become lost behind the clouds, as though ashamed to witness the open fornication on the balcony, and the sea had darkened again, as though it disapproved of Johnny's deep thoughts. It seemed suddenly chilly, and a breeze ruffled the boy's thick black hair. The rapid change in the weather was symptomatic of the swiftly approaching season's end.

Glancing back to his home, Johnny saw that the balcony was now empty again; perhaps they had decided to use the bed after all, he thought acidly. The grand old house loomed as a darker shadow against the dark sky. Ahead of him, the lights of the Boardwalk were dimmed. The ferris wheel rose in a huge circle, its cages covered with canvas against the rain. Within the Casino, the horses of the carousel would be frozen in the silent dark.

Johnny walked slowly, his head bowed, pondering the problems of a suddenly adult life.

Seated at the window of her own bedroom, overlooking the beach, Margaret saw the slender form of her young son walking alone, as he seemed always to be alone, dreaming, longing, hoping. He never seemed to sleep. The sea drew him at all hours of the day and night. He was a true Hawkins, all right. The ebb and flow of the tide seemed to course within his veins. She wiped at the sudden tears in her eyes. What would happen to him now?

Over the sound of the surf, she could still hear

the ominous words of Martin Levine. She had called him to the house because of her concern about the unusual seepage of sea water into the cellars. Levine, an old friend who knew the house well, had conducted a careful examination, checking stresses and structural problems that meant nothing at all to her. His face was grave when he reported his findings, spreading out before her various charts and diagrams that looked like the tracings of a wet spider crawling over pieces of paper.

"I sure as hell don't like to tell you this, Miss Meg," he assured her, biting at his lower lip as he looked down at the drawings he had made, "but I just got no choice."

"That's why I brought you here, Marty," she said, a bit impatiently. "Stop beating around the bush. You never can come right out and tell a body what they want to know."

He peered at her over the dark rims of his glasses. "All right, Miss Meg. I know there's no sense in trying to fool you, anyway. The truth is, the house is in pretty bad shape."

She snorted at his statement. "That's utter nonsense, and you know it. There isn't a house on this entire stretch that's as solidly built as this one."

He nodded, and the strip of hair he carefully combed from one side to the other in an attempt to decrease the size of his bald-spot, fell over the back of his head. "I know that. You're right there, and I ain't about to argue the point with you. This house was built real solid. But you see, Miss Meg, a lot of years have gone by since Captain Nathaniel built this here place, and while the house may seem as sound as the day he opened its doors, the trouble is, well, he just didn't choose very wisely about where to put it."

"The point was the only logical place for the house," Margaret insisted. "If you want to have a house by the sea, you build it as close to the sea as you can."

"But you've got to know what you're building on," Levine insisted. "Captain Nathaniel didn't know very much about that, and either his builders were as ignorant as he was about the ground formation, or maybe they just didn't bother to tell him. You see, the Captain had the mistaken idea, and so do most of the people hereabouts, that the point here is made out of solid rock. Well, it ain't. The rock goes pretty deep right at the end of the point, but there's less and less of it as you move in closer to shore. The top layer of shale rock further back from the end of the point rests on a bed of hard-packed sand. A good builder would never have set a house on top of it. For more than a hundred years now, that sand has been bearing the pressure of this big old house while the sea has been eating away at it."

"What does that mean?"

"It means, Miss Meg, that the foundations beneath this house are finally giving way. It's not safe any more."

"Well, then shore it up or something, do whatever you do in cases like this. I don't know anything about such things. How much will it cost me?"

He shook his head. "No, Miss Meg. Sorry. Can't do it. The weakening of the sand has distorted some of the primary timbers and they're about to give way. I won't involve you in all kinds of technical jargon, Miss Meg, but the important thing is that once the sand goes—and it's going, believe me—the whole point goes with it."

She looked at him, her eyes narrowing, feeling the slightest touch of fear. "What are you trying to tell me, Marty?"

Levine paused, adjusting his glasses, drew a handkerchief from his pocket and ran it across his nose. "Well, Miss Meg, I don't quite know how to say it. . . ."

"Just say it." She was becoming seriously alarmed.

"Well, I suppose I could be wrong, of course, and I hope I am, but I sure as hell don't think I am. I'll have some consultants in from the city, some architectural experts, probably can get them here in the next couple of weeks or so, and we'll have a real, complete examination, make sure about everything." He shook his head again, looking at the charts. "I guess we'll have to get divers, and take a look down there beneath the foundation, but from what I can see . . . Well, Miss Meg, from what I can see, I'm afraid the house just isn't safe any more. You know the winter storms we get hereabouts; I don't know that the house will be able to stand up to them for another season." He hesitated again, pursing his mouth and shaking his head. "If the other members of the committee agree with me, Miss Meg, I'm afraid the place will have to be condemned."

There it was. So many dreams. So many years. And then nothing. The house . . . The Cloud . . . the showplace of Hawkins' Cove . . . the greatest memorial to old Captain Nathaniel . . . will have to be condemned.

Slowly, Margaret lowered the window and closed out the sound of the enemy sea.

# Part III

# Meetings

# CHAPTER ELEVEN

The golden rim of the morning sun timidly raised itself above the horizon, as though uncertain of its reception after the violence of the evening before. The beach was still deserted, the sand white, pure and untrammeled, waiting for ·the tread of thousands of perspiring feet. The waves fell almost caressingly onto the sand; sea and sand were having their last moments of solitary love before the return of the next quiet evening. The air was fresh and pure, cleansed by the sweep of the storm, and the morning was lazily quiet.

The Boardwalk, washed clean by the night's rain, was almost empty. A few lone pigeons and gulls wheeled over the barren boards, too early to be fed; it would be several hours before the children would drop their greasy French Fries and bits of frankfurther rolls onto the wooden walkway. A few sand crabs skittered across the beach. One or two solitary couples slowly walked along the Boardwalk, intent on their own conversation, or merely enjoying the freshness of a bright new morning.

The lowered doors of one of the Boardwalk restaurants suddenly moved on well-oiled wheels and the proprietor stepped out onto the Boardwalk, his chest expanding to take in his early morning ration of pure sea air. He glanced out to sea, to the rising orb of the great sun, and then up to the white sky, with a practiced eye. It would be another bitch of a day, and already there had been radio warnings of another approaching storm. Well, it would be good for business as long as it lasted, at any rate. He turned into the shadow of the unlighted restaurant and called out in a loud, rasping voice.

"Emily! You got the breakfast menus ready yet?"

A short time later, Emily Dunleavy sat at the counter, her chin cupped in her hands, and stared listlessly out to sea. It was nearly seven o'clock in the morning now, and more people were beginning to appear on the Boardwalk, those who appreciated the freshness of the air and the soothing quiet before the influx of bathers and sun-worshipers and Boardwalk strollers. She yawned and stretched, wishing she could have slept just an hour or so longer. She had gone to the dance at the Casino last night and left shortly after eleven; even so, this morning it had seemed she would never be able to get out of her bed. She hadn't had a very good time last night, anyway.

Emily was nineteen, a fresh-faced blonde girl with clear green eyes. In the fall, she would enter the local hospital to begin her nurse's training. This was her last really free summer, and she was taking full advantage of it by having as good a time as possible while working as a waitress to help pay for her schooling in the fall. She lived with her parents and a younger sister in a small, neat and comfortable house in Hawkins' Cove, not very far from the Boardwalk. Her father was a conductor on the railroad, and she had a single older brother, married and living in the City. She had lived here all her life, and she loved it all, the town, the people, the sea. Always a popular girl, she had never lacked either friends or dates, and was active in the youth circles of the Catholic Church in which she had been reared. It was inconceivable to her that she would ever live anywhere else.

Her thoughts were interrupted when a portly, middle-aged woman approached the restaurant, closely followed by her shadow of a husband. The woman hesitated for a moment, looking with obvious mistrust at her surroundings, at the rows of tables lining the interior of the restaurant and the tables outside on the Boardwalk, their colorful umbrellas not yet in place. She sniffed with displeasure at the display of salt-water taffy and took one of the outside tables. Although considerably overweight and old enough to know better, she had squeezed into lavender shorts and a canary-yellow halter. A straw cap with a green plastic visor perched on her graying head, and a pince-nez balanced precariously on her hawk-like nose. As she took her seat, she heavily dropped a large leather bag into the chair beside her.

Her husband was a small man dressed uncomfortably in white shorts that revealed his scrawny legs. A tired gray moustache—a last pitiful attempt to assert his masculinity—drooped dejectedly over a mouth that seldom opened except to agree with his wife's remarks.

Emily rose quickly from the counter and approached the couple, carrying two menus. "Good morning," she brightly greeted them.

After a nervous glance at his wife, the man replied with a timid "Morning." The woman immediately applied herself to the menu, holding her head back slightly and peering with narrowed eyes at the print.

"Lovely morning, isn't it?" Emily asked.

The woman grunted at the remark, which apparently was either too self-evident or too argumentative for agreement, and the man said nothing further. Emily hesitated for a moment, shrugged, and returned to the counter for water. After placing the glasses before the couple, she poised over her order pad with a sharply pointed yellow pencil.

"And what will it be this morning?" she asked. "Hot cakes, perhaps with good, crisp bacon. A good breakfast is very important, you know."

The man looked up quickly, obviously pleased by her suggestion. "Yes. . . ."

"Nonsense!" the woman snorted. "Worst possible way to start a day, a heavy breakfast like that. Be bilious all morning. I'll have a glass of tomato juice and scrambled eggs, toast and coffee."

"Yes, Ma'am."

"The coffee now. Good and hot. Black, no sugar."

"Yes, Ma'am." Emily quickly placed the order on her pad, then turned to the husband. "And what would you like sir?"

"He'd like the same!" The woman ordered

before the man could speak, and the moustache, which seemed to have perked up with attention, sagged again. "I want the eggs nice and fluffy, and none of those dried-up powdered eggs, either. I know the difference, mind you. I want them nice and fresh."

"Oh, yes, Ma'am," Emily assured her. "Our eggs here are always strictly fresh, Ma'am."

The woman snorted again; her pince-nez seemed to bounce on her nose. "Well, that remains to be seen. Never yet saw a place like this that didn't try to take advantage of a body. Figure you're here on a vacation and will eat anything; won't be coming back again, prob'ly, so it don't matter. And I won't accept them if they're watery, mind you. Nice and fluffy. And light toast. Light. And fresh, not yesterday's shingels."

Emily flipped her pad and placed the order with the chef, making the woman's demands very clearly understood, then resumed her seat at the counter. Her only customers sat wordlessly, their faces betraying established boredom and a certain mutual hostility. The man gazed out to sea, and Emily sensed a certain wistfulness in his face.

As she followed the husband's eyes to the hazy horizon, Emily noticed a lone figure slouched on a bench with his feet propped up against the railing, a sailor in a spotless white uniform. His white hat was perched rakishly on the back of his blond head, but there seemed about him an air of—well, melancholy was the first word that came to her.

"Emily!" The chef's voice was an irritated shout. "What's 'a matter, daydreaming? Eggs'll get cold. She'll murder you."

Emily roused herself and took the twin breakfasts from the shelf, her quick glance noting that

211

her order had been filled as placed. The woman eyed her carefully as she placed the food before them, and called to Emily as she turned away.

"Just one moment, there!"

Emily turned back. "Yes, Ma'am?"

"Look at that toast."

Emily looked at the lightly toasted, buttered and cut slices but failed to understand the complaint. "Yes, Ma'am? You wanted it light, I believe."

"Now, Martha . . ." the husband gently interposed.

"Don't you 'Now Martha' me, Henry!" the wife ordered. "I wanted light toast, but not served on a filthy dish."

On a second, closer look, Emily detected a slight smudge on the dish, a bit of fluff undoubtedly blown there by the light breeze. "I'm terribly sorry," she apologized. "I'll get you another dish, if you like."

"If I like! Why, I never heard of such a thing!"

"You must remember, Ma'am," Emily cautioned, striving to maintain her temper, "that you are out of doors here, and a speck of dust might easily. . . ."

"That's no excuse for filth! Bring me another, and make it fast. And not just another dish, but another order of toast as well. Lord knows what's been dropped on this one!"

With a slight sigh, Emily replaced the toast and only then noticed that the lone sailor from the bench had taken a table near the entrance. Handing him a glass of water and a menu, she attempted once again to give a cheery "good morning," and was pleased when the sailor's face brightened with a friendly smile.

"Good morning," he responded, opening the menu. With a quick, somewhat mischievous glance at the breakfasting couple, he remarked, "I do believe there is a smudge of grease on this menu, Miss. My goodness, if your menus are so filthy, what must your food be like?"

"If it will please you, sir," Emily offered, falling in with his light spirits, "I'll dust the food myself with a feather duster before bringing it to you." She lowered her voice and looked at the solemnly eating couple; the woman, with an expression of distaste, was turning the scrambled eggs with her fork. "You heard."

He nodded. "I guess the whole Boardwalk heard. Nice way to start a day, isn't it?"

"Well, other customers make up for it."

They smiled at each other. "What do you suggest?"

"Hot cakes and sausages," she promptly replied. "They really are very good. But I warn you that a certain nameless party claims only lunatics eat such heavy breakfasts."

"Well, suppose you bring an order to this lunatic."

"I trust you won't object to being bilious all day long?"

He smiled again. "Not at all. It just so happens that I'm always at my very best when I'm bilious. And I would also like some orange juice, toast and tea, please."

"Coming right up!"

As she walked from the sailor's table, she felt his eyes appraising her. She ignored the whispered comment that "they always flirt with the sailors" as she passed the other occupied table, and found herself humming. She placed the new order,

213

poured a glass of orange juice and a cup of tea and returned to the sailor's table.

"Going to be a nice day, isn't it?" he asked.

"Lovely," she replied. "But hot. Probably rain again later."

He grinned, and dimples appeared on either side of his mouth. "Can't have everything."

He seemed now quite pleased and cheerful and yet, seated once more at the counter, Emily watched the sudden shadow return to his attractive face. He stared out to sea, a slight frown puckering his broad forehead, eating automatically, picking at his food. There was a restlessness in his eyes; he seemed displeased with himself.

The truth was that at that moment Michael was very displeased with himself indeed. He was thinking of Paul and the two girls, whom he had left asleep, completely sated by their orgasms of the early morning hours. Awakening early and seeing the naked menage, remembering in particular the crude coupling on the balcony, he had felt a certain overpowering disgust and had quickly left the room to walk alone in the fresh sea air. He felt unclean. He supposed by now Paul had managed somehow to get the two whores safely out of the hotel, and he probably would be wondering what had happened to Michael.

It would be just as well to keep out of Paul's way for a couple of hours. Paul could never understand Michael's sense of guilt after such incidents. Sated, after the night's debauch, Michael was simply not himself this morning, but Paul would predict a swift return to "normal" as the sense of guilt faded and the old desires built up again.

Was he right, Michael wondered? Was it merely the reaction of a former Puritan who had loosened up? Somehow, he wasn't sure. He felt there was something different about it this time. The strength of this particular reaction surprised him. By now, he should be well over that sort of thing. Christ, he had done it often enough since that first time in Puerto Rico! Why still this feeling of shame and guilt? It was juvenile, but that did not dissipate the feeling. There was something unmanly about it all. Perhaps that bothered him as much as the reaction itself.

The disputing couple had completed their breakfast and, still determined to be friendly, Emily smiled as she handed the husband their checks.

"I hope you enjoyed your breakfast," she remarked.

"The coffee was too weak and the eggs were cold; the toast was hard," the woman complained as she snatched the checks from her husband's hand, subjecting the slips of paper to extreme scrutiny. "Disgraceful! The prices they charge at these places are positively outrageous. Just because people are on vacation, they try to rob them!"

Emily took the bill extended to her, changed it at the cash register, and wordlessly handed the woman the coins. Rising haughtily from her chair, the woman dropped two dimes to the table.

"Come along, Henry," she ordered with a peremptory movement of her hand. "Tomorrow we'll try that place further down the Boardwalk, where I wanted to go to begin with; it might at least be *clean!*" and without another glance, she started on her way.

Henry hesitated for the briefest moment, glancing nervously at his wife; then he winked at Emily, whispered, "I thought the eggs were just fine," and cautiously dropped another quarter to the table.

"There, you see, the old guy does have some spirit after all," Michael remarked when Emily returned to his table.

"He should have had a bit more spunk twenty years ago," Emily mentioned, watching the little man sprint dutifully after his wife who, with lavender buttocks bouncing, sailed down the Boardwalk like a clipper ship before a sou'wester.

"How do you suppose they'll look on the beach together?" Michael asked. "He could sit in her shadow, and they wouldn't need an umbrella!"

They looked at each other and simultaneously burst into laughter. When the laughing stopped, their eyes were still joined, and somehow the next words sounded very serious.

"What's your name?" he asked.

"Emily."

"Mine's Michael, Emily, and I guess I shouldn't ask this, but what time do you finish here?"

The Boardwalk shops opened their shutters for another day. The restaurants were soon filled and the odor of food floated out onto the humid air. People began their aimless strolling along the boards, gazing out to sea, buying picture postcards, waiting for the bath-houses to open. The younger folk had a game of miniature golf while they waited; the children tried the kiddie rides. The elderly couples sat quiet and contented on the benches.

Johnny was already at the bathhouses, preparing for the opening at ten o'clock. There seemed an air of expectancy about the long rows of open-doored white booths, as they waited for the day's influx of bathers. Before the gate was opened, the lockerboys glanced quickly into each booth to pick up the miscellany that was invariably left behind from the previous day, books, loose change, a stray sock. These were placed in the Lost and Found Department, but few of them were ever claimed, their owners probably long gone before the loss was discovered; they were auctioned off at the end of the season or, if of no use, merely tossed away.

Johnny paused in one of the compartments whose wall contained some chalk-scrawled obscene grafitti, incuding figures depicting two men engaged in a sexual act and the words MAKE DATE; beneath this, in another hand, was written MONDAY 3:00 HERE. Such things were common on the walls of the booths, and Johnny had never before paid them very much attention. Somehow, today, it made him feel uncomfortable. When the walls became too heavily marked with such artwork, they were wiped clean, presenting a fresh slate for future pornographers.

"Hey, Johnny, look at what I found!" Jimmy called to him from the next aisle, then appeared holding a long wet rubber tube gingerly between his fingers.

Johnny made a face of disgust. "Christ! Throw it away!"

With a slight chuckle, Jimmy tossed the article into a nearby rubbish can. "At least somebody had a good time here yesterday!" He looked more closely at his friend. "Say, you don't look so good, Johnny. Something bothering you?"

Johnny shook his head. "No. I'm okay. What

should be bothering me?" The sun glittering on the sea hurt his eyes, and he pulled his dark glasses from his waistband. "Say, Jimmy . . ."

"Yeah?"

"I've been thinking about what you said yesterday . . ."

"Don't tell me I talked some sense into you?"

"Well . . ." There was one final moment of hesitation before Johnny finally took the plunge. "Are you really sure it's perfectly safe? I don't want to get into any trouble, and I sure don't want to lose my job; they wouldn't take me back next summer, either, if I got caught. But I sure could use some extra money. If I can't get that boat in the next couple of weeks or so, I'll have to wait until next summer."

"Take my word for it, Johnny," Jimmy assured him. "Nothing will go wrong. Nobody's ever gonna know about it. Would I wanna get my best friend in trouble?"

Johnny took a deep breath; he knew he couldn't turn back after this. "Well . . . okay, then. I'll look in at some of the guys if they want me to, and if they'll pay me for looking at them." He looked at Jimmy with a stern expression. "But that's all, Jimmy. I won't . . . do anything."

"So, who the hell said anything about doing anything?" Jimmy asked irately, as though the possibility of such a thing had never even occurred to him. "You can make a few extra bucks a day just by looking. All you do is stand in front of the door, see. The guy opens it just a little bit, just so's you can look in and see him naked. Say something nice about it, how he's hung, what a good time he could give the girls, you know. That's all they want. Then he slips you a bill and closes the door again. Nothin' to it. Real easy!"

"Well, okay. I'll try it, anyway. I don't suppose it can do any real harm. Let me know. . . ."

# CHAPTER TWELVE

Ethel Hawkins sat alone on the front verandah of The Cloud, her white hair defiantly coiffed in the tight little ringlets of her childhood, her heavily wrinkled hands clasped contentedly in the lap of her simple print dress. The rocking chair in the right corner of the verandah was always reserved exclusively for her use, and here she could be seen in the early mornings and the late afternoons, rocking gently, sometimes languidly caressing the still air with a worn and faded bamboo fan her father had brought home for her many years ago. Usually she had a tall glass of iced lemonade at her side. She preferred this particular corner of the verandah for a very definite reason; from this vantage point, she could see three different locations: the sea itself, then a long stretch of beach and, in the distance, the Boardwalk.

Although Ethel was now nearly ninety years of age, she missed little. Age had considerably slowed her physical activities, mentally she was almost as alert as ever. As was the way with most people in their attitudes towards the very old, everyone treated her with the greatest condescension, almost as though she were a child, as though a woman of ninety must revert to the thoughts and habits of a five-year old. She was quite willing to accept this attitude, for it sometimes gave her extra consideration, which was always nice to have, and which she felt a woman of her age deserved. People were forever rushing to help her up and down the stairs, to open a door, to fetch her newspapers and magazines, or to place a cushion behind her back and a sweater about her shoulders. She could really quite easily do all these things for herself, but it was nice to be waited on. She was proud of her years, and had no patience with those who attempted to make light of them with protestations that she was really ninety years young.

"Nonsense!" Ethel would snort. "Ninety years is not young, and anyone who says it is has got to be a damned fool. All this business about being young at ninety is so I won't let myself realize I'm not far from the grave. Well, I'm not, and I know it. I'm a very old woman, and I'm proud of it, and don't you dare to lop off so much as one single year of my ninety!"

She was a careful observer of all that went on about her. Although she wore steel-rimmed spectacles, her eyesight was still remarkably good, and her hearing was still keen, although she liked to pretend that she was the slightest bit deaf; she managed to hear a great deal more that way. She knew more than Margaret did about what went on in the old house.

For instance, she was aware that the two sailors on the top floor had managed to smuggle girls into their room last night. Unable to sleep, she had, as was not at all unusual, spent a considerable part of the evening right here in her rocking chair, and had seen them climbing up the tree to the balcony, the girls rather clumsy and foolishly feminine, relying on the helping hands of the boys, who constantly shushed them into silence. She knew, too, that although one of the sailors had already left for the Boardwalk, the other one was still up there, and she supposed the two girls were still there as well. This knowledge did not shock her in the least. Ethel had lived among seamen all her life; she knew their customs, their habits and their needs. You couldn't expect a sailor to be a saint. He worked hard at sea, and when he was ashore he wanted a good time, he wanted liquor, and he wanted women. It had been that way in her father's time, and she didn't suppose the sailors of today were very much different.

Her father's time! Ethel's smile became touched with a warm remembrance and her eyes turned to the burnished sheen of the sea. She could almost hear his voice in the rooms behind her. She remembered the days when she would scramble up to the Widow's Walk after her mother to stand braced against the wind waiting for that first thrilling glimpse of the great white sails of his ship. Oh, the excitement then, the dashing about the house, the eagerness to see what he had brought them. And then the embrace of those powerful arms and the tickle of salt-encrusted whiskers on her face! What times they were!

She moved her head to look down to the beach, already dotted with bathers. How different it all

223

was now! Then the sand had been smooth and white, marked only by the passage of gulls and sandcrabs, colored only by the detritus washed up by the tide. . . .

She shook her head impatiently. These lapses into the past were an ominous sign of her advanced age, and lately they had been coming all too frequently. She didn't like it.

The door swung open and the other sailor, smartly turned out in a spotless uniform, looking fresh and young and handsome, his blue eyes gleaming, stepped out to the verandah and stood for a moment, breathing the clean salted air. Ethel eyed him appreciatively, thinking here was a young man who would have been very much at home in the hearty masculine world of Captain Nathaniel. And in the world of women, too. He looked out to the sun and she noticed his slight frown as he saw the early haze.

"Young man!" she called.

He turned at the sound of her voice, and seeing the small white-haired figure comfortably ensconced in her large rocking-chair, smiled at her. "Morning."

She raised her small, slightly arthritic hand and motioned him to her. "Come here, young man," she ordered, assuming the privilege of the very old to command the young. "I want to have a word with you."

Paul obligingly joined her, taking the chair the old woman indicated.

"I am Mrs. Hawkins. I own this house."

"How do you do?" (He was a polite young man, too, and that was very good. Too many young people today have no manners, and very little patience with the elderly.) "I'm Paul Adranopolis.

I don't own much of anything. I'm just staying here."

She looked at him sharply over the rims of her glasses; he seemed fresh and alert after what must have been an extremely busy evening. "And what happened to the girls?"

Delighted, she saw he was startled by her unexpected knowledge. A slight red shading rose in his face, and this pleased her, too; nowadays it was considered a sign of weakness for a man to blush, but to Ethel it was an indication of finer feelings.

"Ma'am?" he asked.

"Oh, now, don't you pretend with me, young man. I mean those two girls you had in your room last night, you and your friend," Ethel responded, knowing that she was actually shocking this young man; old women were not supposed to know about such things. He was being put to the acid test now. If he fumbled and stuttered and tried to deny what she had said, then he was not the man she took him for.

But he did no such thing. He grinned broadly, and there was a wonderful purity in that smile that did not at all accord with his activities of the night before.

"Now, how did you know about that?" he asked.

"I know about a great many things, young man," Ethel firmly assured him. "Just because I'm old, don't think I'm stupid. I'm not blind either. But you needn't be afraid of my knowledge; I know how to keep a secret. I merely want to know what's happened to those two girls. How do you plan to get them out of here without anyone seeing them?"

"You really don't quite see everything, do you,

225

Ma'am?" Paul asked, a twinkle in his eyes. "They've already been gone for some time. The same way they came."

"The tree?"

Paul laughed again. "I guess you don't miss much at that, do you, Mrs. Hawkins?"

"When you reach my age, there's very little you can do with yourself, except to watch the foolishness of the younger people who think they know everything and who really should know better. What you did was very foolish, and not at all nice. A girl who has been so generous to you deserves better treatment than to be scooted out of a window and down an old tree trunk like a cat-burglar or a squirrel." She glanced around to assure herself that no one was within hearing. "There is generally no one in the front lobby between 5:45 and 6:00 each morning. My daughter has left the desk to open the kitchen and the clerk hasn't come on duty yet, our icthyologist or whatever he is has already left the house, the help is straightening up whatever has to be straightened up, and most of the other guests are still asleep. You might remember that in the future, young man."

"You're very understanding, Ma'am," Paul commented.

"Understanding, pish!" she retorted. "Women shouldn't be treated merely as playthings, that's all. I know I wouldn't much like the idea of sliding down a tree trunk, when there's a perfectly good staircase to be used. It's downright degrading. Now you listen to me!"

"I surely will. I give you my word," Paul promised, smiling and placing one hand on his heart. "No more tree trunks."

Ethel raised a cautioning finger. "Mind, now, that doesn't at all mean I approve of such conduct to begin with! It really is quite disgraceful."

Paul hung his head in simulated shame, but did not miss the glint in the old woman's eyes; she must have been something in her younger years! "Yes, you're quite right, Ma'am. Disgraceful!"

She looked at him for a moment, then remarked, "I note you haven't promised not to do it again!"

"Oh, Mrs. Hawkins, surely you wouldn't want me to risk a lie, would you? How can I tell about the future! I might just be fortunate enough to come across another woman as kind and understanding as you are!"

"Flattery!" Her fan became considerably more agitated. "Well, at least you haven't the gall to call me beautiful. Such nonsense! It only makes me realize how much time has gone by. A woman of my age, beautiful! To tell you the honest truth, I never really was a beauty, anyway, although there were times . . . oh, yes, there were times indeed . . . Well, get along now, I won't keep you. Have a good time."

With another smile and a cheerful wave of his hand, Paul vaulted over the porch railing and headed for the Boardwalk. Ethel watched him go; she was pleased with her young sailor.

She noticed again the slight haze on the sea, and frowned with irritation. What was this peculiar feeling of uneasiness that had touched her for the past couple of days, the nagging worry, almost like a premonition? There was something in the air, certainly. Bad weather coming, no doubt of it; the radio already had the first warnings of a major storm moving up the coast from the south. Early in the season for that sort of thing. Of course, she didn't have to be told this by someone in a radio station; she had lived long enough by the sea to be able to read the signs for herself. Weather was a funny thing, particularly near the sea. The elements seemed in constant war with each other.

The horizon was empty this morning; there was a loneliness about the sea without ships. The sun glinted brightly on the placid water, and the haze blurred the line between sea and sky. It was going to be a blister of a day.

"Here's your lemonade, mother."

Margaret came through the door, carrying a glass of lemonade on a tray. Ethel took the glass and indicated the chair the sailor had just vacated. "Sit with me for a spell, Margaret."

"I've an awful lot of work to do, mother," Margaret objected, while easing her bulk into the tightness of the armchair. "It's going to be very hot again. Radio says a storm's coming."

"I could have told them that," Ethel stated, "and then they wouldn't have to spend all that money on useless equipment. They always say a storm's coming; never one far away during this time of year. Anyway, they're right. Probably won't be for some time, though, maybe not before tomorrow."

Margaret frowned with concern. "Oh, dear, I do hope it won't interfere with the Festival. It isn't nearly as pleasant or comfortable indoors."

"I haven't seen Johnny this morning," Ethel mentioned.

"I haven't, either. He must have left early."

"Margaret, there is something troubling that boy."

Margaret nodded, her eyes concerned. "Yes. I

think you're right. He came in very late last night, soaked to the skin. He sat for hours out there on the beach, in spite of the rain; I could see him from my window. I'm afraid he'll be coming down with a cold."

"That isn't at all what I mean," Ethel remarked somewhat testily. "A little water never hurt anybody, 'specially this time of year. This is something else. That boy has something on his mind."

Margaret sighed. "Oh, I suppose it's that boat of his again. I don't imagine he ever really thinks of anything else."

"It's only natural; he's a Hawkins. A boy who lives by the sea should have a boat of his own, especially when he loves the sea the way Johnny does. And his blood demands it."

"But they really are terribly expensive, mother, and Johnny just hasn't been able to get the money together."

"Then lend it to him."

"Now, mother, you know perfectly well I've offered it many times," Margaret reminded her. "He simply won't take it. He says this is something he has to do himself."

Ethel nodded her head in satisfaction, and contradicted herself. "He's perfectly right. The boy has character. He's like his great-grandfather. Whatever's troubling him now, he'll manage to clear up by himself. I must have a good long talk with that boy one of these days. He spends too much time down on the beach; I really hardly ever get to see him."

Margaret squirmed slightly and managed to lift her large body out of the confining chair. "I must get back inside. Can I bring you something else, mother?"

Ethel shook her head. "No, no, I'm quite all right, dear."

Margaret paused in the open doorway and looked up again at the blue-white sky. "I wish it would storm and get it over with." Seeing a movement inside, she held the door open for Karen, who wheeled herself slowly out to the verandah, a book and a package of cigarettes on her blanketed lap.

"Good morning, Miss Meg," she greeted the older woman.

"Good morning, Karen. I hope you had a good night."

"Oh, yes, quite, thank you. I find rain so restful. I don't mind it the way others do." She gazed out to sea, and a vague smile crossed her face. "Do you know, that weekend Jeff and I spent here, it rained almost the entire time, and we could spend hardly any time at all on the beach. Oh, Jeff was positively furious, but I really didn't mind it at all. Rain is so . . . oh, I don't know, it's really so romantic, don't you think?"

Ethel frowned with irritation; she'd already had more than enough of the dead lover. "Where is your mother, Karen?"

"Oh, mother's already gone into town. You know how she loves her shopping."

"Yes. You're left alone a good deal of the time, aren't you?"

"Oh, I don't mind that at all," Karen assured her. "I have my books . . . and I do like to remember."

Ethel glanced down to the Boardwalk. Although it was still early, there were a number of strollers, and the first brightly colored beach umbrellas were beginning to appear on the sand.

It would be a busy day down there, with the heat rising so early. Where did they all come from? Where was the smooth, vacant beach of her childhood? While she looked, the ferris wheel began to turn on the first of its countless revolutions of the day. She had never been on a ferris wheel.

Karen lighted a cigarette and opened her book. Ethel glanced at her, puzzled as always in the presence of this unfortunate girl. She had been very different indeed on that weekend with her Jeff.

"What are you reading this morning, dear?" she asked.

Keeping her place with one finger, Karen closed the book and glanced at the spine, then favored Ethel with one of her special smiles of doleful romance.

"It's *Wuthering Heights*. Oh, I know it isn't the kind of book you're supposed to read these days, and I've read it many times before, but I never do seem to tire of it. Heathcliffe and Cathy! It's so moving, so romantic and so . . . oh, so sad. As a matter of fact, Jeff gave me this very volume himself, right here, on that rainy morning . . ."

Ethel let the girl ramble on about her dead beloved Jeff, and she scarcely heard the words. They had long become familiar to her, and it didn't seem to matter to Karen that she was not being listened to; she found pleasure merely in the repetition. While she talked, Ethel watched her closely. She saw the pale face come suddenly alive, the eyes for once alert and sparkling, the mouth smiling and even laughing in remembrance of those dead times. Ethel frowned, troubled by a recurring thought.

231

There was something unnatural about Karen's
sorrow. . . .

Steve awakened that morning with a heavy
pounding in his head, and a harsh dry taste in his
mouth. He put his hands to his head for a moment
and sat quite still, trying to recall the events of the
previous evening, but he remembered only too
much beer and a recurrence of that terrible haunt-
ing dream. He should have known better than to
drink so much. Unwinding should go only so far.

He rose unsteadily to his feet and stepped out
onto the balcony. The bright sun sharpened his
headache; shielding his eyes, he looked down to
the Boardwalk and the stream of life flowing along
it. Hearing the soft murmur of voices beneath
him, he bent slightly over the balcony and could
just see old Mrs. Hawkins at her usual post in the
rocking-chair, talking with someone who was out
of his line of vision; he heard a young male voice.

A cold shower and clean clothing improved his
spirits, if not his headache. He was startled to see
it was already past ten o'clock; no point in going to
the beach now until after lunch. A stroll along the
Boardwalk, perhaps a bit of miniature golf, then
the afternoon at the beach. And the evening? He
shied away from the thought of it.

As he stepped onto the verandah, the full heat of
the sun struck him, and he felt slightly wilted.
Christ, it wasn't even noontime yet! It was really
going to be a bitch of a day!

"Good morning, Mr. Conroy!"

Steve smiled at Ethel Hawkins; they were old
friends. "Why, good morning to you, Mrs.
Hawkins," he returned, walking with a faint
apologetic smile past the girl in her wheelchair.

232

Hadn't she been sitting there at the time of his arrival? "It's nice to see you again."

"My daughter told me you were here," Ethel informed him. "I was hoping you'd be back with us this summer."

"Where else would I go?" he asked. "This is like home."

Ethel called over to the girl in the wheelchair. "Karen Fraser, I'd like you to meet Steve Conroy, in case you haven't met before."

The girl lowered her book briefly and looked at him; she was obviously not interested. "How do you do?"

"Miss Fraser and her mother have been coming back here several years now, although I don't believe you have met before."

"No. I haven't had that pleasure," Steve commented. "How are you, Miss Fraser?"

With a slight smile and no further comment, Karen returned to the slender book she was reading; she seemed to become immediately absorbed.

"Well, I'm afraid I've already lost a good bit of the morning," Steve remarked, "so, if you don't mind . . ."

"By all means, my boy; by all means. But one of these afternoons before you leave, we must sit down over a glass of good old lemonade and have a nice, long talk."

"I'd like that very much," Steve assured her.

With a noncommital "Nice meeting you" to Karen, Steve stepped from the verandah and started for the Boardwalk, already quite crowded with much the same groups he had seen the day before—disgruntled parents, screaming children, middle-aged couples trying to recapture their lost

233

youth, although they sensed it was already much too late. And then there were the same teenagers, behaving as though they owned the world. Perhaps they did.

Steve smiled to himself. Why was it that he always looked at the unpleasant aspects of life? It was entirely possible that a lot of these Boardwalk strollers were really enjoying themselves. More than he was, at any rate.

He dropped in at one of the open-air restaurants and ordered a light breakfast, served to him by a wholesome, pleasant young girl he could not recall having seen before. He lingered over his aromatic hot coffee, gazing vacantly out to sea over the mass of bathers who clung to the guide-ropes in the water. There was a considerable swell, probably a remnant of last night's storm. The sounds of the Boardwalk seemed to be strangely muted, and the line of the horizon wavered in the heat.

He set his cup down with a clink and lighted a cigarette. Damn it, this brooding, this melancholy could have gone on in the city at considerably less expense. Why had he come here in the first place? Oh, yes, to think about his problems. He could think about them just as clearly—or just as muddily—at home. What was there to think about, anyway? He was really only running away from himself. He should by this time realize that it just didn't work. He only took his loneliness, his restlessness and unhappiness along with him wherever he went. He was what he was, and nothing could change that. He was really no different from those Boardwalk strollers he held in such contempt, who were forever searching for their lost hopes. He would have to live with his guilt, accept it, and manage the best he could. Don't some people have to be content with a little less than happiness in life? Why should he make matters even more difficult for himself than they were? Life could be shit, but what else was there?

He finished his breakfast, received a pleasant "come again" smile from the waitress, and strolled farther down the Boardwalk, feeling the hot sun on his back. Before the large Seaquarium the billboard displayed the usual playful seals, the leaping porpoises, the toothed shark, and blurbs about the unfathomable wonders of the deep. None of it had any particular interest for him, and he had, he suddenly realized, never even entered the place before. He hesitated a moment. It might at least be a bit cooler inside. It was too early for lunch, and the heat did not suggest Boardwalk strolling. He purchased a ticket at the cashier's booth and entered the building.

He found himself in an enormous single chamber with plastered walls, large green-tinted windows and a glass domed roof. The entire chamber was occupied by a huge sunken tank, whose green water reflected waveringly on the walls. To his right, a broad stairway led up to a second floor in the area beyond the dome, and a small balcony that encircled the tank. There were perhaps two dozen people milling about or leaning against the tank railings, and another half dozen or so staring down into the tank from the balcony.

He leaned over the railing and looked into the green water of the tank. He found nothing of any particular interest. Horseshoe crabs crawled spider-like along the cement bottom, their many legs moving rhythmically. A wide variety of fish— he had never known one species from another—

swam through water so clear that everything could be seen in detail, provided you were interested in the first place. Steve began to wonder why he had come in here. Oh, yes, it was cooler. But not much.

"Good morning, ladies and gentlemen."

Steve glanced to the far side of the pool and saw a tall man in his early thirties, standing with a microphone in his hand. He wore white slacks and an open-throated blue shirt; the smile was broad and friendly in a strong, angular face deeply bronzed by the sun.

"My name is Greg Christopher, and if you'll stick with me for a little while, I'd like to take you on a tour of our Seaquarium and tell you a little about our exhibits. Should you have any questions at all, please don't hesitate to ask, and I'll do my best to answer them. Now, if you'll all come down to the far end of the tank here, we'll begin with the seals. It's just about feeding time, and if I know them as well as I think I do, they'll be getting impatient . . ."

There was really nothing else to do at the moment, so Steve automatically followed the little group on its tour about the premises. He was surprised to find his interest growing, kindled by their guide's personality and expertise. Christopher spoke pleasantly, his diction indicating both intelligence and training; occasionally a lighter comment provoked smiles, without lowering the scholarly content of his talk. He did not talk down to his visitors, but treated them like intelligent people who were sincerely interested in what he had to tell them. Obviously knowledgeable about his subject, he appeared eager to share his lore with the group around him. Those who

236

indicated particular interest were rewarded by his special attention. He was a born lecturer, Steve decided.

After the ear-splitting feeding of the seals, Greg conducted his group about the tank, pointing out the various creatures moving silently and sinuously through the green water. Climbing to the second floor, he explained the curiosities of the sea-horses and pointed out the razor-like teeth of the piranha.

Aware of Steve's silent interest, Greg sensed something vaguely familiar in the man who followed on the fringe of the group, slightly apart from the others.

When the group dispersed in the second floor shell room to return to the varied interests of the great tank, Steve remained behind, wandering about and examining with interest some of the strange and fanciful forms filling the glass show-cases. Squatting in one corner of the room like a fugitive from some tale of science-fiction horror, was a monstrous pink and white clam shell, its thick white lips seeming to curl in derision.

"I don't know how much truth there is in it, but I was told that this particular shell took three native lives in the waters about Samoa."

Smiling, Steve turned to the guide. "I can well believe it. Anyway, I wouldn't care to have my leg caught between those jaws."

"It would give you a pretty nasty bruise, at the least. I'm not inclined to trust the story though; the natives are too familiar with these monsters for three of them to be so careless." Greg crossed his arms and leaned against the railing before the window, looking with interest at Steve. "Enjoy the lecture?"

"Yes, I did," Steve assured him. "Frankly, I didn't really expect to, but I did."

"You seemed interested in the reactions of the group; I saw you watch their faces."

Steve smiled. "I enjoy watching people, seeing the way they react. A tribute to your talk, believe me; most of them were intent on what you were saying. You made the sea extremely interesting."

Greg glanced through the window at the water beyond the beach. "I'm afraid I can't take much credit for that," he laughed, a pleasantly rich chuckle. "The sea was interesting long before I began talking about it. Be a pretty poor lecturer to make it anything else."

"You enjoy your work, don't you?"

Greg turned again, nodding. "I'm one of those rare and fortunate people who happen to be doing exactly what they want to be doing." He took a package of cigarettes from his shirt pocket, offered Steve one and took one himself. "I've told you before," he said, flicking the lighter for Steve, "but on a more personal level, my name's Greg."

Steve blew the smoke away from them. "I'm Steve Conroy."

The grasp of the hands was firm and warm. "Hi. I've been trying to think. Haven't I seen you somewhere before."

"Well, I haven't been in here before," Steve mentioned, "although I'm at the Cove every summer. I arrived only yesterday."

"Oh, I don't mean in here, but it seems to me . . ."

"Maybe it was on the Boardwalk."

"Could be, I guess, although I really spend as little time as possible down there. It gets a little routine after a while. This place isn't a playground for me, you know; it's where I work." A picture suddenly came to his mind of a figure sprawled on a staircase. "Say, aren't you staying at The Cloud?"

"Why, yes, I am."

"Then that's where I saw you," Greg remarked. "I live there myself." He smiled slightly, and his light eyes twinkled. "I don't mean to be undiplomatic, but I believe you had a little trouble negotiating the stairs last night."

Steve flushed and Greg chuckled again, but there was a warmth and friendliness in that laugh that suddenly made Steve feel less lonely. . . .

# CHAPTER THIRTEEN

Johnny was not having a particularly pleasant day of it, and he went about his duties with a surliness that was unusual in him, speaking very little to his fellow locker-boys, ever returning to his chair on the balcony where he could stare out to sea.

Despite the agreement he had made with Jimmy, Johnny was still uneasy as he nervously prepared for the moment when Jimmy would advise him he had his first "special customer." The sense of guilt remained, and the inner conflict in which he repeatedly weighed the pros and cons of the matter, was still not quite decided. He had spent long hours of self-argument on the beach during the rains of the previous evening, and it was not until the early hours of the morning that he had at last decided to go along with Jimmy's suggestion.

Still, all through that morning he was confused with doubts while he automatically fullfilled his duties at the bath house. He told himself this uncertainty was foolish. So it was kind of gross to look at naked men but, like Jimmy said, what actual harm could it do to him or anyone? It wasn't as though he liked it; he was doing it strictly for the money, which would be put to a very good use. It wasn't like looking at nude woman. This would get him the boat and it would harm nobody. After all, he had seen lots of naked men before, so why should there be such a difference, just because he was taking money for doing it?

But there was a difference, and he really couldn't ignore it. Strange though it seemed, simply looking at these men in a state of nudity would give them sexual pleasure, and he was accepting money for it. Wasn't there a name for people like that?

He was still pondering when, a little after noon, Jimmy called to him.

"I've got one for you, Johnny. Okay?"

After the last brief moment of hesitation, Johnny replied, in his best macho bass, "Sure, Jimmy."

"He wanted me to take a look, but I've already seen him, and I said you would do it," Jimmy explained. "They like it better if it's someone they haven't shown it to before."

"What do I do?"

Jimmy cautiously motioned Johnny behind a row of lockers where they could not be seen or overheard. "He'll give you a dollar if you'll just take a look at him." He paused, then added, with a suggestively raised eyebrow. "He'll make it two bucks if you'll show him what you've got."

"No!" Johnny's voice cracked. "I told you that before! I'll look, that's all!"

Jimmy raised his hands in a gesture of self-defense. "Okay, okay, for Christ's sake, don't get so excited. I told him I didn't think you would, but he wanted me to ask, anyway."

"Where is he?"

"Number thirty-four," Jimmy replied. "Just knock on the door twice, and he'll open it for you. When he's through, he'll slip you the bill and close the door."

Johnny narrowed his eyes slightly. "What do you mean, when he's through?"

"You know," Jimmy responded vaguely, "when he thinks you've had a really good look."

Johnny walked slowly down the aisles, the whitened floorboards hot under his bare feet. He pulled down the green visor of his cap to shield his eyes and suddenly felt like a character in a spy novel. There was no one in sight, and he was glad of this, certain that one look at his face would betray his obscene purpose. He wanted to get this over with; the first time would most likely be the most difficult.

He paused before the designated booth. The door was locked, but below it he could see two bare feet, each with five toes, thin ankles and scraggly dark hair. There never was anything particularly attractive about feet; did he expect these to look any different? Slowly he raised his hand and rapped twice on the white wood. The door opened very slowly, cautiously, and Johnny peered inside. The naked man was tall and dark, probably in his early forties. His face was very lean, his nose unattractively prominent; he had a considerable paunch and his chest, belly, arms and legs were covered with black fur. He smiled when he saw Johnny, and his wet pink tongue darted excitedly over his thick lips.

"Take a good look, kid," he urged, his voice low and tense. "Not bad, eh?"

Forcing his eyes to look at the man, Johnny managed a faint, sickly grin, but said nothing. Running his eyes hungrily over Johnny's slender young body, the man began to masturbate.

"Come and do it for me," he urged in a nervous whisper. "It'll be quicker."

Feeling slightly sick, afraid to trust his own voice, Johnny shook his head.

"Come on. What's the harm? Your friend did it."

"No." He was going to throw up.

"I'll give you five bucks."

"I agreed only to look," Johnny insisted; his own voice sounded tight and strange to him.

"Then how about showing me . . ."

"No! Give me my dollar!"

The man hesitated, then reached into the pocket of his trousers hanging on the wall and tossed Johnny a dollar bill. "Take it, you stupid kid, and get the fuck out of here."

Johnny quickly picked up the bill from where it had landed, stuffed it into his jeans; kicked the door shut and, still feeling squeamish, returned to his seat on the balcony. So that's what it was like. Well, it had given him a dollar.

Jimmy rushed to him the moment he was free. "Well, how was it?" he asked, eager for details.

"Stupid," Johnny replied harshly. "What kind of nuts are they, anyway?"

"What's the difference?" Jimmy asked. "It's an easy buck."

"You said I'd only have to look at him," Johnny said accusingly. "You didn't tell me I'd have to watch him play with himself. And he wanted to give me five bucks if I'd jerk him off."

"You should have taken it. They're so hot, it only takes a few seconds."

"You did it."

Jimmy shrugged. "Sure I did. Lots of times. So what the hell? Did it hurt me? I don't see my hand turning green."

"Well, I won't do it, and I'm not gonna tell you again."

"All right, all right, don't get so goddamned uptight about it. So, you made an extra buck, didn't you? Wanna know when I can get you another one?"

Johnny frowned and slouched down in his chair, bringing the visor down low over his eyes. "Yeah. Okay. Sure. Why the hell not? If they're so damned dumb to pay money for it, I'll take it."

After all, it was an extra buck. If you've done it once, there was no reason why you shouldn't do it again.


Michael was waiting outside the restaurant where he'd had breakfast, at exactly two o'clock that afternoon, unusually exhilarated by the possibilities of the day. The lurid memories of the previous night's debauchery had faded, and now his thoughts centered entirely on Emily. There was nothing blatantly sexual in these thoughts; Emily was a different kind of girl.

She joined him, smiled brightly, looked fresh

and youthful, her fair hair gleaming in the sun, her bathing things carried in a small bag dangling from her right wrist. She was surprised at herself. It was not her general practice to go on dates with a boy she didn't even know, but somehow she felt no qualms about Michael.

"Hi!" she called.

"Hello! Ready?"

She tapped her bag. "Sure am. It doesn't take much to carry a girl's swimming stuff these days!"

"That's what I call a promising statement!" he countered, and they both laughed.

They were not disappointed in that lovely sunny afternoon. They romped in the surf, played tag on the beach, talked, laughed, sang a bit, even dozed during the hottest and laziest time of the afternoon. They were young and attractive, both good to look at in their brief swim suits—Michael lean and heard; Emily slender, high-breasted and golden from the sun.

Michael told her all about the family farm in Ohio, about his parents, his life in the navy (with certain careful omissions), and his still vague plans for the future. Emily told him all about the Air Force brother whom she adored, and of her own ambition to become a nurse. The time passed quickly, and before the afternoon had ended, they were chatting comfortably like old friends.

During the afternoon Michael entertained a few fleeting thoughts about Paul. He had no notion of Paul's plans for the day. It was not unusual for them to go their separate ways during the day but always, through some tacit agreement, they would get together in the evening for the usual sexual frolics.

That was what now concerned Michael. Paul

would be expecting him some time before evening to begin making the necessary "arrangements:" i.e., picking up a couple of girls. His uneasiness now was not due to that stuffy middle-class morality that Paul so often derided. Nor was it that irritating sense of guilt that invariably followed their sexual excursions. It was just that Michael would much prefer to spend a quiet evening alone with Emily, perhaps dinner and a movie and later a casual stroll along the Boardwalk. Paul wouldn't understand that. A girl was good for one purpose, and one purpose alone. Michael angrily shook his head. He suddenly didn't want to see Paul, particularly just now. He would feel ashamed of him.

Steve lay sunning himself on the beach near Michael and Emily, surprised to see the sailor in company with the wholesome young girl who had served his breakfast that morning; she was very unlike the girls he had seen with the sailors the day before. He vaguely wondered what had happened to the other sailor, as he glanced at the young couple. Their carefree laughter sharpened the edge of his own loneliness.

Scratching absently in the sand, Steve looked over the congested beach. This was not a very good place to be alone, he decided, and he felt very much alone indeed. All about him were couples, trios, family groups, but he was unable to spot anyone else who seemed to be completely alone. Young couples who fancied themselves in love—at least for the day—lying side-by-side, their healthy young bodies already tanned to a rich bronze or still glistening with protective lotions; young men tussling in good natured horseplay, whistling at the passing girls; older couples seated passively under their beach umbrellas, carefully watching the activities of their children or grandchildren . . . friends . . . comrades . . . lovers. Only he was alone.

He turned over on his stomach and feeling the heat on his bare back, wondered what splotchy pattern the sun might produce there. It was difficult to smear sun-tan lotion over your own back.

Oh, hell, back to the alone bit again. Was he already beginning to feel sorry for himself?

He rose and began to walk slowly along the beach, skirting the sand castles built by the children just at the waterline. Memories stirred again. How many times had he and his sister built just such childish fantasies, creating intricate mud-packed passages through which, at the ultimate moment, the water would rush and curl in a miniature disastrous flood? It was nice to know children could still find pleasure in such innocent enjoyment.

Steve moved away from the roped-in bathing area to the more deserted stretch of the beach just beyond, where the stone jetty pushed its dark thumb into the sea. He glanced up at the motionless figures lining the jetty with their fishing-poles extended, like a row of gargoyles on a Medieval cathedral. He had never gone in for this masculine pastime, just as he had never cared for such spectator sports as baseball and football. Perhaps that had all been an unnoticed indication. A sign warned bare-footed bathers not to walk out onto the jetty; the slippery rocks were dangerous.

He stood on the beach, watching the waves dash upon the rocks and toss lace-curtains of salt spray into the air. The smooth, porpoise-humped rocks glistened in the bright sunshine as though coated with quicksilver. There were a couple of low shadows on the horizon, ships underway, either heading for port or beginning their journey across the open seas, and he wondered vaguely about the lives of those on board. It was extremely hot, and the sky was almost white, the color sucked out of it by the heat. The beach noises about him seemed to have little reality or connection with the scene.

A wave broke against his feet, recoiled and rushed, hissing with foam and salt, back into the fold of the sea. Steve seated himself on the wet sand, his arms wrapped about his knees, clad only in bathing trunks and an invisible mantle of loneliness.

Paul leaned against the frankfurter stand, munching on a hot-dog that had yellowed his fingers with mustard, pleasantly aware of the admiring glances from the girls passing by. He knew he looked good in his tight white uniform, and the knowledge pleased him.

As a matter of fact, just about everything pleased him just now. It was a bright, hot day, the atmosphere still holding just a hint of the wonderful fresh salt air. He had a well-filled wallet, he had just had a really good lay, and all was well with his world. Before scampering down the tree like a pair of sated monkeys, both girls had indicated their eagerness to repeat the episode again this evening. Paul was still a bit uncertain about this; he preferred variety, and was certain he would be able to pick up something new and fresh for the evening. It was a problem that could be resolved any time during the day. No big hurry. He stretched expansively. Yes, sir, this was the life for him! Why should he ever want to give it all up to return to that stinking slum from which he had come? Not him!

Just now, he was a little pissed-off about Michael. Where the hell had he got himself to, anyway? Probably off somewhere in a blue funk, whipping himself for the undoubted pleasures of last evening. Too bad he wasn't Catholic; he might then at least ease his conscience by going to confession. Father, forgive me, for I have sinned, and I sure as shit enjoyed it! Grant me forgiveness so I can start with a clean slate and do it all over again tonight.

Strange he hadn't yet run into Michael; there weren't that many places he could have gone. Michael's conscience was a constant source of irritation to Paul, and on more than one occasion he had even thought of making the scene without his friend. Why the hell should anyone feel so god-damned guilty about enjoying a hot piece of ass whenever you could get it? Sure beat playing with yourself. But, still, Michael was a good kid, once he got over the Jesus-forgive-me business, and the broads really went for him. Paul smiled. That always meant two for each of them.

Paul carefully wiped his fingers on the paper napkin, checked to make certain no mustard had smeared his uniform, and sauntered slowly along the Boardwalk, returning the half-smiles of the timid and not-so-timid girls who passed, keeping an eye out for his wayward friend. He picked up an order of French Fries, heavily salted them, and sat on a bench with his legs propped up on the iron railing. He was always hungry as a bear after a night of rousing sex. Luckily, it didn't go to his belly; his body had never yet disappointed anyone.

Looking over the scene, Paul was unimpressed by what he saw stretched out on the beach. It always seemed to him that women who revealed the most in skimpy suits had the least to offer, and vice versa. It was always good leaving a little bit to the imagination, at least until that exciting ultimate moment when you saw it all; discovery was half the fun. Michael was amazed that Paul always steered clear of the nude beaches, unable to understand you could get too much of a good thing. Most of the girls on the beach down there were either too scrawny or overweight; the grateful kind, he thought with a touch of sarcasm. The few who might have been interesting were not alone.

The sea was roughing up, and the number of bathers was beginning to diminish, although the beach itself remained crowded. A freighter etched against the white horizon seemed to be standing quite motionless, but when he returned his eyes to it minutes later, it had moved a considerable distance on its way. For a moment, Paul considered returning to his room for his bathing trunks (he could show those squealing chicks what a real man looked like!) but the long walk deterred him. By the time he got back, there wouldn't be enough left of the afternoon to make it worthwhile. Besides, he still saw nothing to draw him to the beach. It would be a waste of valuable time that should be devoted to the delights of the chase.

A lifeguard walked by, and Paul ran his eyes appreciatively over the firm, deeply bronzed muscular form, like a contestant sizing up the

251

opposition. That was the kind of job to have, nothing to do all day but sit up there on a bench, blow a whistle, yell at the kids, and look at half-naked girls. He was willing to bet they got plenty of it, too; girls go wild over built lifeguards.

It was several moments before Paul realized the youth over to his left, stretched face down on the large colored blanket, was his buddy Michael, his bare back already revealing the pink signs of sunburn. And it was another moment before he came to the rather startling conclusion that Michael was not alone. Lying beside him on the blanket, wearing a light blue abbreviated bikini that revealed a form just about perfect in its slender shapeliness, was a young girl whose blonde hair fell loosely over smooth, tan shoulders. She also lay on her stomach with her head on her arms, and her face turned toward Michael. Their legs touched below the knee; although he could not hear the sound, Paul saw they were laughing. Their faces revealed obvious pleasure in each other's company.

Paul studied them for a moment, peering around the constantly moving forms that obscured his vision. Michael had never been very successful in making contact with girls without Paul's expert guidance; he was just too damned shy to carry it off alone. How had this happened? Perhaps some of the teaching of the master had got through, after all.

Paul frowned slightly, suddenly aware of a peculiar sense of irritation as the girl threw her head back and laughed and Michael, also laughing, turned over on his back and reached out for her hand. There was something—something so damned wholesome about them, so innocent, these two young people enjoying a day at the beach. Why should he be so displeased at the sight?

With a quick movement, he crumpled the paper cup of fries, indifferently dropping it to the Boardwalk. Wiping the salt from his hands, he vaulted easily over the railing, hitting lightly on the soft sand. Walking was difficult in shoes, and his progress was slow and clumsy as he started for the couple, who remained unaware of his approach. He stood over them for a moment, appreciating the form in the blue bikini.

"Hi there, buddy!"

The boy's blond head turned swiftly in his direction, as though Michael was startled, and the bright smile seemed for a moment to freeze on his face; Paul was surprised to note a flush of instant displeasure. The girl looked up too, and Paul noted the freshness of her face with its bright eyes, generous red lips, and clear skin.

"Oh. Hi, Paul." Michael's voice was less than enthusiastic.

"Where ya been, buddy?" Paul asked. "I've been looking all over for you."

"I've been right here on the beach." Michael hesitated for a moment, then turned to the girl. "Emily, this is my friend, Paul. This is Emily."

Smiling broadly, Paul greeted, "Well, hello! So this is what an Emily looks like!"

Emily's smile was warm, friendly, and completely trusting. "Hello, Paul."

Without waiting for an invitation which, he suspected would not be offered, Paul dropped to the sand, folding his legs under him. "You should have told me you were coming out here to the beach, Michael; I'd have got my suit, too."

253

"You weren't there when I got back to the room."

"Could've left a note. I wasn't gone long." He glanced at Michael and added, with a conspiratorial grin, "I had a little unfinished business to attend to."

"I didn't think of it."

Michael's tone was suddenly sullen; he was obviously not pleased by his friend's unexpected appearance. He had never been competition for Paul. Michael was the quiet one, and it took a time for him to feel really at ease with a strange girl, whereas Paul instantly dazzled with his looks, his charm and his personality. At this particular moment, it was a most disquieting thought.

Paul now turned the full force of his charm on Michael's companion. "Now, Emily, tell me all about yourself, and let's get better acquainted."

# CHAPTER FOURTEEN

Steve walked slowly over the hot sand and onto the cold wet concrete steps leading down to the underpass beneath the Boardwalk. His shoulders felt sore, and he wondered if he'd had too much sun. That would mean a sleepless night. Well, perhaps that would be better than the dream-haunted sleep to which he had lately become accustomed.

The damp underpass was chilly, and the slimy wetness of the floor was unpleasant to his bare feet; he shivered slightly. A mother headed for the beach with her two small children, all three burdened with rubber tubes, robes and towels, sand buckets and shovels; their wooden bath shoes clacked noisily on the cement, and Steve swallowed a curse when one of the metal sand buckets banged his leg as they passed. He walked quickly through the tunnel and up the wooden steps to the bath house. Johnny leaped quickly from the chair he had been straddling.

"Hello, Mr. Conroy." He flashed the boyish grin Steve always found so charming. "Nice to see you again."

Steve returned the smile; he had always liked Johnny. "Good to see you, too, Johnny. How's the boat coming?"

A peculiar expression entered the boy's dark eyes. "Might get it yet before the season's over—if the heat keeps up like this."

"Glad to hear it, Johnny."

Steve entered the wooden locker room and closed the door behind him. He lifted the towel from its hook on the wall, drying off the small amount of moisture that still clung to his back and chest. Straining a bit, he pulled the damp trunks down over his thighs and dried his body, brushing away clumps of sand.

He wasn't feeling particularly satisfied with himself. Here was another afternoon ended, and another night to begin. So what? As he stepped into his clothes and gathered his things together, he again felt the beginnings of depression, then remembered that he had agreed to meet Greg Christopher for a drink after the Seaquarium had closed. That would help. At least he wouldn't be alone this evening.

He vaguely wondered why the heat was still so intense. By this time of day, it should have eased off a bit. The radio predicted another storm moving up the coast. He walked along the Boardwalk, suddenly feeling almost overwhelmingly sleepy. Probably the effects of the sun. It might be a good idea to go back to his room for a short nap before dinner. He wanted to be alert this evening with Greg.

Ethel Hawkins was seated in her usual place on the verandah, the ever-present glass of lemonade at her side. As Steve mounted the steps and started for the door, she called to him.

"Oh, Mr. Conroy!"

Smiling, Steve turned. "Yes, Mrs. Hawkins?"

"Won't you sit and chat for a moment?" she invited, indicating the empty chair at her side. "It's been a long afternoon, and I haven't had a soul to talk with."

Aware of his weariness, Steve hesitated, but he disliked to disappoint the old woman; he took the chair. "Isn't it a bit too hot out here for you, Mrs. Hawkins?"

She shook her white head, bouncing some of the tight little curls. "Oh, my, no," she assured him, although there was the gleam of perspiration on her forehead. "I really don't mind it in the least. I've been out here on much hotter days than this. The summers really aren't at all like they used to be, you know; nor the winters, for that matter. People just can't take it any more, I suppose. They've been spoiled, that's the trouble. Feel too warm, turn on the air conditioning; too chilly, just inch up the thermostat. Can't put up with the natural weather conditions any more. Why, I remember summers when there was barely as much as a drop of rain, when the sun glared on the sea bright enough to blind you, and the sand was too hot to walk on in your bare feet, when the flowers wilted and the grass turned yellow, and winters when this house trembled in one storm after another. And they were real storms, too, let me

257

tell you, when Nature just took this old earth in her teeth and shook it like a cat will shake a mouse." She peered at him over the rim of her spectacles and suddenly asked, "You aren't married yet, are you, Mr. Conroy?"

Startled by this abrupt transition of thought, Steve replied, "Why, no, I'm not."

She leaned back in her chair and began to rock again, her head nodding. "I was just thinking how strange it is. This house is filled with unmarried people. There's Karen Fraser on the first floor—you remember, I introduced you just this morning—and then there's that nice Greg Christopher on the top floor, and the two young sailors. Times do change, I suppose. People just don't seem as interested in marriage nowadays as they used to be. Time was, that was all that really mattered. Marry and raise a family. Now all people are interested in is having a good time before they settle down, if they do at all. This business about living together . . ." She shook her head. "I don't know. It just doesn't seem right somehow." She sighed. "In my day it was a disgrace to reach twenty-one and still not be married, especially for a girl. Old maids, that's what they were. Do they still use that word?"

Steve smiled. "I imagine you have seen a great many changes, haven't you?"

"Oh, yes, yes indeed I have. A great many. Not all of them good, but not all of them bad, either. Your mother killed herself, didn't she?"

Again, the abrupt change of subject startled him, and he looked up at her, momentarily speechless.

"Oh, I know, I've become a meddlesome old woman, but if there is one privilege the aged should have, it should be the right to meddle to a certain extent. It must have been a very painful and difficult time for you."

He nodded. "Yes, it was."

"I remember your mother very well. A good woman, perhaps a little too good. Nothing mattered to her but her family. People like that are a bit too vulnerable." She smiled fondly, her lined face gentle. "Oh, I remember all of you, your handsome father, you and your sister when you were little. A nice family. I suppose you blame yourself for your mother's death, for one reason or another."

He paused briefly. "Perhaps I have good reason."

She took a sip of lemonade and sank back in the chair, her hand only slightly wafting the bamboo fan before her face. She was silent for several moments, as though she had momentarily forgotten that she was no longer alone.

"I've been noticing you. There's something troubling you, Mr. Conroy, something that's making you unhappy. I suppose it's because you do feel guilty about your mother's death. But you mustn't, you know. I don't know what happened or how, but most of us do wrong at some time or other in our lives, some of us even quite frequently. It's a part of the price we have to pay just for living; not really much to ask, I suppose. If we do wrong unintentionally, we shouldn't be blamed too much; it's the purposeful, intended wrong that creates so much trouble in the world. Even so, sometimes even our most innocent mistakes effect the lives of others, and that can be unfortunate, of course. But when that does happen, we mustn't spend the remainder of our lives blaming ourselves. We must take life as it comes. There's just nothing we can do about what is past, and life is too short for that kind of guilt." She looked at him and smiled. "Yes, even at my age, I can say life is too short. Not while we're living it, perhaps, but when we look back and remember, it seems that everything happened only yesterday, and suddenly we realize there will be no more memories to add to the treasured store."

She paused for a moment, saddened by her own thoughts. She waved the fan at a passing fly; then her piercing eyes looked at Steve again.

"You probably wonder what I know of such things. There has been much sorrow in this old house, Mr. Conroy, and I've seen most of it. There is little an old woman like myself can do but just sit and watch and listen. In one way or another, I have shared in the unhappiness of all those who have come to this great old house. For instance, just look out there."

Steve followed the direction of her gaze down the gentle slope from the house to the end of the point. Karen Fraser was seated in her wheelchair, staring out at the empty sea; an older woman, much more smartly dressed than the drab figure in the chair, stood motionless behind her.

"That poor girl should have been married several years ago, but the man she loved died in an automobile accident. She herself hasn't walked since and her incapacity has made her mother as much a prisoner as she is. And there's a sorrow about Greg Christopher, too. Have you met him, by the way?" When Steve nodded, she continued. "I don't know what it is, but there is something there. Even one of our young sailors. I saw him standing on the beach very early this morning, all alone . . ." She sighed and resumed her gentle rocking. "Oh, yes, there has been sorrow here. Have you ever been up on the Widow's Walk, Mr. Conroy?"

He shook his head. "No, I haven't."

She remembered. "Oh, no, that's right, the Walk is kept closed now. Not safe, supposedly, but that's not the real reason. It's—too personal a place for us. You know about that, don't you?"

He nodded, saying nothing, realizing the old woman wanted to talk.

"The last time I was up there—oh, so very long ago—I was still just a small child. I found my father standing there all alone, staring out to the sea he loved so passionately, his arm about the telescope. He often went up there just to be alone with the sea, to look out at the vast expanse of water on which he had spent all his life, to remember his voyages, his adventures. And, oh, he was so proud of that telescope! It was the very best that money could buy—brought ships so close, you could almost reach out to touch them— and he installed it there himself, bolted it in position where he wanted it, so as to give the best possible sweep of the horizon. He would spend hours at a time polishing the brass until it gleamed so brightly in the sun that you could hardly look at it. I suppose it's all tarnished now . . ."

She shook her head and her lined old face relaxed until it seemed again the face of a child. Her voice was soft with remembrance.

"That was a beautifully clear, cool night. The sea was just beginning its seasonal change, from blue to colder gray-green. The sky was clear and full of stars; the moon shone on the water like a mirage. I used to think there were dancing fairies out there, clad in bright silver, until I realized it was what the moon could do to the sea. Oh, it was a really beautiful night!"

She fell silent for another moment, and her eyes briefly closed; she had traveled back nearly eighty years in time.

"I approached my father, chattering about the sea, the night, the weather. When he made no reply, I looked up at him. His eyes were staring out to the horizon; perhaps they were seeing again those majestic ships on which he had sailed. Well . . ." Her voice softened. "He was seeing nothing else. There was a small hole in his right temple, and a thick trickle of blood that looked black in the silver light of the moon. It was only then that I noticed the revolver at his feet. In the noise of the surf, we in the house had heard nothing at all. I stood there for nearly fifteen minutes, all alone with him, doing nothing, just holding his cold hand and whispering goodbye. I remember a breeze, very gentle, almost caressing, that ruffled his hair, as a mother will ruffle her child's hair in a gesture of love. I never went up there again . . ." She sighed. "Oh, yes, this house has known its sorrows."

Steve saw her pale blue eyes shimmer with tears behind the glasses she wore. The thin, almost translucent hand holding the fan was still; the world seemed to have stopped to listen to her story.

"Why are you telling me this, Mrs. Hawkins?" Steve asked.

The old face was suddenly brightened by her wonderfully gentle smile. "Because I feel you have sorrow, too."

262

"Perhaps I do."

"Of course you do. We all do. And we all feel our lives will somehow stop because of it. I knew that night that I could never sing or smile or dance again, never love the sea, never feel gay or carefree again. But I did. More than three-quarters of a century have passed. I can remember now—oh, not without sorrow, perhaps, but with less pain. Sorrow is like the memory of pain."

Steve spoke now without hesitation. "My mother took her life because of something I had done, something she could not accept."

"That was most unfortunate," Ethel mused. "And perhaps very unfair. Sometimes love can be too demanding. We do what we must, Steve." He didn't notice how easily she slipped into use of his given name. "We must all live our own lives; that surely is our inalienable right. Sometimes this brings sorrow, to others as well as to ourselves, but that's all part of the human experience, and we can't change ourselves because of it. Those who love us should realize that, and accept it. Love must never become so possessive that it attempts to alter what we are, or it isn't love."

They were both silent for several moments, hearing only the rhythmic creaking of the old woman's rocking chair and the ever present murmur of the surf. The pair out on the point were heading back towards the house, the older woman wheeling the chair across the rock and sand.

"There's a storm coming, don't you think?" Steve asked at last.

Ethel glanced up at the heat-whitened sky. "Oh, yes, there's no question about that. The air is heavy. The sea looks slick, restless, tossing in its bed like a child with the croupe. Not before some time tomorrow, I should say."

Steve rose as the two women came closer to the house; he wanted to avoid further conversation and introductions. "Well, I spent some of the afternoon on the beach, and I'm a little tired. Think I'll try for a nap before going to dinner."

Ethel smiled. "It's a nice way to tire oneself, isn't it? When you reach my age, you sleep as little as possible." She reached out and, taking his hand, pressed it warmly. "You're a fine boy, Steve. I like you. Remember, what happened . . . happened."

He smiled. "Thank you." And he bent and lightly kissed her weathered cheek.

Steve found his room hot and stuffy, so he stripped to his shorts and flung himself onto the bed, thinking over what Ethel Hawkins had said. How much did she really know, he wondered? Would she be quite so tolerant if she knew the real reason behind his mother's death? She could not know, of course. Yet he wondered if perhaps the old developed certain insights into life that younger people did not have. He had often thought himself about what she said, about not assuming too much blame for what had happened. It would be comforting, if he could make himself accept it.

Ethel's words suggested another inference. Had his mother's suicide perhaps been a dramatic protest, an attempt to place upon him a burden of guilt to carry about for the rest of his life? Had his mother planned to extend her possessiveness even beyond the grave? The possibility had come to him many times, and the thought was frightening. He had even found himself wondering whether his mother had not really intended to go quite so far, but merely to frighten him and bring him back home. That was the most uncomfortable thought of all.

It didn't really matter, of course. Argue as he might, the fact remained unchanged: his mother, a kindly and loving woman, was dead because of him.

Steve struggled with these thoughts until he fell into a light, restless sleep.

From the verandah Ethel Hawkins watched Karen and her mother returning to the house; the spume-covered point of land was the farthest Karen would venture from the house throughout her stay at The Cloud. Ethel's sharp blue eyes peered intently at the crippled girl, again attempting to fathom that indefineable quality that did not ring true. A special ramp had been constructed alongside the stairs for Karen's chair, and Linda encountered no difficulty in returning her daughter to the verandah.

"Won't you sit out here for a little while, Karen?" Linda asked, her voice almost pleading.

Karen smiled and shook her head. "I don't believe so, mother. Sitting in the sun always tires me. I think I'll go on inside."

"I could read to you for a little, dear. Some poetry, perhaps?"

The girl shook her head. "No, thank you."

"Why don't I come with you and sit for a while, then? We could do some crossword puzzles together."

"Mother, please." Karen's tone was that of an annoyed adult talking to a bothersome child. "I prefer to be alone, if you don't mind."

She wheeled herself slowly through the open

265

door and on to her room. Linda looked after her daughter, both concern and annoyance in her face; she sighed, shrugged her shoulders, and seated herself beside Ethel.

"Why do I always insist? It annoys her so. Now she'll go into her room, lower all the blinds, turn on the phonograph and daydream before that damned portrait!"

"Perhaps it takes her into a happier world," Ethel suggested.

"She already spends too much of her time in that world. I wonder how long it will be before she can no longer tell the difference between what is real and what is fantasy."

"Will she really never walk again?" Ethel asked.

Linda shrugged. "The doctors can't say, or they won't commit themselves. All we can do is hope, and be as kind and understanding as possible."

"Sometimes people live too much on kindness."

"What do you mean?"

"Oh, nothing, really. It's just that sometimes perhaps too much kindness may not always be a good thing."

Linda was surprised. "Mrs. Hawkins, Karen is my daughter!"

"Yes, yes. Of course. Yes, that does make a difference, doesn't it?" She began to fan herself more vigorously.

It was a strange evening that fell upon Hawkins' Cove. A gauze veil seemed to come between the sun and the earth, casting a sickly yellow glow upon all the world. The sea moved in long, sluggish swells. The heat grew even more intense, and the humidity increased uncomfortably.

"It's so quiet," Johnny muttered; the locker

rooms had now been closed for the day, and he and Jimmy were seated on one of the Boardwalk benches, having a cigarette together before going home. "You almost feel like you shouldn't even talk. Bet there's a hell of a storm coming."

"No clouds," Jimmy mentioned. "Look at that sky. Clear. You can't have a storm with no clouds."

"Doesn't take long for 'em to come up."

After a moment's silence, Jimmy asked, "How much did you make today, Johnny? How many'd you look at."

"Six," Johnny replied. "A buck from each."

Feeling now completely vindicated, Jimmy enthusiastically turned to his friend, placing one arm along the back of the bench. "See? What did I tell you? Is that an easy way to make a buck, or is that an easy way to make a buck?"

"It's disgusting," Johnny insisted. "Those guys are sick."

"Oh, shit, what's the difference, as long as they're willing to pay? Some of these guys are here for a couple weeks at a time, and when they know you'll look at 'em, they keep comin' back. You'll be making more dough every week; just wait and see." He looked closely at his friend. "Did you play with any of them?"

"I told you I wouldn't do that! That would make me as sick as they are!"

"Awe, you just wait," Jimmy confidently predicted. "Sometimes the guys aren't really half bad. Not always fat and old and flabby. You get the real athletic types who got somethin' to show. Then it's not so bad, and you can make really good money. Shit, feels just like your own, anyway."

Johnny turned on him, his face angry. "I don't

want to hear any more about this! I'm not queer!"

"Okay, okay! But you'll have your boat in no time now, Johnny, if you just stick with me," Jimmy promised him. "Guess you'd really like that, wouldn't you?"

Johnny raised his eyes to the magnet of the sea, and the look of dreamers returned to his face as he visualized himself gently bobbing up and down on that calm mirror-like surface.

"Yeah," he agreed, nodding slowly. "Yeah, that would really be something!"

"Hope you'll take me out on it once in a while, buddy."

"Sure. Sure I will, Jimmy," Johnny promised. "Of course. You're my best friend. Almost," he added, suddenly thinking of Greg.

"Well, it won't be long now," Jimmy again promised. "Say, I gotta go. I was late last night, and the old lady really lit into me. See you tomorrow."

Johnny scarcely heard his friend's goodbye. He was dreaming about his boat, and how to get it fast.

There was still too much he couldn't understand about this business with Jimmy and the patrons of the bath houses. Fairies. Queers. Old men masturbating while young boys watched. Supposedly healthy and normal young men proudly displaying their sex organs and paying to have others look at them. Athletes whose only interest was in bodies as strong and impressive as their own. You were supposed to be able to tell about such people, pick them out of a crowd from the way they talked and behaved, the limp wrists, the feminine movements, the lisping. Well, weren't you?

Suddenly realizing he was quite alone, Johnny

crossed to a nearby hot-dog stand, ordered a hamburger and a coke, and watched the vacationists walk by somewhat slowed by the oppressive heat. He ran his eyes over the men and boys, and found himself wondering about them. How could you tell? One attractive man in his late twenties whom Johnny had looked at in the nude walked past without a sign of recognition. No one would have guessed it.

When he had finished his hamburger, he dropped in at the Seaquarium, returning the wave of welcome he always received from the cashier, who had standing instructions to admit him at any time. Greg had just completed another tour and was in the rear room, preparing fish-heads for the next feeding. He looked up and smiled when his young friend entered.

"Hi, there, Johnny. Hot enough for you?"

"Radio says there's a storm coming."

Greg hesitated for a moment in his work and, raising his head, glanced through the small window above the sink. "Hell, don't need any radio to tell you that. There's sure something coming. Even the fish are restless." He shrugged. "Can't tell. Maybe it'll blow over. Happens this time of year."

He bent over the sink again, and Johnny found himself looking at the broad shoulders, the tanned bare arms with the lightest fuzz of golden hair; his eyes wandered to the light khaki trousers that tightly covered the slim buttocks. He quickly turned away, suddenly ashamed of his thoughts as he found himself wondering what Greg would look like standing naked in one of the bath houses . . .

"How did you do today, Johnny?" Greg asked,

his back still turned.

"I . . . Pretty good."

"Glad to hear it. What's chances of getting the boat by the end of the season?"

"I might do it. Sure hope so."

"Good. Then maybe you can get out and pick up some real exhibits for me." He laughed. "I think the whole town's wondering about that boat of yours." Turning, he smiled broadly, and Johnny was surprised to see his face was as friendly as ever; nothing showed, then? Greg turned off the water and removed his bucket from the sink. "Well, time to feed those monsters of mine. Come on with me."

"No. No, thanks. I'll be getting on home. Mom's complaining that I eat Boardwalk junk too much."

"Okay. See you, kid."

Swinging the bucket, Greg started back to the pool, while Johnny looked after him, feeling guilty and ashamed.

# CHAPTER FIFTEEN

The large steel ferris-wheel moved slowly in its monotonous circle, the cages with their rows of benches carried up, around and down. Most of them were empty just now—business would pick up again after the dinner hour—but the wheel never stopped except to load and unload. A nervous mother with her wriggling children occupied the yellow car, and in the blue one a small boy tried to spit on the roof as the wheel carried them through the slit opening, out and over the Casino. Two young lovers with their arms about each other, quite oblivious to all about them, were in the red cage, and a middle-aged woman occupied the green car, in rapt conversation with a little dog she held to her bosom, occasionally lifting it for a glimpse of the sights.

As his cage moved up into the open, rising above the Casino's great red roof, Steve glanced out to the shimmering surface of the sea. It was strangely quiet up here as the cage moved steadily higher above everything. The pinging noises of the pinball machines, the shouting and crying children, the oompah-pah waltzes of the carousel, all faded into something but dimly heard, as though through a closed door of time. The people on the Boardwalk moved like puppets without their strings. The entire horizon was dominated by the sea, expansive, blue-white, pure, clean. What was the population of the sea, he wondered? How many different races of fish did the seas of the world contain? Could you speak of 'races' in that kind of life? Perhaps all fish were of but one race but different forms. Ridiculous thought.

He sank back onto the hard wooden bench, leaning one arm on the side of the cage, and let his mind wander freely. How many lives had the sea claimed since the first ancestors of the human race had lifted themselves from the primeval ooze to face the uncertainties of existence on the still-smouldering land? What was the sea after all but one vast watery graveyard? But then, wasn't the entire world on which we live a gigantic grave-yard, an enormous round mauseoleum spinning about in space, heavy with its load of dead, moving in its eternal circle until, some day, even that would come to an end? Every living creature, everything born on the surface or under it, be it man, animal, insect, bird, fish, all died and made the earth their grave. What horrors would the eye of man behold if suddenly all the seas were dried up and their beds exposed? The valleys, the mountains, the ruins of ships from Phoenician galleys to the Titanic, aircraft that had plunged from their own element to the hostile world of the fish, tumbled columns of long-lost civilizations, the silent desertion of Atlantis, the countless ruins of what had once been men.

Steve cursed lightly. Time was beginning to hang heavy on his hands again; he was feeling bored and lonely. The sun was moving ever closer to the horizon, as though eager to drown itself in the sea, but still the time was passing too slowly. The wheel came to a stop, with his own carriage at its summit. He looked down at the roof, at the doll-like people on the Boardwalk, the sea, the many-colored lights of the carousel below him, the calm water of the inner lagoon, and he felt suddenly absurdly frightened. The car swung slightly back and forth, and he imagined it breaking from its cables and plunging down, down, down . . . .

The wheel started again. When his car reached the bottom, Steve signaled to the operator to be stopped. He gratefully stepped from the cage and the silence of that strange upper world and back to the more familiar and somehow comforting noise and bedlam of the fun-house and pin-ball machines.

Karen sat alone in the soothing silence of her sacred inner sanctum; once again, time had stopped for her. There was not a sound from other areas of the house. The room in which she had already sat for half an hour was hot and stuffy; the closed windows that kept out the harsh noises also imprisoned the heat. She could have opened the windows—the outside noises could not have been that distracting—but that would have seriously marred the almost religious aspect of her shrine. It would have permitted the outer world to enter. Perhaps discomfort was part of the true religious experience. Perhaps one's thoughts drifted more easily to God on the rising waves of torpid air.

Yet Karen's thoughts were not directed to God, at least not in the traditional sense. She had long since abandoned Him, or was it that He had abandoned her? If God were truly the kind, loving Father she had been taught about in her Sunday School days, then surely he would not have permitted her to suffer as she had, and if He were not kind, then surely He was not worthy of adoration. Love and worship are properly directed to the truly generous, noble, and good. People were often harsh and cruel, but God should not be so. You weren't supposed to queston, but her mind refused to be still. She had once known a man who was truly good and kind, and it was to him and to him alone that her dreams and prayers were directed.

The music moved into the final movement of Franck's Symphony in D Minor, the chords thundering as richly as though heard in a great Gothic cathedral.

She looked again to the portrait on the wall, and her mind remembered Jeff's arms about her, his warm lips on hers, the strength of his hands. Many times—particularly on their memorable weekend here at Hawkins' Cove—Jeff had urged her to the final intimacy, but she had always refused. It would not be right. If he truly loved her, he would not suggest it. It showed a lack of true respect. The time would come, but under the right and proper circumstances. Where would be the joy of union after marriage if they knew the intimacies before they had become truly one?

And how bitterly she regretted that moralistic stance. Now the time would never come. Never. Now she would never know what it was to be sexually possessed by a man, never thrill to the pressure of his naked body on her own, never feel the love surging between them as their bodies moved in unison in the rhythms of sexual love. How often she dreamed of it in the lonely nights, how often she lay alone in her bed, burning with desire for a man who no longer existed, her mind filled with hazy images of Jeffrey lying beside her, caressing her, possessing her straining body. She moaned in her sleep at such times, a deep lament for something lost forever.

"Why did I disappoint you so?" she whispered to the portrait as she had on so many, uncounted periods of adoration. "I should have given myself to you, completely and unreservedly, as you wanted me to do. I belonged to you; it could not have been wrong. It would have given me so much more to remember, and memories are all I have left of you now!"

She leaned her head against the back of the wheel chair and closed her eyes, losing herself in the sonorous sounds of the music and the wraith-like memories of the past. She no longer worried whether or not they were all actually true memories; she was really no longer able to recall which scenes had actually happened and which were fantasy. All brought her a measure of happiness.

The music came to an end. The sharp click of the stereo turning itself off brought her instantly out of her reverie and back into the present. She opened her eyes, sighed, and glanced at her watch. Almost forty-five minutes. She smiled at the portrait—Jeff always seemed to smile back at her—and then wheeled herself into the sitting room. Her afternoon devotions were over.

It was a trifle cooler in the sitting room; Linda had left the door open to catch a breath of air, and Karen could see into the empty foyer. The front door of the house was also open, propped by an old pirate's head made of extremely heavy iron, giving her a clear view to the beach and the sand beyond. Once she and Jeff had walked there, hand in hand, discussing the future; or was that just another of the fantasies? She wheeled herself to the far side of the room and the open window that looked out over the Boardwalk. She could faintly hear the sound of the calliope.

She became sharply aware of the complete silence of the old house. There was not even the creaking of timbers, and no sound of voice or footstep. That was, for many, another advantage of The Cloud enjoyed over the larger, more modern hotels down on the Boardwalk; it was not always bustling with the movement of restless guests and employees. Solitude could be a blessing at times but it, too, often became tiresome; when she was alone for too long, there was no one to give her pity.

Feeling a sudden urgent need for a cigarette, Karen wheeled herself to the coffee-table in the center of the room and raised the lid of the cigarette box; it was empty. The box beside the couch was empty as well. Annoyed, she cast her eyes about the room, hoping her mother had somewhere left a loose pack. She spotted one on the mantel.

She turned her chair and wheeled herself across

the room, and then stopped. The fireplace stood on a small tiled platform that was just a trifle too high for the wheels of her chair. Exasperated, she looked up to the cigarettes just out of her reach. She hesitated for a moment. There certainly was no one about; the house was too silent. She had the peculiar feeling of being totally and absolutely alone. Quickly, she set aside the light blanket that always covered her legs.

As Ethel crossed the silent and empty lobby on her way back to the rocking chair on the verandah, her attention was caught by an unexpected movement sensed rather than seen through the open door of the Fraser apartment. She knew Linda had gone into town and Karen was in her own room; for a moment, she feared an intruder. Carefully, she moved behind the shelter of the open door, peering through the narrow crack between the door and the jamb, and watched as Karen Fraser rose from her chair and walked, easily and with no trace of pain or difficulty, to the mantel and casually lighted a cigarette.

Johnny stood alone on the Widow's Walk. Next to the beaches themselves, this was his favorite place of sanctuary, his personal redoubt for serious thinking. No one else ever came up here, with the exception of his mother, and Greg Christopher. The Walk was closed to the guests of the house, supposedly because it was considered no longer safe but really because this was of all areas of the house the most sacred to the family.

The Widow's Walk provided Johnny with another precious link to the past. It seemed to him that the aura of his great-grandfather, Captain Nathaniel Hawkins himself, still lingered about the exposed platform. Johnny would not have been at all surprised to come up here on some dark night and see the Captain standing with legs spread wide and hands clasped behind his back as he stared out to the empty sea in search of some phantom vessel. Sometimes, on cold windy nights, Johnny fancied he heard the Captain's voice shouting orders to prepare his vessel for the gale.

More than anything in his life, Johnny regretted never having known his great-grandfather. His father had died when Johnny was a small child; he could remember him only as a pleasant man with a gentle smile. In any event, his father would surely not have been the same as the Captain. He had not really been a man of the sea, he thus could not really have understood. There was a large oil-painting of Captain Nathaniel hanging on the wall in his grandmother's room, and Johnny often went there just to look at it—the big, bearded man with eyes that seemed to flash with a lightning of their own, a man accustomed to giving orders and having them instantly obeyed.

And yet, Johnny sensed there was more to the Captain than just this awesome figure of authority. The expression of those deep eyes, the slight curve of the lips, suggested soften qualities that were probably carefully concealed. Such a man would have understood Johnny's urgings and desires.

Johnny had never before so keenly felt the need for discussion and confidence, for he was still deeply disturbed by the events of the day. He sensed, somehow, that his life had been permanently changed by the day's unorthodox activities, whether for good or ill, and he would never again be quite the same.

He no longer questioned the right or wrong of what he had done; that dilemma, at least, had been resolved. While he did not regret the extra money he had earned, he knew that he had been wrong in accepting Jimmy's proposition. There was no question but that he would put the extra money to good use, and he considered himself already too mature to be disturbed by questions of morality or a sense of guilt. His current uneasiness really lay much deeper than that, in the peculiar and unexpected confusion of thoughts that had arisen as a direct result of the day's psuedo-sexual activities. What had happened had challenged beliefs and understandings he had held since earliest childhood and had raised questions much more involved than simply those of right or wrong. He was simply too young to cope alone with the chaotic new aspects of life that had suddenly been presented to him.

The incidents of that day had really not been quite as bad as he had feared they might be. He had looked rather contemptuously at several naked men who stood in the narrow booth, hairy, flabby, pot-bellied, reeking from more than one kind of heat, proudly displaying to him their unremarkable private parts. Most of them fiercely, heatedly, almost desperately and, in at least one instance, threateningly, urged him to touch them or to expose himself to their lustful eyes. To all of these, he had returned an unequivocal "no." He had simply stood there for a few moments, watching them with total disinterest, then collected his dollar and forgotten the incident. They were totally unimportant to him save as a means of making extra money. Perverts, most of them approaching or beyond middle age. It was a silly but an easy way to make a buck.

By mid-afternoon he had easily tossed aside the question of morality that had been bothering him. The uneasy guilt was replaced by a sense of foolishness, then by contempt toward those who so demeaned themselves, then simply by total indifference.

But toward the end of the afternoon, Jimmy sent him to another "special customer." When the door was opened to his knock, there stood a smiling young man in his early twenties, attractive and wholesome, powerfully built, his well-formed body firm and smooth, his belly flat, his legs and arms muscular and glowing with health and vitality. He showed his impressive equipment to Johnny without the least trace of embarrassment. For the first time, Johnny watched until his patron was through.

So they were not all alike. There were some like this one, the clean-cut college type. Yet basically they were all the same, weren't they? They were all perverts, and there was no difference between them. But what if this one, this attractive young man not many years older than himself, had asked him to—well, to "do something"—for some extra money? It had been easy to refuse the others, but would he as quickly have rejected this one?

And that was where a new fear had suddenly entered his mind, for Johnny found that he was now doubting even himself. Would he actually have said yes to such a suggestion from this Joe-college? Had he actually been tempted? This new question, this terrible possibility, had been burning in his mind all the remainder of the afternoon. He had always thought you had to be born that way. He had done it to girls more than once beneath the Boardwalk; wasn't that clear enough evidence that he was as normal as anyone? Surely such a person couldn't suddenly just turn—queer?

Johnny looked out again to the sea, leaden, sluggish, beneath a sky that had turned a sickly, peculiar shade of yellow. The air was heavy, as pregnant with storm as his own disordered thoughts.

If only there were someone he could talk to, someone he might expect to understand. But who was there he could turn to with such terrible fears and doubts? Certainly not his mother, nor his grandmother, nor any woman; this was a man's problem. Jimmy? He would merely be amused, and from what Johnny had learned about Jimmy during the course of the day, it was apparent that his friend was not as completely normal as he had always thought him to be.

Greg Christopher? Johnny instinctively felt that here was the one person who might really understand his problem and try to help him, but his mind instantly shied away from the possibility. Greg Christopher was Johnny's idol, and you can not, and do not, reveal to your idol the flaws in your own character, not if you wish to preserve his respect. Talking to Greg would be the most impossible of all.

The door behind him opened and his mother stepped onto the Walk, panting considerably from the effort of the long climb, one hand pressed painfully to her heaving bosom; in this weather there was always a moustache of moisture on her upper lip.

"I didn't know you were here, Johnny," she said, unaware that this raised an immediate question in his mind as to the reasons for her climb. "Have you had something to eat?"

"Yes." He nodded. "I had something on the Boardwalk."

"I do wish you wouldn't eat so much of that fast-food stuff, dear," she complained. "A growing boy like you needs something more substantial. You should come home more often for a really good meal."

"I wasn't that hungry, Mom," he explained. "I had enough."

There was a moment of uncomfortable silence between them; the older he became, the more difficult it seemed for Margaret to talk with her son.

"Did you have a good day, dear?"

He nodded again. "Had a good crowd on the beach; a really hot day like this helps."

Margaret walked to the edge of the Widow's Walk and glanced over towards the Boardwalk, careful not to stand too close to the railed edge, for she suffered from vertigo. From this height and distance, the strollers looked like a dark undulating ribbon.

"Why do all those people come here, I wonder?" she mused. "So many of them seem unhappy."

She turned again and looked at her son, aware that he was not really listening to her. Johnny stood with one arm crooked about the telescope staring out to sea, his eyes shadowed and troubled.

Put him in different clothes, she thought, put a beard on his face, and he might be the Captain himself. She sensed again that uneasy feeling that something was making her son very unhappy. There were times when she so wished he were still just her little boy, so she could take him to her bosom and comfort him as she used to do. Those days were long past. Could this trouble, whatever it might be, be of her own doing? Had she become too busy running The Cloud to give him the attention he needed?

"I was talking with grandmother about you today, Johnny," she said, desperately turning to the one topic that never failed to interest him, "and she feels just the same way I do, that you should have that boat of yours before the end of this season. Autumn is such a lovely time on the sea."

"No, Mom," Johnny said again. "You know I don't want it that way. I can wait a little longer. Besides I don't think it really will be much longer. A few more days like today, and I'll be able to put down the first payment myself, and I won't have any trouble with the rest of them. I've been doing a lot of—extra work down at the bath house, getting some extra money. I'm sure I can manage by the time this season's over. Thanks, anyway."

He stood with his dark hair blowing in the slight breeze, looking so very young that Margaret found herself again recalling those wonderful days of his childhood. She put a hand on her son's strong arm and smiled through a sudden veil of tears.

"Grandmother says you're so very much like her father, Johnny. He would have been so proud of you!"

The boy smiled. "If only I could sail in the kind of ships he knew! That's when sailing was really sailing! I guess I was just born too late."

Margaret returned his smile; this was the old, familiar Johnny. "Oh, I think you'll generally find it's best to have been born in your own time. We often glamorize the times we haven't known. At least you can be certain of one thing, Johnny; the ships may have changed, but the sea today is pretty much the same."

"Yes, that's right." He nodded and turned his head away. "Yeah, the sea really never changes, does it?"

Margaret looked closely at the strong profile, at the forehead with its new furrows of worry, at the dark eyes that seemed always clouded with trouble.

"Johnny, is there anything wrong?"

He turned to her again, and she could see evasion in his eyes. "Wrong? What do you mean? What should be wrong?"

"I don't know," she confessed, perhaps feeling a trifle foolish; why was it so difficult for a mother to speak with her son? "You just haven't been quite yourself for the past few days. I just think there may be something on your mind."

He shook his head. "No. I'm all right."

"You know enough to come to me if there should be something that troubles you, don't you? I . . . I would always do anything I could to help you. If your father . . ."

Smiling, he lightly kissed her cheek. "Of course, Mom. I know. Don't worry about me."

She looked at him for another moment, sensing that something had happened to her son during this summer that made Johnny no longer a boy, and yet not quite a man. She turned to the door.

"Are you sure you don't want a little something to eat, dear?"

He shook his head again, and a wave of hair fell boyishly over his forehead, making him look suddenly young once again. "Maybe a little later, Mom. I'll just stay up here a while longer; it's cooler."

She paused in the doorway and looked back at him. His profile sharply etched against the yellowed sky reminded her of all the portraits she had seen of Captain Natheniel.

Margaret slowly descended the stairs to her duties below, and Johnny turned once again to stare out to sea.

There were few activities that brought Linda Fraser more pleasure than shopping. Browsing through the stores, fingering the soft materials of a dress, trying on a pair of shoes or a ridiculously frilly hat, these represented for Linda more than the ordinary instinctive feminine desire for new things and the pleasure of spending money.

For Linda, shopping was a necessary catharsis, providing her with a few hours of forgetfulness, when the ever-present problem of her crippled daughter receded for a time. These shopping sprees had become a daily ritual by now; fortunately for her, Hawkins' Cove featured a number of fine shops. Immediately after breakfast every morning, when Karen either returned to her room or sat on the verandah with her book, Linda put on her best hat and headed for the shopping district. She didn't always buy something; that wasn't at all necessary. The important thing was that it gave her a few hours in bright, cheerful surroundings, and above all a time to mix with people who were pleasant, courteous, and not burdened by problems.

Linda wouldn't admit even to herself that the most important aspect of the shopping sprees was that they were a respite from the doleful, often suffocating presence of her only daughter.

To round out her day's brief journey into the world of reality, just before returning to The Cloud, Linda always dropped in at Ricardo's, a charming little Italian restaurant near the Seaquarium, just for some of their delicious espresso coffee. She was well known there, and a table was always reserved for her each afternoon at the same time, at the window overlooking the lagoon. She would sit there for exactly one hour with just two cups of espresso. Then she would return to the prison her daughter had created for both of them.

Linda seemed to feel an exceptional weariness this afternoon. She had not slept well the previous night, the humidity was uncomfortable. The unhealthy yellow of the sky cast a peculiar jaundiced hue over the calm lagoon. The miniature Mississippi showboat, filled with noisy children, was on its way to the other side of the small pond, and several swan-boats followed like courtiers in its wake. Small motorboats crisscrossed the surface like over-sized water beetles.

Despite the heat, there was a certain feeling in the air that this summer would soon be over. Linda slowly sipped her espresso, depressed by the approaching season's end. Summer at Hawkins' Cove provided her with at least a period of some variety, but once the season was over she and Karen would return to their home, and the stultifying routine would begin all over again. Through the long, dark winter the three of them would sit together in the living room, watching the empty, meaningless days pass slowly by, viewing insipid television programs, working jigsaw and cross-word puzzles, merely waiting for the return of the summer.

She sighed. The endless cycle of boredom and monotony. The endless and the unchanging. Oh, there were frequent invitations (although not quite as frequent as in the past), but somehow it had never seemed right to leave Karen alone. Karen would insist upon her going, of course, and in the beginning they had actually often done so, but there was always in Karen's insistence that little tone of accusation that aroused a sense of guilt. Were she and her husband fated to spend the remainder of their once full lives ensnared in the gloomy world of their only daughter's neurosis?

Linda sharply returned the small cup to its saucer, reminding herself that she must not blame Karen. Karen had lost her one love, and now she would never walk again, she would spend the remainder of her life tied to a wheel chair. Surely it was not too much to ask of her own parents that they stay with her and bring into her life whatever pleasure they could provide? She and Charles still had their own companionship and the love that had kept them together for so many years. What did the poor girl have? Only her parents. How often Linda shied away from frightening thoughts of the day when neither she nor Charles would still be here to care for Karen. What would happen to her then? Financially, of course, she would always be well cared for, but would that be enough?

Oh, Karen was so to be pitied, and surely that was the least a mother could give. The poor girl desperately needed love, kindness and understanding.

"Sometimes people live too much on kindness."

The thought thus expressed by Ethel Hawkins was not a completely new one to Linda, but she had always suppressed it under a deep sense of guilt. Karen was her own and only daughter, and if the girl couldn't depend on her mother, to whom could she turn?

But now, for just a moment, Linda permitted her mind to run over the forbidden suggestion. Was there really such a thing as too much kindness, too much pity, too much understanding? Could there be too much of those emotions that kept people together? Was it perhaps time now for Karen to snap herself out of this dream world and realize that many years of life still remained to her and it was entirely up to her to bring some meaning into those years? Could she really be content to spend all those remaining years in a fantasy world of misty memories and doleful sorrow, worshiping the shadow of a dead man? Other women had known tragedy but they managed, somehow, to pick up the pieces of a shattered life and begin anew. Couldn't Karen do the same? After all, Karen had a fine mind. (How often had Linda found comfort in that phrase?) There was much that she could do.

Linda had tried, many times, to make Karen understand all this, but to no avail. Karen either refused to listen to her sound arguments or had some counter-argument of her own. What could she, a helpless cripple, do? When Linda tried to point out that she was not really helpless at all and that there were women even more seriously handicapped who made useful and happy lives for themselves, Karen merely smiled her sad smile and said those women were obviously far more clever than she. As for meeting new people or returning to her old friends, this no longer interested her. She said she didn't want to cause embarrassment to others, and her unfortunate condition was certain to do so. She had all she now really wanted in life. She had her kindly parents and her precious memories. She needed nothing more.

And so, Karen spent her time in sick devotions to a dead man, and Linda accepted the imprisonment forced upon her by her love.

Linda finished her second cup of coffee and was politely bowed out of the restaurant by Ricardo himself. She walked slowly along the shore of the lagoon and over to the Boardwalk. As she was passing the Seaquarium, she saw Greg Christopher just leaving the building.

"Hello, Mrs. Fraser," he smiled broadly, joining her. "It isn't often I have the pleasure of running into you like this. Shopping again, I suppose?"

Linda returned his smile; she had always liked this young man. "More like window-shopping, I'm afraid; I haven't bought a single thing. Well, it's my only vice, you know."

"And how was Roberto's espresso this afternoon?"

She was surprised by this knowledge of her activities. "You don't miss very much, do you?"

He smiled again. "Roberto happens to be a very good friend of mine, and he's told me you're one of his favorite customers."

"I'm flattered," she admitted, and was. "Not much of a customer, I'm afraid; all I have is espresso. He couldn't very well survive on customers like me. His espresso is delicious, though." She nodded to the Seaquarium. "But shouldn't you be hard at work at this time of day?"

"Oh, I feel I deserve a few minutes off now and then. Between hours, I like to run out for an orange drink. With all the talking I do, my throat can get very dry. Won't you join me?"

"Why, I'd love to," Linda agreed, suppressing an impulse to glance at her watch. "It's a long time since I've had a drink with a handsome young man!"

Linda seated herself on one of the benches facing the sun, while Greg excused himself and threaded his way through the crowd to a softdrink stand, returning in a few moments with two paper cups brimming with juice, one of which he handed to Linda as he seated himself at her side.

"What do you think of this weather, Mr. Christopher?" Linda asked, glancing up at the heavily clouded sky. "Very peculiar, isn't it? There isn't even the breath of a breeze. There's a strange . . . silence."

Greg nodded. "There's a storm on the way."

"A bad one?"

He shrugged. "That's hard to tell. Hit down the coast, and there was a bit of flooding, but I'm sure it's nothing to worry about. The storms during the season are really nothing compared to what we have in the winter. Real nor'easterns, Captain Nathaniel would have called them. Sometimes you can't even approach the Boardwalk, what with the wind, the spray, the rising tides."

"It must be rather uncomfortable at The Cloud in a storm like that," Linda mentioned, "exposed the way it is."

Greg shook his head. "Not really. It's gone

through about a century of that sort of thing, and I suppose it'll go through a lot more; it's a solid house." He smiled. "Sounds rather nice to be in the comfortable warmth of The Cloud and hear the wind roaring around you."

A little boy and girl, fully and neatly dressed, stood near the breaking waves on the beach, holding tightly onto each other; the girl's skirt was raised high, as though she feared the water might suddenly rise and wet her. They screamed with delight as a wave tumbled towards them, and dashed quickly out of reach of its cascading wetness. Had Karen ever played that way?

"Well, the summer will be over soon, now," Linda sighed, wiping at her lips with the paper napkin. "What do you do then, Mr. Christopher? I suppose the Seaquarium is closed once the season is over?"

"Yes, we close down right after Labor Day," he confirmed. "It just doesn't pay to keep it open off-season; not enough customers. But there's always plenty to do to keep busy. The fish still have to be cared for, of course, there are new exhibits to be prepared, the whole building has to be cleaned and painted for the next season. And speaking of exhibits, I don't believe you've ever been in to see the place, have you?"

She shook her head, slightly embarrassed. "No, I confess I haven't. I've always meant to drop in, but what with one thing and another, I just somehow haven't managed to get around to it. I don't like to leave my daughter alone too much, you know."

"Yes, of course." He looked closely and for the first time noticed the faint lines of weariness about

Linda's mouth, and what seemed a sad resignation in her eyes. "And how is Karen now, Mrs. Fraser?" He suddenly realized that although he had been seeing Karen at The Cloud for the past several summers, he had scarcely spoken with her, aside from the usual amenities. "Any improvement?"

Linda made a vague motion with her hand. "Oh, I'm afraid things just don't change very much for my poor girl. She stays pretty much the same. I suppose that should be enough for us; we shouldn't complain, as long as she's no worse."

"Well, why don't you just bring her to the exhibit with you?" Greg suggested. "We could easily carry her up the stairs, chair and all, and I'm certain she would find it interesting."

Linda sighed again and shook her head. "Oh, believe me, I wish I could. But I'm afraid Karen just doesn't care to go out anywhere. She's quite content just to stay up there on the verandah and read her books and stare out to sea. She does go down to the end of the point each day, but outside of that . . . well, that's really all she wants."

"But do you really think it's good to shut herself up that way?" He put a hand on Linda's arm. "Please understand, I don't mean to pry . . ."

"Of course not; I appreciate your interest. I know it's very bad for Karen, of course, living as she does." Linda's tone carried a note of severity that surprised Greg. "But what can I do? I talk to her, I try to reason with her, but it simply does no good. She wants only to live by herself, with her memories." Her lips tightened almost imperceptibly. "With her dreadful memories."

Greg raised his eyebrows at this; he had never before heard Linda talk this way. "Her dreadful memories, Mrs. Fraser? It seems rather strange to talk that way about memories of love."

"Perhaps. But this is . . . different." She frowned and bit her lip, suddenly anxious to make herself clearly understood. "There's something frightening about this continuing love affair of hers. It's almost like a sickness. Oh, please, understand me, I liked Jeffrey very much. He was really a fine boy, and I was very pleased about him and Karen. Karen, you know, was never really popular with the boys. She was always so retiring. But since Jeffrey's death, Karen has turned the memory of that brief love into something almost unwholesome. After all, it's been several years now. Surely it's time she began to forget. I never realized how destructive love can be."

"And yet, it never is really a simple thing to forget, is it?" He spoke softly, remembering memories of his own.

"Oh, I don't mean she should completely forget Jeffrey and what they were to each other," Linda replied. "Of course not. If you really love someone, there is no way that you can forget that love, no matter how much time has gone by. But remembrance, after a time, should become a comforting feeling. It's not like that with my daughter. She has turned her memories into a fetish, almost into a cancer eating at her spirits."

There was a touch of anger in her voice that again surprised Greg. He felt Linda had probably been wanting to say these words for some time. She would never have said them to Karen, probably not even to her husband. Still, the anger was touched with sorrow.

"Perhaps if I were to extend a personal invitation . . ."

Linda was silent for a moment, and slowly he saw the anger, the hardness and the irritation fade from her face, leaving only that constant expression of sorrow that had always been there. She smiled and patted his hand.

"Thank you very much, Mr. Christopher; you've very kind. Forgive me for unburdening myself this way; sometimes it does help to get out the words that can't easily be said to others. When I look around me, at the people here enjoying themselves, and I think of my daughter . . . Well, I'm afraid there simply isn't anything we can do but wait and hope. It's really all up to Karen herself. Perhaps one day . . . ."

They sat together in silence for a moment longer, finishing their orange drinks, feeling the unrelieved heat of the dying afternoon, and then Linda rose, tossing her empty cup into a nearby wire basket.

"Well, thank you again, Mr. Christopher; it's really been very nice talking with you. Now I must get back to Karen before she begins to wonder what's happened to me."

"I do hope you'll be able to drop in to see the exhibit before you return home," he reminded her.

"I will," she promised, nodding decisively. "Yes, I'll be certain to do that; I'd really like very much to see it." She smiled and extended her hand to him. "You mustn't pay too much attention to an old woman's complaints. It's a very hot day, you know, and that makes one rather irritable."

She started slowly back down the Boardwalk towards the tall Victorian house, back to her crippled daughter, back to her prison.

# CHAPTER SIXTEEN

Steve was in front of the Seaquarium promptly at ten o'clock that evening, waiting for Greg. The lights still glowed in the building, but the heavy chain had been drawn across the entrance and the cashier's booth was dark. Greg was probably seeing that everything was in order before leaving. Steve lighted a cigarette, leaned against the railing in front of the entrance, and gazed out to sea.

There had still been no relief in the humid sultry weather with the setting of the sun, and Steve was perspiring in spite of his light clothing. There was neither moon nor stars, and it was impossible to distinguish the horizon. Looking across the ghostly white sands of the deserted beach, Steve could see only black velvet. The tumbling cascade of the surf and the occasional gleam of white wave crests were the only indication of the immense body of water that stretched before him.

The Boardwalk seemed strangely quiet; many

people, warned of the approaching storm by the weather forecasters, had returned home early, disgruntled by a second night of bad weather. The amusements were not doing their usual brisk business; the ferris wheel moved in its melancholy orbit with empty cages. The people lining the railing stared into the curtain of blackness that restricted the world. Without the reflection of distant city lights, the darkness over the sea was absolute and impenetrable.

Steve settled himself on a bench and propped his feet against the railing. He, too, was feeling somewhat uneasy, but his discomfort had little to do with the threatening weather. He was uncertain about what he was doing this evening.

Oppressed by his sense of guilt since the death of his mother, Steve had completely withdrawn into himself for the past few years, avoiding all social contact. He had even come to believe his mother's assertion that his relations with others had caused his problems. It was not that he feared—or even wanted—anything out of relations with others. Giving up friends and social activities was all part of his self-imposed penance. Perhaps it was a foolish and empty gesture, coming much too late, but some form of atonement had seemed necessary. It was something he simply had to do.

And yet, he had not hesitated to accept Greg's unexpected invitation for this evening. Was it possible he was finally beginning to realize he had punished himself long enough and could now begin living again? Or was it just that the loneliness was growing too intense for him to bear? There could be nothing wrong in accepting an invitation for a quiet drink. What was he afraid of? He was not looking for anything. Perhaps it was simply time for him to begin to laugh again.

One by one, the lights in the Seaquarium winked and went out. In a few moments he saw Greg, lightly dressed in slacks and an open sportshirt, step through the door, lock it behind him and, with a wave of his hand, start towards him. Steve rose as he approached.

"Glad to see you're here," Greg announced, extending his hand. "I was afraid you might have changed your mind."

Steve smiled, taking the strong hand in his. "Not polite to break an appointment. Besides, I wanted to come."

"Have a drink?"

"Sure thing."

"How about The Buccaneer?" Greg suggested.

Steve smiled again. "That place was my downfall last night, but okay with me."

"They've got a pretty good combo, if you like that sort of thing."

"Oh, so that's what the noise was all about; I thought it was just the swirling of my head. Sounds like you don't particularly care for combo music."

Greg shrugged. "No, not particularly; not my kind. But it's not a bad place. They have a singer who's a good friend of mine, and she'll be pleased to see us. At least, the place is air-conditioned."

They started along the Boardwalk to the tall, plush hotel just beyond the lagoon. Steve thrust his hands into his pockets and was aware of a feeling of deep satisfaction, something he had not experienced in far too long a time. Their steps echoed on the worn wooden boards; the heat seemed to have pressed a blanket of silence upon everything.

"Where'd everybody go?" Steve wondered, glancing at the comparatively few people strolling the Boardwalk. "I don't believe I've ever seen the Boardwalk so deserted this time of night."

"That's true," Greg agreed. "The merchants are having a pretty rough time of it today. The Seaquarium dropped off badly, too." He glanced at the black starless sky. "The weather, I suppose. Something uncomfortable in the air drives a lot of people home. I don't know why, but people have the idea that a storm at the seashore is much more dangerous than anywhere else. The alarmists at the weather bureau don't help, of course; they like to build these things up, knowing people do enjoy hearing bad news. This storm won't even be here for another twenty-four hours or so, at the earliest."

The lounge of The Buccaneer was dimly lighted and nicely appointed, but somehow too large and noisy to provide an air of intimacy. The large bar was circular in form and thus quite convenient for making "contacts;" a quartet performed rather jarringly on a platform in the bar's center. They took seats in a booth as far from the noise as possible and ordered cold beer. It seemed the only possible drink in such weather. Steve sensed something familiar in a heavyset man seated in one of the darker booths along the wall. He recognized Clayton from the bar car on the train. He was seated with one arm about the bare shoulders of a very blonde, much too young girl, and despite the air-conditioning, his face gleamed with perspiration. He whispered something into the girl's ear, and they both laughed loudly. Catching sight of Steve, Clayton winked again like a pornographic doll, nodded his head to his companion and rather obscenely ran his tongue over his thick lips. Seeing Steve's male companion, he lost interest and returned to his flirtation. Pretending not to have seen him, Steve took a long, satisfying drink of the ice-cold beer.

"You enjoy your work at the Seaquarium, don't you?" he asked.

Licking at the foam on his lips, Greg nodded. "Yeah, I really do. I'm content to be where I am, doing what I'm doing. Oh, of course, I can think of some improvements . . . a bigger tank, some really unusual exhibits, but we're doing all right. What more can I ask?"

"Most people manage to think of something," Steve remarked. "I suppose the human race is chronically difficult to please."

"What do you do, Steve?"

Steve was suddenly absurdly embarrassed by the prosiac nature of his own means of making a living. "Nothing nearly as interesting as you, I'm afraid. I've a fairly good position with an insurance agency."

"No dreams? No further ambitions?"

Steve frowned slightly. "I guess not. Not any more, at any rate." He raised his voice to be heard above the supposed music of the combo, who had swung into a particularly raucous rock number. "I used to, of course, like everyone else. Travel to the four corners of the earth, adventure, that sort of thing. I wanted to be an archaeologist, then an artist, an actor, finally a writer."

"What happened?"

"I grew up, I guess. I saw myself getting older and accomplishing nothing. Now I just want to make enough money to live on fairly comfortably, and do pretty much as I please, and I've managed that."

"Married?"

Steve shook his head. "No. I was once, some years ago, but it was pretty bad, and it didn't last long. I don't think I'd care to try it again. I have an apartment of my own in the city, and it wouldn't be easy to change my solitary habits at this stage. How about you?"

"I live here all year 'round now," Greg told him. "My work's become a full-year business. Never been married, and never expect to be. Guess some people just aren't meant for it."

"Were you in the service?" Steve asked, and did not miss the momentary hesitation before Greg replied.

"Yeah. Vietnam. You?"

"Nothing like that. I was in the navy for a while."

"Like it?"

Steve shook his head. "No. I suppose it isn't really a bad life, if you like regimentation and not having to think for yourself." He smiled and added, "Like marriage, maybe; as you say, some people just aren't meant for it." He drank again, and Greg signaled for two more beers. "I've always liked the sea, though. It must be nice, living here all year."

"It gets a little solitary in the winter," Greg pointed out with a smile. "Don't get many visitors then, only the locals. Some of the hotels even close down."

"That wouldn't bother me," Steve assured him. "I've always liked being alone. I've had lots of it; it's one of the things you just get used to."

Sensing a sudden touch of sadness in his voice, Greg looked more closely at Steve; the room was too dark for him to distinguish any shadings in Steve's face.

"I wonder if there may be some things you never really get used to. But it isn't bad here, and of course I've got plenty to do to keep me busy; that goes on, no matter what the season." He paused to light a cigarette. "There's something restful about the sea in the colder months of the year, even if the water is more violent. It has a color, a vigorousness about it that it doesn't have in summer. It's like people who slow down in the heat of the summer months, and only really get back to normal when the colder weather sets in. Maybe it's the absence of people that makes it so nice. Have you been here before?"

Steve nodded. "Many times. Used to come down here with my family every summer when I was a kid."

"Your family dead?"

Steve drank again before responding, and Greg could see the subject was an unpleasant one for him; a burst of the music drowned out his reply.

"Sorry," Greg said. "This isn't the best place in the world for a quiet conversation."

"I said my parents are dead. My sister lives out of state, and I don't get to see very much of her. How about you?"

Greg thoughtfully blew through his lips. "I'm an only child. My parents live some distance away, and I don't see much of them, either." The music of the combo stopped at this point and Greg glanced at the performing platform; the group was leaving. "It's time for Bea's turn, the singer I told you about."

The combo's place on the platform was now assumed by a pair clad in costumes of the Gay Nineties. At the piano sat a small, wiry man, the gray hairs outnumbering the black on his bullet-shaped head, his bow tie clipped in a perfectly straight line, green elastic garters on his shirt sleeves, a red-ribboned straw hat perched jauntily on his head. The singer, a flamboyant vocalist of what is affectionately (or contemptuously, depending on your point of view) referred to as of the "old school," whom Steve vaguely remembered from his prior visit, stood at the microphone, her ample figure tightly encased in a black sequined gown, her long golden hair elaborately curled and topped with enormous feathers, her round powdered face bright and shining with enthusiasm and friendliness.

"Bea and Joe," Greg identified them. "They've been working here for eight summers now, and Bea always swears this is her last."

"Why?" Steve asked. "She must have something, if they keep bringing her back."

Greg stared into his glass of beer for a moment before responding, and his voice had suddenly become serious.

"Well, Steve, like most of us, Bea has an ambition that just won't leave her alone. She wants to sing opera. With the end of every summer, she announces she won't be back next season because she's leaving all this behind and going into the work she feels she's really suited for. Either she's planning to join some opera troupe, or she's going off to Europe to study. Of course, she's always right back up there when the place opens again."

"Is she good?"

"In this sort of thing, she's up there next to Tessie O'Shea. When it comes to opera . . . well . . ."

"And she doesn't know it?"

"Oh, I suppose she does, but knowing it and admitting it are two different things. Her defense is to talk constantly about her plans, to anyone who will listen. She has to hold on to her dreams, like we all do." He looked up at the singer and returned her warm, welcoming smile. "I wonder how much longer she'll be able to manage that."

They were silent as Bea sang and Steve, intrigued by Greg's account of the woman and her dreams, listened with close attention. He noted immediately that Joe did surprisingly well with the somewhat out-of-tune piano, swinging into any tune the singer began, his stubby fingers never still, satisfying most requests thrown their way. Bea's songs were beerhall sentimental favorites, Irish ballads, cry-in-your-beer laments. She sang them in a loud and brassy fashion, without artistic contrivance, as they were meant to be sung, her rich and fullbodied voice rarely required the amplification of her microphone. She obviously enjoyed herself, and that enjoyment was transmitted to the audience, most of whom paused in their conversation to listen and cheer her on as she stood waving her feather boa, swaying her broad hips, her face shining with pleasure. She was a delight.

The set lasted for half an hour, and when it was over and the singer prepared to leave the platform, Greg raised his hand to her. "You don't mind if I ask her over for a moment, do you? She'd be disappointed if I didn't."

305

"No, of course not," Steve assured her. "I'd like to meet her."

Her pink plumes bouncing jauntily, her face brightened by a warm smile, Bea approached the table, brushing her flowing boas behind her, as Steve and Greg rose from their seats. "Why, hello there, Greg," she greeted in her musical voice. "Nice to see you again."

Greg offered her a chair. "How are you, Bea?"

"Just fine, Greg." She carefully arranged her voluminous skirts and seated herself; the air suddenly became pleasantly more fragrant. "And you? Haven't seen much of you lately."

"Very busy season," he informed her. "There's always lots to do. This is Steve Conroy. Steve, this is Beatrice."

Bea extended a rather plump, heavily ringed hand, and smiled again. "Stage name, of course. Real one ends in a 'ski.' Too long for a marquee and nobody can pronounce it, anyway. Glad to meet you."

"Thank you," Steve responded, holding the hand for a moment. "I really enjoyed your singing."

Pleased, Bea bowed her head as the two men returned to their seats. "Thank you, kind sir. It's always nice to be appreciated. Here on vacation, Steve?"

"More or less," Steve replied.

"He's staying at The Cloud," Greg offered.

"Good! I'm singing there at the Festival tomorrow evening. You'll be there?"

"Now I will, yes."

"Why can't you ever say nice things like that?" she asked, turning to Greg and lightly slapping his hand. "What do you think of Hawkins' Cove, Steve?"

"Oh, it's nothing new to me," he assured her. "I've been coming here since I was a kid; it has a kind of special meaning for me. I've always liked it. Sorry I never seemed to get around to seeing you before, but I never really patronized this place."

"Well, I'm glad you managed to get around to it now," Bea said, "because it'll be your last chance."

Under the table, Steve felt the pressure of Greg's leg against his own, while a smile crossed his lips. "Why is that, Bea? Going away?"

Bea put a graceful beringed hand to her carefully dressed hair; the hand was surprisingly slender for one of her size. "As a matter of fact, I am, Greg. This will finally be my last summer here. Next year I'll be with an opera troupe out on the coast. Season starts in May, through October. Everything's just about set, all I have to do is sign the papers. When I finish here on Labor Day, I'm through with this sort of thing. I'll spend the winter studying. And only real music, not the crap I sing here."

"Oh, come on, now, be honest," Greg protested. "You know you enjoy singing this so-called crap."

"Well, maybe." She shrugged her shoulders. "I suppose I enjoy singing just about anything, and I like making people happy. But this isn't real music. Anybody can do what I'm doing here."

"But not half as well," Greg insisted. "Not everybody has your flair, Bea."

"Well, of course not!" Bea agreed, then laughed

307

heartily at her own conceit, her beautiful white hand again slapping Greg's. "You see, you can say nice things if you've a mind to!"

"Won't you have a drink?"

She shook her head. "No, thanks, dear. Send one over to Joe, though, if you'd like; he'll appreciate it more than I would."

Greg caught the attention of the bartender and pointed to the accompanist, who was seated alone in a booth apart, poring over his music; the familiar sign was easily interpreted.

"I should imagine they'll miss you here," Steve said, turning again to the singer.

"I hope they will," she assured him. "I've been here long enough to be declared a local treasure. But they'll forget soon enough. They'll get someone else, a little younger, prettier, a little smaller in the weight department, and poor old Bea will become nothing but a hazy memory."

"Oh, now it's time to cut the bull, Bea," Greg said, looking at her with an affectionate smile. "You'll be right back at the old stand next summer, singing your heart out up there on the platform, and we'll all be glad to see you."

"In other words, you don't believe me?"

"You're the girl who's cried 'goodbye' once too often. You'll never leave us, Bea. It's your home; you'd be lost anywhere else."

Bea pretended irritation, but Steve could see the slight twitch of pleased humor at the corners of her mouth. "Well, we'll see, we'll see!" She looked at Greg for a moment, frowned, and added, "No, somehow I know I won't be back, Greg; I just feel it." She rose from her chair. "Well, dears, nice talking with you, but the combo's about to start, and I want to preserve my hearing." She smiled, leaning closer to Steve. "That's just between us music lovers, of course!"

With a swirl of her spangled skirts, she was gone, stopping at various tables to greet other friends as she returned to her dressing room and the raucous music began again.

"She's delightful!" Steve commented.

"More so the better you know her. She really would be missed if she were to leave here. But no fear of that. She'll be back." He frowned; for a moment his voice again lost its lightness. "She's got to come back. She can't risk facing the truth." He tossed off his sudden gloom with a light laugh. "What the hell, let's have another beer!"

The two sailors walked in silence for a time, each busy with his own thoughts, and only the gentle surge of the surf disturbed them. It had been a rather curious evening for them, and Paul in particular was not very happy about it. He was galled by the omission of that sexual activity so important to his good humor, and he was displeased by his friend's strange attitude. Paul had tagged along with Michael and Emily from the time he met them on the beach, although Michael was obviously not particularly pleased to have his company, something Paul simply found impossible to understand; it had never happened to him before. They'd had dinner together and then gone to a movie. Throughout, Michael had been rather sullen and difficult, and it was only towards the end of the evening that Paul suddenly realized Emily had already become someone quite special to his friend.

The situation at first amused Paul. Michael was really incredibly naive. Had he learned nothing from their association, from all the girls they'd screwed together? Sure, this Emily seemed a nice enough kid, and she probably was fairly decent, like so many nice girls were, to a point. To a point. That was the crux of the matter. Paul wasn't fooled by her, or by any dame. He had seen and known too many of them. They were all the same. Even the most supposedly decent would put out at the right time to the right guy, and he saw no reason to believe that Emily was any different.

It had in fact not been a particularly pleasant evening for Michael, but Paul's presence was only part of it, for he was struggling with an emotional problem he had not encountered before. He could not quite understand his feelings towards Emily, this strange combination of tenderness, of concern, of a peculiar desire to protect. (That was silly, of course; protect against what or whom?) It seemed more closely connected, in some strange way, with home, the farm, the purity of his own family, than with the attitudes he had always held towards the girls he had known with Paul, the only girls, in fact, that he had ever really known. He found himself purposely turning his mind from any intrusive thoughts of lust and intimacy that had, since his entrance into the navy, become natural for him whenever he was with a girl. He stumbled mentally over the world "love." That was just silly. It couldn't be. It was much too soon for anything like that. Well, wasn't it? He frankly didn't know. He had never been in love.

Paul hadn't been very much help. In view of his worldliness in matters of girls, he should have realized that Michael and Emily preferred to be alone, but once he had found them on the beach, he had insisted on remaining with them, through dinner (even picking up the tab) and the movie. It wasn't possible he didn't sense that this was a different situation from their usual roll in the hay. For the first time since that day in the square at Ponce, Michael found himself actually irritated by Paul's presence.

No, he had to be honest. It was more than just this unwelcome intrusion. Paul was too attractive, too charming. The girls always went for him without even really noticing Michael. It came now as something of a revelation to Michael, he had never before been really concerned about his friend's impact on someone else. Jealousy was an experience unpleasantly new to him.

Paul felt something had to be said. "You really go for her?"

Michael nodded. "I guess I do."

Paul scratched his head in bewilderment. "I don't know. Maybe I just don't understand. We've known lots of girls before. What makes this one so special?"

"She just is, that's all." Michael looked intently at his friend, the sharp profile strong and white against the dark sky; he could understand why the girls always went for Paul. "We're buddies Paul, and I want it to stay that way. I don't want any trouble between us." He felt a bit embarrassed. "Keep your hands off, will you?"

Paul slowed his step; frowning, he looked down the beach. He had never heard Michael speak this way before; hell, he'd only known the girl for one day! "Sure, Mike, if that's the way you want it."

"It's the way I want it," Michael assured

311

him and, automatically added, "It's Michael, not Mike."

Paul shrugged. "Well, okay then. I can get lots of others." He extended his hand, which Michael gladly took in his own.

They were close to the house now, moving in a dark and sibilantly silent world. Both felt unusually tired, and the silence was somehow comforting, as was the renewed feeling of companionship between them. Michael reached into his waistband and took out his handkerchief, running it across the perspiration on his face.

"Christ, it's hot as hell!"

Paul glanced up towards their dark window, and chuckled. "It's gonna seem funny to sleep alone tonight."

"Do you good to give it a rest," Michael smiled.

"Maybe so," Paul agreed, "but it sure as hell won't be nearly as much fun. Hell, if word about this gets around, it's apt to ruin my reputation."

They both laughed, and as they walked on, Paul placed a warm hand on his friend's shoulder; the brief strain between them was gone. They walked on in silence again for several steps until Paul, again glancing at the house, spoke his thoughts.

"I wonder what she's like."

"Who?" Michael asked.

Paul nodded to a lighted window on the first floor. "That crippled girl in there."

"Oh, come on, Paul, you're not thinking . . ."

Paul laughed. "Shit, no!"

"I didn't even notice she's crippled," Michael admitted.

Paul nodded. "I notice everything about a girl the first time I meet her, no matter what she's like.

She sits in a wheel chair." He thoughtfully pursed his lips. "There's something funny about her."

"How, funny? Just because she didn't get all hot and bothered when she saw you?"

Paul grinned. "Don't be so sure; sometimes they hide it." He continued after a moment. "I don't know, there's something—well, funny there. Did you take a good look at her? Hell, she's no chicken, sure, but she's not as old as she looks. And she never seems to go anyplace. . . ."

"How can she? She can't walk."

"That doesn't have to stop her. There are lots of people who can't walk, but they don't lock themselves up the way she does. She could wheel herself down to the Boardwalk with no trouble, couldn't she, or have her mother wheel her? All she does is go down to the end of the point in the morning and look at the ocean. And that expression on her face, as though she isn't even there, as though she's miles away. Maybe years away."

"We don't know what's behind it all," Michael mentioned.

"Yeah. I suppose. Shit, the way she lives, she might just as well be dead."

They mounted the steps and Michael suggested they have a cigarette before going up to the warm bedroom. They sat side by side on the top step, silent for the moment, staring out at the curtain of smothering blackness, feeling some of the depression of the humid atmosphere. Only the ever present sound of the sea disturbed the silence. The entire world seemed to be asleep. Or dead.

"Your hitch is up in a couple months, isn't it?" Paul asked.

"Yeah. Yours will be soon, too."

313

"Another six months for me. Gonna sign up again?"

After a moment, Michel replied. "I don't know. How about you?"

"Sure thing." Paul shrugged. "Why not? What the fuck else is there for me to do? Go back to that fucking sewer I came from, fight with my sister, watch my mother drink herself to death, wait for my old man to get out of jail, and maybe go right back in again? Shit, I'm better off where I am now."

"I've been thinking about it some," Michael confessed. "I just don't know, not yet. I'd like to go to school someplace, maybe learn a profession. Maybe agriculture school. Settle down. Be nice to have a home of my own some place. I could always go back to the farm. Be mine some day, I guess."

Paul looked at him, uneasy and vaguely displeased. "You've never talked like this before."

"Maybe I never felt like this before."

"It's that Emily, isn't it?"

A long drag on his cigarette brightened the fine, somewhat delicate features of Michael's face. "Maybe. Part of it, anyway. When you meet a girl like that, Paul, your thoughts change. Things look a lot different."

"Can't prove it by me. Gotta be an idiot to base your whole life on one broad," Paul insisted. "There's not a woman born who won't trick and fool a man whenever she gets the chance."

"Maybe the kind you've known, Paul," Michael agreed. "But not Emily."

"How the hell can you tell that?" Paul demanded, becoming impatient and increasingly more disturbed by his friend's peculiar new

314

attitude. "Oh, shit, Michael, you know a girl for one day and already you're settling down with her and raising kids!"

"Maybe that's the way it's supposed to happen, Paul," Michael told him, determined not to permit Paul's words to raise his anger again. "You just . . . know. Some day you'll find out."

Irked by the sudden tone of superiority in Michael's tone, Paul said harshly, "Are you trying to tell me about girls, Mike? Hell, I've shacked up with more girls than you'll ever get to know the rest of your life."

"Sure. I know you have," Michael agreed. "The Casanova of the Fleet. You come into sight, and women for miles around start spreading their legs. I'm not talking about that kind of girl, Paul. I'm talking about the kind of girl you fall in love with. That's something different."

For the first time in their relationship, Paul suddenly found himself uncomfortable in Michael's company. His friend had changed; in a matter of a few hours, he had suddenly entered a new world, and Paul suspected that he himself would never be able to follow him there.

"I'll miss you if you don't sign up again."

"I'll miss you, too, Paul," Michael assured him. "But what the hell, we'll keep in touch, write, see each other sometimes."

"Yeah. Sure you will." Famous last words, he thought. Everyone who ever wore a uniform had said the same words to his buddy and sincerely meant them . . . at the time.

Paul flicked his cigarette down the steps and rose to his feet. "I guess I'm kinda tired. Think I'll turn in. Coming?"

"In a minute," Michael replied.

Paul looked down for a moment at the seated form of his friend, remembering their nights in Rio, in Trinidad, in New York, wondering who would take Michael's place on future nights in other parts of the world. Would it really be the same? He stepped quickly into the silent house and moved slowly up the stairs, suddenly very tired. Tired or the beginning of loneliness?

Michael sat alone on the steps. There was a great deal he had to think about. Life had suddenly become very much more serious for him; he felt he had grown considerably older in the course of this single eventful day.

He was certain of one thing: he was right about Emily. She was different. This was the kind of girl he would like to have for his own. He smiled slightly. Yes, the kind of girl he could even take home to mother, and that couldn't be said about any of the other girls he and Paul had known. Just how serious was he willing to get? Hell, the entire business might prove to be nothing but a big bust. Emily might not even feel the same way, although he suspected she did.

His cigarette made a broad red-tipped arc on its way to the beach. He sighed, rose and stood for a moment on the top step, stretching himself, silently cursing the heat.

"You're quite right, young man." The voice came to him from the shadowed dark corner of the verandah.

"I beg your pardon?"

He moved closer to the voice, walking down the verandah. He could vaguely see someone was sitting in the rocking chair against the wall.

"Don't think I've been eavesdropping, young man. I've just been sitting out here for hours, looking at the night. It's too hot for sleep. I couldn't help overhearing your conversation."

"I'm afraid I don't . . ."

"I'm Mrs. Hawkins. Old Mrs. Hawkins. I know it's very dark here, unless you're accustomed to it, as I am. You're the blond sailor, aren't you? I haven't met you as yet. I know your friend, and I rather like him, even though I don't approve of some of his views."

"My name's Michael."

"Good name. Simple. Solid. Nothing fancy like so many of the silly names you hear nowadays. Reminds you of knights and chivalry. I had a nice chat with your friend just this morning. You mustn't think I'm prying, young man. I always have to remind people of that. An old woman like me doesn't care to spend too much time sleeping and I like to sit out here at night in the dark, all by myself and look at the sea, even if I can't really see it. It's restful after all the noise and confusion of the day. I've grown up by the sea, you know. It's a very strange night, isn't it?"

"Yes, it's very uncomfortable," Michael agreed.

"Women . . . of a certain kind . . . are very important to your friend, aren't they?"

Michael leaned against the verandah railing and crossed his arms; his eyes, now more accustomed to staring into the darkness under the verandah, could just make out the form of the little old woman rocking gently in her chair. "I'm afraid so."

"Oh, that's nothing to be ashamed of," Ethel insisted. "I like a man with an honest appetite for women. Within reason, of course; everything must be within reason. Today it's supposed to be immoral, but I say it's right smack against human nature for a man not to lift a skirt when he can."

Michael laughed.

"I don't shock you, I hope?" she asked, joining him in his laughter. "Old people are allowed a little extra liberty in speaking, and I take all the extras I can get. I'm afraid that sometimes I take advantage of it just to shock people a little. Of course, I suppose some of my terms may be a bit antiquated."

"No, I'm not shocked at all," Michael assured her. "It's just that morals and that sort of thing aren't quite as strict today as you seem to think they are."

"Well, that may be," she agreed. "It's easy for me to get out of touch with things, sitting in this house all day long. Still, you are quite right, you know. There's a time for fun, and then there's a time when you just want to find the right girl and settle down with her. Your friend will come to it himself, in time. I hope it won't be too late. He's really a very nice boy."

"He's had an unfortunate background," Michael explained. "That probably makes a difference."

"Of course it does. That only makes it all the more difficult but more important, too. You hear a great deal of nonsense about such backgrounds instilling character in a person, as if those who are more fortunate have no need of character. But it's boys like your friend who really need love, more than anyone, and who spend all their time looking for it, but always in the wrong places, because they don't even realize that's what they really want. They think one woman after another will always satisfy them, but that isn't so. Not in the long run. We all of us need something lasting,

318

something that gives us purpose and a sure, solid source of happiness. Too often it's just too late before such people realize they've been searching in the wrong way."

There was a sudden flash of lightning that for a moment fully revealed the gentle old woman, all white; for a moment, Michael had the frightening thought that he was talking with a ghost.

"Maybe the storm's going to break at last," he mentioned, staring up into the re-darkened sky.

"No, no," Ethel assured him. "Not for a while yet. You learn to tell, when you live by the sea as long as I have. These storms like to tease us, to remind us that we have no control over them. They hover about our heads for a while, and then break when we least expect it. That was just heat lightning; no thunder. The storm is still a ways off. We're just being prepared for it . . . Well, I won't keep you any longer, young man. You're probably tired; even the young can feel the effects of too much heat. Go on to your bed and your pleasant dreams. May they all come true."

"Thank you, Ma'am. You're very kind."

"I'm too old to be anything but kind," Ethel chuckled, "so I might just as well be kind. Be sure to bring that girl of yours to the Festival tomorrow night; I want to meet her."

"I'll do that," he promised. "Good night, Mrs. Hawkins."

"Good night, my boy. Good night."

Michael left the old woman alone in the dark and went upstairs. The room was in darkness and Paul was already in his own bed, breathing evenly, although Michael somehow doubted that he was already asleep. Nevertheless, he undressed in the dark so as not to disturb him. Perhaps he felt embarrassed by the events of the day and wanted to avoid any further discussion. He seemed to feel Paul's eyes on him, and he wondered what his friend was thinking.

Ethel remained alone on the verandah while the great house slipped into slumber. She had her thoughts for company, through those long and lonely hours of the darkness.

# CHAPTER SEVENTEEN

Margaret slipped out of her bed and reached for the faded robe hung over the back of the chair. It was useless to try to sleep. She had lain for hours, staring into the darkness, tossing and squirming, the perspiration-dampened sheets gathering beneath her in uncomfortable lumps. It was the heat, she told herself; who could sleep in such humidity? Her windows were wide open, but there was not even the hint of a breeze over the ocean. Again she thought that perhaps air-conditioning might not be such a bad idea, then dismissed the thought. It hardly mattered any longer.

No, it was not the heat at all, she finally admitted to herself. Her mind was too full, she was too worried. Sleep will come to the weary no matter what the weather, but it flees from those with a guilty conscience or a troubled heart. It was no use to go on trying.

Wrapping her robe about herself, she softly opened the door and passed through the corridor into the silent sitting room, where the two lamps kept burning throughout the night cast dark shadows up to the lofty ceiling. The lobby was empty, as she expected; the night clerk slept comfortably in his chair behind the desk. For a moment, she thought of awakening and reprimanding him, but what was the purpose? There was little enough for him to do at this time of night, anyway.

Passing along beside the desk, she opened the door leading down into the cellar, pressed the light-switch and carefully started down the rickety wooden steps, leaning on the shaky railing. Silence somehow always seemed more intense in the cellar of the house. Perhaps it was the gathered dust, the stillness of the many years that accumulates in places that are but little used. The cellar was musty, as though the same air that Captain Natheniel had breathed still lurked in its dark corners.

She stopped at the foot of the stairs and peered with narrowed eyes into the darkness. The dim light cast shadows upon the wine racks, the asbestos-covered heating pipes, the pot-bellied furnace (she had long been meaning to install a more modern system of heating), and the jumbled mass of discarded materials that cellars accumulate over a century. Everything seemed in order. There was not a sound.

Margaret's steps made only a whisper as she crossed the cold stone floor to the far wall against which the sea had battered now for a hundred years. Reaching out her hand, she lightly touched the wall with her fingers. Was there just the slightest trace of moisture, or was it merely the cold of the stone? The wall felt so firm, so solid, as though it had been mortared into place only yesterday. She could not feel that weakening that Martin had warned her about. The floor upon which she stood, surely it was as sturdy as when first put into its place?

She stepped back again and stared into the shadows. She could not see these things, but perhaps others could. What looked normal and safe to her perhaps revealed its flaws only to trained eyes. The house was crumbling. That's what they said. Not only Martin, but those other experts whom he had called upon for consultation.

"Nothing can be done about it. This just isn't the place for a house of this kind. Surprised it's stood as long as it has. Nope, sorry Mrs. Hawkins, but it's too dangerous. Not only to yourself, but to all about here. Got to condemn it. Maybe we can shore it up to keep it in place through the winter, but in the spring it'll have to come down. I wouldn't recommend you spend the winter here, though. Can't tell what these coast storms will do to the place . . ."

Margaret had been listening to the radio all day, tuned to the weather reports. There was a storm moving up the coast toward them right now, with heavy rains, strong winds and high tides. Nothing like those dangerous winter storms, of course, but, still, it did make one a bit uneasy.

The news was not really all that sudden. For some time now, she had sensed stresses in the house that seemed rather ominous, but she had postponed any action first until spring, then until summer, then until the end of the season. Perhaps she had known all along and was merely trying desperately to postpone the inevitable. If we ignore something long enough, it may go away of its own, and there we would be, feeling rather foolish, having worried ourselves sick for no reason at all.

But now she knew there was reason enough. After a hundred years, the sea which Captain Nathaniel had so magnificently mastered, had finally struck back in the way that would have hurt him the most. As always, the sea would be the victor. They would all have to leave. They would have to surrender to the sea that point of land upon which their family had lived through so many years. The wrecking ball would crash into the sides of the house, the timbers would crumble, and this old house of so many memories would slip into the cold embrace of the sea. . . .

The cellar was silent, save for the somewhat muted roaring of the sea and the gentle sound of a woman's tears.

Dawn was already beginning to brighten the cloud-covered sky when Greg and Steve finally left the lounge of The Buccaneer. Feeling a bit heady from the considerable amount of beer they had consumed, they started along the Boardwalk back toward The Cloud. The slightest touch of a morning breeze had moved in from the northeast, but it was like a breath blown over a blazing fire, and it brought little comfort. The Boardwalk was deserted at this early hour. Gulls wheeled over the empty stretch of beach; a sole fisherman sat motionless on the jetty, connected to the mysteries of the sea by the fragile contact of his line.

They stopped for a moment at the railing and looked out to the sea. The horizon could just be discerned in the faint light of dawn, and the sea and sky were uniform in their grayness. The thick clouds were swollen but motionless.

Greg leaned with both hands against the railing and stared into the silent grayness. "Mile after mile after mile," he muttered, "filled with an inconceivable variety of life. Rather hard to imagine, isn't it?"

"You know a great deal about it, don't you?" Steve asked.

Greg shrugged. "It's my business. But there's a hell of a lot I've still got to learn. I suppose I have time." His voice lowered. "I've got nothing but time."

"Do I detect just a hint of bitterness?" Steve asked with a slight smile.

Greg returned the smile. "I suppose so. Maybe I'm looking for sympathy."

"Okay. What do you want sympathy for?"

"I don't even know," Greg laughed. "Maybe for life in general. It can all seem so . . . pointless. No!" he quickly added. "That sounds trite and juvenile. I guess I really don't know what I mean. The dawn does it to me."

"Hey, you're the guy who's completely satisfied with his life, remember?"

"What the hell, so I lied a little. I wonder if anyone is every completely satisfied with life."

"You're doing exactly the kind of work you want to do, and doing it well. Doesn't that mean something?"

"Oh, sure," Greg agreed. "At least, it helps. It makes the dissatisfaction a little easier to bear."

"What else do you want?"

There was a slight pause. "What do I want?" Greg mused for a moment, as they watched the seemingly slow progress of a large black ship on the horizon. "Nothing unusual, I suppose. Companionship. A certain amount of love. A sense that what I'm doing is really important. Oh, shit, I don't know. Maybe that's why I don't expect to find it." Smiling, he turned to Steve. "It's the surroundings, the dawn, the silence. It has that effect on the human race. A primeval yearning going back to our earliest beginnings. Like the subconscious desire to return to the safety of the womb. What the hell, it all ends the same way. Begins in the womb and ends in the tomb; funny the words should be so similar."

They continued along the Boardwalk, a bit unsteady after their liquid evening. They felt little need for talk, and the silence was comforting to them. It was long since Steve had strolled in such wordless companionship with anyone. They reached the termination of the Boardwalk and, abandoning the single road that curved out to the point, started along the hard-packed sand. The Hawkins house loomed against the brightening gray sky like a misty sketch on the paper jacket of a Gothic thriller. Steve glanced up to the gabled roof as they approached. The pointed iron spikes of the Widow's Walk were like rusted spears aimed at the gray underbelly of the sky.

"Widow's Walks have always fascinated me," he mentioned. "They seem to have an inescapable aura of the past about them. I imagine you would have a nice view from up there."

"Never been up?"

Steve shook his head.

"The door is right next to my own room," Greg told him. "I go up there quite often. It's cool, gets the breeze from all sides. It's off limits to the other guests, but Miss Meg doesn't mind my using it. I'd be glad to show it to you, but I'm afraid the view wouldn't be very impressive on such a cloudy morning."

"I'd like to see it anyway," Steve mentioned. "I prefer cloudy mornings to bright and sunny ones."

"So do I," Greg laughed. "Especially right at dawn. They seem quieter, more restful, urging people to relax just a little longer before starting in with the problems of another day."

"We're not the only ones, either," Steve mentioned, and indicated a solitary form walking slowly on the beach on the far side of the house. "That's Johnny, isn't it? Doesn't that kid ever sleep?"

"The resilience of the young, I suppose. He's sort of a strange kid, anyway—sensitive, moody. But I like him. He's a little mixed up, and I think he's got a touch of hero-worship where I'm concerned. He's quite a help at the Seaquarium. A lot of the horseshoe crabs are his catches, you know. We've really got more of them then we need, but I don't like to disappoint him. He's nuts about the sea. I've been sort of hoping that some day he might come in with me; I could use a really good all-time assistant."

They talked more softly as they mounted the stairs of the deserted verandah; Greg noticed Ethel's rocking chair was empty. The lobby was also deserted, save for the clerk who sat asleep behind the desk. They climbed quietly up the stairs.

"Come on up," Greg suggested. "I'll show you the Walk."

They climbed past the second level and on up to the floor where Greg lived.

"This is my room here," Greg said, indicating his door. "The stairs to the walk are right here." He opened a smaller neighboring door, disclosing a brief flight of dark, extremely narrow steps. "There's no light, and the stairs are a bit tricky; here, better give me your hand."

Steve felt Greg's firm grip on his hand, and he stumbled his way slowly behind him up the stairs, aided only slightly by the faint light through the open door. There was a mustiness in the air, as though the past had gathered here to preserve its memories. In a moment, he felt the sultry morning heat on his face again.

"Well, here we are," Greg announced.

They were suddenly thrust into a world of grayness. The lower, hovering clouds seemed almost close enough to touch; their gray edges enclosed patches of ominous black, here and there streaked with a dash of billious yellow. The rolling swells of the sea were more easily observed from this vantage point, moving gently in humped rolls like the backs of a school of great white whales. The beach was empty, and from their position the Boardwalk could not be seen, lending a stronger affinity with the past, when this lonely platform had so often been the scene of anxiety, concern and hope. At this level, the air seemed slightly less heavy.

The beer suddenly went to Steve's head again. He had a sense of dangling unsafely from some great height, and put out a hand to grasp Greg's arm until the spell of vertigo passed.

"It's . . . a little unsettling."

"Yes, it's really higher than you might think from below," Greg conceded. "Sometimes, when my room gets just too hot for sleeping, I spend the night up here."

Steve suddenly became aware that he was still holding Greg's arm, and the realization was strangely embarrassing. He released himself and walked up to the telescope. Its stand was rusted, and there were green stains upon the black tubing itself.

"Is this any good?" he asked.

"You better believe it," Greg replied. "It's getting a little battered now, as you can see, but there's nothing wrong with the lens. Finely ground, from Europe somewhere. It's quite powerful, as you would expect from the good Captain Nathaniel." He glanced out at the gray horizon. "Look. There's a freighter out there. We should be able to pick it up. Let me get to it."

Steve made way for Greg as he stepped up to the instrument. His eye fixed to the glass, Greg quickly and expertly whirled the telescope until he found his sighting and then, with intense concentration, placed the scope in position.

"There. That's it. Take a look."

Steve placed his eyes to the surprisingly cold rim of the telescope, but could see nothing but the gray swells of the sea, almost close enough to feel their spray. "I don't see a thing," he said. "You sure it's working?"

Greg laughed. "Landlubber! You don't speak of a telescope as 'working;' it's not one of those Boardwalk viewers where you have to drop a quarter into a slot before you can see anything. You've nudged it off center; just a little touch can do that. Here, let me show you."

Greg stood behind Steve and, placing his arms

about him, grasped the telescope with both hands, attempting to move the dark tube into proper position again. His cheek brushed against Steve, and Steve felt himself flush at the expected contact.

"There. I think that's got it now," Greg said, holding the telescope in position. "Just hold it steady, and if you still don't see anything, move it very slightly to the left, and then very slightly to the right, until you get the ship in the sight. Just slightly, now; it can't be off by more than a hair."

Steve at first still could see nothing, only the gray union of sea and sky, and he felt childishly embarrassed at his inability to do what Greg had so easily done. He moved the tube first a bit to the left, as instructed, but found only the same gray emptiness; very slowly, with Greg's hands still tightly holding the tube to prevent too strong a movement, he inched to the right. The large freighter suddenly sprang into his view, so unexpectedly close and large that Steve was startled; it seemed that the great iron ship was headed directly towards him. He recoiled a step and fell heavily against Greg, whose arms still encircled both him and the telescope.

"I'm . . . I'm sorry," he stammered, confused and startled. "I didn't expect it to be that close."

Greg said nothing, and Steve suddenly felt the tightening of his strong arms and Greg's warm, beer-scented breath on his flushed face. He turned his head and found himself looking directly into Greg's eyes, eyes that revealed a peculiar mixture of surprise and seriousness. The face came closer to him, and then Steve felt Greg's warm, moist lips on his own, briefly, lightly, and then they were removed again.

They stood looking at each other, silent, both

startled by what had occurred and then without speaking, almost without thinking, as though it were the only really natural thing to do, still looking into those deep eyes, Steve drew his arms about Greg and held him close. Greg's lips first touched his cheek and then slid again to his mouth. Steve returned the kiss; their lips parted and Steve tasted the wetness of Greg's mouth. They stood in a tight embrace, their mouths and bodies joined, and in the distance they but faintly heard a low rumble of thunder.

They separated and looked at each other, a completely new feeling between them.

"I didn't expect that," Greg said, frowning slightly. "And I certainly didn't plan it."

"Neither did I," Steve assured him. "But I don't care."

"I didn't bring you up here to seduce you," Greg added with a slight smile, then said more seriously, "Will you go downstairs with me?"

Steve nodded. "Of course."

Greg took his hand again, holding it tightly in his own, and guided Steve down the dark, narrow stairway and into his room.

The wave crashed against the sand and rushed hungrily up the beach, hissing in fury, to lap at Johnny's sandaled feet, but he was scarcely aware of the sudden wetness. He sat quite motionless on his bit of driftwood, his face towards the house, as though turned to stone by what he had seen, and watched Greg and Steve leave the Widow's Walk and disappear down the stairs. Too intent on viewing the freighter as it moved slowly across the horizon, they had quite forgotten about Johnny, and in their unexpected intimacy they did not realize the boy was still on the beach before the house, where he had glanced up and seen the embrace, the kiss . . .

Johnny rose somewhat unsteadily to his feet, nervously running his hands over his jeans and licking at his suddenly dry, salty lips. He had been mistaken, of course. With his mind so deeply preoccupied with problems of his own, he had only imagined or perhaps had misconstrued what he had seen. The light was still not very good. Perhaps it was two other people, not those he suspected.

No. Only Greg was permitted on the Widow's Walk, and the light was not so dim that he could not recognize the familiar form and clothing of his friend.

He slowly began to walk towards the house, his eyes fixed on the third floor, Greg's floor, and he trembled slightly as he imagined what might even now be going on up there. He shook his head unbelievingly, feeling like a traitor to the friendship Greg had always shown him. It could not be, simply could not be. No, not Greg. Surely his eyes had played a trick on him. Greg and Steve had been at the telescope, looking out to the horizon. The telescope was rusted and sometimes difficult to manage, and probably Steve was completely inexperienced with such things and needed Greg's help. The uncertain light, his rather awkward vantage point on the beach, his mental hang-up about the gays at the lockers, all had provided him with a distortion of what had actually happened.

He paused before the silent house. No one was yet stirring, and all was dark except the permanent lights on the ground floor. The first flush of morning had softened the harsh brown angles of the building, touching the house with a tint of gray. Johnny had always liked the house at dawn; it seemed serene, in touch with the past, as though only at this moment could past and present merge harmoniously into one.

Glancing to the left, he looked at the large tree with its broad spreading branches coming close to the little balconies on each floor. One of the larger limbs moved for a short distance almost parallel to the third floor, sweeping past the room occupied by the sailors and then almost touching the windows of Greg's room; he wondered vaguely if that had been the means by which the sailors had introduced the two whores into their rooms.

Johnny had often played in the tree as a child, moving from one great branch to another, pretending he was scampering in the rigging of his great-grandfather's ship.

He would have to know the truth. He could not add this sudden uncertainty about his friend to the confusion in his mind. It might be disloyal and dishonest, but he had to know.

Nimbly, on practiced feet, he began to climb the tree. For a moment he was a little boy again, with the wind and the branches whispering about him, and an imaginary deck weaving beneath him. But he was not a boy now; that had all changed within the past hours. He was aware only of a sick feeling in the pit of his stomach.

He paused for a moment when he reached the window of the sailors' room, fearful they might be awake and see him in the tree, but through the slowly increasing light he saw them in their beds, asleep and alone.

He hesitated again when he was almost opposite Greg's room; the French doors of the balcony stood wide open to catch any vagrant breezes. He felt again that he was doing wrong. He was prying into matters that were not his concern. He paused, leaning heavily against the gnarled limb, looking down at the ground below. He suddenly wanted to turn back, again trying to convince himself that he was wrong. Let things be as they had been, don't change things, let life go on its orderly course. Something in him did not want to know the truth, but the part of him that had to know was stronger.

Without a sound, he scrambled along the final limb and dropped lightly down onto the balcony, quickly pressing himself against the wall, out of range of the opened windows. A slight breeze moved through the branches of the tree, and the leaves seemed to whisper to each other, as though scandalized by his behavior. He thought he heard a sound in the room, and drew carefully closer to the open doors. Listening, he heard nothing, Careful to keep his body as close as possible to the wall, he turned his head very slightly so his eyes peered directly into the room.

Greg and Steve were lying naked in the bed, their bodies tightly joined, their hands busily, hungrily caressing each other.

Johnny leaned his head back against the wall, and silent tears began to run down his face.

As a new dawn brightened the clouded sky and shimmered upon the sullen sea, the old Hawkins house was silent, standing like a lone sentinel on the small point of land jutting out to sea.

There was as yet no movement in the second floor room where the two young sailors, so different a breed from those spawned within this house, lay in the unrelieved heat of that morning.

Michael lay with his eyes open, staring at the brightening ceiling, thinking of Emily, planning for their second day together, wondering about the future, building his suddenly innocent fantasies. He glanced over to the other bed and saw that Paul, too, lay awake.

"I thought you were still asleep," Michael remarked. "It's early."

"You should be asleep too," Paul replied.

"Don't feel much like it."

"Thinking about her?" Paul's voice was not friendly.

"Yeah. Guess so."

There was the sudden flare of a struck match beside him as Paul lighted a cigarette. He handed it to Michael, then lit another for himself; he raised himself against the headboard of the bed, crossing his hands on his bare chest.

"Christ, it's rough sleeping alone," he cursed. "I almost ended up playing with myself, and that's something I haven't had to do for a hell of a lot of years."

"Don't be such an animal," Michael muttered with a slight touch of irritation.

"Now I'm an animal!" Paul laughed good-naturedly. "Last night you were right there pumping along beside me."

"Oh, go to sleep," Michael urged.

"Too goddamn hot," Paul complained. "Wish to hell this storm would get itself over with; might cool off a little."

Linda Fraser had also awakened at an early hour; it had become a habit with her. She too lay staring up at the ceiling in the custom of all insomniacs, thinking of her daughter in the next room.

At that same moment, Karen was asleep with the smile of memory on her face. She was unaware that the light beneath the portrait of her beloved had somehow become extinguished.

Margaret Hawkins had finally fallen into a troubled sleep, her cheeks still stained by the tears she had shed in the solitude of the cellars. The smooth course of her life had been unalterably changed. The house, Johnny, and her mother were the greatest treasures of her life; how much longer would she have them? She stirred in her sleep, her restless mind thronging with fears and worries. They would still, at least, have tomorrow. The day of the Festival. The last Festival at Hawkins' Cloud. They would still have that.

Exhausted, their bodies streaming with perspiration, Steve and Greg lay back, side by side, on the rumpled bed. Neither spoke for a moment, sated and unashamedly happy about what had so unexpectedly developed between them. Steve reached out and took Greg's hand, holding it tightly in his, and moved his leg so that it touched him.

"I'm glad of it," he said.

"So am I. Maybe this is what I've needed all along. I feel less alone."

"I've never felt quite like this before," Steve confessed. "I don't know what words to use . . ."

Greg chuckled, and Steve thought it one of the most pleasant sounds he had ever heard. "You mean the old joke about don't spoil it by talking about love?"

"Maybe."

"I'm not sure of what it is, myself, Steve. It's so easy, at this moment, lying here naked together, feeling the way we do, to use terms that we might not want to use later. Why don't we just wait and see? It's only been the first time. This night will happen again."

Steve put a hand to Greg's body and gently caressed him. "Yes, I know it will."

He bent over and kissed Greg on the lips, feeling the warm hands running hungrily over his entire body. He took the cigarette from Greg's hand and clumsily crushed it out in the ashtray, not even feeling the slight burning of his fingers in his excitement. As he put his arms about Steve and pressed him close again, Greg glanced towards the window and, for one startling moment, imagined he saw the agony-etched face of Johnny looking in at them. A guilty conscience? He dismissed the thought when Steve's lips again found his.

Old Ethel Hawkins rocked gently in her chair on the verandah. Again unable to sleep, she had come out once more to be alone and to listen to the sea. There was a subdued peacefulness about the breaking of the waves at this time of morning, as though they were still half-asleep.

How many years had she sat here, how many mornings in the bright, golden flush of another silent dawn? There were tears in Ethel's eyes, filling and over-flowing the lids, rolling gently down her lined face, for the thought had suddenly come to her that this might be her last morning to watch the dawn creeping silently over the sea.

The silence of the dark, musty cellars of the old house was suddenly broken by a new sound that did not belong there. It was the steadily increasing trickle of water.

# Part IV

# Friends and Lovers

# CHAPTER EIGHTEEN

The uncomfortable premonition of danger, which had so suddenly come upon Ethel Hawkins in the early hours of that morning, remained with her throughout that peculiar, sultry day, creating within her an unusual heaviness of spirit that she could not shake. With the rising of the sun, the color of the drably gray sky strangely changed. Concealed behind the thick banked puffs of scruffy gray cloud, the sun still lent its own peculiar hue to the ominously quiet landscape. The broad, gently heaving sea shone with the hot lustre of burnished brass armor, and the sands of the beach seemed to shimmer and buckle like molton metal. Even the clouds themselves were daubed with the approach of dawn, but its breath remained suffocatingly hot and it provided little relief. As the trees bent and waved before its pressure, they seemed to whisper to each other secrets never to be known by mortals.

Ethel still sat alone on the verandah as the morning broke at last, cloaked in her strange air of melancholy, rocking very gently, lulled by the creaking of her chair and the rhythm of the surf, gathering about her memories that she feared would shortly cease to exist. Such a precious store to be forever lost!

She shook her head with an expression of irritation. Why all these thoughts of dying, this heaviness of heart and dreariness of mind? Must a yellow sky and an approaching storm necessarily mean the end of her world? Oh, she had seen both skies and storms in her day! Skies as black as sin, rent asunder by blinding pitchforks of lightning, screaming with the anger of all the Furies, when the sea seemed to rise on massive streaming hind legs and hurl itself with uncontrollable anger upon the land, when the water rose over the slightly raised ground of the point to the very foot of the verandah steps, as though determined to enter the house itself, and the salt-laced foam crashed against the house with such force that the sturdy structure trembled either with fear or defiance, when the very beach was lost beneath angry, foaming, churning green-white water. Yes, those were storms! Even the sea seemed somehow tamer nowadays.

Ethel tried again to shake off that mantle of deep depression. She was growing foolish in her old age; it was time she stopped this meandering. Old people lived too much in the past, but then, where else could they live?

A slow smile crossed her small face as she suddenly remembered the significance of this particular day; it was the one day of the year to which she looked forward with unalloyed

342

pleasure. At her age, it was important to grasp every bit of pleasure that came your way, for you could never be certain of another tomorrow, even without the added problems of the weather. This was the day of the Hawkins Festival in honor of her beloved father.

She glanced up with a smile when her daughter stepped through the front entrance. Margaret was concerned and upset, and worry was all too apparent in her troubled eyes and the little lines forming about her mouth. She stood for a moment on the top step, one hand resting on the time-scarred wooden column, the other on her ample hip, looking up at the gray-yellow sky; a large circle of perspiration already stained the back of her gay print dress.

"I did so hope the storm would have gotten itself over with by this evening," she complained, "but I suppose it won't break before evening. What a pity it had to be today!"

"What does the radio say?" Ethel asked.

"What it's been saying for the past twenty-four hours," Margaret replied with some irritation. "The storm slowed down during the night, but now it's on the move again, headed right for us. Strong winds and high tides, with heavy rain." She frowned with her own inner concern. "All small craft have been ordered back into port. I don't like the sound of that."

"We've had storms before, Meg," Ethel reminded her, "and much worse than this one."

"Yes, I know, but . . ." Her mind flitted briefly to the dark, damp cellar, and she stubbornly forced her thoughts away; this was not a day for gloom. "Today of all days! That means we'll just have to hold the Festival indoors. It's so much

343

nicer out there on the point, with the lanterns and the tables and the dance platform, and the fresh sea air; everything seems so cramped and stuffy inside." She shrugged her broad shoulders. "Well, I suppose it can't be helped, can it? I just hope the weather won't keep people away." She turned and looked at her mother; Ethel was staring out to the sea with an unusual vagueness in her face. "You look very tired this morning, mother. Is there anything wrong?"

"Oh, no," Ethel assured her with a smile that was meant to be comforting, but somehow seemed only wearied. "No, of course not, dear. I just didn't sleep at all well last night, that's all. It's probably the weather. It's so . . . heavy."

"You haven't had your breakfast yet, have you?" Margaret asked. "I could bring you something out here; it's so much more comfortable than indoors."

"I really don't much care for anything, dear. I'll just have a cup of tea, if you don't mind."

"Of course." Margaret paused once more at the door and glanced back at the turgid, heavy sea. "The water looks like it'll start to boiling at any moment. I doubt that Johnny will have a very good day today, even if the storm does hold off a while yet. I'll bring your tea right away, mother. Then we must get started on the decorations."

The door closed behind her. A lone gull wheeled smoothly across the sky, its white wings and body touched with the amber that seemed to bathe all the world on this peculiar morning. It swooped gently, hovered over the water for just a moment, then raised itself and headed toward the Boardwalk, as though suddenly desirous of company. No one really likes being alone, Ethel thought to

344

herself. The spume of breaking waves rose like a heavy lace curtain over the end of the point; the sea was growing rougher as the wind increased.

Johnny came slowly around the house, wearing only shorts and a T-shirt, his feet bare, ready to begin his day at the lockers; he paused when his grandmother called to him. Smiling, he vaulted easily over the bannister and bent to kiss her lined cheek.

"Are you leaving so early, Johnny?" she asked.

The boy nodded. "I might just as well, Gram. I want to be there as soon as we open. If there's any swimming, it will be early in the day, before people really begin to feel uneasy about the storm."

Noting the unusual darkness under her grandson's eyes, Ethel asked, "Is there something troubling you, Johnny? You just don't look at all well these days, dear. I do hope you're not coming down with something."

"No, no, I'm all right." His tone seemed evasive. "It's just too hot, I guess. I wasn't able to sleep at all last night."

"Did anyone, I wonder?" Ethel mused. "I don't suppose you'll be very busy today, at that; a lot of people will stay away from the beach." She smiled and shook her head at the folly of humanity. "Oh, people scare so easily. A storm suddenly reminds them that they aren't really masters of their fate after all, and they find the thought very unsettling. Most people will get out of the water even during a light shower, as though there is danger for them when the water from the sky touches the water they're bathing in."

"I'll do all right, anyway," Johnny assured her, and there was a sudden adult hardness in his voice and in his dark, deep eyes that disturbed Ethel; she wondered what was concealed behind his words. "There are still those who go to the beach no matter what the weather; they're here for the beach, and nothing's gonna keep them away from it." He had begun to turn away, then turned back, smiling in a manner that had little of the boy about it. "I'll be getting that boat real soon now, Gram, by the end of the season, anyway. I was thinking of dropping into Sternberg's this afternoon to see if they'd hold it for me a couple of weeks, until I can put down the desposit."

"Oh, I'm so glad to hear that, Johnny," Ethel remarked. "You should have had it long before this."

"I would have, if I'd been smart."

Ethel looked after her grandson again as he vaulted over the bannister—he seemed totally unaware of the existence of stairs—and continued on his way, and she wondered again at the peculiar harshness of his words and the strangeness of his manner during the past few days. Perhaps it was only her imagination. Her mind of late had certainly been working overtime.

Sighing slightly, she rested her head back against the chair and wearily closed her eyes. Now she could shut out the harsh unnatural yellow glare of the sky and, perhaps, forget that strange sense of foreboding that had filled her all through the hot, silent night. She could remember more easily now those happier times of her childhood, her beloved father, the excitement of his return from another voyage, the comfortable feeling of his powerful arms about her, holding her close in a bear hug because she was the dearest thing in all his life, yes, dearer even than his great white ship with the painted smiling figurehead that bowed into the white froth of the sea and rose again with the water streaming down her face and over her full breasts like a Nereid in her bath. . . .

A hand gently shook her shoulder, and Ethel looked up into her daughter's face; there was unconcealed concern in Margaret's eyes.

"Are you all right, mother?" Margaret asked. "You didn't answer me."

"Oh . . ." Ethel gathered her thoughts again and laughed with a slight embarrassment. "I'm sorry, Meg. I must have dozed off for a moment."

"Here's your tea, mother," Margaret said, avoiding Ethel's eyes as she placed the tray on the small table beside the rocking chair. Her mother had more and more of late fallen into the habit of these brief but intense dozings. Whenever she spoke to others of her concern for her mother's increasing frailty, they always made some remark about "Well, after all, she is ninety years old," as if that would make it easier to lose her.

Ethel took the small cup and saucer in her hand. It trembled slightly and some of the amber liquid poured into the saucer . . . and, leaning back again began her slow, steady rocking; there was a vagueness in her face this morning that disturbed her daughter. For a moment, there was no sound but the surf and the creaking of the chair.

"Well, Meg," Ethel mused, lowering the cup back into the saucer, "another Festival. How many does that make, I wonder? I've really quite lost track of them." (She herself had begun them many years earlier.) "Oh, Daddy would have been so proud to be remembered in this way. How he would have enjoyed himself at these parties! He did so love partying, you know. He loved to dance and to laugh, to have this house filled with people having a good time!" She sipped the tea again and sadly shook her head. "What a pity he can't be here, isn't it, dear?"

"Why . . . yes, mother. Yes. It is a pity."

Ethel raised a thin, heavily lined and blue-veined hand to her face and closed her eyes; her delicate fingers trembled for a moment at her pale lips. "Yes. Yes." Slowly, she nodded her head; her eyes remained closed. "Well, such things can't always be helped, I suppose." She was silent for a moment, and when she spoke again, her voice sounded suddenly younger, and a strangely childish smile played across her lips. "Sometimes the winds, or the currents . . . well, sometimes they just aren't right. They can be very stubborn, you know, almost spiteful, as though they just don't want the ship to come home again. And then, of course, it is such a long journey! That doesn't bother Daddy, though, not any of it. No, sir! Oh, Daddy's more than a match for any mean old sea." Her eyes opened, suddenly bright with a new idea, but they seemed strangely out of focus, as though they were looking into a different time; she placed a finger to her lips again, biting its end slightly as with a nervous excitement. "Oh, maybe I should go upstairs now. It really isn't too early . . ."

"Upstairs, mother?" Margaret bent over her, suddenly feeling alarm. "Upstairs?"

"Yes." Ethel's lined face became flushed with sudden eagerness; her eyes shone like those of a happy child. "Up to the Walk. There may already be some sign of him, you know . . . the top of his mast, or the white flash of his sail against the sky. Oh, you know he'll be expecting me to be up there.

348

He'll be on the bridge, and as soon as he's in range, he'll turn his glass towards the house, and he'll be so terribly disappointed if he doesn't see me up there . . ."

She moved as though to rise from her chair, and Margaret's eyes filled with tears as she took the old woman's hand in hers, holding it firmly and gently running her fingers over the worn, almost translucent back. "Oh, no, Ethel, no, not just yet," she said softly, speaking to the child of eighty years earlier. "It's still too soon. You have plenty of time. Why don't you just sit here a little longer? You're very tired, dear."

The phantom girlishness faded like a light slowly dimmed, and age returned to Ethel as she sank back again with a heavy sigh. "Yes, I suppose you're right. I am very tired. Oh, I'm always terribly tired these days. The days seem so long, and I never do seem to sleep really well any more. That's strange, isn't it? I always used to sleep so well. I'm . . . I'm . . ."

She stopped, and her face became clouded with confusion. She frowned and licked her lips, her pale eyes darting about as though she were only now suddenly aware of her surroundings. She looked up at her daughter, and a veil seemed to pass quickly before her eyes.

"Oh . . . Oh . . . Oh, dear . . . Sometimes it's so difficult to remember. I'm getting very old, aren't I? Sometimes . . . I can't quite understand what is today and what was yesterday." Slowly, the confusion cleared and she returned the loving pressure of her hand, smiling comfortingly.

"Don't be concerned about it, Margaret dear. I'm afraid I was wandering a bit, wasn't I?"

"A bit, mother," Margaret replied, trying to

hold back her tears. Why must the old become so old? "Just a bit, dear."

Ethel took a deep beath and seemed to brace herself, determined to have no more of this nonsense; her mouth became firm. "Well, that's over now. I'm quite all right again, really I am. Don't you go and worry your head about me, now, especially today. You just get back to your work and I'll sit here for a while. If it gets too hot, I'll go back inside and lie down a bit."

"You're certain you'll be all right?"

"Oh, my yes, of course I'll be all right. Yes, yes, yes. Quite all right, dear. Unless there's something I can do to help you . . ."

"Oh, no, mother, we'll manage just fine . . ."

"Well, if you're sure . . ."

"Yes, dear."

Ethel sipped her tea, once again in full control of herself. "Yes, I'm quite all right now. You don't have to stay with me any longer. I know you have a great deal to do."

Still slightly uneasy about Ethel's lapse of time-memory, Margaret moved slowly to the door. When she looked back again, Ethel was once more rocking in her chair and gazing placidly out to sea.

Steve had been awake for some time, but he lay still now, listening to Greg's quiet, regular breathing. It was bright daylight by this time, but there was a peculiar yellowish glow to the room and the heat was still intense; his bare chest gleamed with perspiration.

He turned his head and looked at Greg lying naked beside him, on his back, his strong, clean profile outlined against the yellowish cast of the sky, his body smooth and damp with perspiration.

He slept easily, his full soft lips only slightly parted, his chin firm, his blond hair tousled, the smooth chest moving slightly with his breathing. There was a small brown mole on his chest, beside the left nipple, and Steve had an impulse to lower his head and kiss it, but feared this would awaken him. It was enough to lie here and look at Greg, knowing this was now his. He stretched lazily, feeling a sense of complete and total satisfaction. Then his expression became suddenly serious, and a troubled frown creased his forehead.

So here it was again, what he had been so carefully avoiding since his mother's suicide. The proof was now clear and inescapable. The terrible incident that had caused his family tragedy was not just an isolated matter, not an accident, but a true expression of his own suppressed nature. He had now to confess to what he really was, to his feelings, his emotions, his inclinations. The guilt, the fear, the loneliness, the uncertainty—all were bound up in the concealed yearning, now for the first time in his life given full and complete expression. He could put a word to it now, the word he had all these years been trying to avoid. Homosexual.

And yet lying here beside the naked man who had been his lover during the night, he was unaware of any sense of guilt, and the word he had just applied to himself carried no hint of shame. By some standards, certainly by those of his mother, he had committed a perverted, an unnatural act. Had he picked up a street whore and paid her to share his bed, had he committed adultery with the wife of his best friend, people would have expressed public disapproval, but it would not have been as outrageous as what he had

351

actually done. It would not have been "unnatural." It would merely have proven that he was a man, for all that was worth. You may be forgiven—grudgingly, half-heartedly or admiringly—for anything you may do with a woman, no matter how decadent or depraved, but there is no forgiveness for doing such things with a member of your own sex.

It was a relief to realize that he didn't care any more. He did not feel in any way indecent. He had finally put a word to it, and the word did not disturb him. Homosexual. He was homosexual, and no amount of condemnation from others could possibly change that fact. It was a relief, at last, to admit it to himself. To continue trying to conceal the truth even from himself, as he had in the past, would be an even greater indecency and would destroy him by living a lie, to spend the years building up the unhappiness and frustration to a point of inevitable tragedy. The years since his mother's death had merely been a period of marking time. Now he knew. This morning, for the first time in many years, he was content. Happy? Perhaps. At least, there would now be a new beginning. It explained so much— the failure of his marriage, the constant sense of pressure and uneasiness, the hidden sense of guilt. Now it was over. He knew, and he didn't care if others knew. He would accept the fact and live the remainder of his live accordingly. Had he finally found the answer for which he had come here?

Greg stirred, arched his back and stretched his arms, then opened his eyes. Seeing Steve, he looked slightly bewildered for a moment, then smiled. "Hi."

"Morning," Steve replied, returning the smile. "How are you?"

"How should I be?" Greg returned with another smile. "Great. How about you?"

Steve bent and kissed him, their lips lingering briefly. "Does that answer your question?"

"It'll do for a starter."

Warm and comfortable, Steve lay with his head on Greg's broad chest, sharing the rhythm of his breathing; he could hear the beating of Greg's heart. Did it beat differently this morning? He was certain his did.

"Greg . . . ."

"Yeah?"

"About last night . . ."

Greg ruffled Steve's thick damp hair and laughed; Steve saw the tightening of his stomach muscles. "Oh, come now, you're not going to bring out all sorts of guilt complexes about our having done a terrible thing, and all that sort of shit?" He raised Steve's head in his hands and looked at him with an expression of mock alarm. "Oh, Christ! Don't tell me you're a religious nut? Those are the worst kind, you know; they go wild when they finally get around to it, and then are filled with all sorts of saintly remorse. Want me to go to confession with you? If it'll help, I'll take all the blame on myself. You can always claim I seduced you. Did I, I wonder?"

Steve laughed. "No fear of that, Greg!" He reached to the table and got a cigarette for both of them, then leaned on his elbow, looking at Greg and speaking seriously. "But there's something I want you to know, Greg. A few years ago, my mother committed suicide because she discovered

I was a homosexual. As a matter of fact, I wasn't even sure of it myself at that time. But I did a very foolish thing. Don't ask me why, I couldn't tell you; I'd never done anything like it before. I became involved in a public place with a man who was an undercover cop, and I was arrested. Nothing really came of it, but my mother just couldn't bear the thought that her son was something less than what she considered perfect. She opened the gas jets . . ."

Greg frowned. "I'm sorry to hear that, Steve. It must have been a very difficult thing for you."

"I blamed myself for her death, of course," Steve continued, "and I certainly had good reason to. If I had been like other men, if I'd found a 'nice girl,' married her and settled down with a good job to raise a lovely, respectable family, my mother might still be alive . . ."

"And you would be leading a miserable existence, bringing unhappiness to everyone because of your own concealed frustrations," Greg interrupted. "Steve, that supposedly idyllic life just isn't right for everyone, and the worst thing that someone like you, like ourselves, can do is allow himself to be forced into it. Sure, I can understand your sense of guilt, but does it really make any difference?"

"What do you mean?"

"Did you enjoy it any the less with me last night?"

"No." There was no hesitation in his reply.

"Do you feel guilt about being here in bed with me, right now?"

"Of course not. But I've been so careful, Greg. I've tried to sublimate these—urgings—even though I guess I wasn't fully aware of where they were aimed. I've tried to avoid any possibility of this kind of thing . . ."

"And has the life you've been leading these past years brought your mother back, or changed anything at all except to make you unhappy?"

Steve made no reply.

"Look, Steve, the point I'm trying to make is something you must realize even without my telling you. You simply aren't that kind of man, the so-called acceptable 'normal' man. You aren't alone, you know. I never suspected the same thing about myself, but it answers a lot of questions for me, too. Believe it or not, Steve, last night was the first time I've ever gone to bed with a man, and I think you realize I'm not sorry. I don't care what other people think. People who would condemn us, brand us as effeminates and perverts, could never understand the emotions involved, the need that brought us to this, the loneliness. It would be useless even to try to explain it to them. Things are changing, I suppose, but our Puritanical society is still too rigid to accept people like us. A man has got to be a man, and what we've done is supposedly an insult to masculinity. But we have to live in and for ourselves, and as long as we are true to ourselves, and to each other, we need feel no shame. We are what we are, and that's all there is to it."

They were both silent for a moment. Steve felt the warmth of Greg's strongly comforting arms about him, and realized he had only wanted Greg's confirmation and approval of his own confused thoughts. He had it now. He instinctively knew he would never be uncertain again.

After a moment, Greg said softly, "There's

something I think you should know about me, too, Steve, since we're in this confessional mood. I'm under a very different kind of cloud. I came home from Vietnam with the blackest of marks against me." He put his hand under Steve's chin and looked into his eyes, not quite certain what he expected to find there. "I was taken prisoner by the Vietcong. I made broadcasts for them, anti-American broadcasts. I'm called a coward and a traitor."

"Are you?"

Greg frowned. "I suppose I'm just begging the question if I say it's all a matter of one's own personal interpretation. I did those things I'm accused of, and I've never denied it; I can't. It's the truth. When I returned to my home again, the entire town turned its back on me, all except my mother." He mused a moment. "Strange comparison there, isn't it?"

"My mother abandoned me," Steve confessed. "Your mother did not."

"What made matters even worse, what made the town doubly bitter against me, was that they'd learned that my younger brother Bob had died rather than be forced into doing what I had done. He became a hero, a martyr, and they simply couldn't bear to have me in the same town. Regardless of how stubbornly she believed in me, my mother couldn't combat the town's contempt and my own father's hostility. I had to leave." He looked at Steve. "You've been making love to a coward and a traitor, Steve. You have the same right to despise me as everyone else."

Steve returned his silent stare for a moment, then swung off the bed and walked to the open balcony doors, standing out of view of anyone who might be down below.

"I'm hardly the one to condemn, Greg."

"Why not? Everyone else seems to think he has the right. You're going to say a person who feels responsible for his mother's death shouldn't pass judgment on anyone else, aren't you?"

"Isn't that the truth?"

"No, it's not. The cases are entirely different. What happened to you was—well, it may have been wrong, but the fault wasn't really entirely yours. Whatever happened that night, and afterwards, happened because you couldn't possibly have known the consequences, or you certainly would have acted differently. I knew very well what I was doing. I knew it was wrong and what would be said of me because of it. You're not in the same class with a coward and a traitor. You mustn't let your own feeling of guilt interfere with your thinking."

Steve stood silently, staring out at the turgid sea, and Greg watched him, aware of a sense of dread. From this one evening together, Steve had suddenly become more important to him than anyone else in his life. He had lost before. He didn't want to lose again.

"I don't know you very well yet, Greg," Steve admitted. "But even one night together gives some idea of what a person is like. We talked a lot, you know, we shared our views on things, our attitudes, our standards. Aside from the fact that you turn me on, I think you're quite a guy, someone I'm proud to know." He frowned. "And I think I already know you well enough to feel what you've told me isn't completely convincing. I don't think you're really telling me everything, are you?"

Greg looked at him for a moment, then quietly turned his head away.

"I was completely honest with you," Steve reminded him. "Believe me, it wasn't easy to talk about it. But you're not being as truthful as I was. It seems to me you've left out the most important aspect of all. Why did you do it, Greg?"

Greg sat up in the bed, wrapping his arms about his legs and resting his chin on his knees. "I've never told that to anyone."

"If there's going to be an honest, above-board relationship between us in the future, now's the time to start."

Greg stared at the foot of the bed, struggling with himself, knowing Steve was right. He had just admitted to himself that someone very important had entered his life, and he felt the next moments might well decide whether or not they would have a future together. Caution or honesty? Concealment or truth? What would be the wisest, safest course?

"You never had a brother, did you, Steve?" he asked quietly, without raising his head.

"I've a sister," Steve replied, "but no brother, no."

"Bob and I had a wonderful relationship," Greg continued. "We weren't just brothers, we were the best of friends. There was nothing I wouldn't have done for him, or for that matter, that Bob wouldn't have done for me. I loved and protected him all his life." Greg lay down again, propped up on one elbow, still not looking at Steve, speaking almost as though he were explaining things to himself. "Bob died in the prison camp, and my

358

home town made him into a hero, the only real hero the town'd ever had. He had not given in to the nasty Commie warlords, he had stood firm and steadfast, refusing to bow to their demands, like a real red-blooded American boy. He was a great man, someone to hold up as a model of true Americanism to the young. He was twenty-four years old when he died. He lost two-thirds of the life he should have had."

Greg fell silent for a moment before continuing.

"But his older brother was different. He was a coward. He did what Bob had refused to do. He agreed to make those damaging statements, to denigrate his country. He betrayed those very beliefs for which his younger brother died."

"You've already told me all this, Greg," Steve reminded him.

"Yes, I know." He looked at Steve. "But you see, that wasn't exactly the truth." He looked away again. "If you had a brother, Steve, a younger brother whom you had always loved and cared for as I had Bob, what would you do if that brother crawled to you on his hands and knees, what would you do if he came to you crying, screaming, begging you to save him? I suppose there are tortures even worse than the purely physical. They saw my love for Bob, and they used that love for their own purposes. We can't all be courageous, Steve, we can't all be totally insensible to pain. We can't all be men of iron, can we?" There was a desperation, a pleading in his voice as he looked again to Steve, hoping for agreement.

Steve returned to the bed and sat at Greg's side. "No, of course we can't."

"Bobby wasn't really a coward," Greg insisted, "but he just wasn't the stuff heroes are made of.

He screamed. Oh, my God, how he screamed, again and again. While I was chained to a post directly opposite and they wouldn't let me turn my head away. They taped my eyelids open so I couldn't close my eyes. I had to watch what they did to him."

Steve silently slipped his hand into Greg's and listened; Greg's fingers closed about his hand as though groping for support.

"How long can you hold your hand over an open flame before you have to snatch it away? What if you can't pull it away? What if you have to hold it over the flame until you can smell your own roasting flesh? That was the least of what they did to Bob." He closed his eyes, and his mouth became hard. "God, what they did! Bamboo splinters under the nails, biting ants in his pubic hair, his balls squeezed in a vise . . ."

Steve quickly interrupted the softly hypnotic voice; Greg's eyes were open wide, staring with horror into that terrible past. "Don't tell me any more, Greg."

Greg fell silent, and Steve could see the course of tears on his cheeks. He held the hand more tightly.

"They told me it would all stop if I would only do as they asked," Greg continued. "It was entirely up to me; the choice was my own. You see, I was an officer, and they felt my cooperation would be more important, more effective, and of more use to them than Bob's. But I refused. At first, I refused. I said I wouldn't agree no matter what they did to me. They could only kill me once. They kept on torturing Bob, while I stood and watched. I tried with my own screams to drown out Bob's terrible, agonizing cries; I cursed

360

God, ordering him to let my brother die. They stuffed my mouth with cotton. And then . . ."

He paused for another moment, his throat straining, his face wet. When he continued again, his voice was low and tight with remembered horror, the words unsteady.

"And then, I looked down to see Bob on his hands and knees before me because he could no longer stand, crawling to me, begging me to save him, telling me he couldn't bear it any longer, screaming that I owed it to him, to save him. His eyes were staring out of his head, and he cried and cried. Oh, Christ, I'd never seen anyone beg so!"

He paused again, swallowed, and sighed. A sudden warm breeze came through the open balcony, touched them as though with sympathy, and moved on.

"So, I gave in to them. What else could I do? I couldn't let them—I did what they wanted of me. I made the statements, the broadcasts, I said anything they wanted me to say. I condemned the society into which I had been born, I cursed my country and my people, I repudiated everything I had always believed in."

"But your brother is dead."

Greg nodded. "Oh, yes, he's dead. Bob died exactly ten minutes after I'd finally agreed to do what they asked. But they didn't tell me that, of course. They kept assuring me that Bob was well, and receiving the best of care in the hospital; they promised me I could see him immediately after the broadcast had been made. I should never have believed them, but what else was there for me to do? I was in no position to strike a bargain with them. By the time I learned the truth, it was already too late."

"And then you were released? What happened then?"

"A court martial, of course. They considered there were possible 'extenuating circumstances.' They were quite lenient, really. Only a dishonorable discharge."

Steve frowned. "And when you reached home, why didn't you tell the truth? Why let them think you were a coward?"

"I'm not sure myself," Greg confessed. "When I first learned the opinion everyone had formed about Bob, the business of his being such a hero, I couldn't bring myself to say anything; I started to write the truth several times, but I couldn't put the words on paper. I couldn't write about Bob, and the truth about myself sounded too piously self-defensive. I thought I wouldn't be believed. It could wait until I reached home again; I would find some way to explain it then. But I couldn't do it, even then, not even when I could feel the terrible hatred they all had for me. Bob was dead, after all. I knew he wasn't really a coward; he had simply been carried beyond the limits of his own endurance. We all have such limits, you know, but fortunately few of us are ever taken anywhere near that breaking point. Somehow, the account that reached home had made Bob something he was not. It appeared that he had died gloriously and heroically. Maybe it was true, after all. Bob had died in the service of his country. I couldn't bring myself to destroy that image, that belief. I had life, let my brother have the glory." He looked at Steve. "Was I wrong?"

"I never had a brother," Steve reminded him. "I'm sure what you did took a special kind of courage of its own."

"Later, of course, I couldn't say anything at all. I've often wondered at what point I went wrong. When I came home and said nothing, or when I agreed to do what was demanded of me, regardless of the reason? Shouldn't love of country come even before love of family?"

Anxious to help, to find the right words to ease Greg's confusion, Steve hesitated. "Doesn't it come down to the same thing, Greg? Isn't our respect for the life of the individual one of the beliefs that makes us the people we are? What would really have been gained, had you refused, what purpose would have been served? Bob is dead, and you would certainly have died as well. Oh, I'm sure there are those who wouldn't agree with me. Death before dishonor and all that sort of thing. But I suppose we've grown out of such a code, whether for good or ill. Isn't it possible there's a point where sheer courage becomes foolishness? I don't know. What would I have done under the same circumstances? What would anyone else have done? It's impossible to say. You did what you felt necessary to preserve one very precious life. Because you cared. Perhaps that's one of the greatest differences between us and them. We're men, not machines, not statistics. We know the meaning of love and pity and mercy. We hold sacred the life of every single individual. I think that means a great deal, Greg."

They both fell silent for another moment, while the brassy gold of the strange morning bathed the room in rich amber. Then Greg spoke again.

"You're the only person I've ever told this to, Steve, or ever will. The people back home don't interest me any longer. I'll never be going back there. But your opinion is very important. Does this make a difference?"

Steve looked at him, smiled, and then shook his head. "Greg, I didn't talk with you all night because of your political attitudes, and that certainly had nothing to do with my going to bed with you. Even if I'd know about all this before, it wouldn't have lessened the—the ecstacy—of last night, any more than your knowing about me would have lessened your pleasure. I think we both know there's a lot more to what's happened between us than just sexual satisfaction. But nothing in the past can change it."

Greg sighed again; the relief was evident in his face. "You're right Steve. We've got to be perfectly honest with each other. This may have been just another sexual incident, or it may turn out to be one of the most important things that's ever happened to either one of us. We can't decide here and now; the excitement of it all is still too fresh." He smiled, warmly, affectionately. "Let's wait. Later, when we've come to know each other better, perhaps we can—well, see. Then we can talk about it more." It was good to see the strain fade under his smile. "For now, let's just leave things as they are and enjoy ourselves."

Steve sensed they had already both made the decision implied in Greg's words. "Why not? When do you have to be at the Seaquarium?"

Glancing at his watch, Greg replied, "Oh, I've got a good hour or more yet. How about some breakfast?"

"Sure. I'll take a quick shower." He grinned. "You stay here."

As he passed the dresser, Steve noticed a small printed card propped up against one corner of the mirror. He picked it up and read:

All guests of "The Cloud" are cordially invited to the annual Captain Nathaniel Hawkins Festival commencing at 8:00 P.M. this evening.

Please bring your friends.

"That the Festival announcement?" Greg asked, rising from the bed and approaching Steve.

"Yes," Steve replied, showing him the card.

Greg smiled. "Sticking these little cards on the mirrors of the rooms is just about as far as Miss Meg will allow herself to go in advertising the affair; she just don't feel it's quite proper. It smacks too much of commercialism, and The Cloud just isn't that kind of place, she says. Doesn't need to advertise, anyway; everyone looks forward to the Festival every year."

"What is it?"

"It's really just a big birthday bash to honor the dear departed Captain Nathaniel Hawkins," Greg explained. "Haven't you ever been to one? They've been holding them for as long as I've been here, and a good deal longer than that."

"No." Steve shook his head. "I don't suppose I've ever been here quite this late in the season before."

"Oh, it's nothing very fancy, but it's pleasant enough. If the weather is good—and it sure as hell won't be this evening—it's held right out on the point in front of the house. Otherwise it's held down in the sitting room and lobby. Lanterns, music, drinks, lots of really good food, dancing, entertainment, that sort of thing. Bea's always part of the fun. It's a real birthday party; the only difference is the birthday boy has been dead for a lot of years." He smiled and looked at the card again. "It means a lot to the Hawkins family."

"Do you go?"

"Oh, sure, Miss Meg would be terribly hurt if I didn't, and I'm much too fond of the old girl to hurt her."

"Am I going with you?"

Greg slipped an arm about Steve's waist and drew him closer; the touch of the naked warm flesh was exciting. "You sure as hell better not go with anyone else." He ran his lips across Steve's cheek. "You need a shave."

"And a shower," Steve reminded him. "And I'll sure never get it this way."

"So what? Like I said, I've got a good hour yet. . . ."

# CHAPTER NINETEEN

Part of the ritual of their lives was for Karen and Linda to have their morning coffee together in their own sitting room, since Karen refused to descend to any of the coffee shops on the Boardwalk. This morning routine seldom varied in even the smallest degree, whether they were at home or at Hawkins' Cove. Karen would awaken promptly at eight o'clock, and after making her brief morning toilet, she would spend exactly one half-hour dreaming before the sacred portrait of her lover. Precisely at nine, she would wheel herself into the sitting room where Linda would be waiting with steaming hot coffee, brought from the kitchen. Just like two worn out old spinsters, Linda often told herself; two old maids whose lives are finished and who now have nothing better to do than chat their trivial gossip over their coffee cups.

"Your father called while you were still in your

room," Linda mentioned as she poured the coffee. "He should be here in a few hours."

"That's nice," Karen remarked, absently stirring the coffee, which she had over-sweetened with sugar. "He'll be good company for you."

Linda glanced uneasily at her daughter, hesitated a moment, and then ventured to speak what was on her mind. "Karen . . . please . . . won't you try to be . . ."

"Yes, mother?" There was already an edge to her voice; Karen well knew what was coming.

"Well, when your father gets here, dear, won't you just try to—to show a little interest in things?" Linda was having considerable difficulty, knowing the wrong words would result in a painful scene. "I mean, you know he has so many business problems these days, and he worries so about you . . ."

"There's no reason for him to worry," Karen assured her in a brittle tone. "I'm perfectly all right."

Linda lowered her cup; she was determined to avoid any unpleasantness for her husband, even at the risk of incurring Karen's well-known painful wrath. Her husband's comfort was part of that wifely responsibility which Linda took very seriously.

"I do wish you would just go out a bit, dear. You're really very pale for someone who has spent the entire summer at the shore. Wouldn't a bit of sun do you some good? You could be made very comfortable at the beach, you know, and it would be nice for you to see some people other than just those few here at the house. Oh!" As though just recalling something particularly pleasant, Linda lowered her cup to the table and leaned forward in her chair, smiling broadly. "I meant to tell you yesterday, but it slipped my mind. I was talking with that very nice Greg Christopher, and he made quite a point of inviting both of us personally to visit his Seaquarium. I think he'd be terribly pleased to show us about the place, and they do say he has a very interesting exhibit. And he seems such a nice young man."

"Mother, you know you can go at any time you like," Karen said, somewhat tartly. "You needn't always stay here with me."

"But it's for your sake that I really would like to go," Linda replied. "Why, Karen dear, you haven't been down to the Boardwalk even one single time all summer."

"I don't particularly care for the Boardwalk," Karen countered. "It really doesn't interest me at all."

"But it would do you so much good, Karen! We could go down and sit on one of the benches overlooking the sea, have something to eat in one of those very nice restaurants. Or we could even go to my dear 'Roberto's'; they often ask after you, you know, and they would make you wonderfully welcome; they would treat you royally and, for a change, I'd have lunch there with you." Her voice showed determined enthusiasm. "And then, after lunch, we could drop in at the Seaquarium. . . ."

"Mother, you know it isn't that easy for me to get around!"

Linda flushed. "But that wouldn't create any problems, Karen. It's level just about everywhere, and we could always get someone to help us if we needed it . . ."

"I prefer not to put myself on display, mother!"

"Oh, no, Karen, no one would think that . . ."

"If you don't mind, mother, I'd rather not, really."

"But Karen . . ."

Karen's voice stopped her again, sharp and unpleasant; the cup rattled noisily as she returned it angrily to the saucer. "Mother! Have you forgotten what this place once meant to me? Do you think it would be pleasant for me to go about down there where Jeff and I were once so happy, to see other couples walking arm in arm in the way we did . . ."

She buried her face in her handkerchief and turned her head away; there was the sound of a sob.

"But then why do we come here at all, Karen?" Linda wondered as she had often in the past, shaking her head in confusion. "If it makes you so unhappy . . . well, why do you insist on coming here? Surely it would be better for you if we spent our summers somewhere else. Perhaps in the mountains? Why, we could go anywhere at all, dear. Abroad, if you like. You were always so fond of Vienna . . ."

Karen lowered her handkerchief, revealing a face white and set with pain as she wheeled herself away from the table. She never answered this question. "If you don't mind, mother, I believe I'll just go into my room and lie down for a little while. I've a bit of a headache."

Linda reached out a trembling hand to her daughter, filled with that old familiar sense of guilt. "Oh, Karen, dear, I'm sorry if I . . ."

"That's all right, mother, really," Karen responded in her best martyr's tone as she took the outstretched hand and gently patted it. "It really isn't your fault, I know that. I realize sometimes it's a bit difficult for you."

"Oh, no, no, not at all, dear . . ."

Karen smiled, nodded her head slightly, and wheeled herself back into her room. She turned her chair to the left and paused for a moment, facing the lighted portrait, in what seemed a deliberately theatrical gesture. The door then closed gently behind her.

Linda sat quite still, crushed by this further failure to get her daughter out of the house. Covering her face with both hands, she burst into bitter tears of sorrow and loneliness.


Michael was in the bathroom, shaving. Despite the oppressive atmosphere, he was in the best of spirits, and as the razor ran across his lathered cheeks, he hummed lightly. He had just stepped from a brisk, cold shower; he felt clean, fresh and exhilaratingly alive. Paul was still asleep. It was quite early but Michael found further sleep impossible; he was too excited by the prospects of this new day.

He wiped the remaining lather from his face and left the bathroom. The doors to the balcony stood open and he stepped before them, raising his arms and breathing deeply. It was humid and there was an unhealthy color to the sky, but he knew again that this was going to be a day to be remembered. The song bubbled into his throat, and he quickly converted it to a whistle.

"Only damn fools and bo'sun-mates whistle," came the wry comment behind him.

Paul was still in bed, propped up on the pillows,

looking at him with a touch of undisguised annoyance.

"Oh, hi, Paul. About time you woke up!"

"What the hell are you so happy about this morning?"

"Why shouldn't I be happy?" Michael asked. "It's a beautiful day. Just couldn't be better."

"Oh, shit," Paul responded, reaching for a cigarette. "Looks like a lousy day. I can feel the sweat on my balls already. What's that funny color in the sky?"

Michael smiled again. "You know, you don't look natural. I think this is the first time I've ever seen you wake up alone in a bed."

"Goddamn it, it sure doesn't feel natural," Paul complained.

Michael laughed and stepped to the dresser to comb his hair; seeing the notice about the Festival, he picked it up and read it aloud. "The old lady on the porch mentioned it to me yesterday," he commented. "What do you suppose it's like?"

"What would it be like?" Paul asked sarcastically. "A nice little party where nobody drinks too much and nobody dares say 'shit.' Boring as hell."

"Maybe Emily would like it," Michael mused, looking at the card.

"Yeah. You know, I'll just bet she would."

"You going?"

"Waste my time . . ." Paul began, then paused, thoughtful for a moment. "Well, I don't know. Maybe. Free drinks, I guess, and I suppose a lot of people will be there. Might be able to pick up something interesting. If you two are planning on it, maybe I'll drop in, too. If it's okay?"

"Of course it's okay," Michael assured him. "I'll be glad to see you there, buddy."

"What are you planning today, anyway?" Paul asked. "I suppose it's gonna be a real Emily Day, isn't it?"

Michael nodded. "She doesn't work today. I don't know yet what we'll be doing. We'll go to the beach for a while, I guess. Maybe we'll ride the carousel. Hell, I haven't been on one of those things since I was a kid."

"Sounds like a real swinging time," Paul remarked wryly. "Don't get dizzy, goin' 'round in circles all day."

Michael turned at the only half-hidden reproach in Paul's voice; he felt suddenly guilty about leaving his friend to his own resources. "Why don't you come along, Paul?" There was little invitation in his voice.

Paul laughed, humorlessly. "Be a priest in a whorehouse again? Not me, thanks; had enough of that yesterday. Oh, it was all right," he quickly added. "My fault. I shouldn't have tagged along. I've got to get started on some stuff for tonight. Even you'll start to look good to me if I don't get a piece of ass tonight."

"Why don't you at least meet us for lunch?" Michael suggested, still not wanting to neglect his friend completely. "Or maybe dinner?"

Paul swung his legs over the bed and crushed his cigarette in the ash tray. "No, thanks. You go on and have yourself a good time, Mike."

His spirits slightly deflated, Michael let the offensive nickname pass. He turned apologetically to Paul. "I don't like to run off and leave you alone . . ."

Paul laughed. "Are you kidding? Shit! When

did I ever have any trouble finding somebody to keep me company?"

"Yeah, that's right," Michael quickly agreed, feeling easier. "Sure you don't mind?"

"Get the fuck outa here! You'll miss your date, and I'll get the blame for it. See you at the party tonight, anyway, creepy or not. Hey, didn't I tell you it was a good idea to come here instead of going to New York?"

"That's right," Michael agreed. "Best damned idea you ever had!" He gave himself a last appraisal in the mirror. "See you later tonight, then?"

"Sure."

When the door closed behind Michael, Paul sat for a moment on the edge of the bed, staring moodily down at the carpet, feeling suddenly very much alone. With another curse, he tore himself from the bed and walked over to the balcony. He could see Michael, his step light and carefree, his white hat perched jauntily on the back of his head, walking with a swift and eager step towards the Boardwalk.

Paul frowned. Hell, it wasn't really so much that he objected to being left alone this way. He certainly would have no trouble in finding willing feminine companionship. And yet . . . What the hell was he so upset about?

He would not admit it even to himself. Although he would probably have been too embarrassed to mention it, Paul was genuinely fond of Michael, and suddenly very much concerned about him. He didn't at all like what was happening. He didn't want to see any broad make a fool of his buddy. Michael was naive, an innocent farm boy who knew absolutely nothing about the workings of the minds of the opposite sex. Sure, Emily was a nice enough girl, but Paul remained suspicious. He knew from his own highly erotic life and from a number of unfortunate experiences of his whore of a sister, that the business of man and woman was only a game in which one tried to get the most out of the other. There was always an angle. Sex came first, because that was still the easiest way to snare a man. If she showed any serious intentions once that was over, then you could just bet your ass she was after something.

The trouble was that he didn't yet understand Emily's game, but he was certain there was one, and he was afraid Michael would in some way be hurt by it. He knew Michael hadn't screwed Emily yet—in fact, he doubted that Michael had so much as laid a hand on her—and that was even more confusing. No dame who let herself be picked up by a sailor could be the pure untouched virgin that Emily pretended to me. They just don't make them that way any more, Mack! So why this pose? What was Emily's game? Shit, what was she after?

There had to be a way Paul could alert Michael to the unknown pitfall he was certain Emily was preparing for him. But how and when? Talking would do no good; Michael would never believe him, merely crediting his words to envy or to what he considered Paul's rather jaded opinion of women in general. There would have to be some other way, something that could not leave the slightest doubt in Michael's mind that this Emily —nice, decent, supposedly moral Emily—was really no different from the other girls they had known in every port they had visited, and doubly dangerous because of her apparent air of sweet innocence. Be careful, buddy, you're headed for trouble.

Paul's eyes fell on the Festival notice on the dresser.

The suspended menace of the approaching storm was totally lost on Johnny that morning. He sat at his usual place at the bath house, staring morosely out across the shimmering sand to the yellowed sea, scarcely aware of what was before him. People were already becoming accustomed to the strange heaviness of the day and the weird color of the sky and, despite a general uneasiness, were returning to the lazy routine for which they had come to the shore, trusting the storm to hold its fury a few hours longer. The amusements were well-patronized, although business at the beach had fallen off. Everyone kept an eye or an ear on the weather, pausing at the refreshment stands to listen to the radio news, or gathering about portable radios on the beach.

Johnny couldn't care less about other people's problems, for he was still tangling with a big one of his own. Throughout the day, always before his eyes was that terrible picture of Greg and Steve in bed together, naked, doing things . . .

Johnny was feeling both outraged and cheated, and more than just a little foolish. All day yesterday he had burned with a sense of guilt just because he had taken money to look at naked men. At the Seaquarium he had wondered what Greg's reaction would be, and he even felt ashamed when he glanced at Greg bending over the sink and suddenly wondered what it would be like to look at him naked. It had seemed . . . dirty . . . almost sacrilegious. How could he possibly connect his idol with such indecent thoughts and actions?

And yet, that very same night, Greg had gone so much further than Johnny had even considered going, had actually done those things that Johnny had always considered the sick perversions of dirty old men. He remembered looking at the men on the Boardwalk and wondering how you could tell if they were queer. And here, all along, his hero, Greg Christopher, had been one of them, and he had never even begun to suspect.

If Greg had gone this far why should Johnny feel so guilty about the much more innocent diversions that brought him extra money?

Even more important to his confused mind was the question of how he should feel toward Greg now, how he should act toward him when they met again. The pedestal was gone, of course, for good. You can not surprise your god in bed and expect him to remain a god. Greg had been abruptly lowered from his cloud to a spot considerably nearer to earth. In those few shattering seconds outside Greg's window, Johnny had matured forever beyond the possibility of hero worship.

It was all too new, too unexpected. Johnny's sexual attitudes had always been those of the typical teen-aged American boy who looks on sexual deviation with contempt and loathing. Society taught that the sexual act was for the purpose of procreation, a belief strongly promoted by the church Johnny attended with his mother every Sunday morning. He had believed it once, but such naivete had long passed. Still, even with the rough couplings he had witnessed (and several times experienced) beneath the Boardwalk, that basic possibility was at least there, making such fornication normal and somehow natural. That possibility did not even exist in what was considered perverted sex. A homosexual was neither a man nor a woman. He was a peculiar creature with inclinations that were simply not right. Oh, he and his friends had seen many of them on the beach, and had always mocked them as contemptible, ludicrous misfits to be looked down on and laughed at.

And Greg Christopher was one of them. Did Johnny now feel the same way about his long-time friend? Was he disgusted by him? Must he now class Greg with that unpleasant grouping of "queers" and "fairies?"

Greg certainly seemed the same. He looked like a real, rugged man, not a lisping, effeminate person lusting after young boys. He angrily dismissed the thought that there might have been an ulterior sexual motive in Greg's kindness towards him. Johnny would not believe that. God damn it, if he hadn't seen Greg doing it with his own eyes, he would never have known, suspected or believed anything.

It was none of his business, but Johnny was too young to dismiss it that easily. A teen-aged boy can not so simply toss aside his idol, nor can he lightly dismiss unpleasant things he has learned about him.

At least, there was one matter which had now become clearly resolved in Johnny's mind. He was going to get that boat now. His determination had hardened. It had been partially out of respect for Greg that he had earlier refused Jimmy's offer; it had all seemed somehow disloyal to clean-living

Greg Christopher. Well, the hell with that crap. It was all different now. Greg would have no right to say anything about it even if he should find out.

Johnny was still wrapped in contemplation when Jimmy joined in. "Hope the goddamn storm waits a while longer yet," he remarked as he took a seat beside his friend. "Be real hell for business."

Johnny glanced indifferently at the sky, as though only now becoming aware of its ominous shading; it had not changed since morning. "Won't be here till tonight."

"You sure? Sure as hell hope so." The locker boys were not in the habit of questioning Johnny's knowledge of the sea and the elements. "You still want some extras today, Johnny?"

There was now no hesitation in Johnny's immediate reply. "Damn right I do. All I can get. I'll take a look at anything, if they'll pay. Just let me know."

Somewhat surprised by this instant willingness and by the unusual determination in Johnny's tone, Jimmy looked over at his young friend. "Something wrong, Johnny?"

Johnny shook his head. "What the hell should be wrong?"

Jimmy felt suddenly slightly uncomfortable. "Look, Johnny . . . well, if you don't wanna do it, just say so. Hell, it's okay with me. I just thought I was doing you a favor, that's all . . ."

"Of course I wanna do it," Johnny insisted, suddenly and inexplicably angry. "Why the hell shouldn't I do it? All I have to do is look at some guy's prick, and I get paid for it, that's all. It's sure worth a buck just to take a quick look. And look, Jimmy, if you find any who want to see what I've got, I'll show it to 'em, for an extra buck. Hell, I'm

379

not ashamed of it; better than anything I've seen so far."

"Yeah, Johnny . . . Sure thing. Sure. I'll let you know."

Still confused, Jimmy left Johnny to himself, wondering what could be behind this sudden change of attitude. He knew Johnny had played around with a couple of the girls under the Boardwalk, but he had always been something of a prude, not even cursing the way all the other guys did. What gives, he wondered.

Johnny turned back to the sea leaning his arms on the railing. His handsome young face was angry and determined, his deep dark eyes hard, his fists clenched. God damn it, he was through being a fool! He would show that faggot Greg Christopher, and let him say just one goddamned word to him! He was going to get that goddamned boat of his, and he was going to get it fast!

# CHAPTER TWENTY

The Hawkins' house appeared silent, almost deserted, under the yellow sky. An occasionl gull wheeled about the gabled roof or settled on the gleaming black casing of the telescope as though searching the sea for companions. A bit of contorted driftwood, whitened by salt, was washed up on the beach, only to be carried out again by the next wave; it could wait a bit longer for its final resting place, for it had already been carried on the long journey from the Indies.

Ethel still sat in her chair alone on the verandah, rocking gently with the unhurried rhythm of the aged, half dozing in the heat of the day, her thoughts becoming more and more confused between the past and the present. A fly buzzed persistently about her head, and she half-heartedly brushed it away with the painted fan.

Within, the house hummed with activity as Margaret and her staff prepared for the night's

Festival. Brightly colored paper lanterns dangled in the motionless air, colored paper streamers were twisted from wall to wall, the large portrait of Captain Nathaniel had been brought from Ethel's room and placed in its traditional place of honor in the lobby, where a small bar was also being prepared against the rising wall of the staircase. The air of the kitchen was spiced with the fragrance of cooking delicacies.

Increasingly heavy waves battered against the spit of land upon which the house stood. When Ed left the front desk to descend into the cellar for additional decorations, he noticed the floor was covered with a thin film of water.

Charles Fraser found the old house wrapped in slumberous silence when he reached the Point in the early part of the afternoon; he had managed an earlier train than originally scheduled. Unable to find a free cab at the station, he had walked all the way along the Boardwalk, both hot and tired, wending his way with considerable irritation through the slowly milling crowds, buffeted uncomfortably by the increasing and unpleasantly hot winds. When he reached the end of the Boardwalk, he looked up at the massive old house he now knew so well, setting down his single suitcase and pausing to catch his breath.

Well, here he was again. Over the many years they had been coming here to Hawkins' Cove, he had always enjoyed their stay at The Cloud, but just now, his pleasure was tempered by the knowledge that on the first floor of that vast old pile, his daughter was probably holding her devotions to a dead man.

Throughout his trip on the train, Charles had vainly attempted to subdue the uneasy sense of guilt that had been growing steadily more pronounced as the time approached for his visit to the shore. No one could say he did not love his wife and daughter; they were the very center of his world. But he quite honestly could not enjoy ending his summer here in Karen's depressing company. He admitted, guiltily, he had enjoyed the peace and quiet of their empty home during the absence of his family. Was his irritation justified?

In recent months, he had become more and more abrupt in his relationship with his cripped daughter, and this seriously disturbed him. He felt deeply, sincerely sorry for Karen, of course. But was it not possible for a person so to drown herself in self-pity that her entire focus of life became distorted? Karen seemed to feed on pity as a vampire feeds on blood; she reveled in it, no, she lived for it.

At first, Charles had felt certain that time would cure his daughter's wounds. Surely she would sooner or later realize that life had not ended for her. Karen was, after all, an intelligent person.

To his surprise, it had not happened that way. Several years had now passed, and Karen was still in that wheelchair, and sorrow and pity remained the mainstays of her strangely warped existence. His own attempts to force her back into the world had resulted in periods of hysteria culminating in actual physical illness. He had finally ceased to intervene, cautioning Linda to do the same, and they had again hoped that time would still prove the strongest element in her rehabilitation. It was difficult for them all, but love must also mean a measure of understanding.

As he approached the old house, buffetted by the unusually strong winds sweeping across the open point of land, Charles picked out the form of old Ethel Hawkins seated alone on the verandah, sheltered from the wind by the bulk of the building. She had been in that exact spot every year when he arrived, observing the sea and the Boardwalk.

"And how are you today, Mrs. Hawkins?" he asked as he wearily mounted the worn wooden steps.

"Oh, it's Mr. Fraser! How very nice to see you again! But you are a bit early, aren't you? Your wife doesn't expect you before some time in late afternoon."

Charles removed his hat and wiped the sweatband with his handkerchief. "Yes, I guess I am a bit ahead of myself. I had an opportunity to catch an earlier train. It was so blasted hot in the city, I welcomed the chance to get out here a little sooner." He glanced up at the sky and frowned. "Can't say it's much better here, though. Even the wind doesn't help. Like standing before a funnel of hot air."

Ethel brushed away a strand of hair blown from its proper place. "I'm afraid the wind will soon send me inside. It seems to be searching me out now; takes my breath away."

"I suppose the Festival will be held indoors tonight?"

"Oh, my, yes," she assured him, nodding. "It's a shame, but it can't be helped. But won't you sit here with me for a moment? You look like you could use a little rest."

Charles nodded agreement. "Indeed. And a shower. I had to walk all the way from the station. Couldn't get a damned cab."

"Why, you should have called us, Mr. Fraser," Ethel scolded. "We surely could have arranged to have you picked up; it's really too far to walk from the station, and in this weather, too."

"I knew you'd all be too busy preparing for the Festival; I didn't want to bother you. I've done it before, you know." He added, with a rueful laugh, "I guess I was younger then."

Ethel's expression became a bit more serious, and she spoke after a brief hesitation. "Your wife and daughter are inside having a nap, Mr. Fraser. There is something I would very much like to discuss with you. Look, there's some lemonade right there on the table. I'm sure you would prefer something a bit stronger, but perhaps that will do for the moment?"

"It'll do just fine," he assured her. "Will you have a glass?"

"Yes, please."

Charles removed his jacket, folded it, and placed it carefully over the bannister. He poured two glasses of the lemonade; handing one to Ethel, he took the other and gratefully seated himself in the chair at her side, sighing with the satisfaction of getting off his feet.

"Ah, but that is refreshing," he commented, sipping the drink and licking his lips. "Just nothing like a good, iced drink on a day like this."

Ethel looked over to him and immediately came to the point. "Tell me, Mr. Fraser, just what is wrong with your daughter's legs?"

Surprised at the unexpected question, Charles took a moment to answer. "I really can't tell you, Mrs. Hawkins. She hasn't walked since the accident, you know."

"But what do the doctors say?"

Charles frowned. "We've gone to several, the best in their field, but they can't seeem to agree on a diagnosis. I suppose there are some things that are—well, difficult to pin down."

Ethel stared at him for another moment, at the fleshy, once-handsome face now pink with perspiration and exertion, and Charles began to feel uncomfortable under the intensity of her scrutiny. He again pulled out his handkerchief and ran it across his forehead.

"Mr. Fraser, you know that I am a very old woman, and as I constantly remind everyone, age has certain privileges, and one of them is bluntness of speech."

He lowered his glass; his eyes seemed tired. "You're trying to tell me something . . ."

"You and your wife love Karen very much. I know that. You have both been extremely kind and understanding, devoting yourselves to making life easier and more bearable for her. It can't have been an easy time for you, these past few yeas."

"Of course not. I don't understand . . ."

"Surely you and your wife would do anything in your power to restore Karen to health, both physically and mentally?"

He caught at the last word. "Mentally?"

"You have always tried to overlook that particular aspect of her illness, to conceal it from others, but I know what others do not know. I have seen that shrine where Karen says her daily prayers to the portrait of a dead man."

Charles frowned and, leaning his arms on his legs, clasped his hands together; the whiteness at the knuckles revealed his agitation.

"Yes. You're right, of course. That damned shrine. I'll tell you quite frankly that there have been times when we have feared for Karen's sanity. Oh, it's obvious that the problem with her legs is not a physical one, although we have always pretended that it is. There's no point in going to doctors any more; there's nothing they can do, no physical ailment they can heal."

"A psychiatrist?" Ethel offered, gently.

He shook his head and the light glinted on the increased silver of his dark hair. "She won't hear of it, and we can't force her. I've often thought of demolishing that damned shrine of hers, smashing that blasted portrait, but I'm afraid to. It would destroy the last part of her dream, and I don't know what that would do to her; I don't want to take the chance."

Ethel leaned instantly towards him. "And will you allow her to build all the remainder of her life on that empty dream of hers? Is that the future you want for your daughter?"

Shaking his head again, he replied softly, "No man wants such a life for his only child."

"Then something must be done." He looked up at her, puzzled; Ethel leaned back in her chair again, her mouth firm, the lines about her lips set immovably in a spider-web pattern. "Oh, I know. I'm interfering where I've really no business, but please believe me, I'm not merely a woman who has lived too long and has no other pleasure in life but putting her nose where it isn't wanted. I'm not just making conversation, or being inquisitive. I've a very definite reason for speaking to you in this way. May I go on?"

He waved his hand in agreement.

"I have known your family now for a good many years," she continued. "You first came here when Karen was still a child. I saw her grow up. She came here with that young man of hers the summer of his death, and I have since watched the dark world of sorrow close in about her; I know what that is like, believe me. I think I have the right to look upon you all as old friends."

"Well, of course, Mrs. Hawkins."

She held up one hand. "Please, be patient with me just one moment longer. I'm only saying all this so you will understand why I'm interferring in your private affairs. The truth is, Mr. Fraser, that I am in possession of certain information that throws quite a different light on your daughter's condition."

He felt a strong stirring of alarm, perhaps even the fear of confirmation of his own uncertainties. "I'm afraid I don't understand what you mean."

"I would like a cigarette, if you don't mind, and I wish you would have one yourself."

He extended a cigarette, lighted it for her and, his face now very serious, took one for himself. There seemed something almost ludicrously improper about the prim, tidy, white-haired old woman sitting there in her old-fashioned rocking chair, a glass of iced lemonade at her side, a bamboo fan in one hand, and a cigarette between her thin white lips. She was like a character out of Somerset Maugham.

The wind was beginning to moan as it swept up

the point and attacked the old house. The further side of the verandah was already wet with spray.

Through the light haze of blue-white smoke, Ethel looked at him; he had never before realized how bright her eyes were, despite her advanced years.

"I'm afraid what I'm about to say may sound quite terrible to you, Mr. Fraser," she began softly, "but you must know this. You see, Karen has been lying to you. There is nothing wrong with her legs—absolutely nothing—and she is well aware of it. Karen can walk, Mr. Fraser. She can walk as well as you and I. Far better than I can, for that matter."

He looked at her without speaking, no expression on his perspiring face, the cigarette dangling from between his lips; she thought perhaps he had failed to understand her words.

"Mr. Fraser, she can walk. Your daughter can walk. She is not bound to that wheel chair."

He brushed a hand through his thinning hair, and his breathing seemed more labored. "What do you mean?" His voice was hoarse and trembled slightly. "How do you know?"

"I saw her."

"You saw her?" The tone was incredulous.

Ethel nodded. "Yes. As a matter of fact, it happened only yesterday. You know how sometimes in hot weather the door to your suite is left open to catch whatever little breeze there may be from the lobby. It was in early afternoon. I was returning to my room for a nap—the heat does get to me these days—and as I passed your open door I saw a flicker of movement. I stopped, a bit concerned; I knew your wife was in town, and Karen was the only one there. Karen was seated in

389

her chair before the fireplace, looking up at a pack of cigarettes on the mantel; she wasn't able to reach them from the chair. My eye had been caught by her gesture of throwing aside her blanket." Ethel paused, then spoke very slowly and distinctly. "While I watched, she rose from that chair, walked to the mantel, took the cigarettes, stood there for a moment as she lighted one, and then returned to her chair and re-covered her legs with the blanket."

Charles stared at her, his eyes betraying confusion and disbelief. "Are you . . . certain?" He drew heavily on his cigarette, nervously blowing the smoke from his mouth. "Perhaps she just raised herself and leaned on the chair so she could reach the mantel."

Ethel firmly shook her head. "No. You know that fireplace, Mr. Fraser; she could not possibly reach the mantel from her chair. She stepped out of that chair, she walked, she stood erect, all without support of any kind."

He crushed the cigarette in the ashtray and looked out to the sea that was becoming choppy and whitened with swiftly moving caps. His tongue quickly ran over his lips and he clasped his hands more tightly.

"I don't understand." The voice had become almost a whisper.

"I felt you should know," Ethel said, justifying herself. "I didn't mean to meddle, but . . . ."

"Of course, of course," he said absently, then looked up at her once again. "Have you told Linda?"

"No. I knew you were coming today, and I thought it best for you to speak with your wife. That's why I was so anxious to see you first."

"Yes. Yes . . . I'm glad you did; I appreciate your concern, your interest. Thank you." He rose from his chair and stepped to the edge of the verandah, leaning heavily with both hands on the salt-whitened bannister; there was a circle of wetness on the back of his shirt. "I don't . . . I can't understand. What does it mean?" He raised his head and looked out to sea for an answer, found none, and turned again to face Ethel, who was watching him closely and with some concern. "For years now, Karen has confined herself to that wheelchair, going nowhere, doing nothing with her life, a complete invalid who has lost all interest in life. But if what you say is true, it was all for no reason at all."

"There is a reason for all that we do," Ethel commented, "even if it is not always understood by others."

He found it difficult to speak; a nervous tic had appeared at the corner of his right eye. The pink flush had faded from his face, replaced by the pallor of shock. He quickly again licked his suddenly dried lips.

"In God's name, why? Why has she brought her life, and ours as well, to such a needless standstill? A reason? What reason? My God!"

"What are you going to do?"

"Do?" He turned away and walked to the end of the verandah, then returned and stood before her. She felt pity for the pain in his face. "I don't know. My God, what can I do?"

"It seems to me you must let her know that you have learned the truth," Ethel said thoughtfully, "and that this terrible masquerade of hers is over. But, oh, Mr. Fraser, you must be so very careful! Karen is such a sensitive girl, so easily hurt. We can't know, we can't have the slightest idea, what is behind this. No matter how wrong she has been, you must handle the matter in the best way for her as well as for yourselves. What she has done seems incomprehensible, but now your pity must be stronger than ever before, you must be kinder than you have ever been, you must try to understand more than ever. And then you must make Karen understand how wrong she has been. Oh, Mr. Fraser, how desperately she needs your help now!" She rested a hand on his arm; tears of concern glistened in her eyes. "Talk to her . . . make her see . . . make her understand. Make her feel your love now more than ever before." She removed her hand from his arm, her face became more composed, and she settled back in her chair again and vigorously beat at the air with her fan. "And then—bring her to the Festival."

It was not until they were on the ferris wheel that they finally reached the stage of holding hands; somehow, it had seemed to Michael too forward to do so before. Their yellow carriage carried them high above the roof of the building, and there they were stopped for several moments. They seemed in a quiet world of their own, strangers perhaps from a distant planet looking down upon the race of man at play. The sea was a burnished gold, heaving like the breath of a sick old man. The sky was covered with a thick layer of yellow clouds. The car swayed more than usual, for the wind was stronger at this height, and Michael placed a protecting arm about Emily's shoulders, slowly and carefully, fearing a rebuff; she moved closer to him. He pointed to the dark mass of the Hawkins house looming black against the yellow sky.

"They're having some kind of party over there tonight," he commented.

"Yes, I know. The Festival. It's the old Captain's birthday. They have one every year on this date."

"Ever been to one?"

She shook her head; her blonde hair brushed against his face, leaving behind a marvelously clean fragrance. "No. It isn't the sort of thing you go to by yourself."

"Will you go with me tonight?" he asked.

She turned to him, excited, her eyes sparkling. "Oh, I'd love to! I've always wanted to go to the Festival! Would you really take me?"

"Sure." He grinned. "I've got to. The old lady at the house made me promise."

She was surprised. "You've told her about me?"

Michael grinned. "I've told everybody about you!"

Smiling, Emily moved closer, and the wheel began moving again.

Paul was seated alone at the bar, cupping the cold glass of beer in his warm hands, staring vacantly at the mirror before him, feeling strangely lost and alone. His half-hearted attempts on the Boardwalk to find agreeable, feminine companionship had been unproductive; such a state of afffairs had never happened to him before in his entire life. Oh, there were plenty who gave him the eye, that was for sure, but nothing came of it: either they were too shy to pick up on his follow-through, or they had no time, or they were waiting for someone else. He had even begun making time on the beach with a chick in a hotly revealing bikini, when her boy friend, a big hairy bastard with "no nonsense" in his eyes, came long, and Paul had felt it wiser to look around again. The main trouble seemed to be that no one was alone in this damned place. The girls traveled in pairs. So had he, he ruefully thought, until Michael had deserted him.

In the act of raising the beer to his lips, he glanced at his reflection in the glass and looked at himself with sudden interest, trying to be objective about what he saw. He sure as hell hadn't changed, that was for sure. He was still a hell of a good-looking guy, he had a great personality, a body to get any broad hot. Why, then . . .

He frowned and lowered the glass again, suddenly disturbed by the trend of his thoughts. What the hell was he worrying about? So he hadn't managed to get a broad jumping at him with the snap of his fingers, so what? What the hell did that mean? He hadn't really tried very hard, anyway.

Shit. Yes he had. Perhaps doubly hard, because of that nagging doubt at the back of his mind. He knew what it was. He had suddenly lost confidence in his own sex appeal. Can you beat that? He had lost his self-confidence! The worst thing about it was that he knew why.

His pride had been seriously damaged. It wasn't just that he had been left alone this way, it was something that went much deeper. It was the reason for his being alone that bothered him. Michael had found someone whose company he preferred to his own. They should be together right now, drinking their beers, perhaps with a couple of dames all lined up for the evening. But where was Mike now? Out with some girl, some nice and clean and sweet and wholesome little broad who in the course of a single day had managed to twist him around her little finger.

Not that there was anything wrong with being with a dame, of course. But not like this. You spend time with a girl, maybe you buy her a drink, even a dinner, maybe take her to a movie, and then you screw her and that's that. You don't spend a whole fucking day with her, and then claim you didn't even get in. You spend the day with your buddy setting up things for the evening. You don't just ditch him.

Why should Michael have so lightly tossed him aside for this Emily? They'd always shared everything, including women, but now, this girl he wanted all for himself, Michael did, Paul wasn't good enough this time. Did Mike really think he was fooling his old buddy? You don't spend all that time with one girl without getting what you want. No, he didn't know where or how, but Mike was getting in there and just didn't want to share her with his buddy.

Paul almost angrily ordered another beer. Shit! He was becoming confused. Why should he care so much what Mike was doing now? Why should he miss him, anyway? Christ, he was no fucking queer! He sure as hell didn't need any guy.

Come on, be honest, you old bastard. All's fair in love and war, isn't it? In spite of Michael's feeling for Emily, Paul had immediately made a play for her himself and he hadn't got to first base. Emily preferred Michael, and that just didn't make any goddamned sense. Paul knew he was much better looking than Michael, and when it came to sheer sex appeal, hell, there wasn't any contest! He had turned it all on for Emily yesterday, and what had happened? Nothing! Not a single fucking thing. God damn it, no female had ever done this before, preferring somebody else—Michael or whoever—to him.

He quickly drained his glass and ordered another refill. And no God damn broad was going to do it to him now!

Greg returned to his work at the Seaquarium after meeting Steve for lunch, and Steve headed back to The Cloud, feeling a sudden need to be alone. He walked slowly and thoughtfully, almost unaware of the increasing anger of the elements. He felt there was much he had to think about. Decisions would have to be made. His early-morning certainty and confidence were no longer unchallenged, and he would have to resolve his inner problems before meeting Greg again for dinner and another night together. Before that happened, he had to decide whether or not to take a male lover.

There were several people seated on the verandah when he reached the old house, and for a moment he thought he might pass by and walk on the edge of the promontory to do his thinking undisturbed. Then he happened to glance up to the Widow's Walk, and decided that was where he wanted to go; he was certain Miss Meg wouldn't really mind.

But Ethel motioned to him as he mounted the steps and waved in a brief, hurried gesture, preferring not to be delayed. Seated beside the old woman, in her wheelchair, was Karen Fraser and at her side a somewhat overweight, red-faced, rapidly balding man who was a stranger to Steve.

"Mr. Conroy," Ethel called, "there's someone here I would like you to meet."

Hoping to get this over as quickly as possible, Steve joined the little group, smiling his hellos to Ethel and Karen, but not taking one of the empty chairs; the old woman turned to the stranger.

"This is another of our annual guests," she said to him. "Mr. Charles Fraser, Mr. Steve Conroy. I'm sure you'll be meeting again at the Festival this evening. This is Karen's father, Steve."

Steve took the damp, fleshy hand in his own. "How do you do, Mr. Fraser?"

"Pleased to meet you, Mr. Conroy." But the man did not smile, and there was a look of trouble in his face.

Turing to Karen, Steve commented, "I hope we'll be seeing you at the Festival too, Miss Fraser? I've never yet attended one, but I understand it shouldn't be missed."

Karen smiled wanly, bored but pleased at this attention. "Oh, yes, I suppose I'll be there, for a little while, at least. I can always watch."

Steve did not miss either the tone of self-pity or the sudden frown of displeasure that crossed her father's face at these rather lugubrious words; Charles said nothing as Steve extended his hand again.

"And I'll be seeing you, too, this evening, Mr. Fraser?"

"Yes. Yes, of course." The words were automatic and spoken without enthusiasm.

Steve found the lobby a riot of rather unimaginative but colorful decorations. No one ever accused Margaret of having the touch of an interior decorator, but what she lacked in professional taste and expertise she more than made up in enthusiasm. He waved to her, perched rather precariously on a step-ladder in the sitting room while one of the staff held some pink crepe for her. Mounting the stairs, he felt rather limp and tired. Beyond his own room he moved on to the next floor, pausing for a moment before Greg's door. He tried the knob and found the door unlocked, a pleasant tradition in a house whose pride was in its honesty. He stepped inside, leaving the door slightly ajar behind him.

He stood in the silence of the room. The balcony doors were shut, the light draperies drawn before them, and the room was in semi-darkness. This was Greg's home. He looked at the personal items . . . the toilet articles on the dresser, the books on the shelves of one wall. He touched the shirt, touched everything that belonged to Greg, running his fingers lightly, carressingly over Greg's possessions. Greg wore these things, he touched them, he had found pleasure in them and bought them for himself, they were a measure of his taste and personality. He looked down at the bed where the two of them had lain last night, and put his fingers on the pillow where Greg's head had rested. He remembered the night and felt close to him. Had it been the beginning of anything? He could not believe there was anything wrong in what they had done.

He quietly left the room and softly closed the door behind him, then moved on to the small door to the left and started up the stairs of the Widow's Walk, remembering again the touch of Greg's hand as they had walked up these same stairs the night before.

With her hand on the bannister, Ethel watched

him from the lobby below. She frowned, then nodded her head slightly. Leaning heavily on the slender railing, she started very slowly and heavily up the stairs. Margaret, still engrossed in decorating the sitting room, failed to notice her mother's movements.

Steve stood alone on the Widow's Walk, feeling like a school girl after her first big date, but moved by being here where it had all begun between them. They had stood at the telescope, and suddenly Greg's arms were about him; he seemed to feel again the warmth of the full lips pressed against his own, the pressure of the strong, firm body against his. His fingers touched the telescope. It had a meaning. He laughed in spite of himself. A phallic symbol?

"Am I sorry?" he asked himself. "Am I really sorry it happened? Do I feel shame? Guilt?"

He cupped his hands and, with some difficulty lighted a cigarette; the wind was strong up here. He leaned against the railing, his eyes now down towards the Boardwalk and the green-domed building that housed the Seaquarium where even now Greg was probably talking to a group of tourists about the great mysteries and wonders of the deep, but surely thinking only of him. He briefly wondered what the respectfully listening tourists would think if they knew how Greg had spent last evening.

Greg had spoken truly in saying it was easy to defy convention while they were in bed together, but later thoughts had not been quite so serene. The question of guilt had occupied Steve's mind all through the day. Standing over his mother's coffin he had sworn he would never again be guilty of any act that could possibly cause her pain, and he had firmly kept that vow since her death. Until last night.

Yet he could not deny the happiness the evening had given him. It had been the most thoroughly satisfying sexual experience of his life, and the remembrance of it would always give him pleasure. And if the pleasures of that night could become a permanent part of his life, if he and Greg should discover that they loved each other and wanted to spend their lives together, would that be wrong?

That in itself, of course, would create new problems. If they decided they wanted to be together, one of them would have to change completely his way of living, and Steve knew it would have to be himself. Not that there was anything to bind him so closely to his current mode of living. But Greg's world was here, this was where Greg had made a rewarding life and career for himself, much more so than Steve had managed to do. He could neither ask nor expect Greg to make the transition. No, it would have to be himself.

He was being extremely premature, of course. One night of sexual contact does not necessarily lead to a life-time contract. Not necessarily, anyway.

He was startled when the door opened behind him, and doubly surprised to see the old, bent figure of Ethel Hawkins, her face somewhat red and her breath labored from the effort of climbing the stairs. He knew she had not been here for many years. She feigned surprise when she saw him.

"Oh, I'm sorry, Mr. Conroy," she said lightly. "I didn't realize there was anyone up here. I often come up during the afternoon, you know, just to get above and away from everything." She seemed to find it necessary to compound the lie. "Margaret doesn't know it, of course. She says the stairs are bad for me, too much strain on my heart, you know, but it's really quite all right if I take them nice and slow. It's the only exercise I get, aside from rocking the chair on the verandah, and it does me good."

Steve smiled slightly at the blatant falsehood, and wondered how Ethel had learned he was up here. What could have brought her to the place, up the long and, for her, certainly exhausting flight of stairs, to a spot she had shunned for so many years?

"It's quite windy up here, Mrs. Hawkins," he cautioned, "and it's getting worse. Are you sure you'll be all right?"

She smiled. "Oh, my, don't you worry about me, my boy. I'm accustomed to the elements; the wind doesn't bother me." She moved, nevertheless, to the protection of one of the gables, where the wind could not reach her. "I like it up here, you know. I remember things." Her eyes moved over the platform and to the telescope. "It's like two different worlds. Up here, I can remember the world of my father, the time of the great clipper ships. And down there," she indicated the direction of the Boardwalk, "down there, the world of tinsel and froth, a world which may be more comfortable than the world I knew, but is so shallow and meaningless." She turned and looked at him for a moment; he wondered if she could really see him through the tears. "People too often come here and lose their perspective on life."

"What makes you say that?" he asked, curious.

"Oh, but isn't all that down there really just a make-believe world, after all?" she asked him, "populated by make-believe people? They live here only by and for pleasure . . . bathing, carousel and ferris wheel rides, popcorn and caramel candy. None of it is real. People came here to leave the real world behind and their troubles with it. Too many of them make the same mistake."

"And what mistake is that?"

"They convince themselves that this is the real world after all."

"Perhaps it should be the real world," Steve argued, "if we can make it that way. Perhaps it would be better for all of us. A world of cottoncandy. A world where people do as they please, where they are too busy with pleasure to bother with the cares and the worries of their every day lives."

Ethel shook her head. "Oh, no, no. That makes it all much too simple. Life isn't composed only of pleasure and the realization of beautiful dreams. My father learned that, bless him. When his own dream world—and it was, after all, much closer to reality than the one out there—collapsed, he lacked the strength to make his way in any other world. And so, he died. Yes, he died . . ." She looked over to the telescope again and for a moment placed her finger to her lips. "There are many ways of dying, you know. Those who always take the easy way in life, who want to forget their own responsibilities to themselves and to others, are suffering a form of death all their own. We must all have our dreams, of course, but they must provide us with a world to be lived in only now and again, not for always."

He smiled warmly at the little old woman. "How do you know so much, Mrs. Hawkins?"

"I must," she responded. "There has to be some form of payment for my having occupied space on this earth for so many years, and some kind of responsibility. It would be a great pity for a life spanning close to a century to have been a completely wasted one."

A plane flew noisely above them, trailing a banner advertising the week-end's Casino show. The frightened gulls, squawking their protests in raucus cries of disapproval, rose from their spots on the beach and the pilings, flapping their white wings and wheeling out to sea; the plane disappeared in the burnished sky, the gulls returned to the hard-packed sand and the excrement-stained posts, and there was silence again, save for the low moaning of the wind.

Steve wondered again why Ethel Hawkins had come up here, and at the strangeness of her words, which implied a certain knowledge of his own recent activities that he would prefer no one to possess at this moment. How could she possibly know what had happened between Greg and himself?

"You may be right," he agreed, "but isn't it possible that what begins merely as a form of pleasure, as a dream if you prefer, may become meaningful and more important than anything else in the world? Isn't it possible that even here, in this world devoted to pleasure, we may be fortunate enough to find something, a new reality and a new life, with its own meanings and values, not necessarily less substantial than in the . . . well, call it the real world, if you prefer."

She placed a wrinkled hand on his arm and looked intently into his face, her eyes approving. "I rather expected you to say something like that, young man. And yes, you're right, of course. Even a dream may crystalize into reality, if we're sure, absolutely sure. There are some of us who are that fortunate."

"And if we do find that reality in this supposed dream world?" he asked.

"Oh, then we must grasp it," she responded quickly and firmly. "We must grasp it with both hands and never let it go. But we must be oh, so very sure, or we still will delude only ourselves. If we can indeed find that certainty in spite of the insubstantial world that surrounds us in such places as this, how very fortunate we are! We haven't, any of us, so much true pleasure in our lives that we can afford to miss the least part of it. But we must keep our pleasures in their place, or we will be blinded to the realities with which we all must live. It is so easy to be fooled in a place like this! We must be certain. Only when we have no doubt whatever within ourselves that we have really found a new hope and a new permanence then, oh, then we must hold on . . . hold on very hard indeed . . . ."

Steve's eyes moved down again to the green roof of the Seaquarium, where at this moment was the new reality and happiness he had found. He turned and took the thin old hand in his own and smiled.

"If I am to take my pleasures where I may, then the pleasure I'm most looking forward to just now is a few moments of your company at the Festival this evening."

Her eyes filled again. "The Festival . . ." she muttered. "Yes, yes, of course. This evening."

"Now you must allow me to help you down all those stairs," he insisted. "It's really much too windy for you up here."

Ethel paused at the door, with her hand on Steve's arm, and looked back at the telescope. It had been so many long years. There were so many memories. Where had life gone so swiftly? She seemed to see a dark figure standing with one arm about the telescope, staring out to sea with eyes that saw no more. . . .

# CHAPTER TWENTY-ONE

Johnny waited impatiently throughout the day for his "special customer," carefully eyeing every man who entered the lockers, wondering still if there were some infallible way of determining who was and who was not queer. It seemed impossible. Once, it had been so simple.

His first special was a short man in his early fifties, his legs already old and withered, shaved clean of hair so that the skin shone as though it had been vigorously polished. He fumbled foolishly under a paunch that would not even permit him to see what he was handling. Johnny watched with total indifference, accepted the dollar, and dismissed the person from his mind. Next came a real Milquetoast of a man who wore a large, plain wedding ring on his left hand and whose marriage had probably been a wife-dominated failure, driving him to this empty, perverted manner of relief. The third startled him, for when he opened the locker door he saw a tall, powerfully muscled naked Black with richly bronzed, glowing flesh and enormous parts.

The fourth "special" was the athletic young man whose appearance had so startled and disturbed him the previous day, totally upsetting all his conceptions of the kind of pervert who went in for this sort of indecency. When he saw Johnny, the young man smiled familiarly, and his teeth were white and even.

"Oh, hi," he said, without the slightest trace of embarrassment. "Nice to see you."

"Hello," Johnny said, for the first time feeling decidedly uncomfortable. He could not feel contempt here. This could be Greg.

"Will you watch?"

Johnny nodded. "Okay."

The young man began his manipulation, looking closely at the locker boy, his dark, bright eyes running eagerly over Johnny's trim form. Johnny could not remove Greg from his mind, and the thought was not a pleasant one.

"Will you show it to me?"

Johnny hesitated, then thought again of his fallen idol. "Sure. I'll show you, if you want to see."

He moved closer to the booth, standing with the open doors carefully shielding him from any possible passing eyes, opened his trousers and exposed himself; the man, looking eagerly, increased his own efforts, beginning to perspire and breath heavily.

"Come in here with me," he urged in a taut whisper. "Just for a minute. Come on. I'll give you five dollars."

Johnny hesitated again. Only yesterday, he

would have slammed the door shut in disgust. Yesterday. Then he had been a different person. Things had changed since then. He again envisioned Greg and Steve as he had seen them. The young man's attractive face had become almost ugly in the grip of his lust, his lips wet, his eyes wide. For a brief moment, the face became Greg. Five dollars.

"Okay."

Just as he was about to enter the booth with the anxious, highly excited young man, Johnny saw Jimmy round the corner of the aisle. Quickly, suddenly frightened and ashamed, forgetting all about the dollar that was due him, Johnny adjusted his clothing and kicked the door shut with his foot, directly in the face of the astonished and disappointed young man. Trembling slightly at this near-discovery, Johnny rushed down the aisle to where Jimmy, grinning, waited for him, leaning casually against a closed door and picking his teeth with a wooden toothpick.

"Change your mind, Johnny?" he asked, in a tone heavily laced with sarcasm.

"What do you mean?"

"Come on, Johnny. Shit, you can't fool me. I saw what you were gonna do. You were gonna go in there with him. Why the hell didn't you? I sure don't give a shit. Hell, it won't hurt you to play around with them once in a while." He grinned unpleasantly. "Who knows, you might even like it!"

Johnny turned abruptly away, his face crimson with embarrassment. He heard Jimmy's harsh laughter behind him.

As Ethel was gently counseling Steve on the

Widow's Walk, Greg leaned over the railing of the porpoise pool, absently watching the lithe movements of the playful mammals and pursuing the leaps and turns of his own thoughts. His meditations were not quite so confused and chaotic as Steve's, and his new lover occupied only a margin of his mind.

Greg felt not the slightest sense of guilt over what had happened between him and Steve the night before. He had no one to answer to; he could do as he pleased. He had been through too much, had already suffered too deeply from the condemnation of society, to care about such things any longer. His philosophy had long since become a basically simple one; his behavior was determined by what did and what did not please or interest him. If what he did brought no harm to anyone—except, possibly, to himself, and that was surely no one's business but his own—there was nothing either wrong or improper in his activities. He paused for a moment, thinking of the possibility of bringing harm to Steve, but easily dismissed the thought; if anything, he was merely assisting Steve in finally being true to himself.

Although Greg was somewhat startled by his unexpected revelation of his latent homosexual nature, it did not unduly disturb him. He had never felt any particular revulsion towards homosexuals if, indeed, he had ever paused to give the matter much thought. Most servicemen at one time or another have a brush with the homosexual experience, although what had now happened, of course, went considerably beyond that.

His experiences since his return from Vietnam had had a profound effect on his life and particularly on his attitude toward women. The abrupt defection of the only girl he had ever really loved and in whom he had always placed complete and absolute confidence, had been something of a traumatic shock and had made him extremely wary of entering into intense relationships with other women. There had been occasional sexual contacts with women since that time, but they had been automatic, mechanical, and he understood now why, inexplicably at the time, he had never received the complete gratification he had expected. For some time now, he had been completely celibate.

Greg had never been in love with a man, yet his easy acceptance of this sexual involvement with Steve now made him wonder about many things, particularly about his basic feelings for Bob, whom he had always loved so deeply as a brother. As a brother? Should that emotion have been recognized as the beginnings of a homosexual desire? As adolescents, he and Bob had engaged in the usual sexual experiments together, but never to the point of an ultimate act. Perhaps he had loved Bob more than he realized.

He was willing now to accept without question his suddenly revealed nature, as he had urged Steve to accept his own. If Steve could resolve his own inner uncertainties (which, because of his traumatic sense of guilt about his mother, were naturally more intense than his own), he would not hesitate to form a permanent relationship with him, provided the various problems could be satisfactorily resolved. Loneliness can become trying.

Therefore, it was neither his own reaction nor the question of Steve that at this moment occupied Greg's thoughts, but young Johnny. Johnny, for some inexplicable reason, had been standing on the balcony outside his room last night and thus was a witness to his lovemaking with Steve. Greg was seriously disturbed about the possible repercussions on the boy's impressionable mind. He knew he was Johnny's ideal, the personification of what Johnny himself hoped one day to become. What would be the result of his unexpected discovery of the dents in his knight's shining armor?

Greg considered there were two possible reactions. The first of these—and in all fairness to Johnny, Greg sincerely hoped it would prevail— would be the complete shattering of the hero-image. Johnny's idol had feet of clay. It would be a bitter disillusionment for the boy, but in the long run it would certainly be for the best. He was only seventeen. In time, he might even come to understand and perhaps Greg might regain his friendship.

The second possibility was far more disconcerting. Johnny might still feel that nothing his hero did could be wrong, and in this, as in all other things, he might try to emulate Greg. A boy of Johnny's years has not necessarily formed his own sexual proclivities, and might easily be swayed by admiration for someone else. Greg was quite willing to tangle with these problems for himself, but he did not want the responsibility of pushing a young and highly impressionable boy into the difficult world of the homosexual.

Complete honesty was the only course he could pursue. He would have to speak with Johnny and somehow make him understand, point out to him that each person must live according to his own needs and desires, but that what was right for one was not necessarily right for another. How could he overcome the stringent moral precepts of a boy who had always been taught things were either right or wrong, and no circumstances could alter their classification? Perhaps, in spite of what had happened, Johnny might still respect him enough to listen to his words.

But it was apparent that Johnny was avoiding him. Greg had left messages for him all during the day at various spots along the Boardwalk, asking him to stop in at the Seaquarium some time during the afternoon, but these messages, if Johnny had received them, had been ignored, and Greg hesitated to force the interview by going to the lockers.

The porpoise leaped suddenly from the water and covered Greg with a shower of spray. He stepped back quickly, wiping at his wet clothing. It was feeding time again. His friends in the tank were not concerned with his own mundane problems.

The storm moved steadily closer to Hawkins' Cove, and the radio reports began to sound more alarming in their predictions of the storm's severity. Several vessels not far down the coast were reported in danger from excessively high seas. The winds were gale force, and tides were expected to be unusually high for that time of year. There would certainly be some flooding in the low-lying coastal areas, and it was suggested that everyone remain indoors until the storm had passed. Keep tuned to this station for further reports.

As the skies continued to darken, turning from yellow-gray to purple-streaked black, and the wind whipped the sea into tumbling breakers that dashed furiously upon the base of the old house, preparations for the annual Hawkins Festival were completed. Margaret had half considered postponing the Festival in view of the weather, but had finally decided against doing so. All the arrangements had been made, invitations forwarded, and everyone was looking forward to the gala. Never once had the Festival been either canceled or postponed in all these years. The people hereabouts were accustomed to a bit of weather and would not be deterred by this report of a strong storm moving towards them; the weather people had a habit of exaggerating anyway. No amount of bad weather had ever disturbed Captain Nathaniel, and to postpone these festivities because of a little blow would somehow seem an affront to his name.

The lobby and sitting room were festooned with balloons, crepe streamers, and colored lanterns, resembling a combination children's birthday party and New Year's Eve celebration. At one end of the sitting room a platform had been raised for the small orchestra that would provide the entertainment and music for dancing, while at the far wall was the long buffet table that shortly would groan under an ample spread of foods, punch, and delicacies. For those preferring a stronger liquid refreshment, there was the makeshift but well-stocked bar set up in the lobby. The hotel staff had been supplemented with outside temporary help, all dressed in smart black and red uniforms. While disappointed that the weather had forced the celebration indoors, Margaret was not really concerned that it would effect the attendance; the

Festival was always the most popular event of the season.

She stood now in the center of the dance floor in the sitting room, looking about her with a critical eye that nevertheless sparkled with satisfaction at the pleasant if somewhat amateurish result of her handiwork; Ethel stood with her.

"Well, I really think it looks even better this year than last," Margaret insisted. "Don't you agree, mother?"

Ethel nodded her approval. "Oh, yes dear, it's very nice indeed. But then, of course, you always make it so pretty. You've a knack for that sort of thing, you know. I do hope everyone will be here; you don't suppose the storm will keep them away, do you?"

Margaret moved to the window and glanced up at the angry sky; were those the first light splashes of rain on the glass? "Oh, no, I don't believe so, mother, although if it becomes really bad, some of our guests may want to leave a bit early."

"Well, now, don't you worry about a single thing, dear," Ethel urged, joining her daughter at the window and placing an affectionate hand on her arm. "You know how these weather people always carry on about such things; it's the only way they can get the people to listen to them. Everything is going to be just fine, and everyone will have a wonderful time. They always do."

"I do hope that extra order of olives will arrive in time," Margaret fretted, glancing through to the bar in the lobby. "I just know we won't have nearly enough. Why do I always forget that olives go into martinis as well as in a dish on the table?"

"Well, maybe everyone will prefer lemon twists," Ethel offered.

Margaret was pleased by the possibility. "Oh, do you really think they may, mother?"

Ethel began to giggle at this instant acceptance of her little remark and Margaret, realizing the foolishness of her own response, joined in her laughter, and for several moments the anticipatory tension eased. Margaret laughed with all her body, her ample bosom moving like twin mountains during an earthquake; she gasped for breath and applied her handkerchief to her eyes to wipe away the tears.

"Oh, mother, mother!" she sighed, putting her arm about Ethel's narrow shoulders and hugging her. "You are so good for me! But won't you go and take a little nap, now, before the people start arriving? You have seemed tired these past few days. You've got to promise me not to overdo things this evening, now. I don't want to be worrying about you."

Ethel smiled gently. "Don't you worry about a single thing, Meg; you just enjoy yourself, like everyone else will." She looked at her daughter for a moment, with a strange intensity in her eyes; then she turned, breathing heavily. "Perhaps I will just lie down for a moment or so, that's all, and have a little bit of a rest. Are you certain there's nothing I can do for you?"

"Not a thing, dear; you just go in and lie down."

Ethel lightly kissed her daughter's cheek and turned towards her own room. Watching her move with an almost painful slowness to the rear of the house, moving under the dangling crepe streamers like a lost little girl at a party, Margaret was again reminded that her mother suddenly seemed much older these days.

There was a sudden gust of wind. It struck the house with a force that caused it to tremble. Margaret shuddered slightly. Even the wind sounded lonely.

*Part V*

# The Last Festival

# CHAPTER TWENTY-TWO

The storm finally struck Hawkins' Cove shortly after sunset. As the afternoon moved on towards evening, and the strangely golden color of the sky faded and merged with the creeping darkness of an unusually early twilight, the weather became suddenly calmer. The wind dropped off to a mere hot whispered breath, and the crashing, churning green-white sea seemed to withdraw from the battered beach sands and lessen its fury; the spumed white caps disappeared, and the vast expanse of water became smooth and untroubled.

There were those who insisted, as they had predicted all through the day despite the ominous weather reports, that the storm had now bypassed the town after all.

But those more experienced, those who lived by the sea and knew it in all its changeable moods and attitudes, were not so easily fooled. They knew this was but a brief respite, a moment of rest, a breathing spell. The storm was still out there, waiting, gathering its forces before the great final assault. The sea could not be trusted. It had merely withdrawn its fury to lull man into a false sense of security. At the right moment, it would return. No, the storm had not passed. It had not even begun.

And those who insisted on this warning were proved right. When the wind returned, it screamed in from the sea, pouncing in fury upon the village. The sea roared, raised itself high and crashed down upon the land with such power that the very earth seemed to tremble with fear. The gray clouds had turned a slate black with a sickly shading of yellow and purple; their pregnant bellies burst and poured down upon the land a relentlessly hard, saturating rain that soon created miniature rivers along the deserted Boardwalk. The thunder was infrequent but violent in its rumbling, the lightning blinding in its brilliance. It seemed that only the sea was angry, and its voice was in the wind, demanding that its supremacy be again acknowledged.

This ferocity of the sea seemed to be concentrated on that narrow thumb of dark land where the old Hawkins homestead stood. The waves thundered upon the raised curve of rock, and those still on the verandah of The Cloud could feel the chilling salt spray.

And under cover of all this dark turbulence, as though the storm with its violence were merely as a feint to conceal the sea's true designs, the ocean insiduously worked its anger in more devious ways, digging itself through the softening earth beneath the foundations of the old house, weakening the base upon which the wooden structure stood.

It had been a long battle between the land and the sea, each wearing at the other through the millenia of time. But now the sea was becoming impatient. Man had compounded the offense of building on this spit of land for his own purpose and comfort. Such arrogance could no longer be tolerated. The sea had waited long enough.

Slowly, quietly, using the fury of the storm as a thief uses the concealing cover of a dark night, the sea began to seep into the dark cellars of the house and the earth began to fall away.

In view of the weather, Margaret had finally agreed to start the birthday festivities at an earlier hour than usual and thus most of the guest had arrived before the storm broke. There was always the possibility that the storm would have exhausted itself before it was time to leave, and thus they would in no way be discommoded by the elements. Clad in a black gown that minimized her figure and dramatically set off an exquisite pearl necklace, the last remaining souvenir of Captain Nathaniel's voyages to the Orient, Margaret Hawkins stood in the lobby to greet her guests. They dashed, dripping and wind-blown from the cabs to the protection of the great house. Margaret, as always on this night, glowed with an inner light and warmth; this was to her the most glorious night of the year. How many Festivals had she known and enjoyed? Only she was now aware that this would be the last.

Surprisingly, Paul was one of the earliest arrivals and, even more surprisingly, he was still alone, as he had been all through that frustrating day. He had spent all afternoon traveling from one bar to another, attempting to assuage his injured sense of pride and to drown a vague sense of uneasiness, a feeling that was almost akin to fear. The realization that Michael's new relationship might blossom into something more permanent than just another weekend liaison startled and unnerved Paul. It contradicted his whole understanding of women. Women were meant to be playthings, and not to be taken at all seriously; his own family life had clearly demonstrated the disaster of any permanent connections. Women were only co-combatants in the constant war of the sexes. Michael should have learned that by this time.

Throughout the long afternoon, Paul had vainly attempted to ignore the sudden suspicions that perhaps he was mistaken, that his own almost exclusively sordid experiences with women had blinded him to something better, higher. If he indeed were wrong, then he felt he was lost; he could not change now. His only hope was somehow to prove to Michael—and, above all, to himself—that he was still right.

In this manner had his thoughts run chaotically throughout the afternoon as he wandered from one cocktail lounge to another, his gait becoming less reliable and his thoughts more muddled. By the time he headed back to The Cloud for the Festival, which he had almost forgotten, he was no longer very clear as to where he was going, or why.

Margaret greeted him at the door, extending her hand and smiling warmly; it was evident to her that Paul had been drinking, but she was accustomed to the ways of seamen.

"I'm so glad you decided to come."

"Wouldn't miss it for the world," Paul assured her. His speech was thick, but he still exuded that natural charm which he knew no woman could resist. "Had to have a dance with my hostess." He smiled, flashing his white teeth and emphasizing the deep cleft in his left cheek. "That is, of course, if you've no 'jection to dancin' with a sailor?"

"What kind of grand-daughter would I be to the good Captain in that case?" Margaret asked, still smiling. "I do hope you'll enjoy yourself. There are refreshments inside and (with a slight twinkle in her eyes) a bar right there at the far side of the lobby."

Paul immediately made his way to the bar, collected a drink, and leaned against the wall of the staircase, sipping slowly and carefully eyeing the arriving young girls, not yet having completely abandoned all hopes of finding a willing companion for more interesting activities later on. He was totally unimpressed by what he saw. Like he had told Michael: a real Sunday-school kind of party. There were several couples already on the dance floor in the other room, moving rather listlessly to the adequate if uninspired music; others chatted in chairs lining the walls. All as proper as a church social, and just about as exciting.

Carrying his drink, Paul skirted the dance floor and moved to the large windows overlooking the approach from the Boardwalk in time to see Michael and Emily moving quickly up the walk, rather ineffectively carrying an umbrella low before them as a shield against the windblown rain. They walked very close together, Michael holding Emily's arm. They seemed to be laughing. What the hell was there to laugh about, on such a wet and miserable night? As he watched them, the umbrella was turned inside out by the wind and, torn from Michael's hand, was carried like a huge broken-winged raven out to sea. The couple made a mad dash for the verandah, still laughing. Paul grudgingly admitted he felt an unexpected pleasure in seeing Michael again. He had missed him. Would you believe it, he mused.

Just a few seconds later, and still laughing in that rather idiotic way young lovers have, Michael and Emily entered the room, brushing at their wet clothing. Emily ran her fingers through her damp hair. Paul noticed she looked exceptionally pretty in a bright yellow dress that brought out her green eyes and emphasized her narrow waist. They spotted Paul at once and unhesitantly made their way to him, both of them smiling and, to all appearances, genuinely glad to see him. Or were they just pretending? There was a slight blur in Paul's vision, and he couldn't be quite certain.

"Well, hello, there, Paul!" Emily greeted, placing her hand on his arm. "We were just talking about you. Where did you keep yourself all day?"

"Out of trouble," Paul assured her. "Hope you were doin' the same." He lightened his rather surly tone with a smile.

"Thought you might join us for dinner," Michael mentioned. "We looked for you at Roberto's."

"Didn't know what time you'd be there," Paul indicated pointedly. He laughed slightly and raised his glass, stumbling a bit against the wall. "To tell you th' truth, I guess I f'got all about dinner!"

Michael looked closely at his friend and frowned; despite all his carousing, Paul seldom got himself into a condition where his drinking became apparent.

"You've been hitting the bars, haven't you?" He laughed uneasily, not wanting to appear critical. "Don't tell me you're all alone? No female companion this evening?"

"I decided it wasn't worth all the trouble; you've already cornered the only really pretty girl in this town," Paul said thickly, not quite succeeding in his attempt to make Emily a gracious bow.

Emily laughed at his compliment, but there was a slight nervousness in her own tone. "If you spend too much time at the bar, how will you be able to dance with me later?"

"No problem 'tall," Paul assured her, bowing again, his intense dark eyes fixed rather too obviously on her breasts. "No problem 'tall. Nothing can stop me from dancin' with a beau'ful woman."

"Yes, and speaking of dancing," Michael said, turning to Emily with his arms extended as the orchestra struck up again. "Why should we waste the music?"

Paul leaned back against the wall and slowly sipped his drink, his eyes on the happy young couple as they joined the other dancers on the small wooden floor. He caught the possessive manner in which Michael slipped his arm about Emily's waist, the intimate way she looked up at him and smiled when he spoke to her, as though she was seeing something wonderful and very special. Michael had changed, somehow. He seemed older, steadier. . . .

Paul finished his drink and lurched slightly as he made his way back to the bar.

Steve was still in his room, dressing. He had done a great deal of serious thinking during the day, particularly after his brief conversation on the widow's walk with Ethel Hawkins, and had finally decided that this shilly-shallying from one side of the argument to the other would accomplish nothing. A decision had to be made, and just before he and Greg had met again for dinner, he had made it. He would find a way to stay with Greg, provided that was what Greg wanted as well. He was still not absolutely certain that this was the wisest course, nor had he managed completely to subdue the pricks of conscience, but he was going to try. Right or wrong, he would do what he wanted to do. The old woman was right. He would take his pleasure and happiness where he found it, hoping it would become a permanent part of his life. He had told Greg of his decision over dinner, and his new lover was as pleased as he. They would figure things out, and they would stay together, at least for now.

There was a soft knock at the door, and Steve flushed with excitement when he heard Greg's voice. "Ready, Steve?"

"Come on in, Greg!"

The door opened and Greg entered, tall and handsome in a light sports jacket, open shirt, and dark trousers. "You're worse than a woman," he complained. "How the hell long does it take you to get dressed, anyway?"

"Got to look right, don't I?" Steve asked, returning to the mirror. "At least be satisfied that it doesn't take me very long to undress."

Greg stepped behind him and slipped an arm about his waist. "I guess these are some of the things I'm going to have to learn about you. You look great, Steve."

Steve smiled at him in the mirror. "You're a bit prejudiced in my favor, but thanks, anyway. Say, how come you're still calling me Steve? Aren't you supposed to call me honey or sweetie or something like that?"

"What do you think I am, a fairy?" Greg responded, and Steve broke into a slight embarrassed laugh when he felt Greg's lips brush across the back o his neck.

"Come on, Greg," he complained. "You start playing around, and we won't ever get downstairs, and how would that look?"

"Frankly, I don't really give a shit. We'd have more fun right here."

Steve pulled a handkerchief from the dresser drawer and carefully arranged it in his breast pocket. "We can't disappoint your friend Miss Meg that way. Besides, the night's just started." He suddenly raised his eyes to meet Greg's in the mirror; Greg could see a mischievous twinkle. "Say, we going to be allowed to dance together?"

Greg laughed. "I wouldn't recommend it. I imagine we'd raise quite a few eyebrows."

"Doesn't seem fair," Steve commented, his lips pursed in a pout. "Nobody says anything when two women dance together."

"Maybe they don't get as hot as we do," Greg responded, adding, "Think about it, kid."

Steve turned and they looked at each other for a

moment without speaking, sensing that wonderfully new intimate understanding that had suddenly become an important part of their relationship. Steve put his arms about Greg and drew him close.

A strong gust of wind struck the side of the house, and the French doors to the balcony burst open and banged noisily against the wall. There was a dazzling flash of lightning, instantly followed by a shattering peal of thunder that seemed to vibrate through the floor. Startled, they broke from their brief embrace.

"I thought you were so damned anxious to get downstairs," Greg laughed. "You'd better make those doors fast, first; they'll let the rain in and ruin the carpeting. Sounds like a hell of a storm building out there."

Charles Fraser stood at the window in the silent Fraser apartment, staring vacantly out into the violent night, watching the branches of the tree whipped angrily by the wind, like arms writhing in fury. In the distance he could see only the brightest lights of the Boardwalk, gleaming almost defiantly through the driving rain and the intense surrounding darkness. The cigarette between his fingers trembled slightly, and there was the faint glint of perspiration on his face that could not be attributed entirely to the heat. Linda stood before the mirror over the mantel, putting the finishing touches to her carefully prepared hair.

"I can not understand what can be taking Karen such a terribly long time," she complained. "She would dress much more quickly if she would only let me help her a bit but, no, she has to do it all herself." She paused and looked into the mirror at her husband. "But I am so pleased she finally agreed to go, even for just a short time. I do think tonight will be good for her, don't you, Charles?" she asked hopefully, having little faith in her own words.

"I hope so," he muttered, his tone carrying little conviction; he might not have heard her.

"Do you know, she hasn't gone out once, not one single time, since we arrived here, except to sit for a short time in the early mornings on the beach in front of the point. And that's all. She hasn't even talked with anyone here, outside of an indifferent 'hello' to someone now and then." She fluffed her hair and carefully examined the coloring of her eyes, moving her little finger about the lids. There was a nervousness about her, and she seemed to be talking merely for the sake of introducing sound into the silent room. "I do believe she's getting worse all the time, more and more completely withdrawing into herself. Oh, I've tried, believe me I've tried, but, well, you know how stubborn Karen can be. No one can tell her anything. Oh, perhaps we should really have gone somewhere else this summer. There are too many memories for her here, you know. Of course, she does seem to thrive on her memories . . ."

The cigarette burned Charles's fingers. He dropped it with a slight curse and turned angrily towards his wife. "For Christ's sake, Linda, will you please stop rattling on this way?"

Linda turned quickly, an expression of complete surprise and indignation on her face; her husband had never before spoken to her in so sharp a tone. "Why, Charles!"

Shaking his head, he complained, "We've been

431

all through this so many times before! It never gets us anywhere. Surely we've had enough of it by now?"

Her mouth still slightly open with surprise, Linda sank slowly to the edge of the couch. "Why, what on earth is wrong with you, Charles? I swear, I've never seen you so cross and irritable. Is it something at the office?"

He shook his head again, sighing with resignation. "No . . . No. I'm sorry. I really didn't mean to snap at you."

Linda looked at her husband for a moment and she could see the concern in his face, the creases of worry on his forehead, the evasive eyes, the light trembling of the hairy hands that always indicated an inner problem. It was evident that he was troubled.

"Charles . . ."

He interrupted her by turning towards the closed door of Karen's room and raising his hand in a gesture of caution. "Here comes Karen now."

The inner door opened and Karen wheeled herself into the large room; she was clad in a dress of pale blue with her father's corsage of pink orchids pinned to her shoulder, and Linda thought briefly that she might have been rather attractive, if only she had done something with her hair and applied a bit of coloring to her pale face.

"Shall we go?" she asked, her voice indicating a total lack of interest in the evening's festivities. "I suppose I'm ready."

"Why, you look just lovely, dear," Linda exclaimed with a forced enthusiasm as she rose from the couch.

Charles hesitated another moment, running his right hand over his trouser leg in a habitual sign of

432

nervousness. His eyes fixed intently on Karen, he followed his wife and daughter to the door. He quickly licked his lips and seemed about to speak, but then changed his mind. With his hand on the doorknob, he paused once again, still wracked with indecision. He spoke then without turning.

"Wait . . ."

"What is it, Charles?" Linda asked. "What are you waiting for?"

Charles turned to them, and both Karen and Linda were startled by the sudden pallor of his heavy face as he again turned his eyes to his seated daughter. Again he began to speak, again stopped; he took a deep breath and licked his dry lips again.

"What on earth . . ." Linda began as she suddenly experienced a slight shiver of inexplicable fear; she had never before seen her husband act so strangely.

Charles leaned forward and placed his hands on the arms of Karen's wheelchair, bringing his face closer to hers. His daughter looked up at him, as bewildered as her mother by this peculiar behaviour.

"We're going to leave the chair behind this time, Karen," he said, very softly, his intent eyes fixed upon hers.

". . . Father?"

His words were now firm and decisive and he spoke slowly, emphasizing each word. "Karen, I want you to get out of this chair and walk into that lobby out there on my arm."

Linda's voice was strident with shock. "Charles! You don't know what you're saying!"

Still bending over his daughter, Charles ignored his wife's words. "Well, Karen?"

A moment longer he leaned over his daughter,

looking sternly into eyes that suddenly held a touch of uncertain fear; then, sighing again, he walked towards the mantel and stood with his back to them, his head bowed. Karen very slowly turned her chair to face him; on the heavy carpeting, the movement made no sound. Linda placed a strengthening hand on her daughter's shoulder; her own face had turned pale.

"I'm waiting, Karen."

"I don't know what you're talking about, Father. What . . . what is it you want?"

"I think you know perfectly well what I'm talking about," Charles responded without turning. "I want you to get out of that damned wheelchair and walk with us out into that lobby."

"Charles, you're out of your mind!" Linda stridently insisted.

Charles turned and looked at his wife; there was no pleasure in his set, white face. "No, Linda, I'm not out of my mind, and Karen knows I'm not." He lowered his eyes to his seated daughter, and they became suddenly soft and filled with compassion. "Karen, I know. You have been lying to us."

"Oh, Charles, Charles!" Linda staggered to a nearby chair and seated herself somewhat unsteadily, her eyes fixed with amazement on her husband. "Charles, I knew something was wrong; you've been acting so strangely since you arrived. But how can you say such a thing, to your own daughter!"

"I can say it because it's the truth," Charles quietly and firmly explained, still staring at the silent seated girl. "You've been lying to us all these years, Karen, and not only about your inability to walk. About everything. Why have you lied to us, dear?"

Karen caught her breath, and the sharp sound seemed unnaturally loud in that suddenly silent room. She looked quickly up at her mother, then turned her head and looked at the closed door, as though hoping for some kind of help from that source. Her eyes gleamed with a sudden fright as she extended her hands to her father; they trembled noticeably.

"Stop it, Father!" she whispered. "Stop it! Please!"

"No, I won't stop, Karen. You know I can't stop now." Charles dropped abruptly to his knees before the chair and took his daughter's white hands in his, holding them close to his breast. "Karen, it's time now that you told us the truth!"

"But I have told you the truth!" Karen insisted, again looking wildly about like a caged and frightened animal. "I've always told you the truth!"

Charles was pleading with her now, and tears stood clearly in his eyes. "Don't you see, dear, it isn't really important that you've deluded your mother and myself; we love you and we can forgive you anything. But just look at what you've done to yourself, Karen! You're beginning to believe your own lies, and you're basing your entire life upon them! You're martyring yourself in the name of a love that existed only in your dreams!"

Karen screamed with a piercingly shrill cry, pulling her hands from her father's grasp, threw them over her ears and shook her head vigorously. "No, no, I won't listen to you any more, I won't listen!"

"Yes you will, Karen; you've got to listen!" Charles forcibly removed her hands and again brought his face, gleaming with perspiration, closer to hers. "You've got to understand, Karen! I know all about it, everything, the entire truth you've never told us. I know you can walk, and I know . . ." he paused only a brief second and brought the words out in a rush, as though relieved to be free of them. " . . . I know Jeff did not propose to you on the night he died."

Her sharp cry, like a call for help, again pierced the tense warm air of the room, and Karen tossed her head from side to side, as though trying to shake his words from her head.

"No, no, that isn't true! You're lying! You're lying!"

"Oh, God, Karen, I only wish I were!" Charles rose from his knees and stood again at the mantel, leaning upon it with his hands and looking down into the cold, dark hearth. "Ethel Hawkins saw you walking in this very room, only yesterday," he said, in a low, almost inaudible voice. "You rose from your chair, you walked over here to the mantel for a cigarette, and then you returned to your chair."

"She was lying!" Linda quickly insisted, rising abruptly to her feet. "Ethel Hawkins is a senile old woman who just wants to make trouble! She's a busybody who pokes her nose into everybody's business. Oh, just wait until I talk to her!"

"That may be so," Charles agreed, "but you and I both know Ethel has probably never told a single lie in her life."

"Then she was imagining it! She's grown so old that she probably sees all sorts of things that aren't there at all! Well, I can tell you one thing: we certainly won't come back here again!"

Charles slowly shook his head. "No. You know

436

that isn't true. Ethel is as sharp-minded as anybody. If she says she saw something, then I believe she did."

"You'll believe her before your own daughter?" Linda demanded in a tone of outraged disbelief.

"In some things, perhaps." He looked again at Karen. "In this instance, yes, because I have learned other things as well. Karen, I know you had a violent argument with Jeff that night, in the garden at the Silverman house. Elizabeth Silverman overheard you."

This mention of her old friend's name had a decided effect on the now frightened girl. Karen slowly lowered her hands and stared at her father. She was breathing heavily now, and her eyes held the realization that it was all over. Her face was suddenly calmer; she was willing to accept it. Denial would be futile.

Charles continued, anxious to bring this painful matter to its conclusion, his voice low and marked with strain; the words could no longer be stopped, although they seemed muffled in the heavy atmosphere of the room.

"It wasn't easy for me to believe what Ethel told me. If it had been anyone else, I would simply have dismissed it. But it wasn't that simple. Oh, Ethel may have her faults, but she's a good, honest woman and she would never have purposely hurt us in this way." He walked to the window and stared into the increasingly stormy night. "I've been thinking about it all day, going back again over that night and over the weeks and months and years that followed. Oh, I've done it before, believe me, not once but many times, always trying to sort it all out and understand exactly what had happened. There always seemed to be so

437

much that didn't fit. Your reaction above all, Karen. Oh, grief was understandable, of course, but somehow there was in your grief something almost forced and unnatural, something theatrically hysterical. More than once it seemed to me you were playing a part. But the thought always made me feel guilty and ashamed. How could I think such a thing about my daughter?"

He paused long enough to light a cigarette; the hand that held the match was unsteady.

"My thoughts always came back to Elizabeth Silverman, and it seemed to me there was something strange there; I think that's been nagging at the back of my mind these past years. Karen, Elizabeth was your closest friend, almost your only friend, in fact. Yet regardless of how often she called at the hospital after the accident, you refused to see her. Oh, all right, you refused to see anybody; your grief was too intense, you merely wanted to be left alone. But Elizabeth could have helped you, comforted you; she was that kind of girl. I remember how strangely relieved you were when she moved out of the state even before you left the hospital. She tried to see you once more before leaving, but you still refused. A strange way to treat so close a friend. You never made the slightest attempt to see her again, and you refused her phone calls. After a while, she stopped writing. Why? Because, in spite of what you told us, Karen, you never answered a single one of her letters. Why? What were you afraid of?"

He stopped again, as though waiting for Karen to say something. His daughter sat now with her face lowered, waiting. There was no protest to his story. She seemed somehow smaller, shrunken, as though the wheelchair had suddenly become too large for her. Linda sat bolt upright in her chair, amazement on her face as she listened to her husband's outrageous words.

"I didn't want to believe Ethel, and I knew there was only one way to be certain," Charles continued. "I did what I should have done a long time ago. I don't know, maybe I was afraid to, perhaps I was cowardly enough to prefer my own shadowy doubts to a terrible certainty. I phoned Elizabeth this afternoon. At first, she was reluctant to talk to me about it, afraid, even after these years and your treatment of her, that she was being disloyal to you. I finally convinced her when I described what Ethel had seen. You see, Karen, Elizabeth realized the story you had told us was not the truth, but she thought that was as far as it went; it never even occurred to her that your entire life had become a lie, any more than it did to any of us. She realized she had to tell the truth now."

He turned slowly, his face drawn and haggard, and looked down again at his daughter, slumped silently in her chair. He dragged heavily on his cigarette, and the tears that sprang into his eyes came from the sting of the smoke that momentarily concealed his face.

"Jeff had found someone else," he said softly.

"No . . . no . . . no . . ." Karen whispered, staring down at the red carpeting with the black figured swirls, her white hands tightly clenching the arms of the chair.

"He told you that evening that he was planning to marry this other girl, whom he had recently met. There was a quarrel, and you asked him to take you home at once. Perhaps you continued the argument in the car, or perhaps Jeff was just too upset to be as careful as he should have been on that rain-slicked part of the highway. The car went off the road . . ."

The silence seemed even more intense after he had stopped talking. Charles reached out a hand to Karen, then drew it back before touching her; his face was filled with pity.

"Isn't that the way it really happened, Karen?"

Linda stared unbelievingly at her daughter; she seemed to be holding her breath, waiting for Karen's next words, perhaps hoping for a denial. The rain hammered against the windows as though it, too, demanded an answer.

Karen sighed slowly, a long-drawn breath that seemed to fill the room. Leaning her head against the back of her chair, she closed her eyes.

"Yes." The word was scarcely spoken. "That's the way it really happened."

"You turned and saw Elizabeth standing very close to where you and Jeff were arguing, and realized she must have heard you. It didn't really bother you then, but it was one of the first things you remembered later. You waited for Elizabeth to speak out, but she said nothing. Out of friendship for you—and Elizabeth is above all a tremendously loyal person—she told no one about what she had heard, waiting for you to speak; perhaps that's why she tried so constantly to see you. Of course, you knew she would be moving within a few days, and so you remained silent and told us nothing; we didn't want to press you, not yet. It was when Elizabeth had finally left the state that you felt secure enough to tell us the story you had decided on. As long as Elizabeth remained silent, no one would know the truth. Why should you face the humiliation of having

440

everyone know you had been rejected? So, you created the myth of a beautiful, tragic romance. You became a martyr to your self-created portrait of love, doomed to spend the remainder of your life in a wheelchair because of the accident that took the life of the young man who would have become your husband on the very night of his death. Your story was accepted without question; no one contradicted you. Only Elizabeth knew the truth, and she remained silent. I have wondered why we never heard anything about the girl Jeff was going to marry, but perhaps he had not yet even asked her; there were many sad people at his funeral, and I suppose she was one of them. As for you, you lied to us all, and you were content to live in that lie."

From beyond the closed door, they could hear the music of the orchestra and the occasional muted sound of laughter. A tear traced its course slowly down Linda's cheek as Karen opened her eyes and looked at her father; a smile of sadness crossed the girl's face.

"Yes," she said softly. "Yes, it's all true. You're right, father. I did lie."

"But why, Karen?" Linda asked. "Why?"

Karen looked from her mother to her father, frowned, and shook her head. "Can I tell you why? Can I make you understand? I wonder."

She rose slowly from the chair in which she had spent her recent years, and walked to the window. She spoke now with her back turned to them, staring into the wild darkness, one hand toying absently with the twisted cord of the Venetian blind.

"You see, it all started between Jeff and myself before you even realized it; perhaps before I did,

441

myself. Actually, there was never anyone for me but Jeff. Oh, I don't mean only during those last months of his life; I mean always. I adored him even as a child. There was something about him. I suppose I was in love with him even in those early years at school. It may have been puppy love, but it never really ended. I didn't take it seriously; it was a dream, a lovely fantasy. Jeff had very little time for me in those days. He was friendly enough, he sometimes tried to be kind, but he scarcely noticed me; there were too many others in his life. The only time he came to me was when he needed help with his studies. Of course, I was always ready to help him, and those hours when we worked together were the only really happy hours I knew. Sometimes he would flash me a smile, or touch my hand, and I . . ." She paused for the briefest moment. "I was so terribly lonely."

"You needn't have been lonely, Karen," Linda insisted. "You could have had many friends, if you'd wanted them. You just didn't seem to be at all interested. I tried . . ."

"Oh, yes, I know," Karen freely admitted. "Even then, I blamed only myself. But you see, I just didn't care about anyone else, only Jeff. Oh, it was all so foolish, so juvenile, but I couldn't help it. Perhaps it was a form of punishment, a masochistic twist in my mind; I enjoyed the pain it gave me, enjoyed even the loneliness. I preferred to stay alone with my dreams of him. Oh, how I dreamed . . . his arms around me, his kisses, his whispered words of love! Do you realize how grateful we should be for a love that is shared? What is it, I wonder, that causes us to love one person so very deeply that nothing else seems to be of any importance? I loved Jeff that way. Perhaps it started as a school-girl crush, but I couldn't forget him, even when he went away, no matter what the years . . ."

"That's enough, Karen," Charles broke in.

She shook her head. "No, father. You've got to know it all now. You have that right." She took a cigarette from the mantel and lighted it before she continued. "Then he came back and we met again, but now everything was different. Perhaps he had matured; I don't suppose I ever did. It was as though he suddenly found something in me that he had never noticed before. Suddenly I found myself in a new, wonderful world. Why, my dreams were actually coming true! We danced, we laughed, he put his arms around me, he . . . kissed me!" Her face glowed with the remembrance; she seemed to have forgotten she was not alone. "And one night, he even asked me to marry him. Oh, yes, he did, he really did; that isn't part of my imaginings. Even my dreams had never permitted me to go that far." She sat on the couch and stared again at the floor. "How quickly the fantasy of dreams can fade! Perhaps I waited too long, perhaps I wanted to hold onto the dream for as long as I possibly could, savor it, cherish it, with the knowledge that now a word from me could make it all permanent reality. I just waited too long. Jeff found someone else."

The discordant tones of a wild rock tune reached them in slightly muted tones from the other room, but they scarcely heard it. Linda left her chair and sat at her daughter's side, silently taking her hand.

"I guess I still don't want to lose that beautiful dream. As long as no one knew Jeff had stopped loving me, perhaps it wasn't really true after all.

Falsehoods can often creep even into your dreams. Those wonderful evenings that we had together were true, but that last evening was an interjection from someone else's nightmare. Let me remember only the earlier times; let me convince myself that I woke up before Jeff and I stepped out onto that terrace and he told me . . . If he'd really loved me only for one single hour, let me remember that hour and forget everything else. Let people look at me with pity because my lover had died, not because his love had faded!"

Karen suddenly buried her face in her hands and began to weep.

"Oh, my poor darling!" Linda breathed, placing an arm about her.

Karen quickly straightened again, moved from under her mother's arm as though she no longer needed nor deserved its protection, and continued her confession.

"While I lay in the hospital, I thought about the future. I imagined the comments I would hear for the remainder of my life: 'Time heals all wounds. She'll get over it. She'll meet someone else.' Perhaps I feared that was true. I didn't want to get over it or want the wound to heal or, above all, to meet someone else. You can't so easily change the habits of a lifetime. I wanted to go on with my dream. If I couldn't walk, no one could expect me to go about and meet others; if I kept myself at home, if I made myself as plain and uninteresting as possible, then I would never run the risk of interesting someone else and losing my dream. People would pity me, always. There would be no mockery, no sarcasm in their pity. I wanted that, and I accepted it from all whom offered it. And I would not lose my dream."

She rose slowly and moved to the door of her room. She seemed somehow more helpless now, and infinitely more pathetic, than she had been in her wheelchair.

"I'm sorry. I know I have been wrong, very wrong. I suppose there does come a time when you've got to stop dreaming." Pausing at the door, she turned and looked at her silent, stricken parents. "But, oh, I did so want it to go on!"

The door of her room closed quietly behind her.

# CHAPTER TWENTY-THREE

Ethel Hawkins had not as yet put in her first appearance at the Festival. She had gone to her room to lie down for a few moments of rest before the delights and rigours of the evening, and was still there when the first guests began to arrive. This was unusual, for she had always made it a point to be in the lobby to greet the very first arrivals, but this evening she felt particularly weary and thought a few more moments would really not make that much difference, as long as Margaret was there to serve as hostess.

She lay fully clothed on her bed and listened to the sounds of the storm, the low growling of the wind, the rumbles of the thunder, the insistent beating of the rain on her windows. Familiar sounds, all of them, which through most of her life had lulled her to sleep. But now sleep would not come. She heard Margaret moving about in her own room, preparing herself for the evening, and then the door of Margaret's room closed softly and her footsteps faded.

For a time, then, the house became silent as sleep itself. Or as death. There was no light in the room. Ethel lay on her back, her hands unconsciously folded across her breast in the attitude of death which, by rights, she should have assumed many years before. Her eyes stared vacantly at the invisible ceiling.

Perhaps old people develop an additional sense, the sense of the future they can never hope to see. After more than ninety years of life, perhaps then there came a special awareness of things and events before they happened.

Ethel felt the heavy pressure of doom upon her, that peculiar feeling that something was going to happen to . . . well, to someone, but she still could not decide at whom the dark finger was pointed. At herself? Perhaps she merely, at long last, sensed her own approaching end. She was not foolish enough to welcome death, but she was now nearing the century mark, and for her to fall into that last sleep would be a loss to no one but herself. At best, she might have a few more months, even perhaps a year or two, of sitting in the rocking chair and looking at the sea. There was no need for her to fear Death or the realization that He could now not be far away.

Her only real concern was for her family, Margaret and Johnny, and for this old house which had meant so much to her all through her life, even during those years of self-imposed exile. Margaret, Johnny, The Cloud. They were all that mattered. They were her world.

She fell finally into a slight doze, and when she

awakened again, the Festival had begun. The sound of music reached her, and she was pleased that her hearing remained acute. She would lie here for just a few moments longer and then go out and join their friends, forget her foolish fears, accept all the inevitable comments about her age and how remarkably well she looked, the gallantry of the gentlemen, the consideration of the women who knew that here, at least, they need fear no competition. It was always nice to be fussed over.

The past swept over her again like the rushing tide of the sea that had formed a symphonic background for her entire life. The music became slower, softer, more sedate, and she imagined herself back more than eighty years, in happier, more carefree days. She saw her father in the center of the sitting room, his bearded face flushed with excitement after a particularly profitable voyage. He wore his dark blue captain's hat pushed back on his shock of graying red hair, and his massive barrel-chest nearly burst the shining gold buttons of his immaculate blue jacket. He towered above all others in the room, raised his glass high, and proposed a toast to yet another journey to the farthest corners of the world. Then the music started and he grasped his wife about her improbably wasp-waist and twirled her about the room until, breathing heavily and laughing with joy, she had to plead with him to stop. Then he stooped to Ethel and lifted her, screaming with delight, high in his arms and asked her what she wanted him to bring his beautiful girl from his next voyage to the far lands —pearls from the Indies, silks from China, scented jewel boxes from Araby. He would shake the house with his deep laughter and tickle her with his beard when he kissed her . . .

And then suddenly the great house was strangely hushed and quiet, and there were no more parties and dancing, no singing and no more laughter, and the music was gone and the whirling guests. Now Captain Nathaniel sat morosely alone at the open window, a half-emptied bottle at his side, staring out at the cruel sea, that vacant sea that had finally cast him aside in its own final triumph over all his conquests, and when one of the new hulking steamers appeared on the blue horizon, he would try to blur the terrible vision with another sip from his bottle, while his wife stood in the doorway wringing her hands, with the tears running down her cheeks, for she knew there was nothing she could do to comfort him.

"They've dirtied the sea with their new mechanical wonders," the captain complained in his strange thickened speech, "just as they have soiled the land. The sea will die now . . ."

And then Ethel climbed again the dark narrow stairs up to the Widow's Walk where she and her mother had so often stood to watch The Cloud go by with her sails high, pure, white and wholesome, and there she found her father, his arm crooked about the telescope, his legs sagging as though in weariness, staring out again to that empty horizon that always drew his eyes. Wanting, somehow, to ease his sadness, yet not quite knowing what words to use, Ethel slipped her little white hand into his big one with the dark hairs on its back, that powerful hand accustomed to the wheel, the hand that had guided his ship all through the teeming oceans of the world, and she felt the strange coldness. Then the moonlight glittered on the blueblack barrel of the revolver at his feet, and turned to a black stream, the curiously narrow trickle of blood that ran slowly, reluctantly, down one side of his face . . .

Ethel rose slowly from her bed, suddenly aware again of the deep weariness that now seemed always to fill her. She sighed and ran her hands over her eyes. The past and the present more and more become one and inseparable. Soon they would merge with her own life, and all the memories would be gone and forgotten.

They would be looking for her now, all their friends, those who respected her as the oldest surviving member of the Hawkins family, the one person who could remember the Captain himself. She switched on the light and began to dress.

No sound or movement disturbed the silence of the Fraser suite. Linda was still seated on the divan where she had been trying to comfort her daughter, staring blankly at nothing, the tears not yet dried on her face, nervously wringing a tear-dampened handkerchief in her hands. Charles, equally silent and immobile, stared through the window, tracing the erratic streams of rain running down the glass against the dim background of the night sky. The door to Karen's room was still firmly closed, and they could hear no sound from behind it. The music of the orchestra reached them faintly, like the background for a dramatic film, but the lightness of the tune seemed misplaced. When Linda spoke, her voice was only another aspect of the silence.

"Did you have to do it, Charles? Did you have to shatter all her dreams?"

Charles turned and looked at her in surprise. "Linda . . ."

"Dreams were all she had."

"Linda, this is absurd!" He left the window and sat beside her. "She was building her entire life on a romantic chapter of the past, placing it on the foundation of the one great single event of her life, enhanced by a lie. How could she have continued that way?"

"I don't know," Linda confessed, shaking her head. "But perhaps we should all merely go through life in the best way we can." She sighed and pressed her handkerchief to her eyes. "Perhaps we should take our happiness in whatever way we can find it."

"No, no, no!" He beat his palms against his legs as though to bring greater force to his words. "Absolutely not! We must live our lives. I mean really live them, whether they are good or bad, happy or sad. We must exist in this world; we can not create one of our own, merely for the sake of closing our eyes to unpleasant reality. I suppose the mindless may be happy in that way, staring at the world through vacant eyes that see only what they want to see. Would you recommend that for all of us?" Rising again, he lighted another cigarette . . . the ashtray near the couch was overflowing with gray-white residue . . . and paced back and forth before the fireplace. "You don't think this was easy for me, do you?"

"But what if Ethel really had been mistaken, Charles? Did you ever think of that?"

He seemed surprised by the question. "No. It didn't even occur to me; I know her too well, and so do you. My only concern was to do the right thing, both for Karen and ourselves. We've known all along that Karen's problem with her legs was not a physical one. We considered it psychosomatic, but what could we have done about it, particularly in those first days? We very nearly lost Karen then, Linda, the night of the accident and for some time after. I know Dr. Guyther was convinced that if she totally lost her will to live at that time, she might very well have followed Jeff. This . . . dream . . . fantasy . . . whatever you want to call it . . . diverted her mind from what happened."

"It still does."

"No," he insisted. "Don't you see, Linda? Even the crippling was a lie. We were willing to accept a psychosomatic problem that prevented Karen from walking, but the problem simply didn't exist. Karen was always able to walk, and she knew it. That's where the danger lies. A lie compounded by another lie, until all her life was composed of that lie. It would have been different if she herself weren't aware of it, but she was. It's over. It has to end."

"But what will happen now, Charles?" She turned to him for the solution, as she had turned to him for solutions all through their life together.

"I don't know. It's up to Karen, isn't it? It depends on her character, her intelligence. It depends on what kind of daughter we have raised."

He was silent for a moment; Linda rose, went to him and put her hand on his arm. She looked deep into his eyes, and he could see there the pleading and the longing for reassurance.

"Have we done the right thing, Charles? Really the right thing?"

He took her face between his hands and she

placed one hand over his; they had always known such warmth and understanding.

"I hope so. Regardless, it had to be done. It should have been done long before now, if only we'd dared and if we had known the truth. We accepted too readily; perhaps it was the easier way. But in spite of all of this, Karen is a mature woman, and an intelligent one. My God, Linda, she was a successful business woman! She has to come to terms with her life. It isn't too late; she's young enough. I think she'll be all right, if we help her as we always have."

"She'll be so ashamed."

"We mustn't let her feel ashamed."

"But how can we help her? What is there we can do for her now? We've taken her world away. How can we give her another to take its place?"

"We can't. She'll have to find that world for herself. We must help her wherever and however we can, but she has to work this out in her own way. Perhaps she should go away for a while, by herself, where she can think things out. Abroad, perhaps. Paris, London."

"She'll have to laugh again, won't she? I wonder if she remembers how."

"She'll learn."

They were both silent with their own thoughts. A gust of wind blew the rain against the window again. Charles started for Karen's room.

"Where are you going?"

"To her," Charles said. "If she has to laugh again, tonight is the time to start. There's a party out there, Linda. She's going to it, and this time she's not going to sit sorrowfully against the wall and watch everyone and accept cluckings of sympathy from a bunch of old hens. She's going to

454

laugh and she's going to dance. This is the beginning of forgetting. We've begun this, and we can't stop now until it's finished."

Charles paused at the door to his daughter's room, raised his hand and knocked softly. There was no response. He hesitated again, then turned the handle of the door and quietly entered the room, closing the door behind him.

Karen stood before the portrait of Jeff, her lowered hands clasped before her, her head raised, her eyes fixed on the handsome, vapid face of the dead man. The small lamp burned on the table beneath the painting as it always had, but another lamp was lighted beside the bed. The room was brighter than Charles had ever seen it before. Karen made no movement when her father approached and, without speaking, stood beside her. She finally spoke without turning, still facing the portrait, her hands now at her side.

"I did love him, father. And he loved me . . . once. For a while."

"I'm certain he did, Karen. It's a wonderful thing to be loved."

She nodded. "Yes. A wonderful thing." After another brief pause, she continued. "Please don't sound so unhappy, father. You've done the right thing, the only possible thing. I know that. Some day I may even be glad of it. I suppose I just didn't have the courage to end it myself. Once the lie had begun, it seemed so much easier just to continue with it. But it was wrong. It was stupid, vain, juvenile, and dangerous. You see, I'm not so enmeshed in my fantasies that I can't see that for myself. I lost Jeff before his car went through the railing at McGarry's Point. If he had lived, I would have had to go on without him, somehow."

"He really wasn't worth all this, Karen."

She turned, her eyes glistening in spite of a small smile. "Oh, no, don't say that." She turned back to the portrait. "Perhaps I've been blaming him, too; that was wrong as well. There's so little sense to love. He couldn't help it if he came to love someone else more than he loved me. It wasn't easy for him to tell me. He tried to be gentle. You may as well know it all, now. He had to get himself half drunk to find the courage to talk to me; that's why we had the accident. He should never have driven that night. I knew it was dangerous to get into the car with him, but I didn't care; so, you see, it was partially my fault, too." She paused, then went on. "He was a fine, warm man, and I'm grateful for having known him, and for the love he gave me. I'll always remember him."

They gazed silently at the portrait of the dead man who had played so important a roll in their lives. Karen slowly reached out her hand.

"But you're right, father. There's a time for remembering, but we mustn't forget the most important time of all is for living."

With a quick motion, she turned out the altar-light, plunging the portrait into semi-darkness, as though a curtain had fallen over the face.

"And now, it's over. Who knows? I may still find someone else. You see, I'm even ready for that now." She turned to her father again, agony in her eyes. "But, oh, what have I done to you and mother all these years? I was so blinded by my own self-pity, I could not see that. How can I ever atone for it?"

He placed his warm hand on her cheek. "By being happy. You're still all that matters to us,

Karen. Discover again what life can be, make yourself happy, and your mother and I will be happy, too."

She kissed him and smiled; although tears sparkled in her eyes, she was no longer so sad.

"And now, shall we go to the party?" she asked, lighter. "If I'm going to be happy again, this is as good a time as any to begin! My goodness, I don't know a thing about all these new dances!"

Charles silently took her hand and together they walked to the door, which Karen opened herself. As they entered the sitting room, Linda rose anxiously, still clasping the handkerchief in her hand. Karen smiled and extended her arms to her mother.

"Mother . . ."

"Oh, my darling!"

"I'm sorry, mother . . . I'm so sorry!"

Linda gathered her daughter in her arms; Karen uttered just one sharp, half-choked sob as she pressed her cheek to her mother's, then she quickly stepped back, holding Linda at arm's length.

"That's enough of this, now," she insisted. "That's all past. It's over now, and I'll find some way to make it up to both of you. Let's not turn this into a soap-opera. We're going to a party!"

Karen linked her arm through her mother's, and they walked together to the door. Charles looked at them, proud and smiling, his face calm once again with his confidence that now all would be well at last. He opened the door for them, and the sound of music entered the room. Linda and Karen paused for just a moment and then stepped into the festive lobby.

\* \* \*

The black daggers moved slowly and relentlessly across the white clock face pockmarked with little black numbers created by man to measure the passing of time—as though time would not pass unless regulated—moving on to the last moment, sliding beyond that brief second when the two erect hands embraced over the figure twelve and then separated to mark the beginning of a new day.

The wind and the sea continued unmercifully to buffet the house, but the gaiety within almost completely drowned out the ominous noises of the storm. Only when a particularly powerful gust of wind caused the old house to tremble were the celebrants reminded that the violence of the weather continued. Those who stepped briefly out onto the verandah for a breath of air noticed that the churning sea had completely covered the bathing beach and now was attacking the Boardwalk itself, smashing angrily against the scarred wood. But this happened during every major storm, and the Boardwalk always managed to turn aside the violence; the waters would recede quickly enough once the storm had finally exhausted itself, and the flotsam washed onto the Boardwalk, up from the silent depths of the sea or carried here from distant parts of the world, would be easily removed. By the next day, two at the most, few signs would remain of the storm's rampage.

The point itself was raised sufficiently to escape the innundation; an occasional larger wave would break triumphantly over the black hump of raised rock and sweep hissingly close to the house, causing squeals of delighted excitement from those watching on the verandah, before the wave lost its strength and, retired back to the sea. There was really no cause for alarm. There had been storms before, although it was rather unusual for so severe a tempest at this time of year.

So it was that the greatest danger went completely unnoticed by those who had their eyes turned only towards the sea, or who were too engrossed in enjoyment to trouble themselves about the weather, and no one was even aware when a large portion of land on the side of the point most exposed to the fierce northern winds slipped and slid into the hungry churning waves, baring to the full fury of the elements a considerable portion of the very foundation of the old house.

But the sea noticed. Eager, exultant, sensing victory at long last, the sea began its final merciless attack on the exposed foundation, and the work of a hundred years ago, constructed by skillfull hands long dead, silently began to crumble.

Bad weather could not dampen the high spirits of the revelers at The Cloud, and all agreed that this was unquestionably the most successful Festival within memory. It was even possible that the foul weather itself helped to create the ambiance, bringing everyone somehow closer together than they would have been if able to wander out about the point. There was a warmth and comfort in the gayly decorated rooms that seemed even cozier whenever one happened to glance through the windows at the stormy darkness outside. Much comment was made concerning the excellence of the refreshments so liberally provided, and the apparently unending supply of cheer dispensed at the bar. There were two orchestras which provided non-stop music for the dancing. Bea, who had for this one night abandoned her Gay Nineties image, had already performed twice, and had been richly rewarded by well deserved applause for the exuberance of her singing. Some were saying the old house had never known a gayer gathering, not even during the days of the old Captain himself.

Margaret was deeply gratified by the success of what she alone knew would be the final Festival at The Cloud. She moved with surprising grace through the mingling crowd, gliding with all sails flying, her face beaming as she graciously accepted all the compliments that came her way. Now and then she tossed a cautious glance towards her mother, for she was not free of the uneasiness she had felt for the old woman during the past couple of days. She had quietly entered Ethel's room just before the beginning of the Festival, and found her sleeping uneasily, muttering about ships and telescopes and dark nights. But Ethel was now ensconced in her great armchair at the far side of the room, regaling her well-wishers with colorful stories about Captain Nathaniel; there seemed no reason to worry about her, at least for this evening.

The most emotional moment of the evening and, for Margaret, the most totally satisfying, had been provided by the Fraser family. There were gasps of surprise and amazement when Karen Fraser walked—actually walked—into the room on her mother's arm. Those who knew of Karen's tragedy gathered about the beaming trio with warm words of congratulations. It is likely that only Ethel doubted Karen's rather vague statement about treatments finally having healed her lameness, and her delighted plan to reveal the happy improvement in her condition during the Festival. With happy tears streaming down her broad face, Margaraet engulfed Karen in her arms and drew her to her immense, warm bosom, thinking what a fitting end this would be for the final Festival at The Cloud, while Charles and Linda Fraser silently smiled their thanks to the old woman seated in her armchair.

But if there was a belle of the ball that evening, it undoubtedly was Emily. Even those who had known the young waitress most of her life agreed she had never appeared so lovely or charming, so appealing or vivacious. The happiness that had so unexpectedly come into her life upon meeting Michael had brought the young girl to a suddenly mature and exciting beauty. She knew somehow that her life had suddenly taken a totally new course, for Michael had now become and would always remain the most important part of it.

Some of the older people, long-time friends of the family and residents of Hawkins' Cove for some generations, had raised their eyes in displeased astonishment upon seeing Emily enter the dance floor on the arm of a sailor. However, Michael had soon enough won the smiling approval of the dowagers with his gentleness, his courtesy, and his touching attention to young Emily.

Unfortunately, the same could not be said of the other sailor who was present, the startlingly handsome young man who appeared to be Michael's friend, but was nothing like him at all. Paul became more of a problem as the evening progressed. He was never without a drink in his

461

hand; his eyes had become glassy, his speech slurred, his step increasingly unsteady. He seemed to be drinking almost defiantly, as though daring anyone to reproach him.

Emily became distinctly uncomfortable under Paul's constant searching gaze; on several occasions he seemed to leer openly at her, his eyes running offensively over her body, giving the impression that he was more familiar with that lovely form than anyone realized. He remained unfailingly polite to Emily, but it was with an exaggerated politeness that seemed something of a mockery. When they danced together—and for Michael's sake, Emily felt she could not refuse him, although drink made him clumsy and difficult to dance with—he held her much too close, his lean, hard body disturbingly pressed against hers, and his eyes perpetually fixed on her breasts. When his conversation dwindled into a string of obscenities, Michael felt it necessary to draw him aside.

"Paul, you're getting drunk as a bitch," he commented in an undertone. "Watch your step, will you?"

Paul grinned, slapping Michael on the back.

"What the hell, we're here for a good time, aren't we?"

"Sure, but we can have a good time without getting pissed and making asses of ourselves," Michael insisted, still anxious to avoid a serious altercation with Paul. "I think you'd better cut down a little, Paul. And I wish you'd watch your language, too."

Paul's voice suddenly became heavy with sarcasm, and his upper lip was raised in a slight sneer. "Oh, I'm offending your girl friend's innocent young ears?"

"Yes, you are," Michael responded somewhat more heatedly. "Emily isn't one of your tramp pick-ups, you know, and she isn't used to that kind of talk."

Paul laughed. "Oh, shit, Mike!" Two women passing glared with distaste at the obviously inebriated sailor. "You didn't get her out of a convent, did you? She's heard the words before; she knows what it's all about."

Michael flushed angrily and his fists automatically clenched as he strained to retain his temper; Paul generally managed to hold his liquor better than he was doing this evening.

"Watch your step, Paul," he cautioned in a tight, threatening whisper. "That's all. Just watch your step."

For a moment there was an aura of tension in the air between them; Paul's rather vague glance seemed to sharpen and harden as he looked at Michael, and his right hand was raised in what might have been the beginning of a dangerous gesture. Slowly, the hand came down, and Paul smiled, his good humor apparently returned.

"Damn, sure, buddy!" he laughed again, shaking his head as though highly amused by Michael's foolish sensitivity. "Sure thing. Say, I don't want you mad at me, buddy; then I'd have nobody to talk to!" He glanced wryly about the room. "Sure as hell ain't nobody else here; what the hell am I doing here, anyway?" He laughed again. "Have a good time, buddy."

As he turned and moved somewhat erratically back toward the lobby bar, allowing a slightly mollified Michael to return to Emily, Paul brushed against Johnny. Standing nearby, the boy had overheard the hotly whispered exchange between the two sailors, but he was not interested in their words. Their problems were not his concern; he had worries enough of his own. And yet, he couldn't help thinking with a rather grim satisfaction that their taut little argument at least revealed the two as real men, not counterfeits who pretended to be something they were not. Like Greg and Steve.

Johnny had always taken pride in the annual Festival, but there was little pleasure for him in the gala this evening. He kept much to himself in a corner of the room, sipping his ginger-ale, responding rather mechanically to the greetings of family friends. Several of his own friends were also present with their dates, but Johnny was not in the mood for the usual badinage and rather abruptly declined the girls' invitations to dance. He had agreed to one dance with his mother as a matter of form, but he felt rather uncomfortable with all those eyes on them, and that was enough. He most carefully avoided the company of his friend Jimmy, who was there with his own girl friend. Jimmy had always loudly boasted that he was screwing her, but Johnny's doubts about that had doubled in the past couple of days. Jimmy knew too much now about Johnny's activities, and Johnny was not comfortable in his friend's company.

At any rate, just now Johnny was interested only in watching his former idol, Greg Christopher.

Greg and Steve spent most of the evening together in quiet conversation. They would occasionally dance with one of the girls, or chat with the older women. They were charming to all, drawing the eyes of the marriageable girls and the pleased smiles of the eager mothers. Johnny wasn't fooled by this for a moment. It was obviously part of the necessary camouflage. There was nothing in their attitude to indicate what they really were.

This was probably what most disturbed Johnny, and he felt a burning anger as he watched Greg dance by, his arm encircling a girl's waist, talking and laughing as though he had nothing to hide. He felt there was somehow something indecent in this; what would these girls say if they were to learn about what these two supposed men had done together just last night in the room upstairs? Would they smile at Greg so charmingly, so obviously eager to make a favorable impression? Would the girls' mothers sit there so smugly pleased as they watched their young daughters in the arms of these handsome, charming, and supposedly eligible young men? His fury grew as he watched Margaret and Greg dance by, both smiling in his direction. Would his mother gaze with such pleasure into Greg's mask of a face and be so willing to have Steve place his arm about her? These women, and particularly his mother, were being degraded. These two guys were a couple of queers; it wouldn't have surprised him to see them dancing together. How could they manage so completely to fool everyone? It shouldn't be permitted. Everyone was entitled to know the truth about these phonies. He wished he could shout it to the entire gathering and have both of them out of his house.

Steve was aware of Johnny's glowering stares, and he wondered about it, then dismissed it as part of a boy's air of superior contempt for such adult affairs. He smiled at Johnny as he danced past him with Bea. He received a dark scowl in return.

Steve found Bea the most delightful woman present. She seemed transformed, somehow younger and more vivacious than before. She wore a simple gown of light green, far more becoming than her garish costume at The Buccaneer. Her singing tonight, while less than operatic, had given him a better impression of her voice; she even hinted she might be induced to try something classical before the evening was over, perhaps the inevitable Butterfly or Tosca. Steve smiled his pleasure at this possibility (it was actually an annual thing), although what he had heard tonight confirmed Greg's opinion of her limitations. The voice was pleasant, the enthusiasm contagious, but this was simply not enough; the pitch was uncertain, the control was weak. Bea was a lovable, charming woman totally wrapped in her dreams, and Steve hoped when the realization finally came to her, it would be in as gentle a manner as possible.

Bea was a marvelous dancer, light on her feet and rhythmic in her movements, as is so often the case with large women. Bea constantly ridiculed her own size: "You can see I was born for Wagner!" She moved easily about the floor, humming softly, smiling and affable, almost beautiful, accepting compliments on her singing. She might have been the hostess of an elegant soiree, a Violetta surrounded by admirers.

She smiled at Steve, tilting her head slightly to one side; there were golden lights in her blonde hair. "This is my kind of life, Steve. This is what I need. No more honkey-tonk audiences whistling and yelling and banging their glasses on the bar. Style, class, dignity; that's what I want. When I leave here this summer . . ."

Steve smiled and held her closer for a moment, refusing to have the pleasure of this evening marred by sad thoughts of impossible dreams. It had been a long time since he had enjoyed himself so much. He had even found it possible to give a friendly smile and quick handshake to Bernie S. Clayton of Wall Street as the beefy stockbrocker danced ponderously with his frowsy blonde companion.

Steve's eyes were never far from Greg, and he found himself boldly casting a fond glance across the room or even making a discreet and apparently accidental contact with his hand. Their eyes and touch seemed to speak a language no one else would be able to understand. Just wait, they said, just wait until this is over. Let us be friendly and charming, let us please these avid young girls and their even more eager mothers, for we both know it means nothing, and soon they will all be gone, the house will be quiet, and we will again be alone together.

Few of the partying guests heeded the increasing violence of the weather. As the evening passed on into the early hours of another morning, the sea continued to vent its fury upon the land. An exceptionally heavy surge of breakers tore away a bit of the Boardwalk near the Casino, but this was scarcely noticed at the time, and there were various calls for assistance from endangered vessels that had failed, despite all the warnings, to reach port before the storm. The radio continued to report gale-force winds and extremely high tides. The storm, however, was expected to abate before dawn. The guests at the Captain Nathaniel Hawkins Festival were too busy to listen to weather reports.

Concerned still, lest something occur to ruin her Festival, Margaret was probably the one most aware of the storm. She would pause in mid-conversation as a strong wind brushed past and briefly buffeted the house. On three occasions, pretending a need for fresh air, she had stepped out onto the verandah, alarmed at the amount of water now rising over the point. But surely the worst of the storm had passed by now, since the report said it would be all over before dawn. She was relieved to note that the weather had no effect whatever on the high spirits of her guests; that would have been a shame. She chided herself for a tendency of watching the time too closely, as though relieved at every hour that passed without incident.

Only Ethel seemed really uneasy. She had tired of telling old tales and now sat silent and alone in her arm chair against the wall, watching and waiting. . . .

It was quieter in the lobby than in the sitting room; here were gathered those guests who preferred something more powerful than the lightly spiked punch provided for the dancers. They lined the small bar and called their orders to the two harried bartenders, or gathered in small groups from which the hum of conversation and the occasional sound of laughter emerged. The railing of the staircase, right to its very top, had been wrapped in light blue crepe. From the large chandelier dangling streamers danced a wild shimmy whenever the door opened to the verandah and the wind blew in.

Michael drew Emily by the hand from the sitting room to two empty chairs set apart against the curvature of the stairway. It was considerably cooler here, and the sound of the storm was muted by the surrounding gaiety and the music from the dance floor. Whenever the outer door was opened, they would stare briefly into the black violence of the night. It was like looking through a time portal into another, darker world. Michael noticed that portions of the marble floor were wet with blown rain.

Emily ran her handkerchief over her perspiring face; her eyes were dancing and her full red lips parted to reveal her perfect white teeth.

"Oh, it's terribly warm in there!" she complained with a light laugh. "It's a relief to feel a breath of air!" She turned eagerly to her escort. "I'm having a wonderful time, Michael!"

Michael smiled, looking at her with undisguised adoration. "Best party I've ever been to," he assured her. "Must be because you're here with me. I don't generally go in much for parties."

"I'm glad, Michael," she said, reaching for his hand.

"Emily . . ."

"Yes?"

"I don't quite know how to say this." He flushed slightly. "I guess I'm not much for words, either."

She laughed again. "Really? I've never yet seen you at a loss for words these two days!"

"Oh, that's just talking. This is . . . different."

She sensed his solemnity, and shared it. "If you have something to say, Michael, well . . . just say it. I'll listen."

"It's just that . . . .Well, my enlistment will be up in a little less than a couple of months now, you know, and I'll be getting out of this uniform . . ."

"Paul says you're going to re-enlist," she interrupted.

He shook his head decisively. "That isn't true; I never told him any such thing. He'd like me to, that's all. I guess maybe I was thinking about it, just a little, but I've changed my mind. I'm getting out. I've had enough. It isn't as though I have nothing to get out for, you know, no reason to leave the service, like Paul. Paul, well, Paul has had a tough life, you know, and he's never had it as good as since he enlisted. He has no reason to leave. But I want to go to school, maybe study agriculture, become a farmer like my family has always been, but a good one, who knows all the modern scientific methods. Guess I'll go back home then and help my father. We've got a nice, big farm, you know, it does real well, and some day it'll be mine."

"It must be very nice where you live," she mused. "It's so far from the sea. Sometimes I get very tired of the sea, the constant pounding of the surf, the salty air . . ."

"Will you go back there with me, Emily?" He blurted out the words, and she suddenly felt perspiration in the hand she held in her own.

Emily didn't answer immediately, but the clasp of her hand tightened. "Michael, we've only . . ."

"Oh, I know what you're going to say," he interrupted with a dismissing wave of his free hand. "All that crap—excuse me—about knowing each other only for a couple of days, and not really knowing each other at all. I can't deny that, of course, but I don't feel it really makes that much difference. Sometimes that's the way these things happen, you know. If you're going to love a person, I figure maybe you know it right from the start. Something I guess just tells you, inside." He looked at her with an expression compounded of ardor, hope and fear. "Something told me, Emily, right from the start, right from the time you brought me my breakfast. It was like you were the one I wanted to share all my breakfasts with." He flushed again at the youthfulness of his words.

"And you want me to say I felt it, too?"

"Didn't you?"

She hesitated again. "I'm not really sure." Hearing his slight sigh of disappointment, she quickly added, "Oh, Michael, I'm not going to talk about being practical and all that sort of thing; I guess I'm still just too young for that, and right now I'm much too happy to be that sensible. I'm terribly flattered that you feel this way about me, and it makes me very happy. I like you more than I've ever liked anyone in my life, Michael. Maybe that's love. If it is, then I've never been in love before. I want to go on knowing you, being with you, whatever that means. But we both should be really absolutely certain, don't you think?"

"Well, of course," he rather grudgingly admitted, nodding. "But I'm as certain right now as I'll ever be."

"I want you to be just as certain six months from now, or a year from now, or many years from now. You have to go back to your ship in the morning, and then you have another couple of months before you're free. It really can't hurt to wait that long before we decide anything, can it?"

He looked at her again, suddenly hopeful. "You mean you'll wait?"

She laughed, touched by his eagerness. "Until the prison gates open and your long sentence is over? It's only two months, Michael. If I can't wait that long, well, then . . . . Besides, you'll have to meet my parents, and I'll have to meet yours . . ."

"We could be very happy together, Emily; I know we could." His words were quick, eager, happy. "My parents will love you, too. And you will like the farm. It's so clean and pure, the sky is so blue, and after the rain there's a fresh smell to the grass. . . ."

She put her fingers to his lips. "I know, Michael. I know."

She moved closer to him, and he put his arms around her. A couple standing by looked at them and one whispered to his companion; they laughed lightly. Neither Michael nor Emily heard the sound. They forgot the music, the violence of the storm, the amused glances as their lips came together. They had found another world, that shining world found by all young lovers who always think theirs alone has been the discovery.

# CHAPTER TWENTY-FOUR

Greg was standing against the wall, talking quietly with Steve during a brief hiatus in the dancing, when he saw Johnny, his face darkly shadowed, suddenly leave the room and head for his family's apartments. Greg had been keenly aware of the boy's eyes fixed upon him all during the course of the evening, curious, watching, cold and, for the first time, distinctly hostile. Greg had been looking all evening for an opportunity to talk with him; now seemed the best time.

"I've got to talk with him, Steve," he excused himself. "I can't let him go on with the kind of thoughts he's been having all day. I'll be right back."

"Okay," Steve agreed; he was aware of the reason for Greg's concern. "I'm going out to the verandah for a bit of air; meet me there."

Politely fending off calls from various friends, Greg wended his way through the dancers and followed Johnny into the muted silence of the rear of the house.

"Johnny!"

The boy turned at the entrance of his own room; he was surprised to see Greg behind him, apparently unaware that he had been followed. "What is it?"

"I'd like to talk to you for a minute."

"What about?" His voice was sullen.

"I think you know what about."

Johnny hesitated, then opened the door to his room. "I don't want to talk. There's nothing to say."

"There's a great deal to say," Greg insisted, joining Johnny at the open door. "We've been friends for a long time, Johnny; I'd like to think we still are. Can I come in? You've never minded before." He smiled slightly, trying to lighten the difficult moment. "I promise you're perfectly safe."

Johnny frowned and somewhat reluctantly opened the door a little wider; he obviously did not appreciate the weak attempt at humor. He seated himself on the bed, while Greg, having closed the door behind him, leaned against the tall dresser, looking seriously at his disturbed young friend. Johnny stared uncomfortably at the floor, his handsome face dark, angry and stubborn. How could you talk to him, Greg wondered. Was he still too young to understand?

"I know you were out on the balcony last night," he began, "and I'm sorry you saw what you saw. You shouldn't have, you know. You had no right to be out there. It's not like you to spy. It wasn't exactly the proper thing to do."

474

"What you were doing wasn't exactly proper, either," Johnny replied in a low tone.

"Don't be too sure of that, Johnny. For some people, it may be the only really proper thing. For me. For Steve. Not necessarily for others, not for you. But that doesn't give you the right to condemn."

Johnny raised his pained eyes to Greg; he twisted his hands nervously and spoke slowly, seriously, as though explaining matters to himself.

"I've always looked up to you, Greg. You were —well, I guess you were someone very special to me, something of an ideal. I've always wanted to be just like you. But I didn't know you were— like that."

Greg hesitated, again searching for the words. How could he explain to this confused young boy the nature he had only so recently discovered in himself?

"Tell me, Johnny, just why have you always admired me? Was it because of my work, because of my knowledge, because you considered my way of life to be one you would like to follow yourself? Or was it because you thought I went to bed with women? I have, Johnny, many times. I think I'm a bit disappointed, Johnny. You see, I thought your liking for me was based on more important factors than my personal sexual attitudes. You aren't a child any longer, Johnny. You're old enough to know things and do things. You have a man's body and a man's urges. What do you do about that? Do you take girls under the Boardwalk at night? Do you masturbate with your friends? I don't know what you do, and I don't give a damn. What's the difference? It has nothing to do with our friendship. It's just none of my business. Just as what I do is none of your business."

"But what you do is . . ." Johnny hesitated.

"Is what, Johnny? Dirty? Obscene? Perversion?"

"Yes. Everybody knows it is."

"Some people think it is," Greg corrected him; then he corrected himself. "No. That's not quite accurate. A lot of people think it is. Well, I suppose that's their prerogative. But they don't have to become involved in it if they feel that way; it doesn't have to affect them at all. But they have no right to tell me I can't do what I feel I must do. Each man has to be himself, Johnny. That's all that matters."

Johnny pounded the bed with his fist. "Shit. Then nothing really matters."

Greg sighed and frowned, again feeling at a loss for words. "I guess I'm not really putting it very well. Some day you'll understand, Johnny . . ."

Johnny rose quickly to his feet. "Oh, crap? Don't tell me I'm too God damned young to understand!"

"You shouldn't be too young, at seventeen," Greg agreed. "But right now you're acting as though you were. Johnny, Johnny . . . I'm not attacking your intelligence. I'm trying to talk to you man to man. It isn't easy to make you . . . to make anyone . . . understand what it is that Steve and I have found together. To a mind trained to believe there is something terribly wrong in such a relationship . . ." He shook his head. "Maybe this sort of thing takes a different kind of understanding, an older kind, a kind that I hope will come to you later. You've got to be a little patient. . . ."

Johnny turned to him, suddenly furious; he had

476

heard that word all too often. "The hell with patience! Why is it, no matter what it is, people tell me I've gotta be patient? What does patience ever get anybody, anyway? I had to be patient about growing up, about wanting to take a job, about getting my boat . . ." His voice choked and he turned away. "I admired you so much, I didn't want to . . . to do things I thought you might not like me to do. I could have had my boat a long time ago, but I thought you wouldn't approve of what I might have to do to get it. I wanted you to like me and maybe even respect me. I didn't want to dirty myself in your eyes, even if you didn't know about it. You were too good, too . . . too God damned decent!" He turned again, his face twisted with pain and anger. "Well, now I know what a damned stupid kid I was! You proved it last night. You showed me! You helped me to grow up, fast! So now I've done it, and I'm not ashamed any more, and I'm gonna get that damned boat, and I don't care what you think about it!"

Greg frowned and moved closer to him. "Done what, Johnny? What are you talking about?"

Johnny laughed harshly; it was no longer a boy's laughter. "Sure, I'll tell you; why shouldn't I? You'd probably like to hear about it. It won't surprise you, now you know what it's all about! I've been making extra money at the bath-house, that's what I've been doing. I've been taking money to watch naked guys play with themselves and jerk off, I've dropped my pants and let them feel me . . ."

Greg brought his hand smartly across Johnny's face; the sound was like the sharp crack of a pistol shot. "Stop that! You don't even know what the hell you're talking about! My God, you are just a kid! What do you know about such things?"

"Oh, it's all right for you, but not for me!"

Greg's sudden anger had become almost uncontrollable. "Are you comparing that kind of toilet filth with what there is between Steve and myself? Christ, you really are too young to understand, aren't you? Can't you see there's a difference, all the difference in the world?"

Blood trickled slowly from the corner of Johnny's mouth; he put up a hand to wipe it away, staring at Greg with a curious mixture of sorrow and loathing. Tears sprang to his eyes, and Greg knew they were not caused by the physical blow he had received.

"You Goddamned queer!" the boy gasped. "You . . . cocksucker!"

With a sharpy cry he ran from the room; Greg heard the house's rear outer door slam behind him.

Greg stood where he was, white and shaken. God, what had he done? He talked about the lack of understanding! How could he ever expect or deserve that from Johnny after this? He was a confused boy who had been rocked out of his adolescence by seeing something he hadn't been meant to see. He should have talked with Johnny calmly, retained his temper, somehow have made him see, explained to him the difference between their activities, but instead. . . .

He felt sick. With a low moan, he suddenly doubled over and vomited on the floor, mixing his tears with the filth that poured from his mouth.

Walter slowly descended the rather rickety wooden stairs into the dark cellar. More wine was needed upstairs, and Walter was the only member of the staff whom Margaret would trust with this all important task. The Hawkins house had always had a particularly well-stocked wine cellar, and Walter prided himself on his exact knowledge of just what was needed and where on the racks it would be found. He reveled in Margaret's implicit trust in him over the course of his many years of service.

Nothing had been done to alter the cellar when the house had been somewhat converted into a hotel, and the large, dusty chamber remained dimly lighted. The stairs were old, made of wood that had long ago begun to decay, and as Walter carefully descended, he reminded himself once again to tell Margaret that something really would have to be done about strengthening them. The cellars were seldom used and only infrequently visited by members of the staff aside from Walter himself, but there was no point in risking anyone's safety, particularly his own. He wondered why it was that nothing had been said about the stairs by the construction experts who had examined the house. Surely anyone could recognize the dangerous state of the stairs? Of course, the primary concern of the examiners had been the foundations upon which the house stood, and perhaps they had not bothered to look at anything else. It suddenly occurred to him that Margaret had said very little to anyone about the results of that examination, merely muttering something about some necessary repairs. That was strange.

Walter had never liked cellars, even though they were supposed to be the man's part of the house, where he had his workshop and tinkered about with things. Cellars were simply too dark, too dank, too filled with the gathered dust and accumulated detritus of too many years. The darker corners could hold too many unpleasant crawling creatures with too many legs. He didn't like the large asbestos furnace pipes with their thick coating of white dust; he recalled his disgust when he had once seen a centipede rippling across one of them. (Centipede or millipede? He wasn't really certain of the difference, and at any rate he was not about to stop and count its legs!) Cellars were altogether too silent, even this one. The gaiety of the party upstairs was muted, but the roar and thunder of the sea seemed much closer. Christ, how it was blowing out there! With all that noise of the party and the pressure of his own responsibilities, he had almost forgotten the storm. It was a blower, all right! The sound irritated him. Walter had really never liked living by the sea, either. He would have preferred the whistle of the wind through a stand of dark pines.

He reached for the bottle of wine and paused as he pulled it from the rack. What was that sound? Water again. No, not the usual sound of the sea; he was accustomed to that, and now scarcely even heard it. That was different, not the constant shushing rhythm, but a trickling sound, more like a rivulet, a stream, and it seemed to grow louder even as he listened to it. It came from somewhere over at the north side of the cellar. Carefully, straining his eyes in the dim light, he approached the far wall, clasping the wine bottle in one hand.

A stream of foaming sea water was issuing through a narrow crack in the masonry of the wall, stretching from the ceiling of the cellar right down to the cement floor itself. The force of the inrushing water seemed to be spreading the narrow opening; the cement at the sides appeared to be crumbling away. Wishing the light were better, Walter looked cautiously about. Something seemed not quite right here, aside from the unexpected incursion of the sea. The space down here seemed somehow to have lessened. It seemed to him that the ceiling just above him was sagging slightly, hanging downward, as though oppressed by the weight above it, or as though it had lost some of the support that had held it in place over the past century.

Walter moved closer and peered at the jointure between the wall and the ceiling. It was so damned dark down here! Wasn't the wall at this point, just where it met the ceiling, less smooth than it had been, wrinkled, as if the weight of the house had squeezed it together? The sea sounded very loud at this point, almost as though there were no wall between them, and each surge of the wind-blown surf spurted more water into the cellar.

Walter curiously reached his hand upward to the top of the wall, and suddenly the entire gray expanse dissolved before his eyes, and he was lost in the tumbling cascade of sea water. The bottle of wine he had been carrying was smashed against the opposite wall and added a touch of blood red to the churning green and white of the gurgling sea.

Leaning against the small bar in the lobby, with another fresh drink cupped in his hand, Paul had been an interested if unwilling spectator to the little tete-a-tete between Michael and Emily; the young couple had been so immersed in their own suddenly revealed emotions that they had failed to notice him. He saw them kiss, warmly and lingeringly, and watched as Emily, after a few further whispered words, started up the stairway, her face radiant. Michael watched her until she disappeared on an upper floor, and his own expression left little doubt as to his feelings. He turned from the stairs and, catching Paul's eye, joined his friend at the bar. Paul was immediately irritated by the smile of almost idiotic contentment on his friend's face.

"You've got lipstick on your mouth," he said drily, as Michael joined him.

Smiling still, Michael took his handkerchief from the waistband of his uniform and wiped at his mouth; he seemed pleased at the light red stain on the white linen.

"Thanks. Believe me, it was a pleasure." He looked at his friend, his face filled with excitement. "You can congratulate me, Paul. Emily and I are going to be married."

"Shit! You're crazy!"

"I expected you to say that," Michael commented, vaguely wondering why Paul suddenly seemed less intoxicated than he had been during the course of the evening; had it all, perhaps, merely been something of a pose? "It's true, anyway."

"You don't know what the hell you're doing," Paul insisted, unexpectedly alarmed by Michael's words. "Hell, you've only known her for . . ."

" . . . for two days," Michael completed the thought for him. "Don't you think I know that, Paul? It just doesn't make any difference to either one of us. We're in love, Paul." There was a trace of wonder in his voice. "I know what I want. Oh, it won't be right away, of course, but when my

482

hitch is up, I'm coming back here for her and I'll take her home with me."

Paul looked at Michael uncertainly for a moment and then leaned against the bar, staring into his drink; a look of smug complacency suddenly entered his face.

"Oh. When your hitch is up? Hell, a lot can happen in a couple of months. You'll change your mind by that time. Another hot night like we had a couple of nights ago, and you'll remember the only thing dames are good for."

Michael shook his head, still smiling with self-assurance. "No, sir, Paul. Everything's different now, my whole life. There won't be any more nights like that. Not for me. There isn't going to be anyone else for me but Emily."

Irritated by Michael's superior smile and suddenly alarmed at the imminent danger of losing his closest friend, Paul said, "Christ, Mike, she's only a . . ."

"Careful, Paul!"

"God damn it, I mean it!" Paul insisted. "She's a nice enough kid, pretty and all that, but they're all alike, Mike. It didn't take her long to make a date with a sailor she'd never even seen before!"

Michael hesitated for a moment, battling with his anger, then placed a hand on Paul's arm; he didn't want to quarrel with his friend on this evening that had brought him so much happiness.

"Paul, you've had too much to drink. You might say something you'll be sorry for. We'll take a walk along the beach tomorrow morning and we'll talk about it. Emily's gone up to our room to freshen up a little. Be nice to her when she comes

483

back down, Paul; that's all I ask for now. Come on outside with me and get some air."

"I've had enough air," Paul mumbled. "I want another drink."

Michael hesitated. "Okay, Paul. Let Emily know where I am when she comes down, will you?"

"Yeah. Yeah, sure."

Michael smiled once more and stepped out to the verandah.

Paul glowered after him. "She's just like all the others," he muttered to himself, glancing angrily up the stairs where Emily had disappeared. "She's out for the same thing they're all after. She wants a man, a husband, somebody to take care of her for the rest of her life, someone she can cheat, whose life she can run for him." His thinking became confused in an alcoholic haze. "She thinks Mike's a soft touch. So God damned decent and pure! Convinced him she won't put out without that fucking ring! She's just like all the rest of 'em and, God damn it, I'm gonna prove it!"

With one quick gulp, he finished his drink and set the glass on the bar. Still somewhat unsteady, he made his way to the foot of the stairs. It seemed to him an impossibly steep ladder, but keeping one hand firmly on the bannister, he managed slowly to maneuver his way up to the second floor. He knew he'd had considerably more to drink than usual, but he prided himself on his capacity. He was certain no one suspected he had overplayed his drunkenness for greater freedom of speech, but he confessed to himself that he felt more unsteady than usual. But, hell, he was never so drunk that he didn't know what he was doing, and he sure as hell knew now.

He moved up to the top floor and stopped before the door of their room, fighting back a sudden wave of nausea. There was no one else on the stairs or the third floor. When he looked down into the well to the lobby floor, the stairs seemed to reel and the colored streamers suspended from the chandelier to writhe and squirm like striped serpents. He could see through the lobby doorway into the sitting room, dizzy with whirling figures. Man and woman. Dancing together. Loving. Marriage. Family. Bullshit. Michael was his best friend. He just didn't know. Dumb kid. Even after all their wild times together, Mike was still hopelessly naive. A stupid kid who was going to let this broad ruin his life. Thinks he can't get it without marrying her. No, Paul decided, he couldn't allow it to happen. Michael wasn't going to get himself snared in the oldest trap of the human race.

He opened the door and quietly entered the room. The light was on in the bathroom and the door was open. He closed the outer door behind him, his back against it, and waited; he felt dizzy.

"Is that you, Michael?" Emily called from the bathroom. "I'll be with you in just a minute." Her laughter was light and happy as she added, "You smeared my lipstick!"

He waited, holding his breath, watching the rain pound on the glass of the balcony doors; a flash of lightning revealed the gauntly twisted branches of the tree he and Micheal had climbed with the two whores just the other night. Just two nights ago. The branches were tossed by the wind as though they, too, were angry.

Emily came from the bathroom, slipping her lipstick back into her bag. Her expectant smile faded sightly when she looked up and saw Paul standing against the closed door; she rather tremulously brought it back again.

"Oh . . . Oh, hello, Paul. I thought it was Michael. What are you doing here?"

Paul grinned. "This is my room, too, you know."

"Why, yes, that's right, isn't it?" She tried to laugh, but there was an uncertainty in the sound. "I'd forgotten." She approached the door, but Paul made no move to get out of her way. She hesitated for a moment, confused. "Please, Paul. Michael's waiting for me."

"Let him wait."

She glanced at him, suddenly uneasy, disturbed by the harshness of his tone. "What do you mean?"

Looking intently at her through eyes that did not quite focus, Paul put an arm around Emily's waist and drew her closer to him; she could feel his lean hard body pressed against her, somehow more unpleasantly suggestive than when they were on the dance floor. She instantly drew back, breaking his hold.

"What do you think you're doing?"

"Want to have a little talk with you, that's all," Paul replied, quickly reaching out a hand to the dresser to steady himself.

"You let me out of this room this minute!"

She reached again for the door, but again he was there before her. He leaned against it once more, effectively blocking her attempt to leave.

"You're drunk, Paul."

"Damn right I'm drunk," he admitted, smiling again. "Maybe. More or less, anyway. But that don't bother me. I can still handle anything that comes up." He laughed, leering unpleasantly. "Say, that's pretty funny, isn't it?"

"Michael is going to be furious about this."

"Shit." He waved his hand. "I can handle Michael any time."

Emily hesitated, uncertain of her next move. "Well, what is it you want?"

"Let's talk about what you want," he countered suggestively.

"I don't know what you mean," she said impatiently.

"What do you want with Mike?"

The question confused her. "I don't really believe that's any of your business, Paul."

"Mike's my buddy. My best friend. I've got to look after him."

"I'm sure Michael is able to take care of himself."

"Not with broads."

Emily laughed. "Oh, yes, I'd forgotten. You're the world's great expert, aren't you?"

"I know a hell of a lot more about them than Mike will ever know," Paul assured her, "and I'm not gonna let any broad make a sucker out of him."

"I resent that!" she flared.

"I don't give a shit what you resent!" he shouted; anger had cleared his speech, and he suddenly seemed cold sober. "You're gonna leave Mike alone!"

"I think Michael should decide that for himself."

"I'm deciding it for him. Sometimes he's just too God damned stupid to know what's good for him."

Her temper flared again. "What right have you to say that? Is Michael stupid simply because he has the sense and the feeling to want to attach

487

himself to one girl, instead of following your example? I happen to love Michael and he loves me, and I hope we're going to be married . . ."

"Take that dress off."

Stunned, she looked at him. "What?"

"I said take that dress off."

"You're out of your mind!"

He approached her, grinning lecherously, his lips gleaming wet, his dark eyes again stripping her of her clothing. Suddenly frightened, Emily backed away from him.

"I don't know what's so damned special about Mike," Paul said, his lips curled derisively, "but I'll show you what it's like with a guy who really knows how to do it. I've seen Mike at work, and he don't take any prizes, believe me. I can give you much better. Hell, I'll make you forget all about Mike fast enough!"

For a moment, amazement overcame her fear. "What unbelieveable conceit!"

"Some guys have got something to be conceited about," he assured her. "I'm one of 'em."

"You're very sure of yourself, aren't you?"

"Never had a single complaint in my life. I've satisfied 'em all, baby, and I'll satisfy you more than Mike or anybody else ever has."

"You drunken scum!" she spat at him. "How could Michael have put up with you all this time? For your information, nobody has ever touched me in that way, and nobody ever will except Michael, when the proper time comes!"

Paul paused for a moment and looked at her, doubtful, obviously impressed by her vehemence. "You mean to tell me you've never been screwed?"

"Don't be obscene!"

"Jesus Christ! What do ya think of that?" Paul

chuckled. "I'm gonna enjoy this even more than I expected. It's been a long time since I've fucked a virgin. Shit, I didn't think there were any left!"

The contempt in Emily's eyes was quickly replaced by fear as Paul came closer to her; she now realized the danger she faced. "Keep away from me, Paul!"

Smiling drunkenly, he moved steadily closer. "Not a chance, baby. This is too good to miss. A real cherry! Relax and enjoy it, like they say. You're one of the lucky ones. You're gonna lose it to a real grade-A expert, baby. I'll have you squealing in no time!"

She was backing against the wall between the bed and the balcony. "What . . . what are you going to do?"

He laughed. "Oh, Christ! You mean you don't know, honey? Still think the stork brings babies? Don't worry about it, I promise to be real gentle."

"No . . . No . . . Paul . . . Please!"

"Like I said, don't be afraid, honey! I know how to take care of things like this." He was breathing heavily, and she could feel his whiskey breath on her face. He reached out and took firm hold of her shoulder, trying to pull her toward him. She drew away and pushed against his chest. He fell heavily back, tottering, and his back heavily struck the closed door; Emily, her dress torn from the shoulder and one breast exposed, stood in the light coming through the balcony doors.

"Michael!" she cried. "Oh, Michael! Help me! Help me!"

Paul steadied himself against the door and shook his head, trying to clear the alcoholic numbness. Emily sobbed and called again for help.

"Won't do you any good, baby," Paul advised

her. "Nobody's gonna hear you in all that noise downstairs. But just to make sure nobody breaks in on our own little party . . ." Reaching behind him, he turned the key in the lock and placed it in the pocket of his blouse.

Emily turned to him. "Please . . . Please . . . Please . . ."

He laughed again. "What's that? Beggin' for it? Don't have to beg, honey. Hell, I never make a dame beg! I'm a most 'bligin' fella. Don't worry, you're gonna get it." His eyes were fastened on the smoothly white exposed breast, and they gleamed with lust. With a sudden lunge he had his arms around her, pressing her against the wall, covering her face and throat with wet kisses and running his tongue over her lips while rubbing his erection against her. "I'm not gonna hurt you, baby. Get into that bed . . ."

She struggled furiously against him, but his arms were firm and powerful, almost crushing the breath out of her as he pressed her to the wall. He tore at her blouse until both firm young breasts were fully exposed. He grabbed at them, and Emily moaned with the sudden dagger of pain that shot through her at his brutal touch. He was slobbering against her, completely out of control, his lust firing his drink-inflamed brain.

"Come on, baby, come on! Don't play cute with me! Oh, Christ, I'm gonna explode!"

She moved her mouth and seized the lobe of his right ear between her teeth, biting down hard until she tasted blood. With a howl of pain, Paul loosened his hold on her, giving her the chance to break away and cross quickly to the other side of the room. He faced her, blood streaming down one cheek, ugly in his anger, his drink and his frustration.

"You God damned cunt!" he gasped. "You'll be sorry you did that! Now I'll tear you apart!"

At that moment, there was a sound on the other side of the door as the knob was turned; the door did not open. Michael's voice called, "Emily! Are you in there?"

"Oh, Michael!" she cried to him, filled with hope at the sound of his voice. "Oh, God, help me, Michael! It's Paul! He's gone out of his mind!"

The door trembled as Michael tried to force it open, then threw his shoulders against the white paneling. "Paul!" he called. "Paul, you leave her alone! Open this door! You touch her, Paul, and I swear to God I'll kill you!"

Paul hesitated, disturbed by the voice and the harsh words from outside the room, suddenly uncertain and a bit lost, looking at the wide-eyed, terrified girl, and at the shaking door. He narrowed his eyes and placed a damp hand to his throbbing head, as though only now beginning to realize the situation. What was he doing in this room, alone with Emily? It was so very hot here, and his head was pounding. No, that wasn't his head, it was someone hammering on the door. Who could it be? It sounded like Mike, like his old buddy Mike. He'll break the door down if he keeps that up, Paul thought. Why doesn't he just come in? This is his room, too. They don't lock the doors in this place. See, the key is in the lock, but they never use it. He looked blearily at the door. There was no key. What happened to the key?

With the sudden strength of fury, Michael again brought his shoulder crashing against the door.

The door burst open and Michael, his eyes wild and his mouth a tight line of fury, literally flew into the room. He immediately saw Emily standing in terror near the balcony, trying to conceal her exposed breasts behind her torn blouse, and Paul standing near the door with bright red blood streaming down his face from a wound in his ear. There could be no question as to what had happened.

"You filthy son of a bitch!" Michael gasped.

With a sudden lunge, he was on top of Paul, hammering away at him with his fists. The alcohol he had consumed all through the day had now caught up with Paul, and he did not fully comprehend what was happening, but he automatically struck back at his unexpected assailant. A quick uppercut of his powerful street-trained fist sent Michael flying across the bed; he landed with a heavy thud against the wall near the bathroom, but sprang quickly to his feet again and struck Paul in the mid-section. With a grunt of pain, Paul doubled over and received another blow on the point of his chin, which sent him reeling against the dresser. Michael leaped again and landed on top of him; together they rolled into the center of the floor. Desperate, Paul reached for Michael's genitals, but Michael warded him off with a knee to Paul's groin, pressing hard. He rose to his feet as Paul rolled over, howling with pain, his hands grasping his injured crotch. Michael stood framed in the light from the open doorway.

Paul looked up at his friend, squinting his eyes as he tried to focus on the dark figure outlined against the brilliant light from the lobby. His mind reached for reality. What was happening?

Michael was his friend, his buddy. Why were they fighting like this?

"Mike . . . Michael . . ." There was a plea in his strained voice. "Buddy . . ."

"I'll kill you for this, Paul," Michael again threatened through tightly clenched teeth.

Paul rose unsteadily to his feet, his uniform now darkly stained with his own blood. He lurched drunkenly towards Michael, moaning with the pain between his legs, his strong hands reaching for Michael's throat, driven now only by the instinct for self-preservation, that same instinct that had made him a fighter in the slum where he had grown up. This was no longer Michael before him; this was an enemy, and Paul's hazy vision converted his friend into a rival on the streets, a rival who would have to be defeated if Paul were ever again to walk with his head high. The rival must be destroyed, ruined, discredited, in order to preserve his own position.

Aware only of his own burning fury, Michael bent low and carefully watched as Paul approached him, bleeding and bleary-eyed, his face a confused mixture of fear and anger. To Michael, too, the immediate past was forgotten, the friendship and camaraderie. Paul had revealed his true colors, his vicious and depraved inner self. It was a battle of Good against Evil.

Emily stood riveted to the spot, one hand to her mouth, the other still attempting to cover her bruised breasts, her eyes wide with the horror that had so unexpectedly entered her life.

Michael quickly moved in and slid his hands behind Paul's staggering form, grasping him firmly by the buttocks and tossing him over his lowered shoulders and through the room's open door. Paul screamed hoarsely as he flew over the balcony railing and plunged down the stairwell to the marble floor of the lobby three stories below.

It was at that precise moment, with a great roar that could be heard even above the loud thunderings of the storm and the brittle cacaphony of gaiety, that the age and weather weakened foundations of the old Hawkins house finally collapsed beneath the constant hammering of the angry sea. Like the insubstantial structure of a child's sand castle, the foundation wall on the northern side of the house crumbled in upon itself, burying Walter in its foamy wake. Suddenly limp in its final surrender after a century of battle, the great old house began to slide easily into the hungry sea that poured like a green-white mountain cascade into the huge opening, sweeping everything before it in the excited fury of its final conquest, rearing and chuckling as it seized once more that territory that was rightly its own, pouring into the crumbling structure, demolishing its walls, floors and ceilings, rending apart that which the unbearable arrogance of man had constructed more than a century before.

The entire point upon which the house stood began then to disintegrate. A huge wave swept across the land as though at the touch of a consuming acid and crashed down upon the house, which trembled and shook like a field mouse in the mouth of an angry terrier. The howling seas crashed through the walls even as the point vanished before the rolling waves and the house began to slide into the cold embrace of the tumbling ocean.

There were screams of horror as Paul's white-uniformed body came hurtling from above onto the lobby floor, striking with a sickening crash into a film of rain water; his blood turned the small pool crimson. Before anyone could bend over the broken, bleeding form, the very floor itself seemed to explode upward into a boiling fury of sea water, and the graceful curved stairway collapsed inward as the sea burst through the wall where Johnny's miniature ships were so proudly displayed. The great crystal chandelier swung crazily and crashed onto the remains of the marble floor, its pointed crystals shooting like daggers into the screaming crowd.

The startled celebrants on the dance floor heard the sudden screams a split second before catastrophe struck them as well. The large room suddenly seemed to fall in upon itself as the ceiling, with all the weight of the floors above it, crashed down upon the dance floor in a choking cloud of dust and plaster, while the entire room suddenly erupted with sea water bursting up through the buckled floor, demolishing the four walls like the sides of a cardboard doll house.

In that split second before the room became a confused mass of churning water, crashing timber and tumbling bodies, Ethel Hawkins saw the culmination of her fears. She glimpsed her daughter Margaret standing in the entrance to the room, and then everything vanished in a swirl of suffocating green wetness.

In the midst of a number on the orchestra platform, Bea screamed and raised her arms in a futile gesture of defense against the dust and debris that fell upon her, and then all was swept away by the sea.

Greg at first thought the sudden, nauseating

upheaval was merely repetition of his inner sickness following the ugly scene with Johnny. He had just raised himself from his knees, the bitter taste of vomit still strong in his mouth as one shaking hand wiped at his wet chin, when a powerful movement of the house knocked him again to the floor. Before he could regain his feet, he was lost in a mass of choking water.

The upper floors of the house, their supports suddenly washed away by the violent encroachment of the sea beneath them, shook and swayed like an Inca rope bridge over an Andean gorge. Emily screamed and Michael reached out to her, but the distance between them was too great and Michael was able only to utter one last cry of despair before he was lost in a churning mass of crushing debris and tumbling green water. The hissing sea lifted Emily like a limp doll and carried her through the ruins of the French doors and over the balcony.

At the moment disaster struck, Steve had stepped onto the verandah for a breath of cool air. The floor seemed to shift under his feet, and he thought, "No more drinks—you've had enough!" Then he saw the approaching doom.

The rounded end of the point, so like the bulbuous head of a rising whale, seemed suddenly to dip beneath the sea, as though the whale were again plunging into the great waves, like a pack of howling white-fanged wolves, swept up the point towards the house, the mass of water tumbling and hissing and curling upon itself in its eagerness to destroy. He could see the land crumbling as the water approached the wooden structure. Behind him he heard the screams of those trapped within and the noise of collapsing timbers.

Caught in the vortex of the double seas moving across the now-submerged land and bursting through the tumbling ruins of the house from either side, Steve was tossed free of the collapsing verandah and into the water that carried him, tumbling over and over and choking for air, away from the house and towards the shoreline, where he was washed beyond the Boardwalk in the final shushing spray of the great destructive wave. Coughing, choking, streaming with water, he turned to look at the house quickly settling into a sea already covered with debris and struggling forms.

Oh, Greg, he thought. Oh, Greg!

When Johnny dashed from his room after the confrontation with Greg, he left the house through the rear door and, totally indifferent to the violence of the storm, walked swiftly with his hands plunged in his pockets towards the empty Boardwalk, buffeted by the strong winds, the rain plastering his thick hair to his head and pressing his clothing to his body as with some sickening kind of wet affection. The sea had crossed from both sides behind the house, but he was unaware that the land between the house and the Boardwalk was covered with a film of water that seeped through his shoes and soaked his feet. He cared now about nothing—not his home, not his family, not his boat, not his juvenile hopes and dreams. It seemed to him in this moment of emotional catastrophe which he was certain would never leave him that life no longer had any true meaning. He had lost his faith. Where was he to find it again?

He had not quite reached the Boardwalk when he heard the strange, violent noises behind him, a tearing, thunderous sound that rose above the conglomerate roarings of the wind, the rain and the sea. He turned quickly and looked behind him. The great old house seemed suddenly to explode into flying bits of wood and swirling curtains of white-spumed water. He stopped for a moment, his eyes wide with horror, sudden fear twisting his insides, and then he began to run back towards the house, his juvenile problems forgotten in the sudden collapse of his material world.

"Oh, God, no!" he screamed. "No, no, no, oh, God, no!" His voice was carried away by the wind and his words were unheard.

The disaster had already brought others upon the scene and Steve, still dazed with his own horror, had quickly joined them in their desperate atempts at rescue, plunging into the tumultuous waters to reach out for those wildly groping hands of the few stunned survivors, drawing them hastily onto shore and out of reach of the hungry sea, providing them with what comfort was available. For many, it was already too late, and there was nothing to be done but to smooth their limbs and close their horror-widened eyes. The sea was filled with those who were beyond help; the waves seemed to play with their bodies, casting them close to the shore and then, with a malicious willfulness, carrying them out again.

When Steve saw Johnny running back toward the disintegrating point, he dashed after him, catching hold of the boy just as he was about to hurl himself into the fuming, debris-strewn water.

"No, Johnny! Don't!"

"My mother! My grandmother!"

"There's nothing you can do!" Steve shouted

above the roar of the storm. "Nothing, Johnny! You can't swim in that sea!"

Johnny looked up into Steve's face, his eyes wide with agonized fear; both rainwater and tears streamed down his cheeks.

"Oh, God! Oh, my God!"

With a quick, convulsive movement, Steve threw his arms around Johnny and pressed the weeping boy's head against his breast. They stood together in the rain and the chaos, while the storm danced its mad triumph about them and, almost with a sigh, the shattered remains of Captain Nathaniel Hawkins' great house slid into the sea.

Slowly, then, the storm passed. The exhausted wind ceased its constant roaring and retired with a last whimper. The sea, having at last proven itself the victor, suddenly forgot its rage. The waves began to recede from the covered beach. The tumbling black clouds dissipated and sneakily moved on their way, as though ashamed of the havoc they had wrought.

Dawn saw the sun rising in a clear blue sky that seemed to have no memory of the violence it had spawned. The weather reports had again proved accurate. The storm was over. It was a beautiful day. The summer should be made of such mornings.

But on this day there were few who appreciated the beauties of the morning, in the deep, stricken silence that had fallen over Hawkins' Cove. Under the clear summer sky, there were too many grim reminders of the terrible havoc that had been wrought in those dark stormy hours. Portions of the Boardwalk had been severely damaged, the salt-whitened boards splintered into so much kindling. The damage would be repaired; it had happened before, and much worse. The Boardwalk would be reconstructed where necessary, the shop fronts would be rebuilt, the shattered windows of the Casino restored. These were among the perils of living by the sea.

It was the destruction of The Cloud that brought the stunned, almost awesome silence and the white faces, for few families resident in the Cove had not suffered in the annihilation of the old house. Debris and wreckage littered the empty beaches and here and there a bloated corpse moved limply with the motion of the surf. The naked form of Bernie S. Clayton of Wall Street was wedged between two large rocks of the fishing jetty. His eyes were open and the wet puffed face with its swollen cheeks more than ever resembled the cherubic features of a staring kewpie doll; hosts of small sand crabs ran hungrily over the pink flesh.

Nothing remained now of the old point or of the great house that had stood upon it for more than a hundred years. Where the land and house had for so long defied the sea, there was now only a mass of twisted wreckage, rising and falling in the tide as though it, too, had traveled halfway across the world to find its place here.

Rescue efforts continued throughout that dreadful night and on into the beautiful morning. Aid was rushed from neighboring towns, and the sun gleamed brightly on the white red-crossed tops of ambulances. There was little enough that could be done. The catastrophe had been too sudden, too complete. To those who survived, it was difficult to realize that it had all been over in a matter of moments. Once the sea had managed at last to gain its hold on the weakened land, it had worked quickly and efficiently, as though afraid the advantage might yet be lost. Like a mighty destructive hand, it had grasped eagerly at the first opening in the land beneath the house and suddenly and instantly torn it apart.

There was little enough hope for survival in that stormy sea. Only those, like Steve, thrown clear of the crushing debris and cast upon the land in an inexplicably kindly movement of the savage sea could hope to see the next dawn, and there were few enough of these. They stood, wrapped in blankets, their white faces forever etched with the horror of what they had seen, soundlessly sipping hot coffee and watching with vacant eyes the attempts to rescue those who might, by some miracle, still be alive.

Painfully silent groups lined the beach and watched with worn and strained faces as limp, wetly-glistening forms were dragged from the sea. Most of these were carried to the makeshift morgue prepared in the Casino. The covered bodies lay in rows like sleeping sentinels while the great steel-and-glass structure echoed with the weeping of those who there found friends and loved ones lost in the debacle.

Steve and Johnny stood together during those terrible hours, united by fear and sorrow, their differences forgotten, indifferent alike to the beauties of the day and the increasing heat of the sun. Tragedy had suddenly, if briefly, made them friends, and it was in Steve's arms that the boy wept unashamedly when his mother's body was found. Margaret looked strangely peaceful, her body unmarred. She was smiling, as though in her last moments she was still pleased by the success of the final Festival in honor of her grandfather.

Emily's parents were among the group that waited silently throughout those long hours, their eyes revealing that mixture of hope and fear that filled all those who waited. When they heard that their daughter had been found farther down the beach, lying not far from the body of a young sailor, they feared first to ask whether she was living or dead. When assured that Emily had miraculously survived, they rushed to her side and felt new agony at the vacant, unknowing expression in their daughter's bright green eyes. It was soon apparent that Emily's mind was gone, unable to survive the horror of what she had suffered. She was to spend the remainder of her life in a twilight world, constantly torn between vague memories of a lost lover, and terrible images of the horror that had followed.

When Karen Fraser was found lying on the beach some distance away, it was at first feared she, too, was dead, but a small flicker of life remained and she returned to consciousness some hours later. The body of Charles Fraser was finally discovered with other bodies pinned beneath a large mass of debris that swirled like a miniature maelstrom upon the former site of the great old house, as though even now the sea could not dislodge it. Linda Fraser, like Steve, was thrown clear of the wreckage and tossed up onto the beach. It was several days before it was determined that she would never walk again. Thus did mother and daughter change places, and a dour, solemn, unsmiling Karen, who often created a sense of sympathy in those who saw her, devoted the remainder of her life to tending her crippled mother. She accepted it as her penance.

By mid-afternoon of that following day, little hope was held that there might be any other survivors, and the gruesome task of removing the dead from the sea continued. The day grew hotter, and now there was not the wisp of a cloud in the sky. The white gulls swooped across the brilliant blue as though confused by the lack of their usual sustenance dropped by visitors to the beach and the Boardwalk. Hawkins' Cove quickly became crowded with avid sightseers who lined the beach and often interfered with rescue operations. One enterprising merchant quickly opened his fast-food stand and was sternly ordered to close.

Steve was again alone by evening; Johnny had been taken away by friends of the family. He wandered aimlessly along the damaged Boardwalk, wondering and grieving. Some time during the day, he had forced himself to eat something from the Red Cross van that had arrived, but he had little enough appetite, and then he seated himself alone on a bench and stared vacantly out to sea, not wanting to think or to remember, his mind dulled by sorrow. The sea was calm again, glinting under the sun. It was as though nothing had happened at all. Could Nature really be so indifferent?

He did not immediately look up when someone sat beside him, and he was startled when he felt a hand on his arm. He turned to see Bea, her right arm in a sling and a plaster near her right eye. Her face was bruised, swollen and discolored. She was wearing a shapeless dress that someone had given her; strangely, it seemed too large for her.

"I don't believe I care for the sea any more," she

said. "It looks so peaceful and beautiful. See how the light sparkles on it, as though it's filled with dancing diamonds. But how angry it can become, how cold and heartless."

"The sea hates man; it will never learn to tolerate us. Well, it was here first, after all." He took her hand in his own. "I'm very glad to see you. I hadn't heard . . ."

"I'm glad to be here," she assured him. "I never believed in miracles, not before. Do you think it will ever be the same here again, anything like it was?"

He shrugged. "People forget. Time, you know."

"I suppose you're right, but I wonder. Once you've seen such fury, are you ever free from the fear of it? Many here will never forget. I suppose last night will be part of my dreams for a long time to come." She sighed. "They haven't found old Ethel Hawkins yet; I don't suppose it's possible that a woman of her age could have survived." She looked more closely at him. "What about Greg?"

He hesitated for a moment, then turned his head away. "Nothing."

She shook her head. "I'm sorry. For you both. I liked Greg very much." She released her hand from his and ran it over her perspiring forehead. "It's a pity about so many of them. I've known a lot of these people since the first summer I came here. Just ordinary people, I suppose, neither better nor worse than others, but people who wanted to live their lives, people who cared about themselves and about others. Why them, I wonder? Why were some chosen to die and some to live? What had they done? And why not you? Or me?"

"The decision of God."

"A cold decision. Or perhaps the fickleness of Fate. Both seem equally indifferent."

"We should be grateful, shouldn't we?" he asked.

"I wonder. Who are we supposed to be grateful to? That unmerciful God you just mentioned? There are many people in Hawkins' Cove who don't think very much of that mercy today. Is it fair to punish the sins of the dead upon the living?"

"We're not supposed to question, are we?"

"Only the mindless never question. This isn't the Dark Ages, after all. Maybe it's time there was more questioning; perhaps He—whoever or whatever He may be—is getting away with too much these days." She smiled wryly. "His eye is on the sparrow, but the sparrow falls, nevertheless."

The dark smudge of a ship appeared on the blue horizon, the first they had seen since the storm; had those on board heard of the disaster and were they perhaps lined at the railings, looking towards them? The world was already returning once more to its regular routine. Bea was right. This shouldn't have happened. But it had.

Bea rose and extended her hand to him. "Well, I wish you—happiness, some day. I'm leaving in the morning."

Rising, he asked, "Will you be back?"

She looked at him, and her eyes filled with tears. "No. Oh, no. I won't be back. No, no. . . ."

She kissed him and walked slowly away. The spring had gone from her walk. She seemed tired and sad. She seemed old.

Steve returned to his seat and suddenly, at last, found himself thinking of Greg.

Greg's body was washed up onto the beach almost three miles from the site of the disaster, and was not found for two days. The creatures of the sea which had held such fascination for him during his life had left little to be identified.

Ethel Hawkins was never found. It was assumed that her body had drifted out to the open sea, towards that distant horizon she had so often gazed upon as a child through the black telescope on the Widow's Walk, watching for the first glimpse of the white sail that announced another journey's end.

It was hot and uncomfortable on the train. The air conditioning was not working properly and the back of his shirt was sticky with perspiration. The conductor had told him there was a tie-up on the line ahead which accounted for the long delay, and they might be as much as an hour late in reaching the city. It didn't really matter.

Steve slouched down in his seat, resting his chin on his hand as he stared at the seaside villages that whizzed past. A book rested in his lap; one finger marked his place. He had read several pages without being really aware of a single word; he had little interest in what he was reading. That didn't matter much, either.

So, he was going back again. Another summer, another dream, and another ending. This one had been different. When would he forget? Could there be a forgetting?

He frowned and closed his eyes, running his damp hand over his forehead. He had developed a headache. Something had struck him while he was in the water—some part of that great house where he had at least known a few brief hours of happiness—and given him a slight concussion. Not very serious, but probably just enough to create headache problems for some time to come. It would serve as a reminder.

It was little enough to suffer; others had suffered much more. At least he could go back. Perhaps nothing would ever really be the same for him, now, but he at least could go back, back to the office, to the over-solicitous sister, to the emptiness of his life.

What of the others? What would become of Johnny, a confused and bewildered boy so suddenly cast into a world he only partially understood. Could he escape the morbid fear that his own sinful activities had, in some part, been responsible for a disaster sent to him as brutal punishment? And Karen and Linda, sentenced to a new form of macabre imprisonment? How long would Bea's dreams be haunted? And the girl Emily, who had found a brief happiness that would remain with her whenever she emerged now and then from the dark shadows of that twilight world in which she now lived? Others, too, who had lost life itself. The two young seamen, Bernie Clayton, so many he had never even known. He was so much more fortunate. Wasn't he?

And Greg. There had been those brief moments when their lives had crossed, one evening and one day, and that was all. Why? Had it really meant something?

The train sped through the marshes, and the sentinel trees lining the route became brilliant smears of green and yellow. They clacked over a narrow inlet and Steve looked down into a rowboat with two lazy fishermen, their poles extended, motionless. Had they been here all this time? Were they aware of nothing that had happened? For some, nothing had changed. A little boy standing beside the track waved to the conductor as they zoomed by. Yes, little boys were still doing that.

Life continued, for those fortunate enough to have it, and there was nothing quite so precious. He knew that. Time of despair will pass, and we realize again that there is nothing quite so wonderful as being alive. Even the lame and the blind, the sick and the weary know this. Morning will always be a "good morning" as long as one is alive to see it. It is only the hopelessly self-pitying who can find nothing in life. Seek and you shall find. More true than most people ever came to realize.

He wondered with Bea why he had been spared. He was not foolish or vain enough to think there was a reason for it, a purpose in it all. Death was as haphazard as life. There was no real meaning to anything. He was alive because he was alive. He could only make the best of it.

Life would never be quite the same, of course. The doubt and uncertainty that had plagued him all these years was gone. Greg had left him with that much. Be true to yourself. He would do that. And, by doing it, he would always remember Greg. He would live the life he was meant to live, without guilt or shame. Some day, perhaps—no, not very soon, but some day—there would be another Greg for him. He would be ready by then.

They would reach the city within the hour. It was a long, hot trip. He raised the book from his lap and tried again to interest himself in the problems and sorrows of its rather insipid characters. The sun glittered brightly on the blue-diamond sea and hurt his eyes.

He lowered the shade.